Sex and Drugs and Squash'n'Roll

by

Aubrey Waddy

Sex And Drugs And Squash'n'Roll

by

Aubrey Waddy

ISBN: 978-0-9570979-0-2

Published by Caught off Court Publishing in conjunction with Writersworld Limited, this book is produced entirely in the UK, is available to order from most book shops in the United Kingdom, and is globally available via UK-based Internet book retailers and www.amazon.com.

Printed and bound by www.printondemand-worldwide.com

www.writersworld.co.uk

WRITERSWORLD
2 Bear Close
Woodstock
Oxfordshire
OX20 1JX
England

The text pages of this book are produced via an independent certification process that ensures the trees from which the paper is produced come from well managed sources that exclude the risk of using illegally logged timber while leaving options to use post-consumer recycled paper as well.

Also by Aubrey Waddy: **Just Desserts** (a revised version of *The Progressive Supper*), ISBN: 978-0-9570979-2-6

About the Author

Aubrey Waddy is perfectly placed to write a scurrilous story about a squash player. His denials about a scurrilous nature lack conviction and his playing experience is extensive. Aubrey's squash was tempered in first grade competition in Sydney and Adelaide in the early 1970s. On returning to England he reached the UK national rankings, was Hampshire county champion in 1973, 1974 and 1975 and county captain in 1980 and 1981. He resumed playing squash in 2007 after a twenty five year retirement, and his relatively low-mileage joints have allowed considerable success in Masters competition. Aubrey gained selection for the 2011 England team that won that year's Over-60s Home International Tournament in Cardiff, and he has notched up a number of Masters wins, including the 2010 English Open Masters and the 2011 Ulster Masters.

Aubrey's lifetime interest in squash gives him an unrivalled insight into the competitive player's mind. This, combined with his passion for weaving words into a story, provide the perfect writing storm for the first novel set in the high energy world of competitive professional squash.

Acknowledgements

Many people have generously contributed their time, thoughts and enthusiasm to this story. Without specifying the elements of the story's title in which their contribution has helped, I'd like to thank:

Gawain Briars
Trevor Cohen
Matt Cook
Harry Leitch
Mick O'Sullivan
Chris Page
Anthony Ricketts

Nick Rider
Wayne Scott
Chris Simpson
Alan Thatcher
Malcolm Willstrop
Jim Zug

Also in the 'unspecified contribution' category, my particular thanks go to John Nimick, my cousin Ro Hume, my son Josh and my dear friend and dear partner Alison Stevenson. On the production side, Graham Cook, Ian Large and Jag Lall have made indispensable contributions to the book and have been a delight to work with. Thanks to them too.

Finally, sincere apologies to anyone I've overlooked. It's my eccentric RAM, emphasis on the *random*, rather than the impact that they've made.

Chapter One

Navel gazing is said to be an aimless pursuit. Not to me, Jolyon Jacks. I was gazing at the navel of Sasha Cremorne from Sydney and my aim was plain.

I was happy to savour the moment. Why hurry? Sasha was stretched out on a king sized bed, hands entwined in the ornate headboard, naked under a duvet that covered her hips. The pillows were scattered. I was also naked and, if you regarded us alphabetically, I was the descending stroke of a wonky capital T. I was pretty motionless, with the exception of my tongue. Sasha's shrouded hips were writhing gently. I recalled a girly thread on Facebook: Why are good sex and a good stew the same? A good stew needs lots of time, lol.

So, according to the thread, did the other activity, the one that didn't customarily take place in the kitchen, ;-). The thread amplified the theme. People could learn a lot from the social media.

More than I'd learned from my parents, of course. They'd been too embarrassed to talk about sex. I'd cottoned on though that spending quality time on Sasha's rounded stomach and the vertical depths of her navel would gain me a Facebook thumbs up. Sasha's navel was decorated, I'd laughed at the discovery a few minutes earlier, with four plain gold rings, at three o'clock, six o'clock, nine o'clock and midday. Well, maybe midnight. I confirmed with my tongue, while the owner sighed above and undulated below, that there was no fluff in there.

Sasha's sighs eventually turned to impatience. "For fuck's sake get on with it." *Hmm, so much for the Facebook theories.*

With anybody else, Sasha's outburst might have been ironic. *For what's sake, Sasha?* I'd learned pretty quickly though that Sasha Cremorne didn't do irony. But hold on, what was this? As I inched the duvet down and started to comply with her request, I found I must have been wrong. At the top of the mound of Sasha's neatly trimmed pubic hair was a small tattoo in a plain font that my English teacher, if she'd been able to conquer her indignation, would have described as sans serif. The tattoo posed the identical question to the one voiced regularly in our hotel lift: 'going down?'

The answer was yes, all the way. And unless Sasha, who up to that point I hadn't known very well, was a good actress, it was obvious she was enjoying the descent as much as I was. And everything that went on afterwards, for far too long.

Far too long? Another yes. I seriously needed the rest. This is embarrassing to explain, but Sasha was already an item, not with me. She had arrived in England a couple of months previously to join her boyfriend Trevor, and the two had been obviously together as Trevor travelled from one PSA tournament to the next, on the opposite side of the world from his Sydney home.

PSA? Professional squash, squash racquets to give it its full name. A minority sport where the rewards for even the leading athletes are disproportionately small, in the context of the enormous effort needed to reach and stay near the top. A thoroughly physical game with a number of physical essentials at the international level: one, years of exhausting conditioning; two, thousands of hours of on-court routines; three, regular weight training; four, interminable stretching to ward off stiffness; five, whole seasons of hard competition; six, the ability to ignore the pain of countless minor injuries; seven, meticulous attention to diet; and eight, no booze. In other words, continuous monkish dedication.

Oh yes, one more: nine, all important: you had to have a good night's sleep before a big match. The next day I was due to play Sasha's boyfriend.

Squash Times, January 2nd

PSA WORLD SERIES FINALS

The finals of the Professional Squash Association World Series return to London next week at the Queen's Club. World number one, American Julio Mattaz, leads an invasion, with the eight competitors reading like a who's who from the top of the world game.

The tournament is played in two leagues of four players. The winners go through to semi finals on Friday, with the final on Saturday evening. In the Mattaz pool are the world number four, the Egyptian, Magdi Gamal, another Egyptian, Hosni el Baradei, ranked six and Frenchman Armand Darnaud, who recently broke into the top ten. Darnaud comes in as a last minute replacement for his compatriot Serge Colson, who had to withdraw with an eye infection.

Pool B consists of the former world champion, South African Jan Berry, ranked two, the Australian Trevor Cooper at three, world number five, Mansoor Ali Khan from Pakistan, and the new English sensation Jolyon Jacks, aged only nineteen. Jacks has burst onto the scene this season and has already beaten Cooper twice in World Series tournaments.

"'ey Jolyon, do you want to 'ave somesing to eat?"

I vaguely realised someone was talking.

"Jolyon, wake up you stupid galah."

It was the evening before the World Series finals and we were sitting around in the lobby of the Hilton Hotel. I had a great mix by Andy C turned up on my iPod and hadn't been paying attention to the general conversation. It was Trevor Cooper shaking me by the shoulder, "Wake up, mate."

Off with the Bose headphones, bought earlier in the year with my first big tournament winnings; I'd upset the seedings by winning in Chennai. Everyone was looking at me.

"Armand's trying to say something." This was *the* Trevor Cooper, no less. Only a year ago I had merely been reading about Trevor in squash magazines and watching him on Sky or the PSA live feed. Now we were in the same tournament, playing each other the following day.

"Armand's dad's here. He's offering to take us for a pizza."

Marcel Darnaud was a legend in squash circles. His son's rise up the world rankings had been almost as rapid as mine, and it was rare to see Armand at a tournament without his father. Plus there was his coach, Lou Kiefer. Lou Gubrious as he was known behind his back, the life and soul of the graveyard. Anyway, Armand's dad was good news, even if he sometimes embarrassed his son with his raucous support and his loud comments on reffing decisions. I knew the Darnauds quite well, having spent some time a couple of months before at their base in Aix-en-Provence, training with Armand.

"Yeah, sounds great," I said. "We going now?"

"We're going in five."

"My fuzzeur come soon," Armand explained as we stood up. His English was rudimentary, but, I had to concede, ahead of my non-existent French.

"And it would be diplomatic to leave your music at home."

Older statesman Trevor. I wasn't sure about Trevor, but let it go.

"'Course, I'll get my jacket." Another recent purchase. People had disapproved of my hoodie, so I'd bought an expensive but totally uncool grey anorak.

When I returned to the lobby the group had expanded; news of Marcel's offer had spread. Marcel himself was talking to a young, curvy girl with lots of make-up and rings in her nose and ears and eyebrows. It was almost easier to list where she didn't have rings. Then there was my coach, Sailor McCann. Sailor had strictly no make-up on, and even more strictly, no rings, apart from a proudly worn wedding band. Sailor's opinion on cosmetic hardware in the face registered high on the Richter scale. Among the others in the lobby, the Aussie Trevor Cooper was standing to one side in a cool suede waistcoat. Zoë Quantock, three times women's world champion no less, was chatting with a woman I didn't know, next to Julio Mattaz.

Marcel's English, in contrast to his son's, was pretty good. "Hey, Jolyon, good to see you, that's everyone, let's go."

Ten minutes later we were seated in an Italian restaurant, with a couple of introductions made, studying menus. The dark haired woman, who had been with Julio and Zoë, turned out to be Ruth Mattaz, Julio's missus. She was quietly American, the complete opposite to her husband. No one actually addressed Mattaz as 'Julio'. He was universally known as Razza or Razz. It hadn't taken me long to find out why once I'd met him: a more vibrant character didn't exist in the squash world. Probably not in any other world. The girl who had been chatting with Marcel was Sasha Cremorne, possibly Trev's girlfriend. She was the younger sister of Ryan, world number twenty five, part of a group of squash-playing Aussies in Europe.

Sailor was talking to Zoë on my left. Zoë looked great I knew, even when she was red-faced and sweaty in the middle of a training session. Now with her hair sorted and some make-up on she was sensational. Razz was opposite Sasha and I was happy to watch her beside me and listen in.

"What do you think of London so far, Sasha?" As always, Razza radiated energy; the way he posed the question, London had to be one of his favourite spots.

Not one of Sasha's. "Cold and wet. It's summer in Sydney and for sure it's light years better than this. I'm into the beach. Your famous River Thames? Ugh, the water's black. It could be crude oil. Give me Coogee Beach, no contest, I'm like, why did I come over to this country?" She theatrically hugged herself and I couldn't help thinking that she needed long arms to get them round everything she had to hug.

"It's your first time in England?"

"Yes, Trev said why not come over, he'll show me round. He's some rellies outside London and he's going to do a month's training here after the World Series. Before going to New York. Ryan too. For some reason they've decided not to go home to train. I think they're mad."

"It can be colder where we come from," Razza said. "Ruth's from New York State and my family's from Salt Lake City."

"I know about New York," Sasha said. "But where's Salt Lake City?"

It was to become clear through the evening that Sasha had bunked off most of her geography lessons. With Coogee Beach nearby, you probably would. A lot of the rest of her schooling seemed to have gone the same way. Not that I could boast about my own school record. The gritty Sussex shingle near my south coast private school hadn't drawn me away, but doing badly with exams had been an effective way of aggravating my mother. Always a powerful motivation.

"Salt Lake City's in Utah," Razza explained. "The western USA, in the Rockies."

"It's a great place for skiing," Ruth said.

Razza laughed. "And not much else."

"Aw come on Razz. You always say it's good for training."

"A New Yorker coming to the defence of little ol' Salt Lake City! But I guess it's true. Nothing else to do there, and forty seven hundred feet, you make your own EPO."

To be fair to Sasha, she appeared to recognise these items as three from a set that totalled twenty six. "EPO, what's that?"

Trevor rolled his eyes. "Oh come on, Sash. I told you about EPO."

Sailor pricked up his ears at the mention of something to do with training and physiology. And hardness. "EPO. It's a hormone that increases your red corpuscles." He noticed Sasha's big eyes glazing over. "Ye could say it strengthens the blood. Good for athletes. Any aerobic sport."

To Sasha's Aussie ear Sailor probably sounded no stranger than I did with my south of England vowels. Me, I often struggled to make out Sailor's guttural utterances. You needed to have grown up in a Glasgow tenement to understand the accent, let alone the vernacular. Sailor looked short and abrasive. That was how he was. Toilet brush abrasive, though I wouldn't put it to him like that. I nearly died every day during his training routines and I didn't want the 'nearly' to disappear.

In height Sailor would have been able to look Sasha straight in the eye. That's if he'd had the strength of will to keep his eyes off her chest. Will was something Sailor didn't lack. I knew that all too well from the gym and the weights room and the four walls of the court where we did our lung busting training routines. *We* did? *I* did, though I'm sure Sailor could have kept up if he'd wanted to.

Sailor went on, "It's a natural hormone, erythropoietin. It's used by middle distance runners and cyclists, especially cyclists. Ye'll know the Tour de France, that sort of thing. Cheating. You inject it. It increases your red blood cells. Then your blood can carry more oxygen and you can run or cycle faster. Or play squash."

"Just another illegal drug," Razza explained.

Sasha looked at him with those expressive blue eyes. Perhaps Sailor would after all aim his gaze at them; they were far from her worst feature, in the middle of fierce competition. "And you make your own EPO? How do you do that?"

"No, only joking," Razza said. "At altitude, like Salt Lake City, you produce more red blood cells naturally, to compensate for the thin air. None of us take anything," he looked round, "do we, fellers? Anyway, the testing's too strict these days. You'd be caught, bound to."

With that the pizzas arrived, baking hot and, to my nose at least, smelling wonderful. As the waiter proudly placed Razza's in front of him Ruth asked, "You're absolutely sure there's no nuts in these? You did check with the chef?"

"Yes, I spoke to him." The waiter, in his mid twenties, sounded as though a PhD was the least of his qualifications. "The chef's very particular with his ingredients. No nuts, guaranteed. No chance."

"Oh Ruth," Marcel exclaimed, "you should have told me. Do you have a nut allergy?" He seemed really concerned.

"No, it's not me, it's Razz."

"Yeah, it's no big deal," Razza said. "I'm always careful. And Ruth is twice as careful for me. And I always have my EpiPen."

"Have you ever had to use it?" Sailor asked.

"A couple of times when I was a kid. Driver of the school bus helped once. My dad was in the military; we travelled around. That's how I got started with squash. Most of the US bases had courts. Anyway, I was new on the base. I'd told the kids but some of them were horsing around with a Snickers bar. Never again. They were more scared than I was. I promise you, one of them wet himself."

"You have to be careful," said Marcel. "I had a patient once, a young woman. She changed her handbag. No EpiPen." He shrugged, a Gallic understatement that hinted, I remembered from a briefing by the school matron, at slow suffocation and a reduction of Marcel's patient list by one.

"Me, I've an allergy to training." Everyone laughed. Brett Hammond hadn't said much up to then. "Supplementary oxygen, EpiPens, you name it, I need it."

"What artificial support do you have, Jolyon?" Trevor asked. "New English wonder kid. What's in the wonder regime?"

I hadn't believed Sailor when he'd predicted that Trevor would start needling me. *Come on, Sailor. That'd be pathetic.* I was surprised to encounter it now, it seemed so childish. I'd never felt that Trevor would become a friend, no chemistry, but he'd been all right up to then, and he was always fair on court in spite of my two wins against him. Fairness on court, I'd learned in my brief time on the circuit, and indeed as a junior, couldn't be guaranteed.

"I just dance hard at raves, Trev, and," I turned to look at Sasha, "avoid being distracted by sexy women. It seems to have worked so far. Oh, and there's the little matter of Sailor, of course."

"Well this is where the big times start, mate. We're going to find out over the next week."

Fortunately we were interrupted by Sasha-the-sexy-woman, who asked with real interest. "Do you go to raves? Proper, like, illegal raves?"

"Legal, illegal, you can always argue about that. But yeah, you won't find me paying out a fortune for Reading or Glastonbury. Corporate crap. Nothing beats a good DJ, a couple of turntables and ten thousand watts blasting out over a field. Shattering the sheep. You get sound systems as big as houses, Sasha, no exaggeration. Welcome to England's green and pleasant land. Don't worry about the River Thames."

"I've read about that stuff. Sounds great and there's nothing quite like that back home. What sort of music are you into?"

"Drum'n'bass, some techno. Not so much gabba."

Her eyes lit up. This appeared to be familiar territory. "I just downloaded this fantastic drum'n'bass mix, something Rat, Ratpack I think..."

"Ratpack? Yeah, I know them. Well, I've met them, in Brighton. They're legends. Been around that long. If you've never seen them, you've never seen nothing."

"It's a them? You know them?" I reclassified Sasha's eyes upwards from strong provincial to genuine international, right up there with her boobs. This was influenced by the fact that they were trained directly on me.

But there's always a but and, on cue, Sailor butted in. "Jolyon used to spend more time raving, if that's the right word, than training." He said the word 'raving' as though its other meaning was child molestation. "Not any more, eh, Jolyon?"

It was more a statement than a question.

"No, Sailor."

Chapter Two

I can remember every metre of the Redbrook Senior Steeplechase that year. I'd started cross country running in the summer, when I was fourteen. My mother wanted me to concentrate on tennis and suddenly I'd had enough of being organised by her. I was the prize exhibit, flashy in the latest Wimbledon kit. *My son's better than yours. AND he looks smarter than your freak on court.* Aces all round, for the proud parent that is, big brownie points in the ladies' section at the club. I'm his *mother!* Status for *me!* Kudos for *me!* Glamour for *me!*

Stuff that.

The problem was, I'd done well in junior tennis tournaments and everyone was feeding off it. Me, I didn't care. I wanted to win my tennis matches but I didn't collapse, or throw tantrums, Timmy, if I lost. I just liked to flog the ball as hard as I could like the tennis gladiators on TV, grunting with each shot, spinning round with a mighty follow through on either side, shirt twisting, shoes scraping. It all came easily to me, forehands, backhands, one handers, two handers, volleys, overheads. It was pure, simple, physical fun.

Running on the other hand, or rather on my two rather small size seven feet, was something I did just for myself. Running was unglamorous: fifteen love to *me*, mother dear, in your Harvey Nicks knickers. Wet mud was involved: thirty love to *me*, mother dear, in your four hundred pound per foot Jimmy Choos. In the summer, after 10K, the white areas of dried sweat stood out on unglamorous tee shirts, no good at all in the forensic detail of your Harrods videocam: forty love to *me*, mother dear. Add in the occasional splashy puke during interval training: ho ho, game to *me!* As in tennis, some runners wore wristbands. Here it was to wipe away not just sweat, an acceptable secretion in the poncy middle England world of tennis, but snot, the branded fashion statement tick smeared with silvery golly.

Running I loved from the day I took it up. Running was downmarket. Running didn't attract a great coop of clucking mother hens, led by the head rooster, my mother.

And I was good at it. The problem with running for me soon turned out to be the others in the school Colts squad, the under sixteens. They *weren't* much good at it. It soon became a chore as I left them behind in training. I didn't want to stay in the pack; there was something I loved about pushing on. Something about fighting through the tiredness, feeling the calves stretch up the hills round Redbrook, feeling the quads strain as you went down the steep gradients. The chalk hills of the South Downs were pretty in picture postcards. They were comfortingly English as illustrations in the Redbrook College prospectus. My mother had persuaded my usually absent father of the attractions of Redbrook soon after I was born, on the basis of her friends' admiration of the glossy brochure. But for cross country running, or even just hiking, the Downs made a tough challenge.

My father was hardly ever around to see me play my sports. That was the

Navy. For tennis at least, my mother was never not around. That was a pain. Often her being around would involve a haranguing for my coach, especially if I wasn't getting twice as much attention as everybody else. It was embarrassing even when I was small, and her unpopularity with the other kids spilled over onto me. On regular occasions at tournaments she acted as an unofficial line-caller, invariably to my benefit. She would never do anything to favour my opponent.

My mother's support didn't extend to cross country, what a surprise. Not even for the highlight of the school running year, 'Steeplechase Weekend'. Strangely, at Redbrook this wasn't one of the big inter-schools races. It was the main house competition in mid November. Running was a major sport at Redbrook, up there with football and cricket for boys and for girls just as important as netball and hockey. Winners of the four races, the girls' and boys' Junior and Senior Steeplechases, had their names celebrated on boards in the main assembly hall, in Gothic gold lettering. The winning houses were also celebrated there. The Junior Boys' Steeplechase, for under sixteens, was a race worth winning, three and a half miles of exposed, undulating downland. The Senior Steeplechase was longer, nearly six gut-busting miles, 10K in the modern jargon, with, in all, more than three hundred metres of ascent. The girls' races were shorter, still with the up and the down of the half accurately named Downs, and run on the following day.

It was my housemaster, the pompous Mr Middleton, who gave me the idea of entering the Senior rather than the Junior Steeplechase.

"I see you've been going well in the junior cross country squad, Jolyon. We haven't won the Junior Steeplechase since I've been housemaster. Eight years now, and it's about time. You're the one."

Stupid fart, 'you're the one', time for a puke. Mr Middleton's bonhomie (I thought of it then as his Ha-Ha-Harry behaviour) masked a highly competitive attitude within the school. Mr Middleton didn't want his pupils to do well for themselves. That was secondary. More important was how they did for Tudor against the other houses. Tudor House, Mr Middleton: Mr Middleton, Tudor House. In the end what he craved was success – for Mr Pompous Middleton. Exam results, sports competitions, top numbers of exclusions for smoking, fewest pupil pregnancies, it didn't matter. Mr Middleton had to be top of the stats. You would hear him boasting to parents or fellow members of the Common Room about Tudor. I couldn't stand the man.

Well, I'd show him. I always got on well with the teachers in the PE Department. Since I'd started running I'd found a friend in Sarah Bristow. Sarah was there three times a week to coach the running. She was a tiny woman, wiry, with amazing bulging gastrocnemius muscles. No amount of slow cooking could ever turn them into a tender stew. Mrs Bristow, Sarah to us runners, had been an international eight hundred metre athlete. I suspect she ran for the exhilaration more than the competition, the joy of running. Maybe she saw something of that in me.

sixty competitors a boost as they got under way. I was well to the right, out of harm's way, and let most of the field charge ahead. As expected they set off much too fast for a 10K race. I heeded Sarah's words, and indeed those of Ron Clarke, and held back, comfortably in the second half of the field. That's where I stayed until we reached the top of the Downs.

The first couple of kilometres were bliss, before the pain started; a piece of piss with the gale behind. In an easy rhythm I began to overtake the runners around me. After twenty minutes, the route plunged off the top of the grassy Down in a steep, chalky five hundred metre decline towards a sharp right turn over a stile. Taking stock for the first time I saw that I had about twenty runners in front of me. At the front, two hundred metres ahead, was a tight bunch of five. That must be Ron and the other 'professionals', as they saw themselves, looking relaxed, arms out for balance on the descent, scanning the track ahead for flints.

The stile marked the end of the soft part of the race. The right turn took you in a southerly direction and for the first time you faced the wind. I couldn't believe the strength of it. What's more, this was still valley, still sheltered. All you could do was put your head down and avoid coming to a complete halt in the fierce gusts. The rain, maybe it was sleet, it was hard to tell, physically stung the skin of your thighs. The runner in front of me was hardly able to get going after the stile and I went round him, ignoring his 'fuck this'.

Along the bottom it was easier if you were right behind someone and I restrained myself from going past the next runner, a big fit rugby player called Lawrence Connaught. But Lawrence was no help when we turned right again after a couple of minutes, over another stile, and faced the bottom of Junior Heartbreak.

Here the wind was worse, slightly from the left. Connaught's main enemy though, I guessed, was his weight, handy if you were a centre three-quarter but the last thing you needed running up a hill. I went past him in thirty metres and then it was just the grind, you against Nature, up the rest of the four hundred metres. I must have gone past seven or eight runners on Junior Heartbreak, but that didn't interest me. I knew now, a happy certainty, that I'd be in the top fifteen at the finish. I wasn't going to be beaten by Nature's strongest weapon, that wind.

The juniors carried straight on at the top of Junior Heartbreak but, directed by an unfortunate teacher posted to make sure no one went in the wrong direction, the seniors turned right again, inland, down another descent, relatively out of the wind, into another fold of the Downs. At the top of Junior Heartbreak I was utterly out of breath, almost retching. I peered forward through the sleet that was now sweeping in white waves across the Downs. The leading bunch had split up. In front now there were only three together, the tall Ron, the tiny Shu Tung and it was probably Charlie Greene, it was hard to tell. Ten metres back was the next runner and ten further away Jeremy De Montfort, who seemed to be going poorly.

The hill down was some relief after the long ascent, with the wind briefly helping again. I went past several of the runners who were between me and Jeremy and regained my breath. Next there was a short flat section before a metal cattle grid and the dreaded left turn at the bottom of Senior Heartbreak.

I don't know who had given the two big climbs their name. They were part of school folklore; everyone talked about the heartbreaks. As I went through the gate just behind Jeremy, I thought the guy who named this had nailed it. He must have coined the name on another horrible November day.

Senior Heartbreak is nearly six hundred metres, something like a ten percent gradient, oblique across the steepest of the local Downs. It's a straight, featureless track where again you needed to take care to avoid the flints, which had twisted many an ankle, and the sheep droppings. There were no sheep about that day; they weren't completely stupid; it was just the intelligent humans, I thought, who were out there.

I rounded Jeremy as I set off up Senior Heartbreak and took up pursuit of a figure I could now see was Jim Hines, bent forward, hardly more than walking. I didn't mind whether I caught Jim or not. I'd use him as a tool in the struggle to get to the top, a trick to take my mind off the prospect of another five hundred and fifty metres of this.

I did soon pass poor Jim, only just picking out his gasped 'fuck this', a unanimous opinion it seemed. Now I was fourth. Amazing, fourth! And I didn't think many, or indeed any, would catch me. Now I could see Charlie Greene, maybe forty metres ahead. He'd been dropped on the heartbreak by Ron and Shu Tung. I used Charlie as the next distraction, focussing on his muddy running shoes, splattered calves and saturated shorts. Halfway up, when he was only five metres ahead, a shocking gust literally stopped us in our tracks. I managed to get going quicker than him and saw the surprise on his face as I went past.

In spite of the wind I was just able to hear a unique message for that afternoon. "Well done," Charlie shouted.

"Yeah," was all I had breath to shout back.

Keep going, keep going. I took a rare look ahead. It was depressing to see how far I still was from the top. My thighs were aching and my lungs were burning. The sleet was lashing my face. The next target was distant.

But look, some good news. Shu Tung Lee, the studious little Malaysian whom I had heard had won a scholarship to Oxford, had got away from Ron Clarke. Ron had told everyone that this year he would win for sure. He had been in an amazing dead heat the previous November with Jim Hines. Jeremy de Montfort was third only a pace behind. For some reason the dead heat had rankled with Ron. This year, he promised, his extra training would let him pull away on Senior Heartbreak, 'if anyone has been able to stay with me until then'.

Heartbreak indeed, on and on. Gut break. Above all lung break. I just couldn't get my breath in the wind. It had reached the stage where I could hardly bring one foot past the other and I was frequently being blown sideways off the track. I didn't look up again on the hill, concentrating on the grey mud just in front of me. Come on. Get your head down. One slippery apology for a stride. Then another. And then another.

When I finally reached the top I felt so awful I thought about giving up. Then, what a surprise. There was Ron Clarke, hardly ten metres away, hands on knees, throwing up. How could I be so close? Maybe he'd been forced to walk some of the hill. He wasn't even managing to walk now.

Ron must have seen me out of the corner of his eye and his look of sheer shock when he saw me was comic. And worth all the effort of that afternoon, no matter what happened. Seeing who it was galvanised Ron and he set off again at a speed I couldn't match. Soon he was twice as far ahead but this didn't trouble me. The look had been enough.

The last part of the Redbrook steeplechase course descends gently for six hundred metres through a large wood, Bright's Down Wood, which provides shelter from the worst of the weather. What a relief. I expected Ron to go further away now. His basic speed was way ahead of mine. But he seemed to be in poor shape. It was hard to tell from behind. You always slipped and staggered when it was wet in Bright's Down Wood. The track was maximally muddy; there were tree roots to negotiate; many of the hazards were hidden by autumn leaves. Ron was navigating like a clown. The strength had gone from his legs and he was moving as though he was drunk.

Not that I was much better. My legs were so tired it was hard to take advantage of the shelter of the trees. But I was developing an unaccustomed feeling. There was a chance I could get past Ron. After the way he'd treated me it was one I wanted to take. This wasn't the joy of running any more. It wasn't Nature I wanted to conquer, it was a single competitor, human, physical. I wanted to humiliate Ron Clarke. What a pleasure, I visualised, to look back at him when I'd passed, and later to laugh about the result in the presence of Sarah Bristow and the others in the running club.

So I forced myself down the twisting track, and started to reel Ron in. I caught him before we were out of the wood and came alongside at a place where the track narrowed. I turned to him to enjoy the moment. If Ron hadn't looked good from behind, he looked dreadful when you saw him close up, slime all over his upper lip, his cheeks an unnatural pink and his eyes screwed in a comic scowl. I knew I had him and started the pathetic acceleration that would take me away.

That was when Ron tripped me.

The bastard! He knocked my trailing foot sideways in the classic children's trick and it caught the back of my other leg. Down I went, skidding for a couple of metres across the leaves before feeling an agonising pain in my hand and rolling over in a deep, flinty rut. Ron's scowl morphed into a twisted smile as he went past and away.

I hardly had the strength to stand up. My right hand had hit a root or a flint and was hurting fiercely. There were no spectators, no one to tell what they'd seen and no one to help me on my way. I heard a runner approaching behind. It was Charlie Greene.

"You okay?" he said as he went past, then a half shouted, "Come on."

It was what I needed. I must have looked a terrible sight when I emerged from the wood. I negotiated the last hundred metres in front of a line of cagouled and anoracked fellow pupils, and a few Burberryed parents. Not a single umbrella had survived. I staggered to the line, enjoying the applause but feeling an incandescent fury. I should have been second, not fourth. And it would have been so sweet to have beaten Ron Arsehole Clarke.

Sarah Bristow was ministering at the finish, her small wet face an exposed oval in a tightly tied waterproof hood. "Well done, Jolyon, fantastic. But look at you, what happened?"

"I slipped in the wood. Seem to have hurt my hand." I'd already decided not to go into the details. Ron would deny it, obviously. But I knew. *And* he knew. *And* I'd remind him whenever I felt like it.

REDBROOK COLLEGE MAGAZINE – WINTER TERM

...Cross Country

The surprise result came in the Senior Steeplechase. It was an appalling November day with a gale coming up the Channel, perfect to test the mettle of the hard guys. The three stars of last year, Ron Clarke, Jim Hines and Jeremy De Montfort, who had fought out that marvellous finish in 'The Great Race', as it has become known, were in the line up for the last time, together with two other county junior athletes, Charlie Greene and Shu Tung Lee. De Montfort was dropped halfway, on Junior Heartbreak, and Greene on Senior Heartbreak. The few hardy spectators were wondering whether another dead heat might be on the cards with Clarke and Lee locked together as if on a training run. But Lee pulled away and went on to win in the slowest time ever recorded for the winner, 42 minutes and 27 seconds.

The surprise package was fourteen year old Jolyon Jacks, who controversially had asked to be moved up from the junior race. At one time Jacks was up to third place, on the killer final stretches of Senior Heartbreak. He eventually finished fourth behind Greene.

After the race Shu Tung congratulated all his fellow competitors. "Everyone who finished was a winner today." A disappointed Clarke said angrily that the conditions had favoured the small runners like Lee and Jacks.

Sore loser.

Chapter Three

"Mum, you know Dave Kemball, the guy who beat me at the South of England Juniors?"

"All squash players look the same to me." Ever the enthusiast, my darling mother.

"Oh come *on*, why are you always so negative? I thought you saw the end of that game when you came to collect me."

"I was having a coffee. I didn't like to see you losing. You never seem to make it past the quarter finals. Not in any of these squash tournaments." 'Squash' said as if it was a specimen bound for the STD clinic in Brighton. "You used to win tennis tournaments. I don't understand you, Jolyon. Just don't understand."

I did the big eye roll. "Look, Mum. It's less than a year since I started playing. I'm fifteen and I've beaten some of the top under seventeens. And Dave was first seed in the Souths. And it was five games, I really pushed him. I beat Gordon Wheating the round before. He was eighth seed and everyone said he should have been higher. I'm doing okay."

"You're doing okay? On a path to where? Sweaty squash club changing rooms. All over England if you're half decent at it, which anyway I doubt. I've always encouraged you, Jolyon. And Adam, he does too."

"Dad? The absent parent. He's hardly ever here."

"Yes him. Your father. The man who pays for your education, remember. Money doesn't grow on trees. He actually likes the idea of you playing squash, I can't see why. Me I'm not having it, not if it ruins everything else. Of course we both want you to do well. But your GCSEs! So disappointing. Disgraceful actually, considering the fees we pay. And you'd seemed to be doing well at Redbrook, the last two years. Until this, this... this business of squash."

Oh dear, the squash rant. Combined of course with its current bosom pal, the GCSE rant. Two rants for the price of one, special offer. They were both so tediously familiar I could recite them myself. And, sure enough, my mother was quickly into her stride. Next would be the A Stars section.

"A Stars are what matters at GCSE." *Bingo!* "That's what they pay attention to at Oxbridge. B grades, C grades, they're way out of it."

A Stars? No I didn't get twelve A Stars for twelve exams like two of the girls in my year, so what? Tedious little swots, those two. The idea of Oxbridge didn't appeal to me, anyway. Stuffed up toffs. Why can't I live my own life, mother dear? But brace yourself now, Jolyon. Here comes the Junior Science Prize section.

"Your father and I were so disappointed you didn't win the Junior Science Prize." *Ding, ding, jackpot, Jolyon can predict the future.* "Mr Rutherford was convinced you would after your mocks." *And look who won it instead.* This was mother's real problem. "That puerile little shit Jimmy Baines got it, didn't he? I can't stand his mother."

No, I hadn't won the Junior Science Prize. Jimmy B had, not a bad sort for a nerd, an absolute whiz with electronic music. He'd hacked into the school network and installed a pirated version of UltraMixer, and he was doing stuff for several London DJs. And no, I hadn't won the Art prize, either. What's that? The Nobel prize? No, another one that had mysteriously eluded me, sorry to effing disappoint you again, mother. I'd got two A Stars, Maths and English. And I hadn't failed anything. And what's wrong with some Cs anyway?

What's wrong with Cs? We know the answer to that, don't we? The nub of the problem. We can't brag about Cs at the tennis club, that's what's wrong. We can't agonise over what university golden Jolyon should apply to. Should it be Oxford or should it be Cambridge? What a quandary. Oh the poor darling, he's finding it hard to make up his mind, Brasenose, that's Oxford or Braised Ears, I think that's Cambridge. Or something. The Isis, darling, that's Oxford. Or the Cam, that's Cambridge. I thought a cam was something in a car engine. Think of the May Balls! What balls? March bollocks to the May Balls. 'My Jane's doing six ASs and she'll probably follow them all through to A2s. The school's going to change the entire curriculum, just for her.' The Jane referred to, that particular goody goody Jane with a habit of squeezing zits in public and absolutely no boobs, is going to be a nuclear scientist *and* a top diplomat *and* an airline pilot *all* at the same time. *And* pull the Duke of Westminster. Dream on. The only success Jane's got coming, Missus, is in the WBC, the World Bulimia Championships. Dead centre of the bowl every time. Huurp! Splash! Awesome, clean as a whistle, not a drop spilt. Your daughter's world class, Missus. That particular Jane had told me she'd been tutored from the age of two to make sure she got a scholarship to Redbrook Junior School. I hadn't admitted that exactly the same thing had been inflicted on me, alphabets, counting, left to right across the expensive paper with the fine art marker pens, all with my mother looking on. She used to scold me if my attention wandered for as much as an instant.

A little bit of my mother's GCSE angst may have been justified, I had to concede. Squash had certainly got me hooked. Squash was so easy. By the end of the summer term, less than a year after I'd started, on a regime of playing all the time, and yes I have to admit that some of that time was GCSE revision time, I'd not only reached a level above anyone else in the school, I'd started to do well in open junior tournaments.

That was where Dave Kemball came in. I'd been furious on losing to Dave at the South of England. For all of five minutes. Unlike most of the juniors after a game, Dave offered to buy me a drink.

"What sort of poison would you like? Strychnine or cyanide?" It wasn't really very funny. It was the way Dave said it, with his easy grin.

"Fuck. Both of them, in a bottle of coke."

Then at the bar I discovered that we liked the same music. Most times it was difficult to talk to Dave. He was always on his iPod, a blank look in his eye, jigging to whatever was playing. He sometimes listened to music when he was knocking up by himself.

After he'd bought me a drink I asked, "What's happened to your iPod?"

"Left it at the hotel. I think. Hope I haven't lost it."

"What do you listen to?"

"Techno, some drum'n'bass. Mixes my mates have done. Or stuff I've done myself."

"Who do you like?"

"You into techno? Rachett. The Geezer. Ant."

"No way! I saw Ant last week in Brighton. It's only a small club but he's mates with one of the organisers. Where do you live?"

"Manchester."

"Is there much on there?"

"Some good nights not far from where we live. Outdoor raves in the summer. I can sometimes get to Leeds, Liverpool, yeah even Nottingham, there's a lot going on."

"Cool. One of my friends spent a year in Nottingham. She was always going on about the Firefly nights."

"Firefly? I've been to one of those. Getting there's the problem. I'll get a provisional on my birthday. It'll be easier when I pass my test."

"You into mixing?"

"Is the sky blue? I got my first decks three years ago."

"What have you got?"

Dave's reply would have made a professional DJ drool. "Technics 1210s, Ortofon needles, Pioneer DMJ 500, Sennheisers."

"Nice. I've got second hand. My stuff's rubbish, Citronics decks and a Behringer mixer. Have you recorded anything?"

"Yeah," I said. "I'd play you some if I had my iPod."

The only problem with Dave was Manchester, a long way from Sussex. So the offer of spending the second half of the summer holiday staying at his house and training with him was immensely attractive. It would be a great place to be and home was a great place not to be.

"It's perfect," Dave said. "I go along to the English Institute for Sport. The Commonwealth Games site."

"What, the Man City ground, Eastlands?"

"That's it. It's where England Squash's based. Really good facilities, plenty of courts. And I get some help from the guys who train the top players. I'm not in a squad or anything, not yet, so it's unofficial. We could practise every day if we wanted."

"I could bring my vinyl."

"Yeah there'd be lots of time. There are some good parties coming up, too. I could easily get you some sets. I know most of the organisers."

"I'll have to speak to my mother."

We exchanged mobile numbers, and I promised to get back to him. I didn't realise what a battle it was going be on the home front, and I had no idea how trivial this battle would seem compared with the one that was to follow.

"Can I go and stay with Dave Kemball in Manchester?"

"Who's he? Oh I know. He's the one who beat you the other day."

"That's right, he's a good guy."

I was helping my mother unpack the monthly ten tons from Waitrose.

"Well your Aunt Phyllis is coming this weekend. But I don't suppose she'd mind if you weren't here." Her voice dropped. "She'd probably be pleased."

"It's not just for the weekend. It's for the rest of the holidays. So we can train together."

"What do you mean the rest of the holidays? You're coming with your father and me to Tuscany. In case you'd forgotten."

Oh dear, I'd put that out of my mind. The annual summer trip with my parents. Somewhere around the age of twelve I'd stopped enjoying holidays with them. One year it had been Geneva, where I speculated my mother had provided a bright scientist from CERN with the inspiration for the Large Hadron Collider. This time Tuscany. My mother had pedantically explained that Tuscany would mean all the glories of Florence. Whoever the fuck Florence was, ha ha. Tuscany. Stuffy nights in uncomfortable hotel rooms, complaints from my parents about the clothes I wanted to wear, *everyone wears shorts for heaven's sake, and no, they don't belt round the waist.* Museums, galleries, uunghhh. Culture! The thought of it made me cringe. There'd be the embarrassment of my inability to communicate in spite of my Grade C GCSE Italian. *'Oh Jolyon, you're such a disappointment.'*

"I just don't want to come."

"We won't even discuss it."

"I was so bored last year."

"Paris. Boring?" She looked to the heavens. "Give me strength."

"You and Dad would be far happier by yourselves."

"I told you. It's not an option. Now, put this sack of potatoes in the shed."

"Mum, I'm sixteen years old. I'll be seventeen in March. No one goes on holiday with their parents when they're sixteen."

"You're being ridiculous, Jolyon. And bloody ungrateful. Most children would give their eye teeth for an opportunity like this." *No, mother. Faced with this opportunity, the 'children' I knew would unanimously hold on, not just to their eye teeth but their molars, their incisors and everything else in their mouth, and opt for the pleasures of home.*

"I'm not a child, Mum."

"Well I've booked everything. I can't change it. So that's the end of it."

Why oh why? I was furious. Why did I have to live the life my parents wanted? Not wanted, determined. Dictated. My friends didn't have to. They didn't go away on family summer holidays. Unless it was somewhere cool, Yosemite, Mallorca maybe. Or unless they had brothers and sisters, that was different. It was possible to find holidays where there were kids of your own age. I could cope with that. The Jacks? We never went anywhere you'd find other kids. Well, not quite true. There had been Mary-Lil in the hotel in Paris, all the way from Washington. No, I should say as she instructed, all the way from Washington *DC.* Trouble was her father had almost caught us indulging in some *pelotage,* as Mary-Lil had gigglingly described it. Her French was far more advanced than mine. Anyway, that was the end of her as a distraction. The whole family had checked out the following morning. *Paris dalliance dents Atlantic alliance.* My mother had given me a stern talking to, *that sort of behaviour is simply unacceptable,* and my father something slightly less stern.

"Well I'm not coming. You can't make me. I'm staying at home."

My mother's reply was almost a shout. "You ungrateful boy. I'll speak to your father. You're coming with us."

"No way."

"Jolyon, come back here. We're going to finish this conversation."

No way!

I slammed the door and thirty seconds later had lost myself in a mix in my bedroom, with the sound turned up to a level I knew would infuriate, cursing the scratchy fader on my piece of shit of a mixer, cursing my bad luck in having such an unbending dragon for a mother and finally just effing in time to the music.

The next morning the saga continued.

"I've had a message back from your father, and he agrees. Obviously we can't force you to come with us. Not physically. But if you don't come you'll have to pay us back for the air ticket and the hotel room. And you'll have to pay for yourself while we're away. I'm not subsidising your, your rebellion."

"That's not fair. You never asked me if I wanted to go to Tuscany. You didn't even tell me you were buying the tickets. And it's not as if you'd make me pay for my food on holiday."

"It's no use arguing. I've made up my... we've made up our minds. If you want to stay at home you can fend for yourself."

It wasn't promising. It wouldn't cost much if I stayed at home while my parents were away, just whatever it took for entertainment plus topping up my pay-as-you-go plus some occasional weed. There was plenty of food, and I did shifts as a dogsbody at the local supermarket. Specifically not Waitrose; I didn't want to bump into my mother and her friends. But I'd need more if I went to Manchester. I did have some money saved from weekend shifts. I was trying to put together enough for a decent set of decks, eleven hundred pounds for the Technics 1210s that Dave had. I didn't know what the tickets to Italy would cost, if my mother followed through with her threat. Money would be a problem, definitely.

But I couldn't not go to Manchester. Missing out on the joys of Florence, six hundred years of historic tedium, was an end in itself. The chance to practise squash every day, more than I'd dreamed of. And someone to mix with, on good gear. There was no argument.

So my next discussion with my mother, when I rolled into the kitchen at midday the following morning, wasn't an easy one. "I just can't believe it," she said. "You're being absolutely ridiculous. I'm lost for words, Jolyon." Three statements, none of them accurate, or certainly not the last. Sure enough, the words she'd lost turned up again pronto. They reappeared in Kalashnikov bursts through the rest of the day. I paid as little attention as I could, but some of the practical ones penetrated.

"And don't expect any help from me getting you to Manchester."

That was a blow. I hadn't thought through the journey to Dave's home.

"Oh Mum. At least you could give me a lift into Brighton."

"Your father and I would be perfectly happy to take you to Gatwick with us. You can still change your mind."

"That's not fair."

"It's your decision."

So it was a blagged lift into Brighton early the next morning, slow coach to Victoria because it was cheaper than the train, and an even slower coach from Victoria all the way to Manchester where I was met in the early evening by Dave and his father, who introduced himself as Russell.

"Well done, Jolyon. That's a bit of a mission. Coach all the way from the south coast?"

"It was okay. I slept a lot of the way. Only trouble was, coming like this, I couldn't bring any vinyl. Too heavy."

"I wouldn't worry. Dave's getting new stuff every other day. I know because he uses my credit card. That reminds me, you owe me twenty quid, Dave."

"I get paid tomorrow. I'll give it to you then."

"What work do you do?" I asked.

"Filing, tidying, general dogsbody at the local surgery. My Mum's a doctor there."

"She uses him if there's a patient who's asked for euthanasia. One look does it."

"Very funny, Dad, very funny."

I felt relieved. Dave's Dad at least was a million miles from my Mum, and by the sound of it his mother was okay too.

Chapter Four

"Hey Jolyon, this way, I want you to meet someone before we head home." It was Russell calling as Dave and I emerged from the changing rooms at the English Institute for Sport. The EIS, I'd discovered, was more or less in the shadow of the Man City football stadium.

"We'll stop off at the canteen before we go. Sailor McCann's there. You must have come across Sailor? The pair of you may be able to get some advice from him, routines and so on. He's not part of the England Squash set up but he's based here and he looks after several top sportsmen, and women. Squash is his main interest, though. It'd be worth meeting him anyway."

"What's he called? Sailor? Does he do white water rafting?"

"Keep any remarks about his name to yourself. You'll see why when you meet him."

Dave's further information about this dude as we walked round to the canteen made me more interested. "You might have seen him at one of the women's tournaments. He's Zoë Quantock's coach."

"Zoë Quantock, flippin' heck! The guy's big time then."

Russell laughed. He had apparently been a county player, strictly amateur, way back, and he was still involved in Lancashire squash. He played occasional matches, he said, for a club called the Jesters. He seemed to know a lot of what went on in the squash world.

"Zoë spent her first year here at about the same age as you. What, it must be nearly five years ago now, well before she broke through. She was already a top junior. Sailor liked the way she played. The main thing he did with her was conditioning. Relentless. But she lapped it up. Four years later, bingo, world champion. A year on from that, the start of this year, world number one."

Anyone who knew anything about squash knew about Zoë Quantock. She had come to the attention of a wider audience too. She was invariably the player that Squash England used in its publicity, golden girl, big time glamour on court, how could anyone so lovely be so tough, *et cetera et cetera*. She'd quickly progressed from three lines in a bottom corner of the sports pages, the usual place for women's and indeed men's squash, to glam pics not far from page three.

It was the middle of the day and the canteen, adjacent to the indoor athletics track, was busy with recreational players. We picked up some drinks and Russell led us across to a table round the side where a small guy in a tee shirt and tracksuit bottoms, number one haircut, was saying something emphatically to an average looking girl in tennis gear. Nice brown legs though. She obviously spent time outside in her shorts because the brown turned pale halfway up her thighs.

"Hi Sailor," Russell said. "Mind if we join you?"

"Russell, be my guest. This is Sarah Wilkins." By the time he'd reached the word 'guest' Sailor had branded himself. He was Scottish. By the time he'd finished 'Wilkins' even my short sixteen years' life experience let me conclude that he wasn't from some poncy sandstone house in Edinburgh. Nine floors up in a Glasgow tower block was more like it.

Russell finished the introductions as we pulled up some more chairs.

"My son, Dave, and this is Jolyon Jacks, all the way from Sussex."

"Jacks," Sailor looked hard at me. "I know a Jacks. Your father wasn't in the Navy, was he?"

"Still is."

"Submarines?"

"Yes, that's him."

"Lieutenant Jacks, stap me vitals! I thought so. You look like him."

"He's a captain now."

"Aye, he's a good man. I'm no' surprised."

"Where did you know him?"

"Faslane. Mebbe fifteen years ago. I was a petty officer on The Renown. Couldn't stand it. Got out as soon as I could."

"He loves it. He's due to retire next year. Says he doesn't know what he'll do."

"Aye, that's the problem for some of them."

"How did you end up here?" Russell asked.

"End up? I used to play squash for the Navy." A slight swelling of the chest. "Won two Navy championships. I went into the Fleet Protection Group. Then four years as a PE instructor after that. Covert forces, special techniques. Hard men."

"That's right. Aren't you a black belt or something?" Russell asked.

"Aye, but I don't use that on Sarah."

Sarah smiled and Dave laughed. "What about on Zoë Quantock? She's awesome."

"Ye don't need anything special for Zoë. Protection from her, mebbe. I've never met anyone so focussed. I spend more time holding her back than pushing her on."

Russell made a joke that Dave and I were soon to regret. "These two need pushing. Could they join your light squad through August?"

I was to become accustomed to the look Sailor gave first Dave, and then me. He had blue eyes that would have appeared tough in a little old nun. Set as they were in his small, hard face, underneath his greying number one, they made an immediate statement about their owner's personal philosophy. Compromise? What's compromise? Giving up? Giving *what*? There was something that frightened me about Sailor McCann's eyes.

"No problem. Three of the squad have dropped out. Summer holidays." He made taking a holiday sound as acceptable as moonlighting on the dole. "It's three times a week. Monday, Wednesday, Friday. Nine o'clock sharp. We start at the courts, finish at the gym. Stop at one."

"And," he looked at us, "make sure you have a decent breakfast. At least an hour before you come."

That was the moment the squash system started to suck me in. Many, I came to learn, would be spat back out. It might only take a month. That was probably best, not too much lost, no scars. Some lasted a year; it was sad if it took that long for you to realise that you couldn't cope. Some took even longer, before being undone by injury or the realisation that no matter how hard they tried, they had a deficit in talent.

Funnily enough, it had been Ron Clarke, the dreaded tripper, who had confirmed my taste for squash.

I had started completely by chance. In the spring following my first Senior Steeplechase, one of the girls in my house at school had challenged me to a game.

"Oh come on, Siobhan, not squash, it's gay."

"No it's not. It's a lot harder than cross country, trust me. You play tennis, don't you? You should be good at squash. And you need to be fit."

"Why would I want to play squash? Running around in circles in a small room."

"Afraid you'll be beaten by a girl?"

Well I wasn't afraid of *that*. *That* wasn't going to happen. *That* I knew.

But, oh dear, a few days later, specifically *that* happened. I was beaten by the self same Siobhan, who was indisputably a girl. Squash was so different from tennis, and Siobhan knew what she was doing. For one thing she kept on playing the ball into the side wall first so it went at an angle towards the front wall and ended up a long way away, too far for me to reach. Then when I stood further up the court to counter this she hit the ball high to the back. I tried hitting it to the back too but it bounced out. Aaarrgh!

That wasn't all. I found when Siobhan hit the ball deep it was different; it caught the side wall first and ended up too close to the back for me to scoop it out. Then she'd play the ball tight to the wall so I couldn't return it without smashing my racquet. When I fluked one close to the wall myself she unerringly picked it off with the end of her much more expensive-looking racquet, back down the wall. Where hooray, I'd miss it.

The worst part, most embarrassing, was the exhaustion. Under Sarah Bristow's direction I could do repeat shuttles up the side of Bright's Down off sixty seconds for twenty minutes. That was gut busting, but I could easily do 5K afterwards across the Downs. I'd done a 20K charity run and felt fine all the way through. I'd beaten the school record in the bleep test. Now as I scrambled with increasing desperation after the nasty little black ball, which Siobhan always seemed to hit to the furthest part of the court, I started to run out of strength. My legs weren't bulky but I always prided myself on their strength. Not now. There was no better phrase, they were turning to jelly.

It was embarrassing afterwards over a can of soft drink. "So that was gay, was it? I thought you were supposed to be fit. Cross country and all that."

"Well I need to practise. It's different from tennis. I couldn't get used to that shot you played onto the side wall."

"That's called a boast. Don't know why."

"A boast, huh. Maybe I'll have a hit by myself. Practise a few boasts. Then I'll play you again."

I liked Siobhan but I didn't like her next suggestion. "Not unless you admit, in the lesson tomorrow, that squash isn't gay."

"As long as you don't brag about the result."

"Well I can hardly say you won."

The humiliation in class the next day was worse than I expected. Never mind the result. Never mind the amusement of my friends that I'd lost to a girl. I was so stiff. I'd never been that stiff. My thighs were stiff, my calves were stiff, my left arm was stiff. And these were trivial compared with how stiff I was in my bum. It was crippling. I moved around the school like a geriatric.

"What did she do to you?"

"I hear you lost to Siobhan at karate."

"Hail the hard guy, squashed by a girl."

"Unexplained teen suicide at Sussex school."

"And after that shameful experience Jolyon Jacks, at the age of only fifteen, made up his mind to become a monk."

Strangely, the monk notion would return a couple of years later, big time. But I had no idea of that then. And as for being squashed by Siobhan, in a physical sense I wouldn't have minded, but she was a year older than me and interested in some dude it the sixth form.

We played again the following week. This time instead of a tracksuit Siobhan was wearing a tight little dress, and I had to fight to maintain a greater interest in the black ball than her white knickers. The small crowd in the gallery, mostly my classmates scenting a humiliation, became an ally: in front of them I couldn't do anything other than try, rather than ogle my opponent. Which I knew they'd be doing from up above, the bastards. At least my angle was better down here.

The result was the same. I did win a few more points, mostly with short straight shots that had the twin advantage of being too far up the court for Siobhan to reach and making her bend a long way in the attempt. I always seemed to end up behind her in the rallies. It was my first lesson in squash tactics, the most important one of all, get in front of your opponent. Not that I realised it then.

"That was a bit better," Siobhan said afterwards.

"Oh, thanks," I replied, "you're hardly warmed up and I'm a river of sweat."

"Girls don't sweat," she said primly. "We perspire."

"Can we have another game?"

"Okay, but after half term. There's a junior county weekend, and then we're going skiing."

The interval to our next game worked to my advantage. Another early lesson that would stand the test of time, the more you prepared the better your results. My father was home at half term. Some Navy planner must have got things wrong and let him out for a change.

"Hey, Dad, I've been playing a bit of squash. You couldn't give me a lesson or two, could you?"

"Oh not squash," my mother said. "It's such a sweaty, proletarian little game. Why don't you get back to tennis, Jolyon? You could still be really good at tennis."

"Come on, Mum. Why is it tennis, tennis, tennis all the time?"

"You're wasting your talent. Rodney Fairbanks said he'd never seen a junior hit the ball as well as you. Bar none. And you've no idea what pleasure it gave me when you beat Jasper von Liebig in that final. His horrible German mother, turning up in her leather trousers. Lording it all over the club."

"You're wasting your talent, can't you see that."

Rodney Fairbanks was employed by the tennis club, lottery funding or something, to coach the juniors. Not my cup of tea, smooth Rodney. Nor were the other boys in the squad.

"How many times do I have to say? I just don't like the other kids. They're all posers." I could have added that their parents were all posers, but that was too close to home. "And so what if I can hit better shots than them. I just don't care. They're all cheats anyway."

The cheats thing was another reason I'd stopped tennis. I'd first noticed it at a big under-eleven tournament in Eastbourne. I'd been having a terrific game, a semi final, against a boy from Shropshire. Quite a few people were watching, including of course my mother. I'd won a long rally to win the first set but my opponent had called my shot out. It had certainly been close to the line but I'd seen it as in.

"That was never out," my mother exploded. "That was your point, Jolyon."

What the heck, I thought. It may have been out. "It's all right, Mum. I'm okay."

Maybe the boy from Shropshire was encouraged by this. His parents tried to shush my mother as she protested more and more loudly at his calls, some of which even I could see were ridiculous. I battled away and managed to reach match point in the third set. My opponent fizzed a ball past me and it landed on the outside of the line.

"That was out," my mother shouted. "Well done, Jolyon."

I was embarrassed. "No, it just caught the line, Mum." It was lucky that she and the other parents were on opposite sides of the court.

Five minutes later I lost, to another dodgy call.

"This is ridiculous," my mother shrieked in a manner that my opponent's parents would have heard if they'd remained in Shropshire. "You should be ashamed of yourself." I heard later that she'd been reported to the Sussex LTA. Not my opponent, though. What he did was the norm. The cheating took off as we got into our tennis teens. First one or two of the kids did it, encouraged it seemed to me by their parents. Then it became an epidemic.

"Well what's this about squash then," my mother went on in our wasting-your-talent discussion. "Why squash? Why do you care about that?"

"Squash is just a bit of a lark. One of the girls at school, she's a county player. She persuaded me to have a game. Then she beat me."

My father had been looking on with an amused air while my mother and I bickered. "It can't do any harm, Shirley. And it won't be long before Jolyon thrashes me at everything, so I ought to take advantage."

"I don't know. It's such a miserable little sport. It's for people who can't make it at tennis. Anyone can hit a squash ball. You'll soon tire of it, Jolyon, mark my words."

I was to get tired that day, but not in the way my mother imagined. My father had been a good player before the absence of courts on nuclear submarines had led him instead to an obsession with working out in gyms. He was also patient when explaining things. I can remember when I was small, learning all about ships, of course, and space shuttles, and bird migration, and indeed when I was a bit older the X chromosome and the difference it makes. 'You find the X in sex, son, and Y, Y is for willie, so to speak.' Plus a lot of far more subtle stuff that I only started to appreciate years later when my testosterone levels had finally fallen below the teenage acne threshold.

So while we were driving to the club my father gave me the basics of squash.

"The secret of running less on the squash court," he said, "is to be in the middle of the court, at the 'T', so your opponent has to run round you."

"I've seen that already. I always seem to be behind Siobhan when we're playing."

"Well, what you've got to learn is to hit the ball tight down the wall. Make sure it goes to the back. Don't hit it across the court. Straight shots good, cross court shots bad. It's as simple as that."

Perhaps it was the simplicity of what my father showed me that day. It really appealed to me. He hit the ball down the wall as he'd explained, and I tried to do the same. I was exhausted after just ten minutes but we played on till the lights went out.

"Well done, it's not going to take you long," my father said as we came off court. "Now you need to work on that."

Two more sessions with my father cured me of any tendency to get stiff, and among other things I came to terms with the need to move away backwards after playing a shot. My father explained the rules in more detail than Siobhan had. His parting words as he headed off for a week of briefings in Portsmouth were, "Keep playing the volleys. If you can volley rather than let the ball go to the back you'll tire your opponent out."

It was all so simple, and so obvious. In theory. I finally managed to fix another game with Siobhan and felt excited on the day, all the way through my morning's timetable, English and Maths, my two least unfavourite subjects. My friends were predictably mocking.

"The only lamb in history that actually returns voluntarily to the slaughter."

"A mutton for punishment."

"Schoolboy in bizarre assisted suicide experiment."

"We'll be there as witnesses. Blake has been nominated to contact the emergency services, if they're needed."

"When they're needed, not if."

I enjoyed the banter because I was confident of winning. Nervous though. It was clear that Siobhan had been playing well within herself during our first two games. How much better would she be when she was pushed? I hoped I hadn't underestimated her.

Disappointingly Siobhan turned up in a tracksuit. I'd been imagining an improved version of the dress.

"Hi Jolyon. Cool shoes."

On my father's suggestion I had bought a pair of proper squash shoes. "No expense spared in pursuit of victory."

Siobhan hit the ball dauntingly well in the knock up. Some of her friends had come along, as well as our classmates, so the gallery was full.

I started the game doing exactly what my father had taught me. And it worked. Siobhan soon peeled her tracksuit bottoms off to reveal a nondescript pair of shorts, boo. And her international class legs, hooray. At game point I hit another accurate short shot. Yesss, got you!

"Let please."

"Uh?"

"Can I have a let. I couldn't get through."

It didn't seem right but I could hardly argue. "All right. Ten eight then?"

I was pissed off, and angrily drilled her return of serve into the tin. Siobhan to serve, an opportunity gone.

Calm down, remember what Dad said. So I did and moments later won the first game. Siobhan was decidedly pink-faced too, surely a good sign. It hadn't been easy, but I was exhilarated. It was the first game of squash I'd ever won.

In the first point of the second game Siobhan was quite far forward. I followed the usual recipe and hit the ball deep. In trying to get back she bumped me with her shoulder, sadly not one of her soft bits.

"That's a let." It was as much an accusation as a clarification, with Siobhan looking directly at me, hand on hip.

Again, it didn't seem right, but I'd no experience of when lets could be claimed. I'd never seen a serious game of squash.

"Okay."

I managed to win the replayed point, but I didn't win another till near the end of the game. Whenever I gained the upper hand Siobhan would contrive a let. She won the game eleven five.

I had to keep my temper, I could see that. The whole thing was going wrong, made worse by cheering in the gallery, all from my friends, and all for Siobhan. Some friends. Three things on the credit side: first, my legs were still feeling good. Second, Siobhan's shade of pink was intensifying. And third, her shapeless tee shirt was starting to get sweaty and clingy.

In the middle of the next game, the next hiccup. Siobhan made no effort to get out of the way when I was set to win the point.

"Is that a let for me?"

"Could you have reached the ball?"

"Reached it? Of course I could."

"All right, let then."

Keep your temper.

I did, just, and overcame what seemed to be a steady stream of injustice to reach ten eight, game ball. Siobhan's movement had started to become laboured, and next point, hopelessly out of position, she lunged into me with her shoulder instead of making a move towards the ball.

"That's my point."

"Your point? What do you mean?"

The hand on the hip again. "You've got to give your opponent every opportunity to reach the ball. And if they're prevented from hitting a winning shot it's their point."

"I can't believe this. You'd never have got that up."

"I was there."

Slow clapping started in the gallery. "Surely it's only a let, at most."

"Not when it's so clear cut."

Keep your temper?

Not a chance, not this time. Ends and tethers, internal eruption, I was gone. I might have dealt with Siobhan without an audience. Normally I could deal with my mates taking the piss. Combined, the provocation was too much. I lost the third game quickly and in the fourth consistently slammed the ball into the tin, losing it eleven nil.

Match to Siobhan. To boos from the gallery I refused to shake hands and left as quickly as I could.

Chapter Five

That should have been the end of a very short-lived career in squash. I'd smashed my racquet on the way home. Nothing would induce me near a court again, let alone onto one, I was so pissed off. A couple of weeks later, though, I was approached by one of the teachers, Mr Feather.

"Someone told me you've started to play squash, Jolyon. I haven't seen you down at the courts."

"Nah, I've decided to stick to running. The rules in squash are too complicated."

"That's a shame. You're a good tennis player, aren't you? And you're obviously fit. It's a good mixture. I always have plenty of players who hit the ball well but so few are prepared to knuckle down. Put in the work. You don't get anywhere in squash without hard work. Sarah Bristow says you really push yourself."

"You've got to want to do it, Mr Feather. And I don't. It doesn't suit my temperament. Anyway, the running's too much fun."

"Come on. Give it a go. You could at least come down to one of our practice sessions."

That was how I found myself six weeks later on court with my running nemesis, Ron Clarke. It was the first round of the annual school squash tournament. Mr Feather had been persuasive. The memory of the game with Siobhan had faded. After a week thinking about it I'd started practising with the school under sixteen squad. The game turned out to be so easy. In tennis if you played a weak shot it tended to be end of point. In squash you had a fair chance of getting back into the rally. It might mean scrambling a bit, but I was good at that. I learned that Siobhan's interpretation of the rules had really been flagrant cheating. There was a logic to the lets and penalty points, and the referee's response of 'no let' was not uncommon. It only took a couple of weeks before I had beaten one of the Colts team.

Ron Clarke was a different proposition though. He played in the senior team, a hobby for him rather than a serious interest, as running was his main sport.

One of the other Colts players commiserated. "You've got Ron Clarke? Bad luck. Everyone reckons he's going to win the whole thing. He's not first seed because he doesn't play all the matches. Cross country. He's classy though. 'Robin I' just doesn't have the shots."

'Robin I', Robin Inglis, played number one in the school team. I'd never seen anyone sweat so much, hardly surprising given the amount of running he did.

Anyway, it was Ron I had to worry about. "Is tripping legal in squash?" I asked with a straight face as we were going on court.

"Don't waste my time. I'm surprised you bothered to enter. I need to be somewhere else so let's get this over with."

"Well, I bothered to enter the Senior Steeplechase."

I got a look, and we started to warm up. My remark about tripping had just been for the fun of it. I wasn't too worried about Ron cheating because there were several players in the gallery. I didn't expect to win, anyway. I was expecting a good lesson.

From the opening points it was clear that a lesson was what I was going to be given, along with as much humiliation as Ron could mete out. I didn't have a clue where he was going to hit the ball. He would shape to play a short shot and flick his wrist at the last moment to send it to the back. "Nice shot, Ron," from the gallery. Or he'd turn the face of his racquet when lining up to hit the ball down the wall and produce a short angled shot, impossible to reach unless I'd anticipated it. "Well done, Ronny, boy." Then he would ponce his way back to the service box with exaggerated condescension, looking up at his watching friends and glaring at me.

I was quickly one game down, eleven one. I left the court to recover my breath and towel off.

This provoked a reaction from Ron. "Come on, Junior. I told you, I need to get away."

Piss off, I thought. The rules give me ninety seconds between games and that's what I'll take. And I'll see how long I can make the whole match last.

Depressingly, the second game started the same as the first. More swaggering from Ron to the gallery. I was well down and starting to get upset, more with myself than Ron, when under pressure I completely mistimed a shot and it arced high into the gallery. I was amazed to see my father up there. I'd mentioned the game in an offhand way but never expected he'd come along. Now I wished I hadn't; it was too embarrassing. As I looked up he mouthed something at me. I made out the word wall. I know, Dad, hit the ball down the wall. *You* come and have a go. However, I concentrated hard on this in the next point and won it with Ron scrambling around the back of the court. Yesss, that was nice. Infuriatingly in the next point one of my shots jammed out instead of hugging the wall and it was a clear penalty point or 'stroke' as I'd learned it was called, to Ron. Then he played two ridiculous fluky drop shots and I'd lost the game.

My father was waiting as I left the court, not what I wanted. "Come on, Dad, this one's going south, just let me get my breath back."

"Listen to me, Jolyon. You've not lost this. Take a look at him."

Ron had also come off court this time, breathing heavily.

"He really had to try in that game. And that point, the one where you rallied at two seven, he didn't like that. Did you notice, he went for a couple of silly shots after that. He fluked them but that won't last.

"Now, you have to show him at the start of this game. He's got to know, this is going to be hard. You're fit enough, I can see the way you're moving. This isn't going to be rocket science. Hit the ball tight down the wall, the harder the better but keep a length. No frills. Don't lose the match. Don't give it to him. Make him earn it."

I wanted to warm the ball up at the start of the game but Ron said, "No, come on, we've had the full break."

So much for my father's plans. Ron hit three good winners with the cold ball. My father's mouthed 'down the wall' was obvious when I looked up, and in the fourth point I got it going, whack, whack, whack. Ron played a good boast but I scrambled it back and then he hit the tin. Yesss.

The next point was the same, and ended in another Ron error. Jeez this was hard, two rallies and I was out of breath. But so was Ron, I could see. He won the next point and wandered all the way up to the front of the court before returning to the service box.

The next point was a mixture of pain and pleasure, pain because it went on and on, pleasure in that it gave me something I'd never experienced, complete control over another individual. The ball had become bouncy with the hard rallying. It was a question of keeping Ron behind me and enjoying the hunted look that was developing on his face. Finally, with a shout, Ron slipped in a corner and hit the ball down.

"Fuck, we need to wipe the court. Bring your towel."

"I'm not using my towel. Get yours."

"For fuck's sake. The court's dangerous"

"I'm not arguing we need to wipe the court. Not with my towel, that's all."

The wiping problem was resolved with a wide mop propped outside. Unfortunately the ball had cooled down and Ron won three quick rallies when we restarted, "Come on, Ronny boy, that's more like it." My brief confidence turned to fear. I was going to lose. But Ron was taking an age between points and I glanced at my father. He rolled his eyes and mouthed his usual message.

Of course it worked. Soon I'd caught up to six all. Ron slipped again in a comic piece of overacting and we had to repeat the court wiping rigmarole. This time I kept hold of the ball during the interruption and hit some hard shots to myself before we restarted. Ron's next gambit was lets. He started to ask for what seemed to me to be ridiculous lets. I argued but remembered Siobhan. I was not going to lose my cool. I played a good drop shot with Ron far in the back of the court, backing away in the prescribed arc towards the T. Ron scrambled forwards far too late into my back.

"Stroke to me," he panted.

"What do mean?" I panted back. "You were nowhere near that."

We argued for a few moments. Then, in contrast to my experience with Siobhan, the gallery came to my aid. They started to boo.

Ron looked up, arms out in a for-heaven's-sake-I'm-innocent gesture. "Come on, that was my point."

Someone said, "You'd never have made that, Ron."

"Well at least it's a let."

In the end we settled for a let and agony, the ball had cooled and I lost the next three rallies. Ten seven, match ball to Ron.

The fear in my belly was horrible. I mustn't lose now. Ron bounced the ball a dozen times in preparing to serve, stood up straight, took an exaggerated breath and hit a hard one straight at me. I stepped back and only just returned it after a limp bounce off the back wall. A couple of shots from both of us down the wall, there was something very dead about the ball, and Ron hit a drop shot. The thing just didn't bounce and my desperate lunge wasn't enough.

A huge roar from the gallery. Ron threw up his arms. I disconsolately picked the ball up. I wanted to shake hands and get out but Ron was milking the moment. I squeezed the ball in frustration.

It was flat.

"The ball's burst," I said, "look. Surely we have to play the point again?"

"What do you mean the ball's burst?"

"See, here. There's a crack along the seam."

"No way, I won that point."

"Come on, surely you can't win a point with a burst ball?"

My father's voice came down from the gallery. "He's right, Ron. You'll have to replay the point."

"Who the fuck are you?"

"It doesn't matter who I am. The rules are clear. You can't win a point with a burst ball. You'll have to get a new one and carry on."

Someone said, "That's Jolyon's dad."

Ron was incredulous. "You mean you're his dad? You've no right to tell us about the rules. I've won the match. That's it."

He walked towards the door.

"Hold it!" My father's voice was not loud but I realised in that moment how he'd made it to captain of a nuclear submarine. "You can walk off the court if you like, Ron, but everyone here will know that you didn't win the match. It's tough that the ball broke, but that's the way it is."

My father's authority was enough to hold sway over a hundred and fifty strong-minded individuals in a nuclear sub. Quite enough for Ron. He shrugged, "Okay, I'll get another ball."

I felt as though I'd escaped a firing squad. The relief was incredible.

However, I was still two games to love and three match balls down. I think Ron realised that he was in a pretty invincible position. My first task was to make sure that the new ball was really hot before we got going again. Ron seemed to understand this and kept on slow balling it back to me. But I hit hard shots back to myself, and there was the added advantage that a new ball always seemed bouncier.

And so it came to Ron's serve.

"Right, match ball," he said.

The gallery was absolutely silent. More ball bouncing, another deep breath, and a high, lobbed serve to my backhand. I was so nervous. Hit it cleanly. Don't let it drop. Down the wall. Ron shaped to play a forehand and turned it into a perfect little boast at the last moment. I reached it on adrenaline alone. It turned into a mammoth point. Ron kept aiming for the single winner he needed. I ran and scrambled and rallied. And I started to get that feeling again, of controlling an individual. The fact that the individual was Ron 'Tripper' Clarke made it all the sweeter. I was not going to lose the rally. I knew it. Then Ron did. In desperation he took one risk too many and hit the tin.

There was huge applause from a now very full gallery.

Ron looked knackered. "Eight ten," I said and prepared to serve. The pattern was the same, Ron going for winners, me driving the ball to the back. He made another mistake.

"Nine ten."

Then another mistake. "Ten all."

A surge of adrenaline. Ron was seriously out of breath. Come on, two points. My serve bounced wide round the back wall, giving Ron several easy options. Maybe I strayed too far across, anticipating a straight return. Whatever it was, I was shocked by an intense pain in my thigh. I'd never felt that before. A hard hit squash ball really hurts. How could he have hit me from there?

"Front wall," Ron said. "Hand out." I was told afterwards that the ball was too far across the court to have hit the front wall directly. In other words it should have been a let, not Ron's point. I started to argue but Ron said, "Definitely front wall," and went to the service box.

Nooooo!

Eleven ten and I was match point down again. My mouth went dry.

Then I lost it mentally as his serve came over. A crucial point, so you had no option, you knew what to do, no risks: hit the ball safely. But the Devil's a clever operator and he's quick to spot a weakness. I'd seen Ron hit enough winning nicks that day. I'd hit them in practice myself. It's just that the risks outweighed the benefits when you were match ball down.

But Old Nick, true to his wicked name, persuaded me to go for a cross court nick.

Crack, such a good contact, the ball in the middle of my racquet's sweet spot. And the ball rolled clean, a dead nick winner. Ron hadn't moved. What an idiot, taking a chance like that. The gallery erupted, eleven all. Ron tried the same thing with my serve and hit the top of the tin. Twelve eleven, sweet.

"Game ball?" I said.

Ron's nod said yes it was game ball. His body language said no he wasn't going to win the point. I served high. He went for the nick again and the ball leapt up off the top of the tin.

Yesss! I was still two games to one down but I left the court in elation.

My father appeared for another word. "Well done. But it's not over. He'll be rattled, sure. Just give him the same formula. If he's going to win he's going to have to rally and rally and rally, no rest, nothing easy, nothing given. Now go and see the ball doesn't get cold."

By the time Ron came back onto the court I'd whacked the ball enough for it to be really bouncy.

"One game to two?" He nodded. "Love all."

I knew the formula. The first point went on for ages, but felt in control. Eventually Ron hit a weak shot into the middle of the court and utterly failed to run for the gentle drop shot that followed. One love.

After that it was no contest. Ron didn't have the heart to rally and he kept failing with attempted outright winners. Flukes won him a couple of points. The game only lasted five minutes. It was two all.

"Same formula," my father said, on his haunches in front of me as I sat in a chair outside the court. "Don't relax. Now, go and make sure the ball doesn't get cold."

Ron put up some token resistance at the start of the fifth game, and briefly led two love thanks to a couple of good shots. But the percentages weren't with those shots. I saw with a sense of triumph how the fight had left him. I'd done that. He was drenched in sweat. I'd *broken* him. It was as physical a beating as if we'd been in a boxing ring. He'd long since stopped meeting my eye when I prepared to serve. Here I was, a non-descript fifteen year old, in total control of a guy three years older, stronger than me if you measured it in a gym, far more successful than me in the school, and, a big bonus, the arsehole who had cheated me in a cross country race only a few months before.

The fifth game didn't last long. Ron looked shattered. At five love, completely out of order as I prepared to serve, I said, "Top of Senior Heartbreak, eh Ron?"

Ooh that was sweet. Right to the end I made him rally. I felt good physically, and was able to scamper for a couple of his desperate attempts at winners. The pleasure at his weak mistake on match ball was more intense than anything I'd ever felt running, light years in front of my best tennis memories.

That was the moment, Ron's ball hitting the tin for the final time, that totally hooked me on squash.

Chapter Six

Russell Kemball delivered Dave and me to the EIS courts at quarter to nine the Monday morning after our chat with Sailor McCann. In the changing rooms were Sailor and four other guys, getting into their squash kit. Sailor's accent seemed even more pronounced as he introduced them. Paul White I'd heard of, an English player who'd made a late breakthrough into the world rankings. The others could have been anyone, Ahmed Enan, who was apparently being supported by the Egyptian squash set up, James Lovegrove, a young English guy, and Riley O'Callaghan, who was as distinctly Irish as Sailor was Scottish.

Sailor addressed Dave and me. "Did you both have breakfast?"

We mumbled that we had. It had been an effort getting up and a further effort getting breakfast down. Our usual morning programme started with bacon butties in front of Extreme Sports on cable TV around twelve o'clock. This morning, on Russell's advice, it had been 7am and wholemeal toast. The Kemballs were a wholemeal family; my tomato ketchup and brown sauce tendencies were frowned upon.

"We're no' fannying about," Sailor went on, "and you need plenty of carbs inside you. We'll talk more about diet later.

"Now, for the three sessions this week I'm just going to see how ye go. I'll adapt your programmes individually when I've had a look at you."

We started with a ten minute jog, and I was awestruck to meet Zoë Quantock. Zoë was one of three women Sailor trained for squash. She must have been twenty or twenty one, with short blonde hair and a body that looked too frail, slim hips, boobs that would have been labelled in the supermarket as no more than 'fun-sized', and a friendly manner. Brilliant smile too when we were introduced, perfect white teeth. Zoë was one of those people who looked better than the sum of their features. She had a presence, charisma, whatever it was. In a world where each new starlet was labelled, tediously, as stunning, *bang, momentary concussion*, the effect that Zoë had was more like *BANG, permanent brain damage, persistent vegetative state*. The other two girls were Louise someone, generic squash slim and tough looking, and an intense black haired girl who spoke her name with exaggerated care, "Carmen Ferrando González." She even spelled it for me, and after I'd come to grips with the way she pronounced the Spanish 'z' I found myself wondering whether a lisp was an advantage in Spain.

After the jog, next on the menu, in one of the courts, was some stretching. Sailor noticed the look that Dave and I exchanged.

"You're only going to hear this from me once, lads. So listen. And remember. Everyone on this court is here for a purpose. Everything each of us do while we're here is for a purpose. Everything we do is done as well as we can. We turn up in clean kit. We make sure the grips on our racquets are new. We tie our shoelaces properly. We get to bed at a sensible time.

"And we stretch well. Stretching helps to prevent injury. It's not part of our match warm up, but we do it in training. Do ye understand?"

We nodded.

"Because if we don't understand, if I see any attitude, and I mean *any*, we're out. Finished. Gone home. Taken up tiddlywinks. Right?"

Sailor's eyes alone would have been enough to convey the message. After that, Dave and I didn't even look at each other. I'd never paid as much attention to stretching as I did over the next twenty minutes.

"Now, we're going to do some court routines. You two," Sailor addressed Dave and me, "have ye done the drive boast routine?"

The answer for Dave was yes and for me was no.

"Okay, each of you pair off with one o' the others."

"Come on," Zoë said to me. I gulped as we headed off to one of the other courts.

"I've never done any court routines. I don't want to mess up on the first morning."

"Don't worry. Sailor does sound a bit fierce. And believe me he is a bit fierce. But as long as you're trying there's no better coach in the world."

I'd never really thought about a woman's voice before. Singers yes, you liked them or you didn't like them, but that was more the whole package, the arrangement and the particular song. Zoë had a rather deep voice for a woman. Deep but sometimes it bounced upwards, gentle but tough underneath so you paid attention. She explained the routine we were going to do, one player on the T driving the ball down the wall and one boasting alternately out of each corner. Zoë started with the driving. I couldn't believe how hard she hit the ball. It was unnatural. After a couple of minutes I was embarrassed. Her shots were so tight I kept on failing to return them, even though I knew where the ball was going.

"Come on, you have a go from the T."

I didn't do any better from the T. Zoë's boasts were either shallow off just the side and front wall, and had me scrambling to drive accurately to the back, or they were more angled and ended up either in or close to the nick. After a couple of minutes of humiliation Zoë stopped.

"This is crap. If this is how you're going to be you won't last five minutes with Sailor. What do you think you're practising, Jolyon?" Normally I'd have been thrilled she'd remembered my name. Now I felt awful. "You're not practising to play practice shots." Her voice had an undertone of contempt. "You're practising to play in a match. This is serious."

She put her hand on her hip. "Have you ever won a game from match ball down? You must have done."

Ron Clarke. I nodded.

"Right. Each one of these routines, front or back, you're match ball down. You're in a final somewhere, you have to win. Like it was in that game, I'm sure you remember it. You can't lose the rally. Can't. That'd be the end of the world. Otherwise this isn't going to be any use. Not to you, certainly not to me. And I'm not here to waste my time. If you can't do any better, I'm out of here. I'll do something by myself."

"Okay," I mumbled. "Let's have another go."

Oh dear. Only five minutes before I'd been thrilled to be going on court, with Zoë Quantock no less, women's world champ. Drop dead gorgeous, too. I really wanted to impress. Now what? Zoë's face was set as hard as Sailor's, and far from being impressed, she was treating me like a teenage dork. Which is what I was.

"Give me the ball," I said. "You go to the back." It would be easier for me to apply pressure from the front, driving the ball deep.

And did I try. I was on to her boasts with everything I had, concentrating as hard as I could, match point down, drilling the ball to a length, get *that*, now get *that*, and *that*. And it worked. In spite of operating only in the front half of the court I was soon quite out of breath. Zoë's skin became damp with sweat. She started wiping her racquet hand on the wall in between rallies.

"That's better. Can you feel it now? Now you're getting some benefit from this. So am I. Five minutes more, I'll drive, you boast. Mix them up, some straighter, some wider."

It was more difficult at the back, but more in fear of Zoë's contempt than anything else I made a huge effort, and was pleased to force an occasional mistake out of her. We duly stopped after five minutes and everyone gathered in the lobby outside the courts. Dave rolled his eyes at me; he'd been paired off with Sailor. He looked hot.

"Right," Sailor said. "We'll do ten minutes of stretching and then the gym."

The first part of the gym programme was basic aerobics on exercise bikes. I could hear my mother going on about her spinning class as Sailor prescribed half an hour of what he said would be light intervals for Dave and myself, "…nothing too strenuous," in our first week. Within a couple of minutes I was inwardly groaning. If this level was not strenuous, what was strenuous going to be? This would have wiped out my mother's class. Next came a half hour of exercises on Pilates balls. In response to Dave's straight-faced enquiry, he was learning fast, Sailor spent a few minutes discussing the importance of core strength.

"Where does Pilates come from?" Dave asked when we were well into the session.

"Don't you read the Bible?" This was Riley, holding a position that suggested he was trying to impregnate his ball.

"What do you mean, the Bible?"

"Pontius Pilate. He had a bad back. He worked out some exercises for it."

"For God's sake, Riley," Zoë said. "Can't you do better than that?"

"Just trying to keep our minds off the inflatable dolls."

"Can it, Riley," Sailor said. "I'll have no filth under my watch."

The physical relationship with the ball was a positive feature of the Pilates.

If I'd had any energy to spare, and wasn't concentrating hard to avoid abuse from Sailor, I'd have been able to appreciate the sight of Louise and Carmen, and particularly Zoë, stretched out on the giant balls. It was serious exercise, though, and as if the Pilates hadn't been enough of a strain, we then did some specific conditioning for our abs away from the balls.

Finally it was more practice on court. This time Dave and I were paired. Sailor told us to alternate, with one player hitting hard, the other taking the ball early but only allowed to hit gently. Even away from Sailor's fierce gaze we both took the routine seriously. Looking back later from the end of the summer I can see how pathetic our efforts were then.

Everyone gathered in the lobby at the end. "You two okay?" Sailor asked us.

"Sort of," I replied. "We're bloody tired. Or I am, anyway."

"Me too," said Dave.

"Ay, ye should be. Recreation this isn't. Is it, Riley?"

"No, Sailor, Sir. This isn't recreation."

"He knows he has to agree with me. Or it's fifty press ups. Now, is anyone having lunch? I'm going to the canteen after a shower."

Why not? Dave and I could set our own schedule. We were taking the bus home. Half an hour later we were gathered round two tables in the canteen with Sailor, Zoë, Carmen, Ahmed and Riley. The others had gone.

"How old are you two?" Sailor asked.

"I'm seventeen next month," Dave said.

"And me in March."

Sailor looked at me. "So ye've a full year more in the under seventeens. And you Davey, ye'll have to move up with the big boys in the New Year. That's okay. If you're interested, I'll look at programmes for both o' you."

"I'd advise against it," Riley said. "Particularly if you've got any hormones. The price of celebrity in the squash world is," he paused dramatically, "celibacy."

"Don't pay any attention to Riley," Zoë said. "He uses squash to mask his lack of success with women."

"Huh, they say I look like George Best. Another Belfast boy. And you know how he got on with the fair sex."

Carmen looked puzzled. "Who is best, Riley?"

"Riley likes to dream," Zoë said. "George Best was a footballer who died of drink, and too many women."

"Anyway," said Riley, "how do you know I'm not gay?"

"Spare us, son, there's ladies here."

"I think you have nothing to worry, eh Riley?" From the way she said it Carmen would not be averse to some worry from Riley. And regarding George Best, it was true. Riley did resemble the pictures I'd seen.

"No, Carmen, I don't worry. And I'm no more gay than the great George." He pretended to collapse in his seat. "But I've no energy, especially after the track session this afternoon."

Dave was impressed. "You doing some *more?*"

"Ay, they've more to do, seekers of success," Sailor said. "Eat up, girls and boys. Get some rest. I'll see you at the track at three thirty.

"And I'll see you two at nine o'clock sharp on Wednesday, okay?"

That evening Russell asked Dave how we'd got on. "Sailor says he's being gentle with us this week. Then he's going to give us individual programmes."

"How was Sailor's gentle?"

"Bloody hard," Dave said. "We did some court routines, after some other stuff. I was with Sailor. Half an hour of that felt like a match."

I confirmed how serious this was going to be. "Zoë threatened to leave the court if I didn't get better. Literally. I'm not joking."

"You were on court with Zoë? What was she like?"

"She hit the ball incredibly hard and incredibly accurately. It was embarrassing at first."

"So it's Wednesday morning then? I can give you a lift."

A little later Dave and I went up to have a mix in his bedroom, but my heart wasn't in it. I was too tired. We'd already talked about importing our mixes into Dave's PC, and Dave wanted to get me started.

"I'll show you how to use the software. PCDJ DEX. It's really cool, dead easy. You can sample and echo and loop, just like that. It doesn't allow clipping. You can change speed without changing pitch. I can find any of my MP3s just like that. It'll do anything you want."

"Nah, let's wait till tomorrow," I said. "Tell you what, though. Can I get onto Facebook on this?" In the quiet of the Kemball's house, miles even from Manchester, I was suddenly aware how out of touch I was going to be with all my friends. My primitive mobile didn't do anything as clever as the Internet.

"Sure. Do you want to log on now?"

"Well, just a quick one."

There wasn't much on my wall, just some information about a free download and some more comments about my Manchester trip. And as I expected, there was a message from Samantha: 'Miss you jolls off on sat to jersey with mum and dad and fifi. Wicked party at jim the tigers but not the same wivout a mix and a seeing to from you.'

Lucky the party hadn't been up here. I'd have been too tired on either count.

Chapter Seven

In the second week I found myself looking back fondly on what we'd done in the first. Dave and I added the afternoon session to what everyone did in the morning. Sometimes this consisted of joining various athletes at the track beside the Institute. Apparently it had been the warm up track for the Commonwealth Games. Warm up, it did what it said on the label when you repeated four-hundred metre intervals. The afternoon alternative was pressure simulation on court, in groups of three. You rotated, with two players applying the pressure for about a minute, while the third hurtled about the court in match point mode. Riley was outstanding at this, but no one matched the intensity that Zoë brought to it. She blanked off any social chit chat for the entire session and she made *me* get tired when I was supposed to be one of the two subjecting *her* to pressure. After about ninety minutes we'd finish off with a jog and a stretch.

I'd used to think that Sarah Bristow's routines on the Downs were hard. Sailor's word for that when I told him about it was 'amateur'. Indeed, Dave and I were the only two in Sailor's squash squad who weren't professional. We soon learned something else. The professionalism extended beyond the courts and the track, as far as your evenings and your diet.

Firstly, Sailor insisted that we drank enough, sometimes glucose drinks but also simply water.

"Dehydration damages performance. You can't afford to be even half a percent dehydrated."

Dave's experience of this was the same as mine. "Pardon me. I seem to spend my whole time pissing on training days."

"Quite right," said Sailor. "Healthy kidneys, it's doing ye no harm."

"Mine are suffering from erosion," said Riley. "It's not long before they'll be washed completely away. And as for my hose..."

"That's enough about your hose, Riley. I'm responsible for the psychological state of these ladies, as well as the physical."

"You're responsible for my physical collapse," said Riley.

Paul White was quieter but he always enjoyed the relaxation at the end of training. "It's a miserable Celtic body, yours Riley. I'm surprised it's lasted this long."

"Watch what you say about us Celts. Celts do hard like no other race." This was Sailor now. I wasn't sure how much of it was banter. I don't think Paul was sure either, and he didn't respond. "With the honourable exception of Zoë here," Sailor went on. "Ye must have some Scots blood, Zoë."

"I don't think so. Pure bred English."

"And what about me?" Carmen asked, nose in the air. "My blood is Castilian."

"I'm just talking about the British Isles here. You can be an honorary Scot, Carmen."

"You, Carmen, can be honorary Irish," Riley said, "and I'd volunteer to instruct you in all the little ways of the Irish, if I had any energy left."

"Oh Riley, are you sure you don't have just a little bit of energy?"

"Can it, Riley," Sailor said. "I'm in loco parentis with Carmen. I made her father a promise."

Carmen pouted and Sailor continued, "So ye still have some energy, Carmen, I'm impressed. I'll specify additional reps for you next time, the four hundreds, I think."

"No that sort of energy, Mister McCann."

"Talking of energy," Sailor addressed Dave and me. "After a hard gym session like we've had today, you need to get protein into you quickly as well as carbs. To restore broken down muscle tissue, ideally within half an hour of stopping."

"Ugh," Dave said. "The last thing I feel like now is eating."

"You don't have to eat. This is the one time you need a supplement drink, with protein."

"And this is when you take..."

"No, Riley, we've all heard your nandrolone jokes. I'll no have any drug jokes in any squad of mine." He paused. "It's. Not. Funny."

It was the way Sailor said it. Even Riley looked embarrassed. Dave and I received some further advice about protein supplements, and Sailor gave us each a five hundred millilitre bottle to try. It didn't taste too foul, and, I reckoned, I was going to have to get used to it. I wanted to do everything by the book.

Well most things by the book. Half an hour later we set out on our bus trip home. At first after Sailor's full day sessions it was all I could do to make it to the bus stop, which was only just outside the Sportcity complex. But now a couple of weeks on, the weariness was starting to feel merely pleasant in a heavy sort of way. It wasn't the same for Dave.

"I'm absolutely, totally fucked," he said as the bus headed east towards the village where the Kemballs lived.

"Have you ever tried weed? I used to sometimes after a long run. It really helps."

"Oh come on. After what Sailor just said? You're a nutter. Where could we get it, anyway?"

Given Dave's reaction I thought it best not to mention that I'd brought an eighth with me when I'd travelled up from home. It had sat unused in a small tin with my wash things. I was missing my regular bung. "No problem getting it around Brighton."

"Do you smoke a lot?"

"Mainly at parties, raves. Sometimes having a mix with my mates."

Mixing hadn't been the same with Dave, in spite of his superb gear.

"I've had it a few times at parties," Dave said. "I've never got it off a dealer."

"A couple of my mates deal. Small quantities. Never any problem getting it," I said.

"We can't, anyway. NRTP."

"Uh?"

"Come on, Jolyon. Aren't you registered?"

"Registered? What's that?"

"Fuck me, you'd better get Sailor to go through it with you. You could have been tested already. At a sanctioned event, that is."

"Seriously? I could have been drug tested?"

"Sure, they can turn up at any sanctioned tournament. Anywhere you get ranking points. And everyone competing has to be registered as well. Squash England does it for squash. They can turn up any time and test you. The very top players have to keep an online file up to date with where they're going to be."

"I didn't know anything about it. So say the South of England, they could turn up there?"

"I can't believe you don't know this. Any big competition."

"I never realised. A bit of weed wouldn't hurt, anyway."

"Weed's a banned substance. There was a French player who was banned for weed. Stephane Gadaffi or something, I think that's what he was called."

"You mean he can't play because he did a little weed?"

"It happened twice with him. I think so. First he was given six months. Yeah, just for cannabis. Then later it was permanent. He was positive for cocaine the second time. He was a good player, too. Top sixty."

"I don't see how weed would make you play any better."

Dave stared at me. "You're not getting it are you. It doesn't matter. There's rules. And think about it, you were talking about weed for recovery after training. You need a reality check. It's anything that helps. It doesn't even have to help. It just anything that's banned."

"Where can I see the list?"

"Like I say, talk to Sailor. I got the whole shit when I first started playing in the under fifteens. We had to register if we were on any medication. For asthma, anything like that. I've never been tested, but it could happen."

I didn't like the way this was sounding. You couldn't enjoy a set at a party without some weed.

After our next session I asked Sailor about the NRTP.

"I can't believe ye've not registered. Ye've played in sanctioned events?"

"He was a private entry," Dave said, and then to me, "You weren't entered by your school, were you?"

"No. I've only played in three tournaments, apart from school ones. I just found out about them and entered myself."

Sailor recovered and became all business-like. "Well, I've no' the time today, but Friday, when we've finished, I'll go through everything with you. The rest of the week's going to be a bit different anyway. Wednesday we're going to do a physical assessment, have a look at your performance levels. That'll take the place of the morning work. And I want all of you to play a competitive game at the end of the session on Friday. You two, Jolyon and Dave, will play together, Carmen, you and Louise, Riley, you play Ahmed, and me and Zoë. I've promised Phil Brennan that the losers will sweep the courts."

"Tough luck, Ahmed," Riley said immediately. "Remember to bring your broom in on Friday."

Ahmed was never one for long speeches, and just smiled. I'd have to bring my broom too. Dave and I had already played several friendlies after our encounter in the South of England. I couldn't get near to troubling him. He had so much control and a wonderful touch. I'd won a couple of games, but there was a gulf between us. At that moment, though, I was more interested in the performance tests and asked Sailor about them.

"You've no' done these before? No' with the cross country? Not even a bleep test?"

"We used to do bleep tests. But I haven't done one for eighteen months. I've got the school record, thirteen."

"Thirteen, not bad, not bad. We do the bleep. We do four tests basically. Five if you count body fat. We start with the jump test." I raised my eyebrows.

"That's self explanatory. Standing jump, off both feet, how high. Then the drop jump. It's much the same, but ye drop off a fixed height of fifty centimetres to set off the jump. This time we don't look at the height, we measure how long you stay in the air, but also how long you've spent on the floor making the jump. The ratio's the important thing. Then the VO_2 max, that's standard, and finally the bleep test. And no, Riley, no jokes please about yours or anyone else's vocabulary."

"Bleep that. That's harassment, Sailor. There's no reason to bleep my vocabulary. You should know that by now."

"In a perfect world you'd have a bleeper permanently assigned to you."

On the way home I asked Dave if he'd done the performance testing.

"I've done bleep tests, my best is thirteen too, and we did the standing jump at school last year. I did thirty eight centimetres."

"Sounds like fun."

"Is it that long since you've done a bleep test? At least with the jumps you don't end up fucked. Interesting to see how we get on."

I was excited at the idea of the testing. We started off on some sophisticated scales that measured not just your weight but percentage of body fat. It was based on electrical resistance, if I understood Sailor properly. Then the standing jump, with your hand chalked to mark your touch on a wall. It took me five attempts to reach my best height, which I was pleased was three centimetres better than Dave's, forty three to forty. Then the drop jump, on an electronic platform that gave a readout of your time while you were actually making the spring and then the interval to landing. After that we divided into two groups, one for the VO_2 max, which included Dave, Carmen, Zoë and myself, and one for the bleep test.

The VO$_2$ max process wasn't comfortable. There were two treadmills, and Carmen and Zoë went first. Sailor had asked Phil Brennan, the manager of the centre, to help with the measurements. The test involved running on a treadmill at increasing speeds until you were exhausted, with a bulky mask over your face that took your exhaled breath via a flexible pipe to a machine that measured volume and the concentrations of oxygen and carbon dioxide. The mask didn't enhance Zoë's looks but neither did it make her running style any less easy. I was sometimes behind her when we jogged on the track, and she was a class apart from the other girls when going flat out. Faster, too. On the treadmill, Zoë just seemed to flow, with perfect balance, eyes fixed in concentration on some feature on the gym wall. Truly international legs. Something about her boobs, too. You didn't need a machine to work that out.

Carmen came off sooner than Zoë. She rested, hands on knees, breathing heavily. A minute later Zoë stopped. They were both dripping. Even with the windows open it was stifling in the gym.

Once the masks had been changed it was the turn of Dave and myself. As I loped along on the treadmill in the early stages I found myself thinking of easy training runs in the South Downs. That wonderful speed, the one you could sustain on a long run, the feeling of having infinite reserves, of just flowing. Soon Sailor increased the treadmill, but it still felt good with the artificial bounce of the rubber surface. We must have been going for fifteen minutes when I saw Dave signal to stop. I was still okay. Sailor upped my speed again and I really started to push. A couple more increases and I was flat out, exhausted. Sailor slowed the machine at my signal and I had the relief of jumping off the treadmill and removing the mask.

"Well done, Jolyon," Zoë said, to my intense pleasure. She handed me a towel as I puffed back to normality. "Sailor tells me that you were a runner before you took up squash."

"Cross country, not sprinting like that. Funny though, I was thinking while I was doing the test that it would be good to do some running again. Not Sailor's four-hundred metre reps. There's nothing like doing it out in the hills."

"I'd be up for that. I do some road running, for stamina, but it can be grim in the streets round where I am. There must be some great runs out in the Pennines."

"I'll find out some more." I said. "I'll let you know on Friday." Running with the women's world champ, that would be a story! My mother would find some way of disparaging it but my father would be impressed. The thought of my mother reminded me that I should phone her. I hadn't spoken to her for a week. By now they'd be in Florence.

Sailor interrupted my thoughts. "Right, time to swap over. You four out in the hall. You all know what to do. I suggest ye change your shirts if ye've spares."

The first bleep test group were sitting on the floor in the hall. Riley was drenched in sweat and Louise was the strong shade of pink I'd come to recognise in a few females. Carmen caught up with us in a fresh bright yellow tee shirt.

"How did you get on?" As usual, she seemed to be addressing Riley more than the others.

"Ahmed's still the champ. Eighteen. And he wasn't trying, I could tell."

Ahmed grinned, nice face, brilliant teeth and the darkest eyes you ever saw. A thick Arabic accent completed the picture. "Big push to stay ahead of you, Riley."

"You're supposed to sweat, Ahmed. I'm going to get a message back to the Egyptian SRA. You're wasting your money, fellas. Ahmed's not trying. He doesn't sweat."

Sailor appeared. "Can it, Riley. Come and breathe your halitosis into my respiration machine."

"I'm not going first. That's Paul and James. Louise and I will go and get a drink and a change of shirt. Separately. And that remark was out of order, Sailor, harassment again. Anyway, my breath's shamrock pure. Isn't it, Carmen?"

"I don't understand sham rock, what rock?" From her grin it was clear Carmen wasn't embarrassed by the implication that she'd been up close with Riley. The first group moved out, with Riley's incessant chatter fading away.

The bleep test set up in the hall was identical to the one I was familiar with from Sarah Bristow. We were going to do the test in tandem. The twenty-metre distances were marked out by two pairs of small cones. There was a cheap CD player plugged into a power point nearby. The test involved running between the markers, to and fro, at a speed set by regular beeps from the CD. Apparently the standard start speed is eight and a half kilometres per hour. After a minute the interval between the beeps is shortened, equivalent to nine kph. Another minute and the time comes down again, nine and a half, and so on. The first levels are a doss, but towards the end it's utterly exhausting as you try to stay ahead of the increasingly dreaded beep.

"I guess Carmen and I had better go first," Zoë said.

When the two girls were ready, Dave pressed the play button on the machine. At the first beep the two girls set off. For seven or eight minutes it was easy and they ran side by side. Zoë made less noise than Carmen, whose feet were starting to stamp at the turns as the intervals shortened. Zoë seemed to glide with minimum effort. At level ten Carmen's breathing became obvious. The only change with Zoë was the concentration on her face. She was doing the test as seriously as everything else in her training. In the twelfth level Carmen was having to work hard. In the thirteenth she fell behind the beep a couple of times, but with obvious effort caught up each time and made it to the end of the interval. There she pulled away gasping with a great shout of, "Yes, my PB."

Zoë was still floating back and forth, the occasional squeak now coming from her shoes at the turns. In the fourteenth she was scrambling at each end in the same manner as in the back corners of the court during a hard point. With much encouragement from Carmen she just completed the fifteenth and stopped, hands on hips, bent over.

"Was that good?" Dave asked, as Zoë stood there hands on knees recovering.

"I've never done thirteen before," said Carmen, and mock punched the air.

Zoë was a little downbeat. "Fifteen's okay. I did sixteen once, last year, at the end of the summer. That was good today. I wasn't feeling great at the start.

"Now, come on, you hunky fellas. Are you ready?"

Dave and I went over to the start cone. I was feeling really nervous, a mixture of anticipation of the hard effort to come and having to do it in front of Zoë. Carmen went over to the CD player, pressed the button, the first beep beeped and we were on our way.

Bleep tests are a bit dull in the early stages. Normally there'd be some banter, but I didn't want Zoë to think I was showing off. Then at about level eight the whole thing narrowed to just Dave and me and the beeps. My legs were feeling so good, and I had a perfect rhythm, twelve strides between the markers and back. Twelve strides and back. Somewhere round level ten my breathing became heavier, and that felt good, too. I wanted to do well and I wanted to beat Dave. And I knew I could do both. The adrenaline I'd felt at the start came back round level thirteen.

"Come on Dave, come on Jolyon." Lots of encouragement from Carmen.

By thirteen Dave's breathing was noticeable, even from the mental zone I was in. He started grunting at the turns in level fourteen, but he made it and then fell away in fifteen and gave up with a shout of 'Ah, I'm finished', after only a couple of beeps. I was feeling under pressure but at the same time I was still feeling good.

"Come on, Jolyon." More of Carmen, jumping up and down.

I made it into level sixteen and it was really hurting. But my legs still felt good in the middle of the pain. Then I fell behind towards the end of the sixteenth. Concentrate. I just got it back, but I was struggling.

Then Zoë's voice. "One more, you big sissy, you're not trying, come on!"

Into the start of seventeen and my lungs were on fire, my legs screaming at me. That was all, I had to stop. But after Zoë's voice I couldn't. She was now making more noise than Carmen. "Match point, Jolyon, match point, you can't give up."

I fell behind and caught it, and fell behind again. Come on, two more lengths. Every part of me was protesting. Last turn, go on. I made it to the final cone of the seventeenth exactly on the beep and collapsed.

"Bloody hell, Jolyon," Dave said when my breathing had slowed. "Bloody hell."

I stood up and Zoë handed me my towel. "That was good. You made an effort there, didn't you? That's the way you do it." What a lovely voice, and voicing those words, too.

We finished the morning with pressure routines. I was poor. The bleep test had taken a lot out of my legs. At lunch in the canteen there wasn't much comment from Sailor. He simply said, "I'll pull together the results for Friday. Go through them with each of you individually. We'll do some hitting routines through the morning, nothing too heavy, and then we'll play the matches in the afternoon."

"What about Jolyon's bleep test?" Dave said.

Sailor looked at me hard. "Aye, a good result. But tests are one thing. No ranking points given for test scores. What's important is winning squash matches."

Chapter Eight

When we went in on the Friday I felt as though I was getting my GCSE results. I knew I'd done well in the bleep test and the jump test but none of us had any idea of our results in the drop jump and the VO_2 max. Sailor was taking about ten minutes to review the tests with each of us, at a table in a corner of the canteen, while the others rotated on two courts with hitting routines. I was last.

"Siddown, Jolyon, son." Sailor took some papers from a beaten up briefcase that I hadn't seen before. He looked unfamiliar in a pair of half moon reading glasses.

"Now, first the overall picture." He looked at me with his diamond eyes. "I'll come straight to the point. I've never seen anything like this. You're a freak, son, a physical freak. How old are you, sixteen and a half?" I nodded.

"If I saw these in an adult with five years of conditioning under his belt I'd be impressed. You don't play football, do you? Stupid question. They'd be drooling over these if you were at one of the academies. Even if ye couldn't kick a ball. Anyway, football's no' the point.

"Now," another pause to look at me over his half moons, "you've still some growing to do, if I remember your father. What's he, six foot?"

"Yeah, but I was always smaller. I'm one seventy three now. Dunno what it is in feet."

"That's about five eight. Some kids, especially girls, they finish their physical development early. But I'd say ye've still some way to go. Strength and endurance, they'll both improve.

"Hold on," he said, "I need a coffee. You too?"

Sailor was back a minute later with the drinks. He looked older and unexpectedly studious, peering through his glasses as he shuffled his print outs.

"Okay, the jump test, you know that. Forty three centimetres. A high jumper, listen to me, a high jumper, would do better, but not by much at your age, great leg power. I say great when we combine it with the reactivity index." He smiled. "Did you think the machine was electrified? You averaged 0.28 seconds contact, that's short, and 0.78 in the air. That's a 2.8 result, just under. That's high jumper territory too: I'd expect a good high jumper to do no more than three."

"What about the VO_2 max?"

"I'm coming to that. VO_2 max is something you're born with as much as anything. But physical activity helps. You understand VO_2 max, don't you? It's the rate your body can take up oxygen and use it. Anyway, you're lucky, son. Your result is eighty three point six. I've never heard of a squash player that high. Riley's the best I've had, seventy seven last year. He's been down a bit this year. Cross country skiers, cyclists, they tend to be best. Miguel Indurain, heard of him?"

I shook my head.

"Great cyclist. Spaniard. Won the Tour de France five times. He recorded ninety six, incredible. Couch potatoes, mebbe forty five.

"But it's not everyone with a high VO_2 max who can perform. Your lactate threshold, that's important, too. We didn't measure that. Involves blood samples. Beyond your lactate threshold you go anaerobic. Your muscle efficiency goes down and you can't sustain the effort. We've a clue to that from your bleep test. Seventeen. Seventeen, son! No one in my group has done a seventeen, certainly not at your age.

"So what this means, my friend," those hard eyes again, "is that you're under performing."

Sailor must have noticed the disappointment in my face.

"No, I can understand it. It's no' bad. How long have you been playing?"

"A bit more than a year, I suppose."

"Well really, it's okay son, you're over performing. Dave tells me you've played a lot of tennis."

"That's right. I never quite got on with it though. It ended up more my mother than me. She wanted me to play."

Sailor nodded. "It had to be a racquet sport. Tennis is for poofters. In my opinion, that is. It seems to attract spoiled brats."

"I used to play badminton, too. I'd play anything. I did gymnastics till I was ten. And swimming."

"And you must have played football."

"Yes, though my prep school did more rugby. I enjoyed that."

"Scrum half?"

"How did you know?"

"It's obvious. Combination of small size and insolence."

"Riley would call that harassment. Child protection issue, since I'm still a minor."

"Can it, sonny. I want to be serious. When I say you're under performing, what I mean is that with your physical attributes, with a full grounding in squash, there's no way you shouldn't be better. I've been watching you these last four weeks. You've already come on but you've a long way to go, so-o-o far. You're a tough little bugger. Yer just raw."

Sailor slowly, deliberately finished his coffee. "The point is, son, for you," he looked at me again, "the sky's the limit. Up there. It's just down to how much you want it. For only twelve months playing squash you've good racquet skills, amazing for such a short time, far better than the average. That must be the tennis and the badminton, and you've got good timing. What I think you'll never have is Ahmed's wrist, or Dave's way with a racquet. They've both been playing since they could stand up. You could do with those skills. We all could. But ye don't *need* them. You can break people down. So in the end the skills work against the player."

"I'm not sure about that. I'll never be able to beat Dave."

"We'll come to Dave in a minute. Have you heard of the South African, Jan Berry?"

"No, I presume he's a squash player."

"Aye, he's currently ranked three in the world. Berry the Hatchet, they call him. The most boring individual on the face of the planet," he laughed, "personally and squash wise. On court? He's relentless. He's short of real talent, nothing in the way of racquet skills. But as I say, he's relentless, a whirlwind. Anyone who plays Jan knows they're going to be put through it. He's onto every ball early, bang down the wall, volley, volley, volley; bang, bang, bang," he made cutting movements with his hand, "length, length, length. Nothing subtle. Nothing fancy. You know if you're going to beat him you're going to have to overcome his will. And he's a hardboiled Afrikaner. Fancy stuff won't beat Jan, not by itself."

Sailor paused and lasered me over his glasses. "You, son, can be better than Jan Berry."

"Me?" I didn't know how to react. It felt weird. What had he said, number three in the world?

"Aye, you. I think so. And this afternoon we're going to find out for sure."

"This afternoon? What do you mean?"

"Nothing fancy. You're going to beat Dave three nil."

I laughed. This was some sort of set up. It was the sort of joke Riley would make.

"Don't laugh son. Here's how you're going to do it. It's all in the first three points. Now, you're a good lad. You and Dave always have fun playing. I've watched you. Dave's a good lad, too. Sure your game's are hard. But they're no' serious. Well this is where they get serious. I don't mind how you are off court. On court, from now on, you're going to be an animal. I couldn't say this to Paul, or to Riley, or to Ahmed. I don't need to say it to Zoë. You have to have the physicality." 'Harv tae harv the phuzzicarlitay', is more how it came out. His accent had become more pronounced.

Sailor took off his glasses and folded them away into a case. "This afternoon, first three points, if you do it right, Dave will know he's going to lose. First three points. Or he'll realise that it's going to have to be a different ball game if he's going to win. He's going to have to dig, dig down deep. He's a good lad, Dave, fantastic talent. But you can squeeze the talent out of him. Like toothpaste. No one can squeeze what you've got out of you. If ye don't want them to, strong enough. It's got to be the wanting. Am I making myself clear?"

"I suppose so. But beating Dave Kemball? I don't know."

"That's the last time I hear you say that. For you, son, the world changes today, or I'm wasting my time with you." He looked at his watch. "One fifty three, August the thirtieth. The world changes now today if ye want it to." He rubbed the side of his face, as though checking his shave.

"First, here's how you win. Simple. In one way it's simple. In another way it'll be the hardest thing you've ever done. You're Jan Berry, mark two. Only you're worse than Jan. Think worse than The Hatchet. From the first point yer going to pressurise Dave, early, early, early. When yer serving, no messing around, no wiping your hand on the wall. Straight into the service box. Ready. Serve. Ready. Serve. Pressure. Give him the message. Pressure. After five minutes ye'll really be feeling it. But you can take that." He smacked the back of his hand on the print outs. "The tests show it. After only four weeks training." He looked away, "I can hardly believe it, a boy operating at that level. Dave will be hurting too, hurting worse. But most of all, he'll be damaged inside. You'll be damaging his psyche. 'What's got into my mate Jolyon? He's a bloody animal today. Oh this is hard.' After only five minutes.

"See?"

I nodded.

"Dave's a good lad. He'll fight. He'll hit a few winners mebbe. He'll rally, he's no' unfit. And he's quick. But as you grind, he'll start to realise." He made a clenched fist gesture against his heart. "This is going to be too hard. And then the mistakes will come. They always do in the end, if you pressurise enough. Too hard. All those wonderful shots you'll never be able to play? They'll find their way into the tin, not the nick. Then you'll win the first game. He'll joke while you towel down. Because believe me, you'll need to towel down. It'll be the eighteenth level in the bleep. *You* won't joke. It'll reinforce the message. 'This is serious. This is business. I make this *my* business, my friend.'

"First three points of the second game, same message. That's when he'll know for sure. That'll confirm it. He's going to lose. And he'll break. I'm telling you. He's a good lad, Dave, but he's no' got what you've got."

I was shocked. It was the intensity as much as the actual words, the way Sailor delivered the message, his piercing eyes. I wasn't convinced though. Dave Kemball was miles ahead of me. I'd tried rallying with him, been there. But he was fit, too. And he was certainly quick, getting to shots he'd no right to. He could always absorb a hard five minutes. Then he had the skill to pull away. I'd tried going for clean winners against him, lazy short cuts. No good those; he was simply better at those. Once after I'd gone one game up he'd beaten me with a stream of clean winners that went right through the next three games.

"I don't know."

"Well, we'll find out, won't we? You do as I say, son, don't mix it up. Just pressure. Pressure, pressure. Berry the Hatchet. Be like Jan Berry. You'll never beat Dave in a game of skill. Not if you play for the next twenty years. But you'll beat him today if you beat him in his mind. The top two inches, that's where you'll win, top two inches.

"And then if ye beat him, no, when ye beat him, I'll want to talk to you, on Monday. A serious talk. Okay?"

"Okay, Sailor."

Wow! Sailor's passion. I was half convinced. Not the rest of it, not Jan Berry, not three in the world convinced, just beating Dave today convinced. Maybe I could do that.

Then it was all happening. We were on court, three minutes into the first game, the score had hardly moved, I was one nil down. Unbelievably, we were in the middle of only our second rally. I'd won the toss and served. The first rally must have gone on for two hundred, maybe two hundred and fifty shots. Eventually a backhand volley from me had jammed out and it had been a clear penalty point to Dave. He smiled as he went to serve.

"Phew, bit fierce, that."

I just looked at him. Now into this second rally I was starting to feel the pain. There's nothing harder in squash than taking the ball early. More physical effort is needed and you have less time to breathe before you're doing it again, less time for oxygen in, less time for carbon dioxide out. A high VO_2 max obviously helps, high lactate threshold too so you don't go anaerobic. The theory's fine, I understood that. The theory gives you high hopes that your opponent is feeling worse. That's the other side, the good side of the taking-the-ball-early equation. Your opponent has less time to get back to the T after his last shot, and if your next shot is tight, he has less time to pick it up. You're pressurising him. In the second rally I had Dave behind me, where I wanted him, volley, volley, volley. He tried floating the ball high down the wall, but I still reached it and volleyed it, push, push, don't wait to take it off the back wall. Eventually Dave only scraped a short straight shot into the middle of the court and I hit it away easily.

Four minutes gone.

One all.

Riley was playing Ahmed in the next court but everyone else had come to watch us. Sailor must have said something. There he was, staring down impassively. After fifteen minutes, I could hardly believe it, we were no further than five all. Dave had quickly realised I was serious, and had cut any errors out of his game. That's good, he's playing my way, I thought. We exchanged the serve a couple more times. Neither of us could establish a lead.

Then suddenly Dave hit a succession of superb shots, including three fabulous, risky dead nicks. Eight five to him. Not good after all. I knew it: Dave had too much class. I remember thinking, this isn't going to work, he's just too good. I looked up at Sailor. An imperceptible nod. I was feeling as bad as level seventeen, breathing heavily, thighs painfully leaden. Come on, at least try. He must be feeling bad too.

He was. The next rally was a huge one, with Dave mainly behind, me mostly where I wanted to be, in front on the T. Then crash, tin. Yesss, he'd tinned! At last. Crazy to try a winner from back there. Hand out, me serving, six eight. Next point the same, another unforced error from Dave. "Come on," he shouted and wiped his hand high on the wall. Next point the same, but it was far shorter.

And so on till the end of the game as Dave's effort collapsed. Game to me, eleven eight, in about twenty minutes, eighteen of which had been the most intense continuous squash I'd ever played.

We left the court for a drink and to wipe away the sweat. "What was that?" Dave asked. "That was a bit fierce."

I didn't reply.

Dave looked hurt. "Okay, be like that." He went back on court and flogged the ball angrily down the wall until I joined him.

"Right, you're one up," he said. "Bring it on."

Yup, I thought. And you're going to have to do something better than the last game. And I don't think you can.

The second was like the first. Dave now realised what he was up against, and he wasn't giving up. If anything I had to dig even deeper. The score hardly advanced for ten minutes. The ball was incredibly hot and bouncy. Then Dave began to delay the start of the next point. No matter how stressed I was feeling, I followed Sailor's prescription and moved promptly in the service box when I was hand in. Dave in contrast would go through a rigmarole of wiping his racquet hand on the court wall, wandering around adjusting his sweat bands, pulling up his socks and tying his shoelaces. There was no marker and still further no referee to remind him that, as the rules said, play had to be continuous. I wasn't troubled, though. I knew it meant I was getting to him, and although I was hurting myself, I was confident of playing through it. A couple of fantastic shots from Dave saw him to a four two lead. Come on, up the pace. Volley, volley, volley.

Then, on cue, the mistakes started. There was another shout from Dave, "Aaahhh!" He looked fiercely up into the lights, as though seeking help from some god, left hand open, expostulating with the deity. I waited patiently in the service box. There were half a dozen of Dave's hand wipes, then the sweatbands, the socks, the laces. It's not going to help, mate. Volley, volley, volley. His deity ignored him and soon Dave was well past his anaerobic threshold again, behind me, retrieving in the back of the court.

Another couple of minutes and I'd won the game, eleven four.

"It's only a practice game," Dave said as we both took a drink.

"I'm practising winning."

I went back on court to warm the ball up. I didn't want to chat.

Dave's resistance lasted for one rally at the start of the third game. Admittedly it was a long one, the usual formula, volley, volley, volley. After that he just tried to hit nicks. One came off, and he served, but that was all. It can only have taken two or three minutes. A final crashing tin and it was match to me, eleven eight, eleven four, eleven one, with the score telling nothing, absolutely nothing, of the story.

We shook hands, and being the decent guy he was, Dave said, "Well played mate," as though he meant it.

The others went to watch Riley and Ahmed's marathon, and we joined them in the gallery. I was done. My legs were absolutely dead. As the adrenaline slipped away my body gave me the message I'd ignored from about the third minute of the first game: that was the hardest physical stress I'd ever been subjected to, or subjected myself to. All right, maybe the Redbrook steeplechase, Senior Heartbreak in the gale, maybe that came close. The steeplechase went on for longer. But it didn't have the intensity of those thirty five minutes on court with Dave Kemball.

"Have you rehydrated?" Sailor addressed both of us. "Take a protein supplement, too. And spend at least ten minutes stretching out before you shower. And you," he said to me when Dave had moved away, "we'll need to talk. After training on Monday."

I had a big smile from Carmen. "Well done. You were very good." And I had a big thrill from Zoë. She looked me directly in the eyes, itself special, and said simply, "That's the way you do it." Riley on the other hand said, "What a little golden boy."

On the bus, with the Pennines glowing in the late afternoon sun, Dave asked the same question as he had after the first game.

"What was that about, then?"

"It was Sailor. After he'd seen the results of the gym tests, he gave me a talking to. He said mine were good, that basically I should play at a faster pace."

"Fuckin' hell, faster pace. You certainly did that. You didn't have to be so offensive about it."

"I think that's the point. The top two inches, Sailor said. Winning mentally he meant, I think."

Dave grinned ruefully. "It comes across as mental. You looked as though you should have been locked up. Mental. You're right though. Have you heard Sailor talking about Zoë? She's mental."

I was happy to talk about Zoë, and we spent the rest of the journey discussing women who played squash. Not from the squash angle, though.

Chapter Nine

Sailor told Dave not to wait for me after we'd showered following the afternoon session on Monday. Dave raised his eyebrows and left with a couple of the others for a meal. I told Sailor I was sorry to be missing the social.

"That's what I want to talk to you about, sit down."

When I was settled he asked, "What do ye want to do in life, son?"

"Do? What do you mean? Career or something?"

"Aye, that's what I mean."

"I'm not sure. Go to university, anyway. I'm good at maths. I like English, too."

"There's no' anything definite, then? The Navy, for instance. Does your father want you to go into the Navy?"

"It's my mother who wants me to do things. Certainly not the Navy. She's always rabbiting on about it, Navy this, Navy that, never complimentary. My dad just laughs. He's a bit more easy going. My mother would like me to do something in the City ideally. She likes the idea of the salaries, big bonuses. She's got a point. I'm not sure if I fancy it though. Then there was the idea that I should become a surgeon. After she'd had her hysterectomy. She must have been impressed," I raised my eyebrows at the 'impressed', "by the guy who did the operation."

"Don't be disrespectful. But I get the picture, ye've no any vocation. And that's good considering what I'm going to say." Sailor paused. "Pay attention to me, son, because I'm serious here.

"How would you like to be world squash champion?"

It took me a moment to digest what he'd said. Sailor was glowering at me.

"World champion? It's pure ridiculous, Sailor, for God's sake. It is ridiculous, isn't it?"

"That's where you're wrong, son. Of course there's many things to go wrong along the way. There's always injuries. There's some Pakistani or Egyptian or Aussie who moves the game on. But you've got it. You can be the one to move the game on. Zoë said to me, and I think the world of Zoë, respect her, Zoë said after your first practice with her, something about your intensity. I've seen that, I've noticed it. You've impressed me here, son. I've been thinking, these last few weeks, shame Jolyon didn't start younger, he could be good."

He reached into his case and pulled out some papers. "Then we did the performance testing. Look at this, standing jump, forty three, drop jump, two point eight, that's ridiculous. Do you want a career as a high jumper? It's yours. Then your VO_2 max, nearly eighty four. Ridiculous, there I'm saying it again. Do you want to be a racing cyclist? Tour de France? And your bleep test, seventeen, you're up there with the academy footballers after they've had two years of training. I mean training for just that kind of effort. That's the one I really like. A big VO_2 max is no good unless you've a high lactate threshold. A big bleep test says you can go on through the pain, the biochemistry pain as well as the physical pain. And all this is on four weeks of training, just four weeks. It's absurd."

I shrugged, feeling a mixture of pride and embarrassment.

"You may shrug, son. You're a frigging physical freak. But that means jack shit if you can't play. I told you, you'll never be an Ahmed. It's too late. But you've good volleys, that's the tennis. And then the game on Friday. I didn't expect you to win the first game. Dave's too good. I thought you might damage him in the first game, and then if you wanted it enough, ye might scrape a game yourself, then two, then mebbe even three. Did you feck! Excuse me. You wiped him out. You did everything I said, only twice as well. Far better than I thought. It was the mental side. Mebbe ye didn't notice. He knew he was in trouble. Early on. See how he rallied. He knew he could beat you, he thought he knew. If he rallied. That lasted for ten minutes. Then he started hoping you'd slow the pace. Hope doesn't win any prizes. That's what it took, ten minutes. The rest was going through the motions."

"It didn't feel like going through the motions. Saturday I was knackered. Sunday, I was so stiff. I was still tired this morning."

"Aye, you youngsters, you always expect something for nothing. This isn't a sport for fairies, son. Haile Gebrselassie, do you think he wasn't tired after his world records? Muhammed Ali, how deep did he have to dig? You watch Zoë before a match. She does more visualising than warming up. Partly it's the tactics, but mainly it's preparing for the physical side.

"Am I getting through, son?"

"I think so. It's so, I dunno, so ridiculous. And if I agree, if I want to do it, how are we going to make it work? I could come up here some weekends in term time. Then most of the holidays. You could give me stuff to do in the week, schedules and so on."

Sailor laughed. "No, no, you're not understanding me. Listen. If you want to do this, there's only one way. You start tomorrow. Here tomorrow, nine o'clock prompt, good breakfast inside you.

"Have ye heard of Edwin Moses?"

I wished I hadn't said it as soon as it came out of my mouth. "The guy in the Bible?"

"I'll ignore that. The winningest track athlete ever. Four hundred metres hurdles, never beat for more than nine years, think of it, nine years. Moses talks about the links in a chain. Each day's training is linked to the last, linked to the next. Ye can't break the chain. It's mental as well as physical. One hundred percent committed, that'll be you. And there'll be no days off. Three sixty five days. It's a leap year next year, three sixty six."

"That's impossible. How could I do my A levels? What would I live on? *Where* would I live? I can't stay with the Kemballs for ever."

"That's some questions ye'll have to answer. As for where ye'd live, you'll stay with Mary and me. I'd expect something for food and such, but no' much.

As for your A levels. It's bye bye to A levels, son. The only way this will work is if you do it one hundred percent. Starting tomorrow, September the third. Mebbe Dave could get away with it, staying on at school, it's hardwired into him, the squash. He's been playing the game since he was eight. Not you. You've too much catching up to do."

I'd thought when he said he'd wanted to see me that Sailor might be proposing a special training programme, something I could do at school, to help bring me along through the juniors. Plus the occasional visit to the Institute. But nothing like this. This was huge. With huge implications. First thing, I'd have to talk to my mother. How was that going to go down? Silly question. And the world champion business? In reality, don't be ridiculous. I used to fantasise a bit about becoming an international, at cross country that is. I was happy to let that happen if it happened. This was different. This meant changing my life. Completely changing my life. What about my friends? What about parties, could I still go to parties? What about mixing? There was no way I could give up mixing.

As these thoughts went through my mind, I realised that 'no way' had to be the only answer. There was just too much to give up. Too much to risk. There'd never been any question that I'd do my A levels, and then something at uni. Another five or six years before I was faced with decisions. Decisions like this one, but when I was grown up, easier then. Moving out of home permanently, moving away from my mother? To be fair, that would be special. In one way. But not really, not yet. My friends at school? Samantha? She was still pissed off about me spending six weeks of the summer in Manchester, but I'd get her over that.

"No, I don't think so, Sailor. Yes I beat Dave, but I'm not that good. It was just one win. Probably won't happen again. And the squash is beside the point anyway. My parents wouldn't go along with it, not me leaving school. I've only got GCSEs."

"I tell you what, son," Sailor sounded almost kindly. "Ye don't have to make up your mind right now this second. You'll have to give your family a call. If ye like I'll speak to your father."

"He's away, you can't reach him."

"All right, you'll think about it tonight. Talk to your mother. Phone me tomorrow, early. If the answer's yes you can come in then. But," he hesitated, "but do me a favour. Think about it seriously. You could be best in the world. World champion, say it, savour it. Jolyon Jacks, squash champion of the world. That's if you start now. There's no slack in the timetable. You're a physical freak. No doubt of that. You're the perfect storm. But in squash terms you're so raw, so raw. I think we can deal with the rawness. But there's no time to waste, and it's going to take your one hundred percent commitment, and I mean one hundred, ninety eight's no' enough, nor's ninety nine."

Sailor stared at me intently. 'World champion'. I did say it, to myself. It sounded ridiculous. Me, world champion? Best in the world? It was a thrilling idea, but crazy. And deeply improbable.

I shrugged. "All right, Sailor, I'll think about it. I'm sure the answer's going to be no. But I'll have a think. And I'll call tomorrow."

As I headed for the changing rooms to get my kit I was surprised to see Zoë, looking hot, in running shoes, coming into the Institute.

"Gosh, you've not gone yet," I said. "You don't stop, do you?"

"Do you think the Aussie girls stop? Do you think Beth LaSalle in New York stops? The Egyptians? Look at it this way. With the time difference the Aussies are always a day's training in front of me. That's the way I think of it. I can't afford to slack. Right now I'm better than them. The results show it, look at the rankings. But if I don't push, every day, I won't stay there."

She bounced a question back to me. "What are you doing, anyway?"

"Bit of a bombshell. Sailor wants me to come up here permanently. Train full time. I could stay at his house, he says, so there'd be somewhere to live. He wants me to make my mind up straight away, like tonight. Fix it with my parents."

I shrugged. "There's no way, not really." The enormity of Sailor's proposal was starting to come through. "I'd have to leave school," I tried to joke, but it wasn't funny. "There would be some benefits."

"Jesus, Jolyon, that's a big one. Tell you what, you don't have to get back to Dave's straight away, do you, right now?"

I shook my head.

"Right, give me ten minutes for a shower. I need to feed. There's an Indian not far away. We'll have a meal, my shout."

"Hey, thanks, that sounds great."

Zoë headed for the changing rooms in her brisk way. In spite of the turmoil I was in, I couldn't help noticing for the umpteenth time her truly international walk, cosmic movement, upright, perfectly balanced, a glide, feet angled at five to one, muscular bum tilting slightly with each step. I hauled my mind off that image, located my phone and called Marion to say I'd be back later. Then I retrieved the image of Zoë's bum and sat down to wait. I wasn't familiar with Indian food. It hadn't featured in my mother's world. I knew it was hot and hoped I wouldn't make a fool of myself.

Chapter Ten

Zoë drove us the half mile to the restaurant in her sponsored BMW. "This is a big perk. I get great lottery money as world champion," those two words again, world champion, "but running a car is expensive."

"Do you have to do anything for it?"

"Nothing in the contract. But twice I've had a hit with a couple of sales people from the garage where this comes from. And the manager asked me to turn up at a new model launch earlier in the year. She's great."

"She?"

"Yes, must be a rarity. She's going places."

"Anyway, I was around. It wasn't a problem. What I do do is let them know, about once a month, how I'm getting on, the local dealer and the UK head office. It's just an email. I send a photo if I have one. They put it up in their show room, at the dealership, and they've used it in the newsletter they send out to customers.

"For me, it's a small price to pay. Well, it's not even that. It's saying thank you, and," she smiled with glee, "I've got this glitzy car."

Zoë was a whole lot better than my mother in the business of driving. She parallel parked easily in a small slot, and a few moments later we were sitting in one of the restaurant's booths, in dim light. The waiter placed a plate of discs in front of us.

"These look like models of sand dunes from a geography lesson," I said.

"They're poppadoms. For heaven's sake, you weren't kidding, were you? Never been inside an Indian? I always try to find Indian restaurants when I'm away at a tournament. You'd be amazed where they crop up."

There was a dish of stuff to go with the poppadoms, divided into compartments. Zoë warned me about one of the substances, dark and mysterious with green lumps in it. I made a total prat of myself by ignoring her. Something as benign sounding as lime pickle? Can't be much wrong with that, come on, Jolyon. After five tearful minutes and absurd volumes of water, plus something called raita from one of the other dishes, I finally erased the mixed concern and amusement from Zoë's face.

"What's the Indian word for napalm?"

"You mean Hindi; maybe Urdu. I've no idea." She studied a menu and ordered several dishes no less mysterious than what I'd seen already.

"There's one main to avoid," she said when the waiter had gone. "I'll point it out. This time listen."

My eyes were still watering. "Don't worry, once burned, twice shy. Anyway, my tear glands are empty."

"Now," she demanded, "tell me all about it. What did Sailor have to say?"

A particular advantage of sitting opposite Zoë with our knees almost touching, was that I could look at her. The tabloid cameramen loved Zoë. She'd come third in the BBC Sports Personality of the Year competition the year after she'd become world champ. The papers had been all over her after that. The vivid yellow dress she'd worn on the night had helped, a second skin. I'd watched the programme and gawped, never imagining that I'd meet the wearer of the dress, still less that I'd be this close to her in a half lit Indian restaurant. Now I tried not to gawp some more, and confined my gaze mainly to her rich brown eyes. Not a problem.

"Well, like I said, Sailor wants me to come up here full time. It's embarrassing. Ridiculous really, he says I could be," I made a pathetic attempt to mimic his accent and his gruff voice, "'wurruld charmpeeyun'."

A half smile and she shook her head. "It's not ridiculous, Jolyon."

Yesss Zoë's eyes. Oh, oh, oh! Dark brown, almost black in that light, intense and no other way of putting it, longingly lovely.

"Well," I managed to say, "even if it's not ridiculous, I can't do it. In practice it's ridiculous. I can't stop school just like that. I can't drop out, no A levels. Most of my friends are down in Sussex. And all this on the basis of one game of squash against Dave Kemball."

"I don't have any A levels," she said. "Do you think everything was clear for me when I committed to full time? Full time squash, full time training? Full time absolutely exclusively nothing else? No time for the rest of life. I was going to be a doctor. My Mum and Dad are both doctors. And one of my brothers. The other one did law. What do you think my father said when I told him? He went ballistic. 'You silly child. It's out of the question. Where's your sense of responsibility?' Stuff like that."

"I'd be more worried what my mother would say."

"Mother, father, same difference. The point is, you've got it. Something inside you. I could tell the first week you were here. You haven't a clue how to play squash, but you can learn that. You hit the ball well enough. Especially volleying. The thing is, I've never seen anyone, any man that is, with your attitude. You cottoned on to the match point thing straight away. The result is, you've got far more out of the last three weeks than any of the others. I'm amazed the way you've come on.

"And then the performance testing. If you want something that really is ridiculous, that's it, your results. You're a freak. You're off the scale."

At that moment a waiter arrived with a pungent trolley of dishes and placed them on aluminium mats under which he lit little candles. One of the dishes came straight out of a pan and was still sizzling. It smelt fantastic.

Zoë smiled at my reaction. "Now we'll seriously see how you cope with the pain barrier. Big time. I'm joking really. She pointed to one of the brown meaty dishes. Just don't take much of this one."

"Why, what is it?"

"Chicken Madras. It's quite spicy."

"They all smell spicy if you ask me."

"Well, help yourself and eat up, I'm starving."

Sixty seconds later I had to ask for more water. Sweat was trickling down the back of my neck, even without the Madras.

"You can't go back home now anyway," Zoë said. "Not if you have any more Indian meals. You'll reek of it, all these spices. From the way you've described her, it sounds as though your mother would throw you out."

"If mothers were Indian food, mine would be the lime pickle."

Zoë's face softened. "Mine would be the raita. She's lovely."

I'd talked about my home set up, and she hers. "The thing that decided me," Zoë said, "in the end, was this. What would I feel when I got to thirty? 'Oh, what a shame I didn't have a real go at it. It's too late now, look at me, five kilos overweight, ten years too old, I'm past it. They said I could have been really good. I wish I'd tried, I really wish I'd really tried.'

"I didn't want that. My dad had always drummed into me, from when I was little, 'Have a go. Go on, Zoë, don't be shy. Have a go'. Well I didn't act shy and I did have a go. I turned it back on him when I told him I wanted to do squash full time. In the end he saw it. He came out to Boston when I won my first world championship. Saw me beat Heba Elkalawy in the final. You know what he said straight after? He gave me a great big hug, me all sweaty, and then looked at me straight and just said, 'You were right'. I knew what he meant. All the nagging, all the guilt they made me feel about doctoring, or rather not doctoring. All gone."

"I'm sure my dad would be pleased," I said. "In the end. I could make him realise. My mother? Something else. I can remember when I was only eight or nine, I heard someone describing her as implacable and I went and looked it up. Implacable. It's totally accurate. She'd just say, 'World champion? In squash? Huh; such a *minority* sport'. She always wanted me to win Wimbledon. Nothing else would do. Olympic Games? Nah. The Open? No way, not golf. Squash? To her squash is the equivalent of a dog turd you find on the sole of your tennis shoe."

"She sounds awful," Zoë said. "But up her, Jolyon. What do *you* want? If a man like Sailor says you could be world champion, you'd better believe it, you've got a chance. It's a possibility, maybe small, but Sailor doesn't say things he doesn't mean. There's maybe only three or four juniors worldwide you could really say that about. You can go back to Sussex next week, and end up what? Another plummy south of England commuter, working too many hours so you can make too much money. You'll never get rich playing squash. Too much travel, too many hotel rooms, too much being dog tired. Too much hurting. Something's always hurting, I'm telling you. But a chance to be the best in the world. Who has that? In a major sport. It's not glamorous, squash. But think how many people play it around the world. It's millions. And you could be the best *one*. Out of all those millions."

"Look, it's eight o'clock. You could call your mother now."

"Not Monday night. It's one of her bridge nights. She doesn't like being interrupted. She turns her mobile off."

What Zoë did next really surprised me. She reached over and put her hand on mine, really gripped it. "For God's sake Jolyon. There's no question. Do you want to be an ordinary this or an ordinary that? All your life? Stuffed up Englishman, anonymous. Twenty five year mortgage. Posh voice. Pinstripe suit. Two point four children. In among the crowd. Single figure golf handicap. An also ran. That's what's in front of you. Or do you want to *be* something? Not for long, maybe.

"But look at me."

I certainly was, almost torched by her passion. "How do you think I feel?" She measured the words. "I feel great. There's all these eminent folks in my family. OBEs, there's a Knight, someone with a Rolls Royce. And then there's me. I'm Zoë Quantock. I'm world flipping squash champion. I'm up there with any of them. Above them. And I tell you what. There's not one of them that wouldn't swap. Not one.

"Do you have any choice?"

Then she realised we were being stared at by a nearby couple and took her hand away. "I've got to go to the loo. Think about it."

I watched her moving in her easy way to the back of the restaurant. Zoë had just demonstrated what you needed. Beyond the talent and the technique and the Sailor stuff. Enthusiasm. Passion. Commitment. The way she spoke, it came across like an explosion. Her passion wasn't for me, unfortunately. It was for what she was doing. For the choice she'd made. I don't think Zoë had a boyfriend. Probably no room for that, not after what I'd just heard. I'd already seen her dedication, day after day. Now she'd shown me where it came from. The question was, could I do the same thing? Could I commit to a goal in the same way?

A waiter came past, balancing several great-smelling dishes for the nearby couple. I wondered what goals he had. Get back home to the sub-continent with a little money? Open a restaurant of his own? Marry sultry Soraya from down the road? That was it, probably, all of it. What goals did *I* have? With a jolt I realised that the only goals I'd ever striven for, cross country being the single notable exception, hadn't been mine at all. They'd been my mother's. Boadicea one day, boa constrictor the next. Laying opposition to waste one day, squeezing the life out of it the next.

The tale for me had started early. Tennis: win the Under Eights at the club. *You could see his talent from the first time he picked up a racquet.* Then the Under Tens. *Apart from his talent he really puts his mind to it, look, so dedicated.* Then the Under Twelves. *Look at that timing, he hardly needs a coach.*

And so on and so on.

Then it was school: lead role in the annual musical. *I think he'll be a baritone when his voice breaks. He's so expressive.*

Tennis again, it wasn't long before it became personal. Specifically I had to beat Quentin Berkeley whenever confronted by the poor boy, preferably six love, six love. *I can't stand that child's mother, such a pushy woman.* Pushy, hark at that!

Then it was a money thing, the TV commercial for boys' jeans: 'Builder's

Denim For Growing Kids. Tear These And Your Money Back. It's Guaranteed!!!' That involved me and two others upside down in a tree. *I'm wondering whether drama school wouldn't suit Jolyon; he was an absolute natural during the filming.* Not to overlook academics, of course: pass the entrance exam for Redbrook School, preferably with a scholarship. *Oh that, the entrance exam? He sailed through that.* Then further tennis: the stifling LTA training camp. *They say he moves like Andy Murray, just look at him.* Full house of A stars at GCSE? Er, no, that didn't happen. *He was forecast to do so much better... hormones; I'm sure, he'll grow through it.*

All my mother's goals. What about mine, my own goals? Good phrase, there were some big own goals, often to spite my mother, the worst being my refusal to play in a tennis match on the afternoon of the FA Cup Final. I wasn't then allowed to watch it on TV. My other goals were nebulous, a foggy horizon whichever way you looked. A levels? Yes, three or four. Shag some girls? Yes, three or four hundred. What else was there? University? Probably. Oxbridge? No way, for obvious reasons connected with my mother's ambitions. Then what? Not the Navy. One thing I was sure of, I wanted to control my own life, not have the military dictate what happened to me.

And now this.

I looked up and Zoë was coming back, a smile on her face. "Careful, you don't want to be pulling a muscle in your brain."

"I was just thinking."

"I could see that. Do you want a dessert, or a coffee?"

"Do they do tea? A tea would be good. I've no room for anything else."

The waiter looked disappointed that we didn't go for one of his kulfis but was mollified by the way Zoë apologised.

"Well," she said, "did any conclusions emerge from all that thinking?"

"You've made it so obvious. I really like playing squash. It's something *I* want to do. Not something someone else expects me to do. For one thing, there's nothing like the feeling of getting on top of someone, breaking them down. Breaking their will, I suppose. It happened to me once, big time, when I'd just started playing, at school. That was the game that really got me started. And it happened on Friday, against Dave. Don't get me wrong, I really like Dave, he's a great guy. But it was that feeling, I guess it's what boxers feel, it's very raw. To lose isn't an option, that's being *beaten.* You've *got* to win, and there's this other guy in the way, tough luck. And then you get on top.

"I enjoyed squash from the start, the grind. It's like a long uphill run, uphill into the wind. But there's shots to enjoy at the same time. I guess seeing how it worked out against Dave, exactly the way Sailor said it would after the gym tests, how to convert them into something on court, I didn't expect that."

"I knew you'd beat Dave," Zoë said. "Not on Friday, I didn't think it would be then. It was obvious you had it in you, the way you've trained, the way you can volley, so early. Then, on Friday, that was brutal. You have to have the brutality."

"At least I've inherited something worthwhile from my mother."

Zoë laughed. "Don't knock it. You should be grateful. And Sailor's good. He must have seen it in you."

"He said that about you, something about brutal."

Zoë gazed at the maroon wallpaper over my right shoulder, far away. "It is brutal, but it's got to be economical. Otherwise you tire yourself out too much. Lots of the girls can do a game, or two games, at the same pace as me. The way Sailor explained it, if you've got really good functional stability, you don't waste anything in the way you move. So you can sustain a higher pace for longer. You can't teach that. Apparently it comes from the way you grow up. I did lots of tennis, too, like you. And I did gymnastics, till I was ten or something, but if you think I'm obsessive, you should see women's gymnastics, women's artistic gymnastics as it's called. *That's* brutal. And I did swimming, and I used to love football. Any sport. That's when you develop your functional stability, that's what they say. When you're a kid."

"Funny that," I said. "I did most of those sports. Quite a lot of gymnastics. I do slag my mother off, but she was always organising things for me. I never had any free time. And swimming too, till I was eleven I think, not much after that because it clashed with the tennis."

"Well, you move so well on court. It's funny watching you because, how can I put it, there's all this economy, you glide, but at the same time you look so raw, your choice of shot sometimes. Inexperience."

"Thanks," I said, "rub it in. How about naïve?"

Zoë smiled again. "That's it, perfect, naïve."

"Perfect?"

She laughed. "No, naïve. I'm the one who's perfect. You don't get to be perfect till you're world champ.

"So what's it going to be, young man? Are you going to have a go? Or are you going to be the biggest disappointment in Sailor's life?" Then Zoë added quietly. "And in a way, mine, too."

"It's unfair," I said. "If I was Dave, any of the really good juniors, I could sort of ease into a decision. Why do I have to decide everything now, right now?"

"Sailor was right, as usual," Zoë said. "For you it's the time factor. You've just not played enough squash. It's a gamble. Can you pick up enough of the squash side, the craft? Luckily you do hit the ball well. But forget that stuff. At some stage, no matter who you are, anyone who wants to be best, at squash or any other sport I should think, they have to commit. They have to accept that the next, I dunno, eight, ten years of their life is going to be focussed on just one thing, getting to the top. And then staying there." She grimaced. "Excluding most other things, almost everything else. It may be a bit sudden for you. It is sudden, just this month up here. And maybe it has to be now for you, how old are you, sixteen, seventeen? You look older. Because of your history it has to be now. But everyone has to face the decision.

"Come on," she said, getting up, "I'll pay on the way out, and then I'll drive you back."

"You don't have to do that." I checked my phone for the time. "There's a bus just after nine o'clock."

"It's no problem. And it's crunch time for you. I'll shut up. It'll take, what, twenty minutes to reach the Kemballs? Then Master Jolyon, twenty minutes is what you've got to make up your mind. Twenty minutes will be enough. We don't need to talk. You have to remember, if Sailor said he needs to know by tomorrow, that's it. He never goes back on anything. If you're undecided tomorrow, the chance will be gone. He's like that. I know Sailor very well. As for making up your mind, you've got as much information as you need from outside. You just need to do the inside stuff."

"The inside's stuff's the hard stuff."

"Of course it is. That's the way it is. On court, too."

"Look, really, you don't have to take me."

Maybe Zoë thought I'd bottle out if I went on the bus, and maybe she'd have been right.

"Course not. Anyway, from today, if you're going to go for it, you've got to look after yourself. Plenty of rest, and I mean plenty. That's part of the formula. And I want to see where you're staying if we're going to go running."

"If I decide yes, and if I can get things sorted, my mother, school, the whole lot, I won't be staying with the Kemballs much longer. I'll be moving in with Sailor."

"Well we won't argue tonight. The traffic's gone. I don't suppose it'll take long."

Chapter Eleven

True to her word, Zoë shut up once we were on our way, and I only spoke to give directions. I was daunted by the decision I was faced with. The whole thing was unbelievably sudden. There was no doubt now in my mind that I was going to do it. I'd worked that out while Zoë was in the loo. It was just the upheaval. The battle of wills with my mother for starters. It was lucky I had the time during the drive back. It let me prepare myself for the phone call. It conserved energy after what had been a big, big day. I needed all the energy I had.

As I got out of the car I said, "This is going to be a match point of a phone call."

"Great!" Zoë's face lit up. "You've decided to go for it?"

"Never any doubt really. Just thinking about the alternative, back home, back to school, all stuff I don't want to do. My poxy housemaster. Another two years of my mother. Her on my back, every day."

The moon was coming up over the Pennines, a full moon, and it looked huge, only just above the horizon. On the way up. It seemed a good omen.

"Thanks for the lift, Zoë. And the meal. Big help."

"No problem. Good luck with the call. I'll see you on Wednesday."

She drove off. She was so enormously together, Zoë. It was hard to imagine her with the same uncertainties as me. I envied her. She'd done it, she had the titles and the status. Life was easy, she had the car, the sponsorships. As if all that wasn't enough, she was disturbingly, achingly lovely. The evening had discombobulated me, left me in a turmoil, except it was a double turmoil. Could you be discombob-bobulated, I wondered? There was the squash, daunting if anything could be daunting, and there was Zoë. Which did I want more? More chance to become world champion than Zoë's champion, sadly, and I had to be realistic, what chance was there of that?

I went inside and exchanged greetings with various Kemballs. Dave was only just home and was incredulous.

"Zoë took you out? What was that about? Zoë never socialises."

I mumbled something about needing to eat and put my sweaty gear in the washing machine. Then I cast around for things to delay my trip upstairs. Nothing convenient presented itself. Listlessly I went up. I had to make the call. I caught a glimpse of myself in the mirror. Shell-shocked, and I hadn't even been shelled. Yet. That was about to come. I put my shoes and racquets and kitbag carefully in their appointed places. I picked up various items of clothing. The room was becoming unaccustomedly tidy: you could see the floor. Maybe I could put the call off until first thing in the morning? No, she'd be worse in the morning. Maybe I could just do the whole thing without telling anyone.

Don't be a prat.

Finally I sat down on the bed and took a deep breath. This was going to be an epic. Not in length, if I knew my mother. Storm Force Twelve. In my mother's world, teenagers just didn't drop out of school; it was unthinkable. Teenagers in my mother's world were there to be bragged about, to do all the right things. We had to blaze through our exams, *It's been confirmed in the psychometric tests. He's a genius.' 'Oh genius, oh that, how trivial. Mine does genius in her spare time.'* We had to pull the girls and the boys from the rich families, *'She's going out with Lady Pevensey's son. So young, but they're very much in love.' 'Mine's thick as thieves with Rhiannon de Courtney. She's a friend of, ah, the Windsors.'* We had to make it into the most exclusive magazines, *'Now he's auditioning for a Harry Potter remake.'* We had to carve out colossal careers. *'The first year bonus is said to be six figures. After that, well, the sky's the limit.'* We provided the opportunity to be, and remain, one up.

My plan on the other hand didn't bear thinking about. *'Mine's dropped out of school and gone to live with an awful Glaswegian. I can't understand a word the man says. In Manchester, of all places, Manchester! He's going to become a full time, can you believe this, a full time squash player. Squash for Christ's sake, it's so, it's so proletarian. So ungrateful.'*

I took a deep breath and hit the quick dial code for our landline. Three rings, the breath didn't have to last for long.

"Hello."

This wasn't the neutral hello most people used. It was sentry-at-the-gate hello, who-goes-there hello, and it had better be good at this time of night or I'll drop the portcullis on you hello. The ground rules for the conversation had been set, a presumption of confrontation.

"Hi Mum, it's me."

"Oh, you. It's late, isn't it?"

"I knew you'd be at bridge."

"Well what is it?" Any plans I had to ease into this gently went out the window.

"It's good news, really. It's the squash."

"Squash?" A six letter word. "Why are you calling me about squash at this time of night?"

"It's going so well. I, er, I've been doing better than people expected. It must be all that volleying practice you made me do at tennis."

"Come on Jolyon. Stop beating about the bush. Why are you calling me now?"

"I've been offered the chance to go full time."

"Full time? At squash?" *Waiter, there's a slug in my salad.*

"Yes. Sailor, the coach here, he thinks I've the potential to get to the top."

"Well bully for you. How do you expect to get up to Manchester every weekend for all this full time squash? And you can't stay with the Kemballs for ever. I wouldn't do it for their son if it was the other way round." *Don't worry on that score, Mother, no son of anyone else would want to.*

I gulped. "It's not going to be like that. I'm going to stay up here. With Sailor and his wife. And train full time."

"Bloody hell, Jolyon. That's absurd. What are you going to do for money? And where are you going to go to school?"

"Please understand, Mum. This is full time. I'll be training all day. There won't be time for school."

"Jesus wept. I've never heard anything so absurd. I've no intention of continuing this conversation, not now. You can call me back in the morning. I'll want to know what your plans are for coming home. You've been up there quite long enough, that's clear. Good night."

Bang, the conversation, more accurately the clash, ended. The phone may or may not have survived the return to its cradle. I fell back onto the bed. Zero progress, oh dear. I'd have done no worse if I'd told her I was planning to work in the locality of King's Cross Station as a rent boy. On the credit side? Nothing. Well, not quite nothing. It was a short call and I still had seven minutes credit, ha ha, on my phone. On the debit side? Well, where do you start?

These reflections were interrupted by a knock on the door.

"Hello?" It was Russell. "Are you okay? I wasn't trying to listen, but I couldn't help overhearing some of that. It sounded a bit heated."

He came into the room and I sat up. "Superheated, more like. That was my mother."

"What was it all about?"

It was a relief to have someone to talk to, and Russell might understand. I told him the whole story, from Sailor's proposal right through to my mother's response to the call.

"Bloody hell, Jolyon."

"That's what she said."

"No, I mean, that's fantastic news. If Sailor says that. He's a hard guy to please. That really means something."

"Fat lot of good it's doing me."

"That's the other side. This is a major major decision. And look at it this way. Suppose I had a call from Dave, late one evening, from let's say London. 'I'm like not coming back, Dad, and oh by the way I'm dropping out of school.' I'd lose my rag too. Dave's still a kid, at least in Marion's eyes. I know he's almost grown up. You too. But that's not the way parents see it. I'm not surprised your mother was pissed off."

"But what can I do? I've thought about it, the squash. I really want to do it. The idea I could be up there, right up at the top."

"Dave was pretty impressed on Friday, I must say. When he came home he told me about your game. He said suddenly you were different. He said it felt like he was playing a man, somebody ranked. He really tried. He always does. Especially that first game. He didn't think you could keep it up. In a way he was disappointed. He wants to be good. He is good, for Heaven's sake, bloody good. But he kept on saying 'different', you were different today, Jolyon was different. Up to now he's always known he could beat you."

"He always has."

"The question is, how are we going to manage this, the whole thing? Firstly, you need to consider, are you absolutely sure it's what you want to do? It's a very sudden decision."

"Oh yes. It's definite. I didn't realise how much I was dreading going back till the chance of not going back cropped up. It's a way out in one way, I suppose. And it's me. I'm always doing things because of my mother, her little chess piece, move here, move there. I never let myself realise how much I hated life at home."

"Your father's in the Navy, isn't he?"

"That's right. Submarines. He's not home much. Anyway, what I do, what I've done, is always down to her. I hadn't really thought about it until this, the whole squash thing, came up. Well, I had a bit. She always wanted me to play tennis. Since I was four or five. I was pretty good at tennis. I used to win all the tournaments locally. Down in Sussex. Then into Surrey. I went to LTA sessions. But it was like I was the prize exhibit. I was her, I dunno, her status. I'd hear her, it still makes me cringe, she used to boast about me. So in the end I took up cross country instead. She hated that, hated cross country. It wasn't glamorous somehow. That's true, it isn't glamorous, especially in the winter. There's mud and cold and wet. But I loved it. It was, sort of, well it was for me. And I was good at cross country. Our coach said I could do well in running if I kept at it. I did county stuff, and South of England. The squash came up as a sort of accident. Squash is a bit like cross country. It's so hard. You've got to keep pushing and pushing and the other guy's pushing and pushing back. It's down to your will in the end, and if your will's stronger than his you're going to win. But with squash there's the shots, too, and the fun of just hitting the ball and winning a hard point, and pushing on when you're completely out of breath and completely knackered. I don't think I'll ever be as good as Dave at hitting the ball. Dave's magic. He's like Ahmed. It's just that I'm stronger. And I like the training. I actually enjoy it. Dave doesn't. He pushes himself but he doesn't enjoy it. For me these last few weeks have been fantastic, once I'd got the hang of it, the intensity. Then there's the other guys. Dave's been great. Riley I'm not so sure of but he's such a laugh. Ahmed's a good guy. And Zoë. Seeing what Zoë does, she's the one who's really shown me. Almost more than Sailor. It's her attitude. And what is she? With her attitude, she's the world champion.

"And like I said, this is me, my decision for once, not my mother's. Not anyone else's."

Russell sat down on the bed beside me. He paused before he spoke, and then he spoke slowly. "It's important that your mum and dad get to meet Sailor. As soon as possible. They've got to understand. He's got to make them understand what he sees in you. And they've got to see that you're really committed to this. You have to have them on your side."

"Huh, that's not going to be easy. Firstly, I'm not sure when my dad's back. I think it's something like six weeks from now. As for my mother, well I don't know."

"Put yourself in her shoes. She's bound to be upset. I would be if Dave suddenly decided to give up school, like I said. It's not as if your future's guaranteed. I'm wondering if there's any way you could transfer to a school up here."

"Sailor says I don't have the time. I've got too much catching up to do. I started squash too late."

"We'll see. Don't rule anything out right now. First, you've got to get your mother up here. As soon as possible. She needs to meet Sailor, see the set up. She can come out here and meet Marion and me. It would make sense if she stayed here."

I was embarrassed I hadn't talked about that. "That's something else I wanted to say. It wouldn't be fair, me carrying on staying with you. Sailor says I can live with him."

"I think we could manage. If we got a truck to deliver the food. But you're right. It might make more sense if you were closer in. The buses aren't great out here.

"Look, sleep on it tonight. Call your mother in the morning and see when she can come up."

"I've got to call Sailor, too. He wants a decision tomorrow morning."

"Okay. It's your decision to make, and I can see why you want to do it. I think *I'd* want to do it, if I had the chance. And been good enough. But a few days to sort out the details, make the arrangements, that's not going to make any difference.

"So call your mother, call Sailor. I'm working from home tomorrow. You can let me know where things stand."

I felt a lot better to have someone on my side. I'd seen this horrible void when my mother reacted the way she had. I guess I'd been naïve in expecting to arrange everything with one call home, out of the blue. Maybe that's the way that Sailor thought it could be done. Perhaps that's what he did when he signed up for the Navy. Anyway, Russell's calm presence was making me feel better. And talking to him had made me all the more determined to go for the squash thing rather than struggle on for the next two years at Redbrook.

And with my mother.

When Russell had gone I went through to Dave's room.

"What's your dad do?" I asked.

"He's a lawyer. Family law. He's in a partnership in Manchester."

"Ah. He's good at listening."

"What do you mean?"

I told Dave about my conversation with Sailor.

"World Champion? Sailor says you could be world champion. Phat! You were the genuine article on Friday, rinsed me. I expected you to cave in after ten minutes at that pace. So if he thinks you can be world champion, what's he going to say the next time we play and I wipe you off the court?"

He laughed. "I'm only joking. I don't think I could beat you again. At the moment. Not if you play like that."

I felt bad for Dave. "Fuck the squash," I said. "Let's have a mix."

Dave was even more of a natural at mixing than he was at squash. Everyone said he could make it as a DJ. He had a perfect ear for beat, that wasn't so difficult, but he also could see things in the melody that worked when you dropped. And even the lyrics. He had a ton of vinyl, literally hundreds of discs, and he had an amazing memory. Each track on each disc, he knew where to find them.

So we had a mix and it went really well. We put some of it onto a CD because Dave wanted to take some fresh material to a club he'd been talking to. I went to bed later than I should, but at least I was in a better frame of mind.

Chapter Twelve

First thing in the morning I called Sailor. "So your mother was unhappy at the idea," he said. He sounded gruff. "It's usually the other way round. They're begging me to take their wee bairns."

"Well, it was rather sudden. The thing is, Sailor, I'd like my Mum to come up here, meet you, have a look at the set up. She'll be happier about it then."

"What about your father? He'll get the point. I'd like to speak to your father."

"He's on a tour right now. Not back for six weeks, I think."

"You can contact him."

"I always do it through Mum. I'll phone her now. Is there any bad time for her to visit?"

"No. Next two weeks are clear. We're all here."

"Okay, I'll get back to you."

Thirty seconds later, it took me twenty seconds to raise the nerve, my mother picked up the phone. "What is it?"

"Hi Mum, it's me."

"Oh you. I take it you've come to your senses."

"Hey, don't be like that. I've been trying to arrange for you to come up here. I want you to meet Sailor. You'd understand a bit better then. And when's Dad back? Beginning of October, isn't it?"

"I'm not wasting your father's time on this. And if you think I'm coming up to Manchester, Manchester of all places, to meet some sweaty Jock-the-squash-coach, you've got another think coming. The sooner you come to your senses the better, Jolyon."

Coming up to Manchester. Think *coming*, Jolyon. *Come* back to Brighton. *Come* to your senses. I liked to mentally dissect my mother's words, *Come come, Mum, I'm really not scum. Throw me a crumb, Mum. Don't be so dumb.*

"Your father will be just as adamant as I am. There's no way we'll countenance your stopping school."

Oh eff! Eff off! Not good at all. And she always found a way of making me angry.

"It'd be different if it was tennis. If I was some great white hope at tennis. Then you'd be licking the LTA's arse, and, and arranging for a private tutor or something."

There was a brief pause while the neutrons built up in my mother's plutonium brain. B-a-n-g! F-u-l-l n-u-c-l-e-a-r F-I-S-S-I-O-N! I winced as Chernobyl's reactor number four blasted out of my mobile.

"I – won't – be – spoken – to – like – that!"

Communications from the Ukraine abruptly ceased. The fallout would reach the farthest corners of Europe. My milk, a metaphor my English teacher would have liked, would be poisoned by iodine-131 for the next ten years.

I called back immediately.

"Yes."

Not just 'Yes?' It was a bunker busting 'YES!'

"Look, Mum, I'm sorry. That was rude of me. It's just I've made up my mind about the squash and I can't get you to *listen*. I'm going to do this, you have to understand. No one can physically make me go to school. You can't march me through the gates at Redbrook, not now I've done my GCSEs. There's no law saying I have to do the sixth form. This is a real chance for me, can't you see? A serious chance. And Sailor's big time. He already coaches one world champion. Zoë Quantock. She was on Sports Personality of the Year before Christmas. And Sailor's got such a strong squad here. It's the base for England Squash, too. This isn't some tin pot set up nobody's heard about."

Silence. Now the nuclear winter.

"Please. I'm sure if you came up here you'd understand better. I want you to meet Sailor, talk to him."

"There's no chance of that, Jolyon. This is crazy. There is absolutely no chance."

"What, no chance about you coming up here, or no chance about me doing this?"

"Both. I've heard quite enough of this, this fantasy. I want you to come to your senses and get yourself back down here. Pronto. By next weekend at the latest."

Again the phone went dead. It was half past eight. I was exhausted. I slumped on the bed. A moment later I was roused by a call from downstairs.

"Do you want some breakfast, Jolyon. It sounds as if you need some breakfast."

It was Marion. Russell must have told her what was going on after he'd seen me last night. I wasn't sure if I wanted to eat. My stomach was churning too much. Some tea and some company would be good, though, so I went downstairs. Dave wasn't up yet but Russell came through from his study and the three of us sat down at the kitchen table.

"I take it your mother wasn't receptive," he said rather than asked.

"That's right. She was blank unreceptive."

"What about your father?" Marion asked.

"He's at sea. Not back for six weeks."

"Can't you wait until then? From what you've said, you could work something out with your father. Even if your mother's against it."

"Not really. For one thing, Sailor's said he wants an answer by now, today, this morning. And with Sailor, that's not negotiable. He says I don't have the time. I've got to commit or the offer goes."

"That's Sailor," Russell said.

"Money's going to be important," Marion went on.

I'd thought a lot about money. "That will just about be okay. Sailor says he won't charge me much to live with him. And he says that I'll almost certainly get a lottery grant, assuming I do well in the tournaments this autumn. And the really good thing is, my grandfather's set up a trust, which I get access to when I'm eighteen. My birthday's March the tenth so that's, what, eighteen, nineteen months away. It's a lot of money, half a million quid, something like that. I'd always thought I'd just leave the trust alone for the time being. I didn't think I'd need it, or maybe just something for university. It's not as if my parents have been stingy."

Marion whistled. "Phew, you're a lucky boy. So you've got to get through the next year and a half. After that, it sounds like money won't be an issue."

"The next eighteen months should be all right if you get a lottery grant," Russell said. "They're not big at the bottom level, but your travel to tournaments, accommodation, stuff like that, that's part of the deal, and you should be able to get by otherwise on pocket money really. You won't have time to be out spending, and you should be too tired for anything else anyway. If you're training properly, even girls, ho ho. I know Sailor well enough; it's not going to be a picnic. I bet your mother doesn't realise."

"Go on then," Marion said. "Make the call to Sailor. You'd be welcome to stay here going forward, but I can see Sailor's offer makes more sense." She glanced at Russell. "And if you needed some money in the short term, I'm sure we could help."

I was embarrassed at the Kemball's generosity. "That's so kind. I'd pay you back. If it actually came to it. But I hope not."

At that moment Dave wandered into the kitchen, in his shorts. "What's this? Some big pow wow?"

"No, a social breakfast, which you'd have been welcome to join if you'd got up in time."

Dave smiled. "He kept me up last night. It's his fault." Marion made the obvious point that it hadn't stopped me from getting up.

That reminded me about my situation and I lurched internally. Talk about burning my boats. I wouldn't have been up so soon without the need to call to my mother.

After breakfast I spoke to Sailor. "That's good, son," was all he said when I told him I wanted to take up his offer. Then I explained the problem with my mother. "I can understand. It's no' an easy call. Your father's away? I tell ye what. Ye'll have to go south to pick up stuff. I'll drive you down. I'm sure I can square things with the Captain, but I ought to meet your mother too."

Blimey. The rock going to meet the hard place. Twelve three-minute rounds, bare knuckle. It would be bound to end in a stoppage.

Two days later we set out on the trip. It was a long drive and we arrived in the late afternoon. The last couple of miles were in a dank south coast fog. The rest of the journey had been in brilliant sunshine, with every one of the thirty ambient degrees finding its way into Sailor's old car. No air con. Air con, apparently, was for Sassenach pansies and pouffy Monaco playboys.

The fog was bad enough. The temperature descended further as soon as we went into the house. "I don't have much time, Mr McCann," was my mother's friendly greeting. "And I want you to know straight away, I don't approve of this. At all."

I went away to make some tea, since my mother hadn't offered, and returned with a large pot, some milk and some biscuits. There was an absence of small talk between Sailor and my mother. And large talk, indeed any sort of talk. They were sitting opposite each other on the hard sofas, both straight backed, gazing out of the French windows, an autistic blind date.

Sailor broke combat silence as I poured the tea. "I don't always get the chance to meet the families of my players," he said. "Overseas, Egypt, Pakistan. But I write to them. I understand the responsibilities I have. I make sure they're properly looked after. No messing, no trouble. No polis. Ye can set your mind at rest on that score, Mrs Jacks. I can see you're against this wi' Jolyon. An' I can see why. It's hard to let go at the best o' times. He's just a young lad. But ask yourself this. When did the Captain first go away? When did he leave home? This isn't any different. I know for a fact when he went because he told me. It was his seventeenth birthday. Same as me. Jolyon's no' seventeen, but he's no' far short."

"You can save the speeches, Mr McCann. This is simple madness, no discussion. Jolyon has always been immature. He's never made good choices. I've had to make them for him. I've looked into the whole business of school. There's nothing I can do to prevent my son dropping out. Physically. But I'm sure Adam will be paying you a visit when he's next on leave."

She turned to me and I stared back. How could she be such a cow? I was angry and embarrassed and, I suppose, fearful.

"That's if you're not back here already," she went on. "One thing I'm going to make absolutely clear, Jolyon. You're not going to get a penny out of us. Not till you come to your senses. I'm not going to be party to your squandering your life with this hair-brained fantasy."

"Excuse my abruptness, Mr McCann." Golly, she'd noticed. "There are times when plain speaking is necessary."

Then she unleashed her bombshell. What had gone before was only small arms fire by comparison. Sailor and I had discussed money on the drive down. He was certain that I'd get a small lottery grant as soon as I was regularly reaching the later stages of the big junior tournaments, enough to cover tournament expenses. And I'd told him about my grandfather's trust.

"And one other thing, Jolyon," my mother said in her best House of Lords voice. "I've already spoken to your grandfather. He's in complete agreement. He's going to amend the terms of your trust. The fund now will be controlled by Adam and me on his death, if he lasts till you're over eighteen. It'll be managed at our discretion from then on. And believe you me, you won't see a penny of it, not one penny, until your attitude changes and you've demonstrated that you're going to grow up."

I felt a surge of anger, no, more than that, fury, rage, all of them. It wasn't so much the threat of my losing the legacy, or at least not having access to it for the next however many years, although that was fundamental in terms of the plans I'd made. It was the way my mother said it, and her sheer meanness. She liked to control everything, including her father. Control. I was powerless.

My grandfather on my mother's side was a lovely old man. He was now in his nineties, long widowed, living quietly not so far away from us in a sheltered home. He was still active, and still 'had a long way to go' as he put it. Grandpa had always taken an interest in what I was up to. When I was small he'd been a big factor, a regular factor, in my life. More than my father. He'd talk about things, take me on outings, and, I realised now, he'd give me a break from my mother. He'd made a reasonably sized fortune with an engineering business after the Second World War, and sold the business while he had time to enjoy the proceeds. He and my grandmother had had two daughters. My mother was the older one. Her sister had never married so I was his only grandchild.

Grandpa had first told me about the trust on my twelfth birthday, how he wanted me to use it sensibly, and with a wistful smile, how he'd come back to haunt me if I squandered it. Eighteen sounded a million years away then, and I hadn't thought much about the money until Sailor had made his squash proposal. Then the forthcoming bequest had loomed as a lifeline, even though I knew there would be the possibility of lottery grants in squash if I did well. I'd guessed that my mother wouldn't approve of my dropping out of school, and whatever the reason, she was the one who made the financial decisions in our family. My father just wanted to do his Navy thing, for as long as it allowed him to go to sea. I was coming round to the view that this was the preferred alternative to being on land with my mother. It would be the sea for me too, preferably deep down, or eighteen months at a time on an Antarctic research station, if I'd been married to her. My father was a far less present factor in my day-to-day life than I imagined most fathers were.

"You can stuff the legacy, Mum. You want to place as many obstacles in front of me as you can. Well thank you very much. One more isn't going to make much difference."

My mother stood up. "I will not be spoken to like that. Excuse me, Mr McCann." She glared at me. "You can leave the house, Jolyon. Come back when you want to talk sensibly. And civilly. After a proper apology. I hope that one day you'll see how dismal this whole, this whole tawdry episode has been."

"Come on, Sailor," I said. "There's some stuff I need to pick up." I turned to my mother, who was standing implacably, arms folded, radiating, I don't know, radiating indignation and righteousness and cast iron certainty.

"Is it okay for me to go to my room, mother?"

"That's enough, Jolyon," Sailor said. "Don't be silly."

He grabbed me by the shoulder and with an 'Excuse us, Mrs Jacks' marched me out of the room.

"Where now?"

"Upstairs, first on the left."

In my room, with a stern-faced Sailor looking on, I could hardly control myself. I prowled around, fists clenched. "How could she be like that?" I took a punch at a wardrobe and my fist went straight through the veneer. "Oh fuck, I've cut myself."

"Get a grip on yourself, son. This isn't helping. You'll no' get your mother or me or anyone else to treat you as an adult if you continue to behave like a child. It's time to grow up. Now." I stopped and licked the blood off the gouge in the back of my hand.

"Let's see, what do you need from here?"

It was his air of authority that did it. I realised I was being a pillock. I managed to exit the angry loop and collect my thoughts. "Okay, there's some clothes. My squash kit's all at the Kemballs already. This vinyl and my decks, and the amp and the mixer."

"You pack up your clothes and I'll begin taking stuff out to the car." He made the mistake of starting on the vinyl. "Lord save me, this weighs a ton."

Sailor staggered out with two cases of vinyl and I pulled an old kitbag down from the top of the damaged wardrobe. I worried for a moment about my mother's reaction to the now fenestrated door. Then I thought 'sod you'. I started chucking stuff into the bag. I looked around. What else? Not the trophies all over the mantelpiece and the window sill. It would be a laugh to move them to my mother's bedroom. She was the one they were important to. Not the posters. Not the books. Except the dictionary; I liked having a dictionary. Certainly not the revision texts. Goodbye to all that.

Sailor came back and I started to disconnect my mixing kit. Good point: remember to take the pliers and the screwdrivers. And my Swiss Army knife. My grandfather had given me that, to my mother's audible disapproval, on my tenth birthday.

Sailor looked around the room. "I hope you're planning to leave some of this behind?"

"Don't worry, I'm almost done. Most of this is history."

Then another 'Lord save me'. He was looking at the admittedly impressive straps of copper cabling for my amp and speakers. "Is this thing connected to the National Grid?"

"Don't worry," I semi lied. "It's not for the power; it's the quality of the audio."

"Well there'll be no quality audio thumping out in my house."

"It's okay, I can use headphones."

It took two more trips to the car to transfer the small proportion of my worldly possessions that I wanted with me. I couldn't bring myself to confront my mother again to say goodbye, but Sailor called out as we left, "We're off, Mrs Jacks. I'll call when your husband's home."

Don't bother to see us out, I muttered to myself. I couldn't believe that my mother had been so rude in front of a stranger. She had potential in that direction, and her support for me at junior tennis tournaments could have been dismissed as simply combative, but I'd never witnessed anything like her performance this afternoon.

Sailor efficiently navigated us back onto the M23, pointing north. Our plan originally had been to stay in Sussex overnight, me at home and him with friends in Brighton, but both of us felt deflated. His suggestion that we cut our losses and head straight back to Manchester seemed a good one, even if it meant a lot more miles that evening.

After half an hour's silence I started to apologise, but Sailor cut me short. "Don't worry about it, son. I'm never surprised any more, not by human nature. She's one powerful woman. I've seen her type. Mothers and fathers, it can be either. They have to have control. Did ye hear about Marcel Darnaud the other day?"

I was amazed that Sailor had reached this certainly accurate conclusion about my mother after what, only five minutes in her presence. "That's right," I said. "I'd never really worked it out before. She wants to dictate how every little detail goes down."

"I've seen lots of them like that. In sport. They live out their ambitions through their kids. They try to clear the path for them. Watch out anyone who's in the way. Marcel's the father of a good young French player, Armand Darnaud. Plenty of ability there. The boy's been playing since he was a bairn. His father disgraced himself last week with the marker at a junior tournament."

"Sounds like my mother."

"Ay. With those ones, often as not it's me in the way. I'll no' be having big egos around my kids, any of them."

He glanced in the rear view mirror. We can't have been doing more than sixty miles an hour and traffic was flowing past. "Tell me, son, what do you think's the most important attribute in a top squash player?"

I didn't reply for a moment. "Go on," he insisted, "gimme an answer."

I thought a bit more. "It's so hard physically. It must be fitness, so you can keep on at a high pace. You don't have to have Ahmed's level of skill."

"No," he said. "It's no' physical at all. It's summat you can't see, can't measure. It's a little worm somewhere in the player's head. Something that *drives* them. Point is, no parent's going to put that in their darling bairn's brain. Sure they push. They bully them into training, for a while. They make them run, do sit ups. Enter them in tournaments. But they can't instil the soul. The soul of competition. It comes from inside. You've got that worm, son. Mebbe I can understand your set up now. Well some of it. Your father, your mother. And she's pushed you. And now your pushing back. Harder.

"She'd probably make a fine naval captain," he said with a grimace. "I'm no' surprised your pa likes to be away. There's no room for two captains on one ship."

"It feels strange," I said. "Like I'm cut off. I was so angry. Now it's just empty. And scary."

"Ay, I can see that. Just hang on to what I said on Friday. It'll no' be easy, but let the little worm grow. It's a big decision ye've made, 'specially with no support from home. Let the worm grow, son. Concentrate on getting experience. That's what you lack. You've everything else. The physical stuff? Ye'll take that in your stride."

"I'm worried about money, Sailor. I thought I'd be okay."

"It'll no' be easy, but it's doable. I've had two lads with jack shit, lads who made it. Alan Lindwall, you know how he did. Top twenty for three, mebbe four, years. Before his injury. And Krishnan Singh, a right scally. Krishnan made it with nothing from his folks. And I mean nothing, not a rupee. Darned maharajahs, too. When I first saw Krishnan he was playing with a wooden racquet."

He wiped his hand over his mouth. "It's doable, son. And it's down to you."

We stopped a couple of times on the way back, for food, petrol and to let Sailor stretch his legs. I called the Kemballs and told them about our quick turn around. Some time after midnight I quietly let myself in with the key they'd given me. I'd agreed with Sailor to move over to his place the next day, provided I could get a lift with my stuff.

It was a long time before I went to sleep.

The transfer to Sailor's house turned out to be easy. I hadn't much in the way of personal possessions at the Kemballs, so packing didn't take long. Russell was working from home again and drove me over after the morning traffic had died down. Sailor lived in a quiet road about ten minutes away from the Man City sports complex. It was an ordinary semi, with three bedrooms and a small garden at the back. He'd stayed home to let me in. Once Russell was on his way he showed me round.

I was to be given the third bedroom. It wasn't large, about a third the size of my room at home, but the bed seemed okay. The room had the basics, a wardrobe, a bedside light and a small desk. Sailor had dumped the stuff we'd picked up at home on the floor. 'It gave me a hernia, son.' Sailor's wife apparently worked, so I'd meet her that evening.

"Now, listen to me, here's the rules. My wife is no' a housekeeper."

"What's her name?" Sailor had never spoken about his wife.

"Mary. She works full time. Long hours. I do the housekeeping. So listen carefully. Housekeeping I don't like. So that gives us rule number one. With you here there'll be no extra housekeeping for me. None. You do your own. You make a mess? Ye clear it up. You've dirty laundry? Machine's in the kitchen. Kit? Ye wash it yourself. That's rule number two. No festering kit. Ye change your bed every two weeks. I'll no' have your room turning into a pit. Food. Ye'll eat with us. Breakfast, six thirty."

"Come on! There's no way I can eat breakfast at six thirty."

Sailor gave me a look and repeated in an identical tone, "Breakfast at six thirty. Sharp. And our evening meal's at seven. Ye'll give us fifty pounds a month, for the food, that's rule number three. And rule number four, ye keep your bedroom tidy."

"God. I made up my mind years ago not to go into submarines. My dad showed me round one once. There was no space and it was all so tidy. Not to mention the discipline. Now I find myself in the Manchester equivalent of a submarine."

It might have been a faint smile crossing Sailor's face: "Rule number five, son, no insolence."

"All right, Sailor, not much insolence."

"No insolence." The smile had gone.

"One problem," I continued, "big time, and I should have talked about this while we were driving back. I don't have any money with me at all. You know the situation. I'd ask my mother but I can't imagine she'll give me anything now."

"No, I can see that. I've thought about that, and I've a proposal. Ye'll have to get a job, obviously. Can you swim?"

"Yes, I'm okay at swimming. I used to swim for the club until I was nine or ten. Before my mother decided winning Wimbledon was the only thing for me."

"Good. I know the people at Fallowfield Pool. Hartford Road."

"Where's that?"

"It's no' far. Lifeguarding. Ye can do that as and when. It's no' exciting, but it'll keep ye out of mischief and give you some pocket money."

"That sounds okay, I suppose. Will I get to rescue any drowning teenage girls?"

This time it was a stern look. "That's another thing. No girls here overnight. Ye do that and you're out. Understand? Back home, finished. End of story."

It clearly wasn't the time to ask whether overnight boys would be all right.

"Understand?"

"Yes, Sailor, I understand." I was already starting to wonder about my social life, but breakfast at six thirty wouldn't be compatible with overnight guests anyway.

"Is it six thirty breakfast at weekends, too?"

"Ay, six thirty sharp. Training doesn't stop at weekends."

We were interrupted by a call on my mobile. The screen carried the single word, 'Home'. My mother, uunghhh.

"Hello, Mum."

"Now listen to me, Jolyon, pay attention. I've been to see your grandfather this morning." Blimey, she hadn't wasted any time. "He wants to see you."

"What for? It's hundreds of miles from Manchester and I've only just come back. In case you'd forgotten."

"He can't believe what you're doing." I held the phone away from my ear. "Neither can I, by the way. But he wants to hear about it. Directly from you. In person. He wants to talk about what you're doing. He thinks he can change your mind or something. I tried to tell him he's wasting his time on you, we all are, that's obvious, but he's insistent. Don't get any silly ideas about the trust conditions. That was decided when I spoke to him the other day. His lawyer is dealing with that at the moment. Today. But before he authorises the changes to your trust, he wants to talk to you."

Sailor could clearly hear what my mother was saying. They could probably hear out in the street. "Next weekend," he mouthed. "Do it next weekend. Ye can take the coach."

Chapter Thirteen

So I arranged to travel down to the South coast the following Friday. What a fun journey that would be. Hours of boredom on the M6 and M1, Victoria Coach Station in London and then further hours into Sussex. At least I could actually talk to my grandfather, and tell him myself what I was doing. Explain it to him properly. I didn't have any illusions about getting him to change his mind about the trust fund. Not after my mother had tenderised his attitudes with her steak mallet approach. But I did want to try to make him understand, to lighten the picture my mother would have painted. He of all people would understand.

Sailor suggested I wait to sort out my room till that evening, and we headed off to the EIS. Most of the group were already there, in the middle of some on-court routines. On the way to the changing rooms Sailor said, "I'm going to do some planning for ye this morning. We'll go through it at lunchtime, right."

Lunchtime came, and with it the plans. Sailor had taken over a quiet table at the side of the canteen area. He waved the others away. I'd had a quick shower and brought the tray with our sandwiches, three for me and one for him, and the same ratio of isotonic drink. I'd worked hard to catch up through the morning and was thirstier than I should have been. Sailor put his half moon glasses on and extracted an A4 pad from his battered brief case.

"Right, son, how old are ye now, sixteen?"

"That's right."

"When's your birthday?"

"March the tenth."

He looked down and made a note on his pad. "Excellent."

"Why excellent?"

"It means ye've three British Junior Opens, one at under seventeen, two at under nineteen. The Juniors are played at the start of January so a March birthday's good. That helps me with what we'll do through the autumn. Focus on the under seventeen. Ye should win that, I'm telling you now. We need to build your reputation. If you were Dave, for instance, with lots of experience we might even skip the under seventeen this year and go direct into the under nineteen. But ye could lose early in that. I want ye to win the under seventeen."

I raised my eyebrows.

"Yes," he said. "Without dropping a game."

"What?"

"That's your first target, without dropping a game. That's the first opportunity to show ye've something different.

"And that's the plan. When you start on the professional tour, in the Challenger tournaments, I want people to know about you. You won't win much, at first, but I want people scared at the way ye go about it. Scared about what they have to do to beat you. If you're going to be as successful as you can be in this sport, it'll be because you beat people before you go on court. The top two inches, that's where you've got to beat them. In their minds."

"That's a long way off, Sailor. I know I can get a lot fitter, from what I've done here already. But I've hardly played anyone."

"Can it, son, can it. Ye've got to believe it now." He raised his voice. "Now.

"See, I know what ye can do.

"You've seen what you can do. Mentally.

"You were the same person last week when you beat Dave, same body, same player that had always lost to Dave. But not in the top two inches, that's where you changed.

"Mentally ye were different.

"And see what happened. You wiped him. It's no good now slipping back into the old Jolyon Jacks: talented lad, used to be a tennis player, good runner, little bit o' this, little bit o' that. What you are son, is the winningest squash player on the planet. Winningest ever. Well potentially. Stuff Geoff Hunt. Stuff Jonah Barrington. Stuff Zaman, Shabbana," he counted on his fingers as he ran through the names, "Peter Nicol, Jansher, Jahangir, Jonathan Power, Lincou, Ramy Ashour, all the others, Nick Matthew. It doesn't matter who."

Sailor was staring at me now, his voice rising. He took a breath. "Everything ye do from now on, mentally you're the best. Every training session. Every practice game. Do you hear what I'm saying?"

I nodded.

"Believe it. You believe it, son.

"Now, something else." In a more business-like way Sailor rummaged in his briefcase and came out with a plastic A4 binder. "Ye need to be fully aware, and I mean fully, about drugs. Here's the background, the whole story and it includes the current list of banned substances." He handed me the binder, which had 'UK Sport. Background to Dope Control' on the cover. It was surprisingly thick, maybe twenty pages. Someone took this seriously.

"Keep this. Ye'll need to read it, cover to cover. First things first, are you asthmatic?"

"Me? No." Several of my friends back home had inhalers, even a couple of the runners, but not me.

"That's good. And no' epileptic?"

"No."

"So ye're no' taking any regular medication?"

"No." Not since I stopped doing draw at raves back home, I omitted to add. Hardly medication, I suppose.

"Good. Asthma's the one that can get you. And cold remedies. And food supplements. Asthma, some of the medications are on the banned list but ye can get a so called Therapeutic Use Exemption. You get a note from your doctor. Cold remedies? Don't take 'em. Full stop." He glared at me. "If you're poorly with a cold, come and see me. Do you hear me?"

He stayed fierce. "And food supplements."

"Banned?"

"Not quite. There's just one we consider. The protein drink you've had. That's okay because I say so. People get into all sorts of bother with food supplements. Standard excuse for anyone caught taking steroids." He mimicked a whinging voice, "'I didna know it was in there. I'd never take a drug'. You know what I think of that. No matter what anyone says, ye don't take food supplements. Understand?"

I nodded. "Could we get tested here?"

"Unlikely here out of season. But at a tournament, yes. World championships, always. WADA rules, that's the World Anti-Doping Agency. All sports associations are affiliated. WSF, World Squash Federation, that's us. Junior championships included."

"So there could be testing at any tournament I'm in?"

"Sure, could be. And you'll be in the World Juniors soon enough. Testing in this country's covered by UK Sport. They operate through the UK Anti-Doping organisation, UKAD."

"At last I'll be able to win at Scrabble."

There was a pause. "Son, ye don't seem to understand, this is one subject where there are no jokes. D'ye get me, no jokes?" He tasered me, a twin high voltage beam from hostile blue eyes.

"Do... you... get... me? No jokes."

I nodded again.

"So the answer to your question is yes, you could be tested, at any tournament. Not often in the juniors, but it happens. But it's no' a worry, is it, son? Because you're no' taking anything. Ever? Are ye? In our world, dope is a dirty word. D-o-p-e, four letters. In my squad, dope equals out, final, no excuses, no explanations. I will not be disgraced by anyone in my squad.

"Understand?"

Another nod. Apart from the draw, I'd tried E a few times, and once, what a mistake, I'd snorted some ketamine. Sailor's rules would save money on the E and the draw, and in the case of K, save serious embarrassment. With the ketamine someone had caught me on their mobile, staggering around, gurning like a retard.

Most of all I understood that if I got done for dope I'd have to deal with Sailor. *Gamma ray burst in Manchester, cosmic catastrophe leaves nothing but a smoking hole. No survivors.*

I was glad to meet Sailor's wife when we got back to his place that evening. What a contrast. For a start, she was Irish, with a soft, lilting voice a long way removed from her husband's. Unlike Sailor, she projected a proper education. I asked her what she did and she explained that she was an actuary, working at the head office of a building society in Manchester. That would explain the smartly cut suit she changed out of after Sailor had introduced us. The jeans she came back in probably cost as much as my entire wardrobe, but not as much as the shoes she'd left upstairs in exchange for a smart canvas pair. I knew about shoes. They were one of my mother's obsessions.

Sailor had cooked the evening meal, and true to his word it was ready at seven o'clock prompt. It was some sort of chicken stew containing chickpeas and potatoes and something hot.

"Harissa paste, son, a grand ingredient. I'll rub it into your eyeballs if you slack at training."

Just my *eye*balls? Instead I said, "That's harassment."

"No lad, it's encouragement."

We had sat down in the McCann's dining room, with a proper table cloth and linen napkins. I'd risked a, 'What are these small sheets for?' and Sailor had replied with a 'Remember Rule Number Five, son, no insolence'.

I soon came to realise that Mary McCann was closer in character to Sailor than first impressions suggested. She coolly described having to fire an individual that week for poor performance, and made it sound exactly like Sailor's ejection of a Spanish guy from his squad earlier in the summer. She talked about work stuff that was way over my head, but not, apparently, Sailor's. I started to see him in a different light.

"What are your ambitions, Jolyon?" Mary asked while Sailor was out making coffee.

I thought for a moment, looking down and noticing with relief that I hadn't spilt anything on the tablecloth. Hmm, what *were* my ambitions? I looked back at Mary and she was staring at me.

"I'm going to be world squash champion."

"Yes. Sailor said so." Her eyes looked right inside me. "He gets these things right. Don't let him down." There was every bit as much steel in her delicate Irish as there was in Sailor's harsh Glaswegian.

The only distraction from the routines and the training leading up to Friday was a trip to Fallowfield Pool to meet the manager, Jim Braddock. Jim was a decent fellow who talked me through the NPLQ certification that would qualify me as a lifeguard. I'd have to do a one week course and pass every one of the sections of the assessment. After this and some supervision at the centre, I'd apparently be licensed to fish drowning individuals, of all shapes and sizes, not just the ones I'd chosen, from the pool. Then there'd be the mouth to mouth resuscitation. Looking around at the Pension Club members cruising up and down the pool, at speeds that might have been just detectable with time lapse photography, I hoped again that any drowners would be female, sixteen years old and shaped like Samantha, not sixty six and shaped like a discarded sofa. I didn't mention this to Jim, but signed up for the next NPQL course, which conveniently was only couple of weeks away.

Friday came. I took an early bus into the centre of Manchester to catch the London coach. It only added three or four miles, and a single hour, to the journey. What was another hour? Then it was motorway boredom, relieved to some extent by the mixes in my iPod, recordings Dave and I had made as demos.

I didn't reach Brighton until six o'clock that evening, and spent virtually all my remaining cash on the taxi home. I'd called my mother, admittedly pessimistically, and asked her to meet me. "What do you mean? I'm your mother, Jolyon, not your chauffeur."

The plan was, my mother explained, to visit my grandfather in the morning after breakfast. I'd hoped we could do it that evening so that I start the return journey in good time.

"No, that doesn't suit me," my mother said. "I have a do over in Lewes."

Well do your flipping do.

So I called up Samantha. "Hi, it's me."

"I know it's you. You still come up on my phone because I've not got round to deleting your number. Can't think why. Why haven't you called? And where are you now, anyway?"

This wasn't going well. In fact it was a good question, why I hadn't called. The true answer was that I'd been wrapped up in all the squash stuff. When I'd been thinking of the opposite sex it was invariably of Zoë.

"I've been wanting to call but I wanted to wait till I was back down. I'm at home now. Any chance you could come round? My mother's out."

"That's just like you. You don't do Facebook, don't call for weeks, and when you do it's no warning and you're down here and all you're after is a fuck."

"Hey, that's not true, Sam." Hmm, it was somewhat true. "It's so inconvenient, me being in Manchester, but I really want to see you."

With an empty evening stretching in front of me the idea of seeing Samantha in the flesh, even seeing Samantha's actual flesh if I could persuade her to expose it, was hugely appealing.

"I want to hear how the new term's started," spot the lie, "and what else you've been up to." Another lie. "Come on, Sam. You can show me your new car." True, even if a means to an end.

Samantha had turned seventeen in August and after a blitz of driving lessons had passed her test first time, just before the new term started. Affluent divorced Mummy had come up with a new car for her. I was relieved that I had managed to respond in kind to her text that carried this good news, but regretted now that I hadn't called back straight away to congratulate her. That might have simplified the current conversation and even paved the way to one of our tsunami shags.

"Look, maybe we can sort out a trip for you up to Manchester. At half term or something." Not to stay at the McCanns obviously. Perhaps, I thought, she could stay at the Kemballs. "It's a great scene up there and I'll be playing some sets pretty soon." If I could get away. And if I wasn't too knackered by the training.

"I bet you've got a girlfriend up there. Already."

"That's rubbish, I haven't at all." This time sadly true. I was a million miles from being able to call the only candidate my girlfriend.

"Come on, Sam, I'd love to see you." Another truth. But, I realised with momentary guilt, not on your terms.

"Oh, all right, but I can't stay long."

Yesss!

There was a knock on the door inside ten minutes. I'd always fancied Sam and she looked good as she proudly showed me round her car in the twilight. She took me for a drive up and down the lane, but the thing I noticed most was the way the seat belt bisected her boobs and emphasised them in her skimpy tee shirt.

Back in the house we uncomfortably circled each other in my rather empty bedroom.

"When am I going to see you properly?" Sam demanded.

"Well, we're seeing each other now. And like I said, you can come up to Manchester at half term."

"When are you coming down here again?"

"I'm sure I will for tournaments. And possibly to see my granddad."

"What about me?"

"We could see each other in Manchester."

"Why not here? Why can't you come down at weekends?"

"I can't drive, for one thing. It's a real mission by coach." And the truth is, I wouldn't want to interrupt my training. I moved closer to her, wanting to line up for a snog, but she stepped back.

"You mean the squash is more important than me?"

"Oh come on, Sam. Of course it isn't."

"If it wasn't you'd come and see me."

"That's not fair."

"It's not fair that you've gone away and don't make any effort to see me, even to contact me."

"I've come to see you now. I'm here aren't I?" I sat down on the bed, in the hope she'd join me.

No such luck. She leant against the wall on the other side of the room, arms folded. "You'd have called if you'd been coming to see me. You're here for something else."

"I do have to see my granddad."

"You see, it's not me at all, is it?"

"We're going round in circles, Sam. Why don't you come here and give me a hug?"

"Don't you mean a fuck?"

"Well yes, I really fancy you, you know that. I haven't noticed you not wanting to do it before."

"That was when I thought we were friends."

"We are."

"Not in my book. I've got to go, anyway."

"Oh Sam!"

"It's no good 'Oh Sam-ing' me." She headed out of the door. "It's good bye. Don't bother to call."

I caught up with her at the bottom of the stairs and grabbed her arm. There were tears running down her face. "Don't bother," she said and tried to pull away. I resisted then let her go and she ran out of the front door, slamming it behind her. I heard the car start and drive away with the engine revving hard.

Another link with my Sussex life gone.

Chapter Fourteen

Out of respect for my grandfather I was wearing my smartest tee shirt and had belted my jeans at my waist when I dressed in the morning. They felt uncomfortable as my mother drove us in silence out of the village, but I'd be spared my grandfather's gentle sarcasm.

An old country house and some low outbuildings made up the sheltered housing complex. The car park was some distance away. It was a hazy autumn morning and you could smell the sea on the walk over to the main building through well tended gardens. Inside, the smell changed: disinfectant and old people. This was the nursing home area.

I was feeling nervous. I'd given up hope on the trust; the money would come to me eventually, when my parents died, but that was irrelevant now, a lifetime away. I couldn't care less about my mother's opinion of what I was doing, but I desperately wanted Grandpa to understand. He was the one I'd always hoped to have on the touchline, or at the courtside or the poolside, all through my childhood. He'd encouraged me when I'd done well and sympathised when I'd lost. Grandpa's interest in my sports started with a particular incident when I was just eight. I remember it so clearly. I'd started playing cricket at the end of the previous summer and was desperately looking forward to more the following spring. Grandpa had come out to the local park and had thrown down some balls to me. Then he'd batted to give me a chance at bowling. Finally he said we ought to do some catching practice.

"Right, Go back a bit and throw it to me on the full. Then I'll do the same for you."

I retreated quite a distance and Grandpa said, "Stop, that's far enough. Remember, it's got to reach me on the full."

I carried on backwards. "Don't be silly, Jolyon." Grandpa stood with his hands on his hips. "You won't get it half way."

Finally I stopped, ran a couple of paces and threw as hard as I could. Grandpa's exasperation turned to surprise as the ball sailed over his head and bounced way the far side of him. After trotting back to retrieve the ball he thoughtfully moved closer before throwing it back. It would have done an eight year old boy serious damage arriving from the distance I'd thrown it.

"That's quite a throw you've got," he said as we left the park. "And I'm impressed with your catching, Jolyon. You'll make a good fielder. Fielding's important, not just batting and bowling."

He never gave praise unless he meant it. Praise from Grandpa had even more impact in the absence of any from my mother. Seeing my enjoyment of cricket, he spent a lot of time with me after that on summer evenings, batting and bowling and catching. "You'll never be any good unless you practise," was his mantra. "You'll get out of it whatever you put in to it. Nothing comes free."

We passed the usual uniformed staff and trolleys and morning bustle on the way to Grandpa's apartment. The door was open. He was standing in the main living area, looking out of the window, as always smartly dressed, with well pressed trousers, a jacket and a tie. His white hair was neatly barbered. He was well shaved, no doubt still with the cutthroat razors I remembered with awe from my childhood. How did he not cut himself? It didn't make sense.

Grandpa radiated a sort of flinty energy. In recent years he sometimes used a stick to steady himself going down a slope or when he knew he'd be in a crowd, but he held the stick more as a weapon, not as a hedge against loss of balance. No one would guess his age.

He turned as we entered. Nothing wrong with his hearing. "Hello, Jolyon," and then a frown, "Hello Shirley."

His voice was strong, but the change in tone when he addressed my mother gave me some hope that he wasn't a hundred percent on her side.

"Hello, Grandpa." It was good to see him and we had our usual hug.

"Now, pull up a couple of chairs."

We sat down at the table where Grandpa ate. He moved a neat pile of newspapers out of the way, still The Independent I noticed, how appropriate, and sat on his bed.

"Your mother tells me that you've dropped out of school. I'm not happy to hear that. What's it all about?" No preamble.

"It's not dropped out, Grandpa. That sounds sort of derelict."

"Dropped out is precisely what it is." The first words my mother had uttered since we'd arrived.

"That's not fair. I've got this opportunity, Grandpa. It's a chance to play squash full time. In Manchester."

"Why Manchester?" he asked. "I seem to remember you'd started playing down here."

"There's a coach there, Sailor McCann."

"Out of a Glasgow tenement," my mother said. "It's impossible to understand a word the man's saying."

"Give the boy a chance, Phyllis." My mother touched her hair, a rigid shell, two hours and probably two hundred quid's worth, repeated twice a week in Brighton. She raised her eyes to the ceiling.

"This coach," I went on. "He has some of the best players in the country, and from overseas. And he coaches the women's world champion, Zoë Quantock."

"Is she the woman who won Sports Personality? I think I remember her."

"Yes, that's her, she came third actually. I train with Zoë."

"Well that's not going to see you through the rest of your life, saying you trained with the women's world squash champion."

"Exactly," my mother said.

"The point is, Grandpa, Sailor says I can be world champion too."

"Absolutely absurd," my mother said.

"Shirley, I'm trying to understand what Jolyon's on about. Could you simply give the boy a chance."

"This whole thing is just ridiculous. I don't know why you're wasting your time seeing him."

"Go on, Jolyon. That sounds a bit far fetched, world champion. I thought it was all Pakistanis, the Khans, and the Egyptians."

"It's not like that any more. There are one or two good Pakistanis; lots of Egyptians it's true. The world number one, he's an Egyptian at the moment. But there's Australians; there's a Scot at number nine, Josh McKean, a New Zealander, a guy from Malaysia. It's wide open."

"Right then." It was as if he was rolling up his sleeves. "Let's just suppose for a moment you've got some potential. Sport's a chancy business at the best of times. It's just not clever leaving school without your A levels. For the sake of the two years, it's obvious, you should stay on at school. Play some squash, certainly. But there's no substitute for qualifications. I've hired enough people in my time, I know. Then you can concentrate on the squash, if you still want to. You could put off going to university for a couple of years, have a gap. It wouldn't matter at that stage."

"It doesn't work like that, Grandpa."

"Oh don't be ridiculous, Jolyon." My mother had been silent for all of a minute, probably a record.

"Shirley, I want to hear what the boy has to say. You're not being helpful."

"Now, Jolyon. There's more than an element of truth in what your mother's saying. You are starting to sound ridiculous."

I really wanted to convince him. "It might work, staying at school for another two years, if I'd played lots of squash. But I need to be full time to catch up. I've only really been playing for the last year. Sailor says I shouldn't miss a day from now on."

"Then why does he think you're so good?"

My mother raised her eyes again and made a 'tch' sound, followed by, "Why indeed? Just tell him about the trust, Father, and he'll come to his senses."

"Shirley, you're being conspicuously unhelpful. I'd be grateful if you'd leave us for ten minutes. Out of the room."

Yesss! I doubt if anyone had ever spoken to her like that. My mother looked at him as if he'd accused her of catching gonorrhoea from the meter reader.

"I simply don't understand why you're wasting your time," she said. "But if you want to carry on listening to this drivel, then I agree I'll be better off elsewhere."

She stood up and humphed out of the room, leaving her chair at an untidy angle.

Grandpa just said, "Go on."

"I think it's two things. Firstly, I did really well in the performance testing. Sailor says it's the best he's ever seen."

"Tell me about that."

"Well it's simple. Four tests basically. The standing jump, off both feet, how high." He nodded. "The drop jump. You drop from fifty centimetres and jump as high as you can. This time they measure how long you're in the air after the jump divided by the time you take to do the jump, when your feet are in contact with the mat. Then there's the bleep test."

"I've heard of that one, the bleep test."

"It's really hard. Anyway, I did a seventeen. It's high for someone my age.

"Then the last one's the VO_2 max, which you're more or less born with, Sailor told me. I was over eighty, which is very high again."

"So," he said, "lot's of good performances in some gym tests. How does that translate into world champion?"

"I played my friend, Dave Kemball. He's the guy I was staying with, just outside Manchester. He's really good. Ranked two in the country in the under seventeens. He always used to beat me. We'd have a good game but he just knew too much, too many shots, and he's so fit.

"Anyway, before the game Sailor told me how to beat him. In a way it was beating him mentally first. The top two inches, Sailor says, it's in the mind. Then beat him physically. I wouldn't do it on squash skill, I could never do that with Dave. I just had to use what the gym tests said. In squash that means taking the ball early, that's really hard. But if you can do it it's really hard for your opponent too. That was all I did, pressurise him. It was only thirty five minutes. But I've never been so tired, Grandpa, I was absolutely gone. And I beat him three love."

I sat back, reliving how I'd felt. "It was fantastic. I really like Dave. But I took him on there. I'd never beaten him. It was, I dunno, exhilarating. I controlled him. Then Sailor talking to me afterwards. The idea I could be the best. It's a long way away to go, obviously. But it's worth a try. And to be honest, otherwise I'll just be doing what Mum expects. Dad too, I suppose. But Mum. It's sort of like I'm her little possession, to be displayed everywhere. Look at mine. My one's better than yours. See how well it's doing.

"Well I will be better than anyone's, but she just doesn't seem to like it this way. And I know giving up school doesn't sound clever. And it isn't, I suppose."

Grandpa's blue eyes had never left me. "The quality I value more than anything in a person, Jolyon, and I've told you this before, the best quality of all is enthusiasm. I've been getting worried about you these last couple of years. You've been turning into a typical cynical teenager, always ready to knock something down, never to build it up. I've hated that. It's not how you always used to be. This is the first time I've seen you enthusiastic about anything for ages, the first time in years. When your mother told me about the squash I was angry. It sounded like another stupid step downhill. I realise now it's not that.

"It is a big risk, though. It's a huge risk. Another of my worries has been that all you'll go for is an easy life. Live off what I'm leaving you. Not make anything of yourself. That wouldn't be acceptable. I'd already been wondering about altering the terms of the trust. Eighteen seemed a good idea when I set it up all those years ago when I sold my business. Recently it had started to feel a ridiculously young age, giving you more money than most people could ever spend. I'd wondered about changing it entirely, maybe to forty or something like that. The story your mother told made it easy. You'd get the money in the end; I don't want to give it all away somewhere else. But only after your mother and father had died. And that's decades away."

He sat back and shut his eyes. "I've a confession to make now. I got your mother to tell me who it was putting these daft squash ideas into your head. She tends to slant things, put them the way she sees them. I wanted another angle. I've met Sailor McCann, you know. It had to be the same man. It was an occasion when your father was first at Faslane. Your dad thought the world of Sailor. Well I phoned him yesterday evening. He told me more or less what you've told me. You've really impressed him. More than even the performance assessments, he says there's something inside you. I used to see that when you were small, I thought I did. Then it disappeared. Now I can see it again."

His voice had gone very quiet and I had to lean forward to hear. "I asked Sailor how long it would take you to reach the top. He said even though you're so raw, because with you it's all physical, well not entirely, he did say that you hit the ball very well, 'beautifully correct' I think was his phrase, he said he'd know by the time you were twenty one whether you were going to be a world champ."

There was a long pause, and then he went on. "I asked him about twenty one. I pressed him. He said you had it in you to be world champion, that's a bit open to chance, or world number one, one or the other, by your twenty first birthday.

"Two chances, Jolyon, two chances, world number one or world champ." His eyes held mine. "And that's what I'm going to give you. I'll get my solicitor to redraft the trust. I set it up originally to be flexible, so it won't be a problem legally. If you're world champion, or officially world number one, either's all right, by your twenty first birthday, the money in the trust will come to you then. If you haven't made it by then, well, no gifts from me. The trust will then vest on the death of the second of your parents."

He was still looking at me intently. "I know you'll do it, Jolyon. After talking to Sailor McCann, knowing you as I do. After all those games we used to play. There was never a child who tried so hard to win." He looked away for a moment, maybe into the past. "I'm just hoping that I'll be there to see you do it.

"Now, will you go and find your mother and bring her back. Go on."

It was a relief that I could turn away. I didn't want Grandpa to see the tears in my eyes.

Chapter Fifteen

I got back to the McCann's house after the appointed time for the evening meal, but Sailor had put some food aside. He sat down with me at the kitchen table while I bolted the food down. I'd missed lunch.

"Hard man, your grandfather."

"I was amazed. He told me he'd spoken to you."

"Aye, he had a lot o' questions. We must've spoken for forty five minutes, mebbe an hour."

"How did he get your number?"

"Through your mother, then the Kemballs. I had the impression not much gets in his way."

"He's still so strong. For eighty five."

"Aye, I could feel it. He started off quite aggressive. Like what was I doing ruining your life? What right did I have? He told me he'd been so grateful to his mother when he was a lad. She made him study when he didn't want to. Forced him. She'd seen his talent. He told me he'd been a wild kid. It was her got him into engineering. She never saw his success, though. He's always regretted it.

"I said hold on a minute, Mr Fellows. How d'ye define success? Does it have to be inside the tramlines? Big business success? Academic success, Mr Fellows? Do ye think I've had the academic success? I tell ye what I've had, Mr Fellows. I've had Zoë Quantock. I've had a world champion. That's success."

Sailor stood up, opened one of the kitchen cupboards, took out a bottle of malt whiskey and called out, "Do you want a glass, Mary?"

To my surprise a positive reply came back from the room his wife used as a study.

"Bring two glasses, then." Sailor looked at me. "You'll have a soft drink, son."

A moment later Mrs McCann came in with two crystal glasses and sat down with us. Sailor fetched me a glass of squash and poured tots of whiskey for his wife and himself.

"I was talking about Jolyon's granddad. And education."

"It's Sailor's theme, always," Mrs McCann said, looking at me intently. "I've been so sad, we're both so sad, biggest regret of our lives, we could never have kids. But Sailor has brought more life into the world, more life out of more kids than, I don't know," she gave a wry smile, "the biggest families you see round here. This part of Manchester, very Catholic."

It was an intimate moment. Mary McCann put out her hand and rubbed Sailor's back. "I should know. I come from a Catholic family, four brothers, five sisters. And did my father care about us? Care? No. It was the booze he cared about. Sailor cares far more about each individual in his group than my dad did about any of us."

"Aye," Sailor went on. "I said to your granddad, you're the one for Jolyon. You've the power to encourage your grandson's talent. He'll listen to you.

Your boy has as much potential as anyone on the planet. That much. The whole planet." He looked at me. "I told him Jolyon doesn't realise it yet, he's so raw. But I know. I *know*, son. I told him you tick all the boxes. I told him about Zoë. I knew when Zoë first came to me she was special, what she'd do. The first day. Nobody was aware of her then. Nobody was aware of me. Nobody would listen when I said she should go full time. Her dad kicked up a fuss. Heavy duty. But I was lucky there. It was her decided that, not me.

"Then your granddad asked me, how long is it going to take? How long before he could make it to the top? I said mebbe six years. We'll know by then. He said he knows you, ye'd never be focussed with a target like that. Six years, it's a lifetime. Too long. He asked me, could he do it by the time he's twenty one?

"It's a tough one. I told him I'll know that in twelve months. When I've seen how you come on physically."

"Stop messing around, Sailor," Mrs McCann interrupted. "Sailor told me the other day, before all this came up, he told me he'd bet Jolyon would be number one by his twenty first birthday."

She turned to me. "Once in a blue moon Sailor makes a bet. Only if he knows he's going to win." She laughed. "It hurt him, but he put on a bet, he really did, at Ladbrokes, that Scotland would drop out of the top hundred football countries I think it was, top something anyway, I can't remember. When Berti Vogts took over as manager."

"Bertie who?"

"Of course, you're too young. Boy did it hurt." She smiled. "Scotland were pathetic. But Sailor won his bet." She rubbed his back again. "We're drinking the winnings right now. It wouldn't surprise me if he put a bet on you."

I'd never seen this side of Sailor, a secret life he didn't show his players. "Can it, Mary, that's no' called for. But yes, that's it son, I told you're granddad you'd make it by the time you're twenty one. An' there's my fiver resting on it, good odds.

"An' that was when he told me about the legacy, the trust. How much is it? Two million quid?"

I nodded. "Something like that."

"'Far too much to give to someone before they've achieved anything', your granddad said. 'The boy needs a target', he said. Ye can tell he's old. But there's a spark about him. 'Thank you, Mr McCann', he said. 'I can see how I'm going to manage this now.'"

Sailor was making a fair imitation of the way Grandpa spoke. "'Leaving the money is incidental. He'll get it in the end, anyway. It will be up to him. Whether he gets it on his twenty first birthday. Or later.'"

I nodded. It seemed so enormous, so impossible.

Mary smiled at me this time and ruffled my hair. I might have been embarrassed but I wasn't. "Sailor will do his bit," she said. "The rest is up to you, Jolyon. You've got to do yours. If you want two million quid by the time you're twenty one."

"Given the choice I'd rather be world champion. I want to be like Zoë."

"Aye, that's it, son, but it's both or nothing for you. I promised to keep your granddad up to date. He wants ye to do it. Don't disappoint him."

I didn't sleep well that night, thinking about Grandpa and the challenge. I hadn't been to see him enough recently. It would be even more difficult with me in Manchester. There was a tournament coming up in Brighton soon, a bit Mickey Mouse, but I'd enter it anyway and see him then. I thought about my mother, too. The thing that would impress her, or rather, much better than that, the thing that would mortally piss her off, would be me completing Grandpa's terms for the trust. That would be a grand slam triple bagel, game, set and match to me, mother dear. I'd make a point of buying her a ridiculously expensive present, something she'd hate. Only trouble was, there was a downside to Grandpa's challenge: me not making it. That would be awful, truly awful. How my mother would crow.

I wanted to show Zoë, too. With her in mind I wished I could do it sooner. As for the practicalities, the move from eighteen to twenty one for the trust, that was a problem. I hoped I'd be okay for money. Maybe I'd get something from my father now.

Over the next couple of weeks Sailor mapped out what I'd have to do (I could hardly believe the words) to reach world number one by my twenty first birthday. Reach world number one? Sometimes I thought that three times round Pluto was more likely.

"The big challenge is the ranking points. You have to reach the first round of PSA tournaments to get points. When you've enough points to be ranked you're in the first round automatically. Before that ye can only get into the qualifying. So by the time you've reached the first round you've probably had two hard matches, against young guys as hungry as yerself. Then you end up playing a seed and bang, you're tired, you lose quickly and no' many points. It's hard to make progress."

We were sitting in Sailor's kitchen having a cup of tea. As usual we had had breakfast with Mary at six thirty prompt, six and a half bells or something. She had left for work as usual at about seven, looking very formal and expensive, leaving Sailor and me to clear the dishes away. Sailor often did paperwork then, there seemed to be enormous amounts of it, and sometimes we'd chat about how things were going over a cup of tea before setting off for training.

"How are the points allocated?"

"It depends on the grade of the tournament. We'll go through it when you join the PSA. The tour guide gives the nitty gritty. What ye need to know now, the higher the prize money the more points. Ye'll have to be winning big money tournaments, not just doing well, before yer twenty."

My life fell into its new pattern after that, fierce training with Sailor's squad, good behaviour back home in Sailor's semi, military mealtimes. Matches were important and there were as many as Sailor could find me. If I'm honest, to an outsider it would have been dull, squash and not much else. I had my decks set up in my bedroom but the only way I could mix was through headphones. Although that kept my hand in there was no buzz, no satisfaction in perfectly syncing a bass line unless you could feel it juddering the contents of your chest. There was no one to play a new drop to. And not enough money to buy any vinyl.

Dave had gone back to school, so I'd usually only see him at weekends when he came along to training. I often found myself wishing I could get back with Samantha. My dreams of rescuing voluptuous babes from Fallowfield Pool after I'd got my lifeguard qualification disappeared on about day two. It was dreary sessions of watching pensioners burn off single figure numbers of calories in their forty minute sessions. Mainly they chatted at the shallow end, not doing much swimming. Then there were the frenetic kids' parties. You soon identified the brats you'd happily hold under rather than pull out of the pool.

I was given little sympathy by Sailor when I moaned about this one evening. He'd insisted that I save as much money as possible to pay for trips to tournaments. We were sitting down for our evening meal. As usual, he'd done the cooking, no hardship, the food was never dull.

"What do you expect, son, everything on a plate?"

"Well, that's where this rabbit stew is."

"Rule five, sonny, rule five."

"It's just that it's hard to get to the pool, and then it's tedious, just doing the lifeguarding. You've no idea how dull."

"Start of January, there's the solution. If you do well in Sheffield there'll be a lottery grant for you for sure. Let it be an incentive, son, show the powers that be you've arrived."

Sheffield meant the British Open Junior Championships, just about the biggest junior event on the world calendar. Apparently there was a massive entry, hundreds of kids in each age group. It was too big for a single centre, so it had to be played at three big Sheffield clubs, the Abbeydale, the Hallamshire and the Concord Sports Club. There were four age groups, under thirteen, under fifteen, under seventeen and under nineteen, boys and girls. I would be desperately disappointed if I didn't do well in the under seventeens. That would be a big set back.

"How are lottery grants decided?"

"It's tight now. There used to be more money around. There's a sort of committee. The national coach, and Tim Graham's a bit sharp but he's okay, and four high performance coaches in the regions. Dick Bentley over in Sheffield, you've met him, Alastair Stoogie, Brian Bartholomew in the South East and the fourth's vacant at the moment. They get together regularly and decide who's going to get the support. Dick's the important one as far as you're concerned. If you win the under seventeens you'll definitely get some help."

Dick Bentley had brought the best players in his squad of juniors over to the EIS for an informal match, 'The War of the Roses', a couple of weeks earlier. I was getting used to the historical Lancashire Yorkshire rose rivalry, red for Lancs, white for Yorks. I'd upset Dick by saying that we didn't do pouffy flowers down in Sussex. In the match I'd beaten the Sheffield number one easily, which had apparently made a better impression on him than my attempt at humour.

For me the highlight of the White Rose visit was one of the girls in their team, Paula Bentley, Dick's daughter. Paula made a good impression on all of us, graceful, laughing. And provocative. Paula was well aware of the effect her body had on the opposite sex. In GCSE Geography, I remembered, we'd been taught about a disease called goitre, which used to cause a condition known as Derbyshire Neck. Goitre made your eyes stick out. Riley showed every sign of having goitre whenever Paula was around.

"What's an intelligent boy like you doing full time squash?" Paula had asked me.

"Appearances can be deceptive. My parents were dead disappointed with my GCSEs."

"GCSEs! What about your A levels?"

"I dropped out of school. Didn't do them."

"When was that?"

"Just this summer."

"No! How old are you then?"

"Sixteen. I'm seventeen in March."

"No way! I thought you were much older."

"Well, how old are you?"

Paula provided a diversion from my regular ruminations about Zoë. Paula was just into the under nineteens, her eighteenth birthday apparently on midsummer's day. I stopped myself from replying that she already looked a wicked twenty one, more than one entendre on the wicked. It was several things about her, the cut of her dark hair, short and sophisticated with a long fringe that she kept out of the way on court with a yellow bandeau, her long brown legs, her truly international walk. And her boobs. They'd have been labelled 'Twenty Percent Extra FREE!!!' if you'd seen *them* on a supermarket shelf. I stopped short of explaining this, and from asking whether there would be any special offers. She gave me the feeling she wouldn't have been too offended.

"How much dosh do you get in a grant," I continued with Sailor.

"You don't get any money in your pocket. But you get your travel to major events, and accommodation. Next year's going to be big for you, a fair bit of travel. We'll map out a plan after Sheffield. The grant'll be important. In fact I don't see how you can do it otherwise. We don't want ye having to work all the hours God gives at Fallowfield."

"Too right. That's not a career I'll be moving into when I retire from squash."

"Don't knock it, son, it's a job. And there's still your lodging to pay. I'm hoping you'll get one of the kit manufacturers to sponsor you after Sheffield, some racquets mebbe, but ye still have incidentals to get. Like a razor, for instance. When did you last have a shave? Did your dad no' tell you about puberty and facial hair and things like that?"

"Riley would call that harassment, Sailor. How do you know I'm not growing a beard?"

"Rule number six, son. No beards. Or not if that fluff's the best you can do."

Chapter Sixteen

"There's a blocked toilet in the men's changing room, Jolyon. Go and fix it when you've finished your spell."

I was perched on the observation stand by the side of the Fallowfield Pool, bored out of my mind. I was looking forward to a break from watching elderly swimmers, and to the sandwiches I'd carefully prepared after getting back from training that morning. Sailor's cooking didn't extend to packed evening meals for lowly lifeguards.

The unwelcome instruction about the bog was coming from Anthea, one of the supervisors at the pool. Anthea had an enormously high opinion of Anthea, not shared by me. With anyone else her round face, short brown hair, adequate legs and at least county standard bum, obvious in the tight shorts she wore, would have added up to a classification of All Right. She really looked okay. So did sour milk until you sniffed it.

"Oh come on, Anthea. Why can't Derek do it?" Derek was another lifeguard at the centre, a walking refutation of the theory of Intelligent Design.

"Because I'm telling you to, that's why."

Anthea had a way of winding me up within seconds of any conversation starting. Nothing new today. "I'm due off in fifteen minutes," I said. "Are you sure you don't want me to go and do it now? Then I'd be on time for my tea break."

"No," she looked up at the big clock over the pool. "I'll get Di to take over from you at six o'clock. You can have your break once you've cleared the toilet."

"What about Derek? He's on general duties too."

"Derek isn't feeling too good."

"Derek's always not feeling too good. When he's on duty that is. He's fine any other time."

"Well I've made up my mind, so stop arguing."

Up to then I'd wisely not told anyone at the centre about my plans to leave. But up to then I'd managed to control my temper. Not this time. I let it all go, at a volume my mother would have been proud of, "Thank God I'll be out of this effing place in the new year!"

Now the whole pool knew, and probably everyone in the crèche and the gym and even out in the car park. The swimmers were all suddenly staring at us. I must have been loud. They didn't have their hearing aids on in the pool.

"For God's sake Jolyon," Anthea said, looking around. "Keep your voice down. You're way out of order. I'll have to report this. You'll be up for a disciplinary for sure.

"And don't forget the toilet."

She flounced away round the pool. A couple of minutes later, through the glass barrier that separated the wet and dry sides of the centre, I noticed Anthea chatting with Derek. No sign of anything wrong with him of course.

He pointed at me and they both laughed. It dawned on me then, dead obvious from their body language, they must be an item. What a horrible thought. Derek attracted women in a tanning parlour sort of way. It wouldn't have been his personality; all he had was his overdeveloped body, steroid fit from a seven day a week gym habit. He had the broad shoulders, huge pecs and thick neck of the sweat-stained retards you saw pushing improbable iron in the Fallowfield weights room. In Derek's case it was all emphasised by the tight tee shirts he wore. Just the sort of mindless meat that would attract a fly brain like Anthea. Derek's effectiveness as a fellow dogsbody was in inverse proportion to his muscle bulk.

I'd had a run in with Derek soon after I'd started at the place. There was going to be a large Scouts event after school hours that evening, in the park next to the centre. We'd been told to take several hundred metal chairs outside. The chairs were stored in stacks of ten in a room at the back. I found it hard work from the beginning, on a really hot late summer's day.

Perhaps Derek was feeling the same way. He'd started chuntering as soon as Jim Braddock had given us the job. "Who does he think I am, some no-hope assistant? I've a fucking certificate in sports physiology, that's what I've got. I'm not paid to carry fucking chairs around. And what are you laughing at?" I'd made the mistake of smiling at his tirade. "This is a job for juniors, so get on with it."

I could just about manage three of the chairs at a time. I reckoned Derek could have picked up a whole stack without difficulty, but he was crabbing through the storeroom door with just a single chair in each hand. After fifteen minutes, before we'd completed even a quarter of the job, Anthea came out to see how we were getting on.

"I've strained my left pec," Derek said. "I'll have to stop before I do more damage."

"Okay," Anthea replied. "You carry on, Jolyon. I'll see if I can find someone else."

Derek gave me a smirk. "Get on with it, then. The job needs to be finished by five."

What an idle bastard. "You big girl's blouse," I said. "If you'd been wearing a proper sports bra that wouldn't have happened. Come to think of it, you and my mother, you're about the same size. If it helps, she gets hers from Marks and Spencer's."

In a moment he'd grabbed me by the shirt and lifted me off the ground, "Just don't mess with me, sonny."

I was too pissed off to be worried. "Mind that pec, Derek love. The silicone may leak out."

"You cunt," he hissed and pushed me away. "I'll sort you out later."

"Boys, boys," Anthea said. "Leave it out. Come on Derek. And you, Jolyon, you get on with the chairs."

But I was on a roll. "He's damaged my breast, Anthea, I mean my pectoral.

I can't carry on…" Here I tried to mimic Derek's rather high pitched voice and his Lancashire accent, "in case I do more damage."

Derek's face turned an even deeper shade of red, but Anthea pulled him away. "I said, leave it out. I'll send someone as soon as I can."

In the end, Sarah, one of the fitness instructors, appeared, but I'd done the bulk of the job by then. I was knackered when we finished. It was the start of permanent hostilities between me and Derek. From then on I took every opportunity to bring up the subject of implants, and how clever it was that you couldn't see the scars, and was Derek's poor pectoral still tender, and would it help if I gave it a squeeze.

As for Anthea, it had taken me a little longer to start wishing something awful would happen to her. Our first run-in had been over the till at reception. The end of day balance had been off by small sums on several occasions. Apparently the discrepancies hadn't been enough for anyone to become fussed, but they had been consistently negative. Anthea had raised the matter at the end of my first staff meeting, four weeks after I'd started at Fallowfield.

"Lastly, I think you've all heard, some money's been going from the till, 60p, 50p, not much. We thought it must be a child at first, or even mistakes, the amounts are so small. But that's impossible. No children behind the desk, and the till's always under, not over.

"What I've proposed is, we're giving the thief an opportunity to stop before it gets serious." She looked at me. "We think we know who it is, Jolyon, don't we. It's only happened on your days on. Just stop it now, nothing more said, and I won't have to elevate it to upper management."

That was seriously out of order, and I was livid. A wave of heat washed over my face, made worse by the smiles from the other lifeguards.

"Are you suggesting it was me?" I said, as calmly as I could.

"Not for the record, no one's seen you. It's just obvious, that's all."

"I don't accept that."

"Well then, you can play the detective and find out who it was. Only joking. Just get on with your normal duties and leave the till alone."

Thank goodness I'd be out of the place permanently at the end of February. Roll on the British Open. No pressure, I thought. Sailor was expecting me to win and winning was key to the lottery grant. Not that the grant would add up to free cash. But paying my main expenses would make a huge difference to my finances. Specifically, no more dismal minimum wage lifeguarding. The work at Fallowfield was grim and the company even grimmer.

Typically, Anthea wasn't going to let me forget my outburst. Later the same evening when we were both on duty at Reception she said, "So you're planning to leave, are you?"

"Just as soon as I effing well can. I can't wait to hand in my notice."

"It could happen sooner than you think. The last disciplinary we had, it was someone much better than you, she'd been here for several years. She was fired, just like that. While you're still here with us, if you're still here with us, you'll have to sort out your attitude problem."

Derek had joined us. "Is he bothering you, Anth?" He moved uncomfortably close to me. "You just watch your mouth, Joly-on. You need to learn some manners. Show some respect. Understand?"

"I understand where not to look for an example."

He bumped his chest against me. "Just try it with me, boy, just try it. Just raise your hand."

"No way, not unless you lay off the garlic for a couple of days. I'd be asphyxiated." I turned to Anthea. "Do you have a halitosis fetish or something, Anthea? His breath, fuck's sake. It wouldn't do anything for me."

Two customers walked in at that moment and Derek managed to control himself and pull away. He wandered off, huge thighs rubbing together, no doubt incubating awful fungi. Anthea mouthed something under her breath and booked the customers in.

Afterwards she said, "Don't expect any support from me at your hearing."

Chapter Seventeen

I couldn't wait for the British Open, but before that there was a decent tournament in London and then the Mickey Mouse Championships in Brighton. My training had gone well through the autumn, with a special focus on preparing for the Open at the beginning of January. Even so, Sailor had me ease off training for a couple of days before the London tournament, the Barnes and Barney, or B&B as it was referred to. The tournament was apparently sponsored by a 'hedge fund', whatever that was, and either Mr Barnes or Mr Barney, maybe Mrs B or Mrs B, I didn't know their gender, had an interest in squash.

I'd entered the Under Nineteens rather than the Under Seventeens in the B&B. "Part of the message," was Sailor's comment. "Do well in London an' you'll scare the children in Sheffield." Hmm, what did that make me?

Anyway, I felt really strong when the tournament started. The entry wasn't as large as it would be in a couple of months' time for the Open, although it did include some well-ranked Egyptians among the higher seeds.

Daily Telegraph, November 17th

Jacks Wins Barnes and Barney Junior Championship

In a display of fierce hitting newcomer Jolyon Jacks, not yet seventeen, won the international Barnes and Barney Junior U-19 Tournament at the RAC Club in London. In the final Jacks overpowered the Egyptian junior number five, and number one seed, Salah el Zarka, 11-5, 11-5, 11-3 in just twenty seven minutes. Jacks did not drop a game throughout the tournament. He never looked threatened against el Zarka, and overwhelmed the tiny Egyptian with his fierce pace.

Jacks is coached by Sailor McCann in Manchester. He has surprised observers with a string of impressive results since joining McCann's group in the summer.

Zoë had taken to helping me with the mental preparation for matches, when she wasn't away herself at tournaments. I was amazed how seriously she took every aspect of her squash. Firstly, she had her own internal databank of opponents, and before tournaments with Sailor she would watch videos of the ones she was likely to meet. They would work out where most of their winners came from, how close to the T they moved in down-the-wall rallies, what signs they gave out when they were tiring. I'd seen Zoë win a tournament in Nottingham. She wouldn't talk to anyone for a whole hour before a match. She would just prowl. She was visualising, she told me. Clean ball striking. Good movement. And above all how she would apply the pressure that was the key to her game. I started to do the same thing before matches, with a fast mix in my headphones, taking myself into a zone that excluded everything else, imagining how I would make the game so hard for my opponent he would mentally have given up long before the end of the match.

Before any further matches, though, I had to deal with my disciplinary. I'd no idea of what was coming up. I thought I'd get some sort of a bollocking, with maybe a warning put into my HR file. Then Jim Braddock told me to come to his office.

"Close the door," Jim said, and didn't offer me a seat. He was sitting in the big chair behind his desk, with a couple of folders open in front of him. "I understand this is the third time you've been observed swearing in front of customers, on top of persistent arguing with staff, shoddy work and poor punctuality. Anthea has apologised for not coming to me sooner. I hadn't realised that there've been actual complaints too."

For a moment I was lost for words. Eventually I croaked, "What do you mean, third time? And complaints? That's ridiculous. And late? I've never been late, not once."

"Anthea only told me yesterday. It's all here, in the log, seven entries. On top of that here's the two complaint forms, you know the system, from members of the public." He prodded one of the folders with his finger. "Our customers, Jolyon, we take our customers seriously here."

He opened one of the folders. "September the third, abuse in the canteen area, Mrs Nightingale and Miss Swann. October the twelfth, shouting during Over Sixties Swimming.

"I don't mind doing a favour for Sailor McCann, but I can't go on supporting you, not with this persistent poor behaviour. Especially customer-facing. Your disciplinary's set for next Wednesday. You're not scheduled to be in that day, I've checked. Anthea Trivet has prepared the dossier. We'll start at two fifteen. You'll get a fair hearing, of course. There's a standard company procedure. There'll be a representative from headquarters HR. You're entitled to bring along a representative yourself if you wish, but it has to be a member of staff."

I could hardly take in what he was saying. This was all made up, or virtually all of it. I stood there. If I was out, what would I do for money?

"I have to tell you this," Jim went on. "I'm not optimistic about the outcome. In the meantime," he looked up from the fiction he'd been consulting, "I'm obliged to suspend you from customer-facing duties. As of now."

"But it's not true," I said. "Or hardly any of it. I admit I shouted at Anthea. I was pissed off because she's been giving me all the dross jobs, all of them, while Derek hangs around hardly lifting one of his fat fingers. I had to do extra lifeguard sessions because he said he wasn't feeling good. Then I had to spend most of my tea break unblocking a toilet. But the other stuff, that just didn't happen."

Jim didn't look impressed. "Firstly, if you want to dispute any of the evidence that's brought on Wednesday, that's your prerogative. The incidents have all been logged. Even assuming something's been exaggerated, which I don't believe for one minute, it doesn't look good. Look, here are the two complaints. They're both signed by the customers."

He pushed the file towards me. Sure enough, there they were, separated by another one, referring to 'Faeces in the Men's Dry Side Changing Room'. I knew the cause of that one, a horrible little five year old. Surprise, surprise, it was me who had been given the task of clearing it up, and the little shit, or more accurately the little shitter, had peered round the door while I was doing it. The two complaints about me cross referred to forms that had been sent to head office. They were both initialled by Anthea.

"You'll be given a chance to speak for yourself, of course, and bring any evidence. In the meantime, you'd better keep your nose clean." He closed the files dismissively. "Right now Anthea's got work for you clearing out the gym pit."

I left the centre that night in despair. I didn't need to be a genius to work out that Anthea and Derek had concocted the stories. All except the lifeguarding incident; what a prat, that had been a gift. I'd no idea who Miss Swann and Mrs Nightingale were. Birds of a feather, probably elderly, swimmers maybe. The oldies looked much the same in their swimming hats. I turned to eye the wretched leisure centre after I'd walked through the doors, restrained myself from making a rude gesture at the CCTV camera trained on the forecourt and headed for the bus stop.

Back at Sailor's I went straight to my room, put my headphones on and started a savage mix. Blast everything out of my head. Didn't work. I kept thinking about Derek and Anthea, and how easy it had been for them to manufacture evidence. The only weak point might be Miss Swann and Mrs Nightingale. Maybe I could speak to them. This idea improved the more I thought about it. I could get their numbers from the members' register and at least call them, then even catch one or other at the centre. I was booked in for the evening session the following day and should be able to make the calls in my break.

"I heard from Jim Braddock yesterday evening."

My heart sank. This was an angry Sailor at breakfast, the morning after my meeting with Jim.

"The disciplinary?" I said. The darned disciplinary was going fissile. What if Sailor told Grandpa?

"Aye. Yer an eejit. A complete eejit. I called in a favour with Jim to get you in there."

"But Sailor..."

He wasn't to be interrupted. "Now you've blown it out of the water. Bang, gone." A swing of the hand that knocked the cornflake packet violently onto the unused fourth chair at the table. Cornflakes spilled onto the floor.

"The thing is..."

"I'm a fair man but I won't be made a fool."

"Most of it's a..."

He was shaking a finger at me. "Not me, I won't be made a fool, sonny."

"I know what..."

"Now where does this leave you?"

Mary had kept her head down to this moment, quietly eating her usual one and a half slices of wholemeal toast. She put a restraining hand on Sailor's arm.

"Hold on, Sailor. Jolyon's trying to say something."

Sailor looked at her as if he'd forgotten she was there, and then back at me. "Aye, well what do ye have to say for yerself, son? This is no' a joke."

"What I have to say is that it's mostly untrue. I did shout at one of the supervisors, once. She was being completely unreasonable. But they have me being rude to customers, there's two complaints. They have me being late. I'm never late, not once, but I'm up for poor punctuality. They have me not doing the job properly."

"What's going on, then?" Mary asked.

"Two of them, they've got it in for me. One of the lifeguards. I admit, I did wind him up a bit. It was a month ago now. And Anthea, she's a supervisor, she's been on my back from the first week I was there. She really doesn't like me. She always gives me the crap jobs."

"Son, yer in deep trouble. Ye'll no be making it worse with bad language at my table."

"Sorry. What I'm saying is, she always gives me the worst jobs. Finds ways of making life difficult. I think they've got together and made up a whole lot of stuff."

"Did ye tell Jim?"

"I tried to. He wouldn't listen. He said if I wanted to bring some evidence at the disciplinary I could."

Mary said, "You'll have to do that. You can't let this thing go through."

"I know, but I can't see how. My word against theirs. One thing though. I know who the two people are, the customers, the ones who complained. Well, I know their names, anyway. Not actually them to recognise. I was thinking of finding out their numbers and calling. Or even speaking to them at the centre. Although I'd have to find out who they were."

Sailor gave me one of his gamma ray stares, five seconds of it. "Okay, son. I believe ye. You do that an' I'll give Jim a call. It doesn't sound good though."

That evening I found Miss Swann and Mrs Nightingale in the members' register. During a quiet moment on reception I rang them.

First Miss Swann. "Who's that?" It was a very elderly woman's voice.

"It's the leisure centre at Fallowfield. I want to speak to Miss Swann."

"Sorry, she's not here. She's gone to see her sister."

"When will she be back?"

"Some time next week. Thursday I think."

"You sure it's not before Thursday?"

"I think so. I get so muddled with the days. It's not one of my lottery days.

We were talking about it. Do you want to leave a message?"

"No. No thanks. No message."

No luck there. Maybe I'd do better with Mrs Nightingale.

"Hello."

"Is that Mrs Nightingale?"

"Who wants to know?"

"It's Jolyon from the leisure centre."

"Who?"

A white lie was needed. "It's the manager from the leisure centre. It's about that trouble you had the other day. I wanted to apologise to you and find out if you're all right."

"All right? Course I'm not all right. I've never heard language like that. Not even my brother, and he was a bad one. He was in the army. That big young man. I used to like him. That was when I used to come in regularly."

Ah, my suspicions confirmed. "You mean the one that swore at you?"

"He's a nasty piece of work. He quite frightened me."

"Would you be able to come in and tell me about it? We're having to decide on the right punishment for him."

"Come in? All the way to Fallowfield? Not on your life. I was only there for my granddaughter. It wasn't her fault she spilled that drink. There was no reason to behave like that. I've had quite enough of you and your leisure centre."

The phone went dead. Oh nooo! Mrs Nightingale would have been perfect; it was so frustrating. For a moment I'd had a picture of bringing her in the following Wednesday and showing that at least one of the pieces of evidence against me had been totally made up. Once I'd established that, the disciplinary would surely have fallen apart. Better still, Derek and Anthea would have been in deep doodoo. The only positive point from Mrs Nightingale was the information she's given me. It was obviously Derek who had sworn at her, and from that it confirmed that he and Anthea were prepared to make stuff up to get me into trouble. I suppose I knew that anyway, but this was concrete. If only I could prove it.

I was really depressed as I left Fallowfield that evening. Again I resisted the temptation to star on the CCTV. Jolyon's Got Talent. But why not? I couldn't make things any worse. And I knew that the cameras were hardly ever monitored. The images were displayed together in a crowded pattern of squares on a small CRT behind the reception desk. No one paid much attention. The tapes were stored for a month in the strong room and then re-used. I was thinking about this on the bus when suddenly it occurred to me, what if there was something of Derek's incident with Mrs Nightingale, or even whatever he'd done with Miss Swann, on the CCTV? Trouble was, there was no way I could check. It would take hours to run through the tapes.

I'd been earning as much as possible at Fallowfield to cover the several tournaments that followed the British Open in the spring, so I was back at the centre the following evening. And so unfortunately were Derek and Anthea. They were both nearby on poolside during my first lifeguarding shift.

"What do you think's going to happen to the Jolly Boy at the disciplinary?" Derek asked at a volume I couldn't help but hear over the noisy background of a swimming club training session.

"He's out. It's too many things together. I suppose if we both put in a good word for him, say what a good worker he is, he might get off with a serious warning. Letter from HR, that sort of thing."

"Are we going to do that?"

"I don't know about you, but I'm just going to tell the truth, like a responsible supervisor."

Derek giggled. "And say he's a cunt?"

"I might not use that word. It'd be what Jim would call unprofessional. And I'm always professional here, you know that." Anthea winked at him. "So I'll say he's an arsehole."

They walked away laughing, not realising that they'd just made a big mistake. This was too far, over the top. Suddenly, instead of being angry, I was in match point mode, match point down. I would not lose now. I WOULD NOT LOSE! I was determined with a cold passion. *This* was not wanting to be shown up in training with Zoë. *This* was my match replayed against Ron Clarke. Whatever it took, I was going to beat the two of them.

A little groundwork would be necessary. At breakfast the next morning I told Sailor I'd be staying overnight with the Kemballs. Russell would be picking me up from Fallowfield.

Sailor nodded. "Make sure ye've enough sleep. And don't be late Friday morning."

"Course not."

Chapter Eighteen

Not being late the following morning might be an effort. My shift that evening ended at 10pm. The centre would be closed at eleven. I'd made up my mind to hide somewhere inside till the place was locked up and then spend the night, or however long it took, in the strong room with the CCTV tapes. A video machine in there was available for reviewing them. I didn't know if it was working, but it was used for training so it should be. I probably wouldn't be in great shape for my own training on Friday, but this was match point.

I'd scoped out the CCTV cameras. There were eight of them in and around the centre, all displaying simultaneously on a monitor behind the front desk, out of sight of the customers. The first camera was the one that tempted me when I was leaving the building, outside covering the forecourt. The next was trained on the front desk. One was in the canteen area where I hoped to see Derek's incident with Mrs Nightingale. One covered the entrance to the pool. I hoped to use this to work out the total time Derek and I had spent lifeguarding on the day I shouted at Anthea. One was in the crèche, one outside the gym and two trained on the gallery above the sports hall, at either end. I might even have to come back a second night. What a horrible thought.

Any encouragement I needed with the tapes was provided by Derek that evening. I was knackered after clearing away a hall full of gymnastics apparatus and looking forward to a sit down with my sandwiches. Bad news, Derek was in the staffroom too, having his meal. I went to the fridge for my food and was surprised to see my sandwich box and apple sitting out of the Sainsbury's bag they'd been in. There was no sign of the yoghurt I always finished my meal with. I'd had food nicked before so this wasn't a surprise, just bloody annoying.

As I took my sandwiches out of the fridge, Derek said, "Oh sorry, Jolly Boy, is this your yoghurt?"

It took me an instant to hold back a white hot bolt of rage.

"Looks like it, Derek, old son. No problems though. I've heard yoghurt's good for mammary development and we wouldn't want those big breasts of yours to shrink, would we?"

His face went red, but he did his best. "Ha ha very funny. Who's going to be laughing next week?"

"Next week we'll wait and see. It's tomorrow I'm thinking about. I'll bring raspberry flavoured in tomorrow. It's said to make your nipples stick out, so remember to help yourself."

He half got out of his seat and I hoped for a moment he'd be after me. "I'm going to be so satisfied," he said. "You're going to be dismissed next week. No doubt about it. I'm going to have a big house party in your honour."

"Ooh Derek, you're lovely when you're angry."

That did it. He was after me. Nothing to be gained by a last stand in the staffroom, and I was out of the open door far faster than Derek would ever manage. Unfortunately I almost collided with Jim Braddock, coming the other way. Jim caught me and was just starting with, "What's going on?" when Derek emerged, also at speed, and with impressive momentum. It was his momentum and his lack of agility that did for both Jim and me. The three of us ended up in a tangle on the floor, with Derek coming off worst.

I was on my feet quickly, taking an early chance to make my case. "Sorry Jim, Derek nicked my yoghurt. He can be awfully aggressive."

"Hold on a minute," Jim said as he picked up both himself and his clipboard. "I'm not going to hold an inquest here. Come on, get up, Derek. Now, just cut this out, both of you, understand? I'll see you both in my room in fifteen minutes."

We got a fearful bollocking from Jim when he confronted us in his office. Inevitably the truth didn't emerge, but I managed to provoke Derek into calling me a cunt, in a loud voice, so I felt I came out the better. There was nothing like a little aggravation to speed the passage of the evening. It didn't feel long before I was making a pantomime of saying good night and leaving through the front entrance. I didn't head for the bus stop, but nipped round the back and in through an emergency exit I'd left ajar a little earlier. Then it was just a case of hiding until Dave the duty officer had closed the centre down at eleven. From behind a vaulting horse in the gymnastics storeroom I heard Dave doing his checks at five to eleven. There was some light in the storeroom from the lobby, and this clicked off at eleven. The last thing I could hear was Dave setting the alarm.

Then there was silence.

I gave it five minutes. The first thing I had to do was unset the alarm. I knew the code so that wasn't a problem. Next I collected the key to the strong room from a drawer in the front desk and headed for what was going to be my last hope. I wasn't expecting Derek to be lobbying with Anthea to put in a word for me, and there was no way the little dear herself would say anything positive. On the plus side, I was sure there'd be something on at least one of the tapes. Trouble was, how long would I need to find it?

The strong room contained a Human Resources filing cabinet, properly locked. I assumed Jim Braddock kept the key. There was a safe, some floor-to-ceiling shelving with row upon row of company files and procedures, and my target, a roll-fronted cabinet where the CCTV tapes were stored. These were labelled with their dates, each covering two days, and the location of the camera.

Now that I was in there I was excited. My plan was to photograph the incriminating frames with my mobile. Once I'd produced these at the disciplinary they could review the originals if extra clarity was needed. It would be a delicate matter explaining how I'd tracked down the relevant frames. It could hardly have been during a working shift, but I couldn't imagine that would be an issue if the message from the CCTV was clear.

I'd already decided to start with the canteen tape. My best hope was to show that it was Derek and not me involved in the incident with Mrs Nightingale. Her complaint had been logged on September the third at 11.35am I found the relevant tape and slotted it into the machine. The first image came up. The date and time to the nearest hundredth of a second were digitally displayed at the top right hand side of the screen. It wasn't a moving recording. One image was logged every three seconds, in black and white. Sadly of course, there was no sound.

I quickly got the hang of the display's fast forward, fast back and pause controls and started reviewing the tape from 10am onwards on the third. Through the first hour I watched jerky images of an increasing number of people using the canteen. The quality was mediocre but you could see some detail in the freeze frames, whether a person had a soft drink in a bottle or a hot drink in a cup on their tray, and you'd have been able to recognise most individuals if you happened to know them.

There at last, at 11.03.22, was the meat mountain, no problem in identifying him, apparently talking to Janice, the woman who ran the canteen. I felt a surge of excitement and intently clicked forward, frame by frame. Derek spent some time at the canteen counter. Then Janice was pointing across the canteen with Derek looking in the same direction. Yesss! Two frames later he was paused in front of a woman and a little girl sitting at one of the tables. It looked as though a glass on the table was on its side. Derek stayed there for four frames. He was facing away from the camera, partly obscuring the woman. I clicked back and forward several times in increasing frustration. There was no story. All you could make out was that Derek and the woman seemed to be talking, although a couple of people at nearby tables were turned to them in the last two frames. It could be that the little girl was crying in the last frame before Derek left, but that might be my imagination. If only I could track down the two women at the adjacent table. Sadly there was no chance with the limited time I had before the disciplinary. It would take a major effort just to identify them. The next two frames showed Derek leaving the table. Then he was gone.

Oh dear, it was past midnight, I'd made no progress and my best opportunity had turned out to be useless. Those images would never be accepted as proof that it had been Derek shouting at someone. I wasn't even sure the woman in the images was Mrs Nightingale. Suddenly I felt tired. Training that morning had been intense and I was way beyond my usual ten o'clock bed time, extended to eleven on Fallowfield evenings. My enthusiasm for investigating the other opportunity was waning. I wanted to be able to show that although Derek and I should have been doing roughly equal lifeguarding stints on October the seventeenth, the day I had my run in with Anthea, I had spent far more time at it than him. It wasn't much in the way of mitigation but it would indicate that Anthea was favouring Derek over me.

Going through the tape at the entrance to the pool from 2pm to my 10pm finish was tedious. It wasn't a quick process finding and noting when Derek and I entered the pool area. There was no camera on the pool itself so you had to suppose that the lifeguarding sessions coincided with our ins and outs. I wearily took photos of each relevant frame on my mobile and made notes of the times. It was half past two when I reviewed my notes. Not good news. Although I had indeed spent more time lifeguarding than Derek, it wasn't nearly as clear cut as I'd thought, and certainly not enough to confirm serious favouritism on the part of Anthea.

What to do now? The whole CCTV thing had turned out to be a waste of time, good sleep time too. My prospects at the disciplinary had descended to bleak. There was a vending machine in the lobby and I shambled through to get a Red Bull. As I put the money in I wondered about the change that had been going missing from the till. There was only a small chance of anything showing on the CCTV, why bother? It didn't take much to pocket an occasional 50p during a transaction with a customer. Even if something was there it would be needle and haystack territory.

As I headed back towards the strong room I stopped to look through the glass wall that separated the lobby from the wet side. The pool was eerie without its harsh lighting. There was no hint, apart from the empty lifeguarding stand, that underneath the cover were thousands of gallons of chlorinated water, ready to be weed into by the children of East Manchester. I realised I was standing exactly where Derek and Anthea had been when they laughed at me the evening of my single genuine disciplinary offence. Half a can of Red Bull reinforced the surge of anger I felt. That day was one of the ones when the till hadn't tallied. Come on, match point down, worth having a last go at finding some evidence. Derek's fat-fingered mitt in the till? That would help on Wednesday.

The lobby camera took in the desk, the start of the corridor leading to the changing rooms, the bottom of the staff stairs to the upper floor and the entrance to the admin area. This was separated from the reception desk by a dividing wall on which there was a noticeboard and a big bank of switches that controlled the lights throughout. Derek's shift had started before mine that day but he couldn't have been around at the 6am opening, for about twenty unfortunates in the swimming club, so it was likely that he was on a twelve to eight shift. I fast forwarded the tape to twelve midday and began the tedious process of advancing through the frames slowly enough to have a general idea of what was happening. Derek's first stint on reception was at one o'clock. A lot of punters were coming and going around lunch time. There were many occasions when Derek could have put some change to one side without it being recorded. It was so boring. I finished the Red Bull and nearly packed up right then. My plan was to doss down on some gymnastics mats in the storeroom until five thirty, then let myself out. The duty officer would arrive between five or ten minutes before six so I would be well clear. I was then going to spend the half hour or so before I could reasonably arrive back at Sailor's in an all night café I occasionally went to five minutes from his house. I knew the buses started early so getting back wouldn't be a problem.

I reluctantly decided to carry on as far as the Derek and Anthea incident. Seeing it again would probably prevent me from sleeping, if the gym mats didn't achieve that anyway, but it would be an appropriate end to a fucked up project. Derek had two further spells on reception through the afternoon, neither with any hint of 50p thievery, before at 17.52 22.73 seconds he emerged from Admin and, apparently by chance, met Anthea in front of the glass wall. I clicked slowly though the next couple of minutes. I could make out a blob that was me on the lifeguard stand. As for Derek, his back was turned and Anthea only half in view. Her big-time irritating smile was obvious and there I saw the pointing incident. It was all I could do not to throw the monitor across the strong room, it made me so angry. I carried on clicking forwards, only half watching. A couple of frames later Anthea was walking towards Admin. Next frame Derek followed. In the next they were both stopped behind the dividing wall to Reception, facing each other, quite close, completely out of sight unless someone was coming in or out of Admin. All of a sudden I started to pay attention.

In the next frame, wonder of wonders, they were snogging.

This was a result! The result I absolutely, desperately needed, on par with clear evidence about the Mrs Nightingale incident if I'd been able to get it. Better than that. I clicked back a frame and carefully took a photo. Two clicks on, 17.56 33.46, and they were still snogging. Three frames later, 17.56 42.41, I struck gold. Anthea's hand had very obviously disappeared down the front of Derek's pants. It stayed there for six whole frames, an eighteen second grope, each frame recorded at the highest setting on the passable camera in my mobile. In the next frame Anthea's hand was back out, no doubt smellier than when it went in, and it was only due to the strength of the fabric of Derek's tracky bottoms that his dick wasn't out too. He was side on to the CCTV camera, a perfect profile. The effect of Anthea's manipulations was rigidly obvious. Several frames later Derek went in to Admin, at a guess for a wank in the staff bog, and Anthea disappeared up the stairs.

I rewound the tape and played the sequence again, to convince myself the whole episode hadn't been my imagination. Yesss! It was all there, frame by glorious frame in arty black and white. How stupid could you get? I punched the air a couple of times, here we go, here we go, here we go, checked the pics on my mobile before I shut the video down and tidied up. I didn't want to leave evidence that I'd been in the storeroom.

It was almost 3am when I'd finished, time for a couple of hours' sleep. I managed to get comfortable on the gym mats in the overheated storeroom and the next thing I knew it was half past five with the alarm going off on my phone. I borrowed a spare key to the front entrance from behind Reception, set the alarm, let myself out and locked the door. With any luck no one would notice the missing key, and I'd be able to return it later when I was back for my shift.

Sailor gave me a surprised look when I turned up at around seven. "Russell gave me a lift," I said. I had some breakfast, messed around with Facebook on my laptop and felt surprisingly good when we headed off to the EIS for training. It wasn't my best morning but I got through it and was able to grab a couple more hours sleep before heading off to Fallowfield for my four to ten shift.

I was trying to work out how to let my dear colleagues know about the information I had on them. Derek would be too unpredictable to be given the news about Anthea's feel directly so I waited until I had an opportunity to talk to her. It came with just the two of us in the staffroom, quite late after the swimming club had finished their evening training. I was sitting at the table, having a cup of tea. Anthea was tidying up.

"What's likely to happen at my disciplinary?"

She seemed surprised I was even talking to her. "It's a done deal, must be. Repeated offences, several. You've got to get used to the idea. You're going to be dismissed."

"It would help if you put in some words for me. You know I'm always on time, and I get stuff done."

"What makes you think I'd do that?"

"Maybe you'd have second thoughts."

"Ha, ha."

"It's not as if I was ever misusing company time. Or stealing. You've never proved that business with the till. Or getting caught doing it on the premises."

She looked at me sharply. "What do you mean, doing it?"

"You know, making out. Instant dismissal, that's what the staff handbook says."

She laughed. "No, it's not that. Not you. I can't see anyone wanting it with you."

Oh Anthea darling, you're making this so easy.

"No, I suppose not. It's true there's some of us, like Derek would be another, some of us no one would want to touch. What a loser, Derek. They say big muscly blokes have tiny dicks."

"That's enough. You're not being funny. You're not helping yourself for Wednesday, either."

"I wasn't trying to be funny. I'm surprised you didn't leap to Derek's defence. You know full well how big his dick is." Ooh this was so sweet. "Don't you?"

"Cut it out, Jolyon. If you don't stop right now I'll log this as sexual harassment. Not that one more complaint'll make any difference. You're out and good riddance."

"Only, if I could prove that you were, how can I say it, investigating the size of Derek's miserable little knob on the premises here, do you think they might overlook sexual harassment charges against me? You'd suppose they would. That'd be sexual harassment, much worse, supervisor corrupts poor innocent lifeguard."

"This has gone far enough." She made a move towards the door. "I'll ignore this, but just don't expect any favours on Wednesday. You're history."

"Hey Anthea, stop." I took my mobile out of my pocket. "I'm just wondering if you've seen these pictures. It's Derek and you. I'd no idea you two were so close."

She paused in the doorway. "What do you mean?"

"Come and see. Shame they're not in colour. For your mum and dad, that is. They're awfully sweet. Your family, they'd be so proud if you had one put into a frame."

I'd never seen someone's face fall. It was a metaphor my English teacher had used in class. 'Faces don't literally fall', she'd said. Well Anthea's did. It was comic.

"What are you talking about?"

"Here they are," I said. "There's more than one. Come here and see."

She walked over and stood beside me uncertainly. I pulled out a chair. "Sit down. We don't want you fainting or anything."

"Just show me."

I played the sequence of shots. It hadn't struck me how sordid they were, voyeuristic, a private moment between a girl and a bloke. It should stay private, but it was my lifeline. Anthea sat down in the chair beside me, her hand over her mouth.

"How did you get those?"

"It doesn't matter, does it? I've got them. You wouldn't want the management to see them, would you?"

"That's blackmail."

"Well, yes it is, if you want to put it like that."

"You can't do it. It's, it's illegal."

"Huh, you're one to talk." My sympathy evaporated. "So is making up stories and putting them in the complaints log. You and Derek, you must've thought you were being clever. Well you weren't. If I had more time I'd get more proof. But I don't need that, do I? Like I suggested, you and the meat mountain can put in some words for me. Say what a good worker I am. Say what dragons those two women were. Anything, I don't mind. It's just that it doesn't suit me to have to leave this miserable job at the moment. It's miserable because of miserable pricks like you and Derek. It would be okay otherwise. Anyway, the job suits me so I need help from you at the disciplinary.

"Now, go and find Derek and bring him here. He needs to understand too."

"I can't. He's on lifeguarding."

"Gosh, doing some proper work, that's rare. Well fiddle it. You do that often enough. Put Janice on or something. Go on."

She stood up and headed stiffly out of the room. I was still sitting at the table when a couple of minutes later she returned with Derek, who came straight across the room and stood over me.

"What's this, then, sonny? You been upsetting Anthea? Right? Right? Upsetting Anth? Just listen, sonny, if you been putting yourself about, I'll have you. Just see if I will. I'll make you sorry you ever walked in here."

It was a golden opportunity for Derek baiting, but I wasn't in a position to run, and the running option always had to be available at those times.

"Hey, no Derek, it's okay, I just wanted a chat, sit down."

He looked uncertainly at Anthea.

"That's right, sit down, Derek." She slumped into a chair opposite me, and Derek reluctantly sat between us. "What's it all about, then?"

"What it's about is, I need some help from Anthea, and maybe you if you get involved, at my disciplinary."

"Help you? You must be joking."

"Well no I'm not, see. I was hoping to persuade you."

"What is this, Anth? This prick can't be serious." Anthea remained staring at the table.

"This prick *is* serious," I said. "This prick has some photos on his mobile that you wouldn't want the management to see. This prick was hoping that in exchange for the photos remaining private, Anthea and maybe you, if you could make five consecutive words come out in the right order, would help him with his disciplinary."

"What photos? You better fucking show me, mate. There's no photos'll make me change my mind about you."

"No, I don't think you'll change your mind. Not about me as a person. I think your opinion of that will be reinforced. But about my value as a good colleague, yes.

"Here, have a look."

I ran through the sequence of photos. "You dick, you cunt," he said. "How d'you fucking get those?"

I couldn't **resist**. "With my hermaphrodite skills, Derek dear." No surprise, he looked blank. "That was what Anthea asked," I went on, "but it doesn't matter. The fact is I have them, and if Jim Braddock sees them you'll both be out of here, bang, just like that. Without a reference.

"I'm quite prepared to show the photos to Jim, happy to. You'd be mad to let me, though. This is long term for you and Anthea here. Your career. Hers, anyway." Anthea was still staring at the table. "It makes no sense for you to chuck it away. All I want is a little help. Between you, you made up most of the evidence for my disciplinary. You can't uninvent it but I'm sure that you can persuade the panel or whatever it is that it would be unjust for me to be dismissed. Which after all it would.

"If I had more time I'd find those women who apparently claimed I'd shouted at them. I never did that. So either it never happened, or maybe someone else shouted at them. I think it was you, Derek darling.

"I don't need the ladies, though." I pointed to my mobile. "These are enough. I have Anthea's hand, Exhibit A, inside your pants, Exhibit B. Getting on for half a minute. And oh look, in spite of all the steroids, Exhibit H with Exhibit O, you've got a hard on."

Silence from Derek. Silence from Anthea.

"That's agreed, is it? And don't be in the slightest teensy weensy bit of doubt. I don't mind getting a formal warning from the disciplinary. But if I lose my job, Jim sees these. You'll be out as well, both of you. I don't know if Derek will be involved in the hearing, but obviously you will, Anthea. Derek can back you up if he's called in. The message is, I'm a star, those women were way out of order, there's no way it could have been me with my hand in the till, there's no way the centre can run efficiently without me, *et cetera et cetera*.

"Now, it's knocking off time for me. I'm going to have a shower and piss off home."

I left them at the table, Derek looking at Anthea and Anthea staring at the table. I went into the tiny changing room leading to the staff shower, put my things in my locker, undressed and got into the shower. It felt good to rinse away the tension of that sordid meeting. I couldn't imagine that Derek and Anthea would take any chance of the photos being made public. I might have a rough ride at the disciplinary, but if Anthea stood up for me I should be able to avoid being dismissed.

The first thing I noticed when I stepped out of the shower was that my clothes were on the floor. Why? My locker was open, too. The key, which had been in the pocket of my shorts, was still in the lock.

The rage inside me threatened to burn its way out through my skin. Was it Anthea? Or was it Derek? Derek of course, put up to it by Anthea. I hardly wasted time checking the contents of the locker. I'd left three items in there, my keys, my wallet and my mobile. My wallet was there. So were my keys. My mobile was not.

Along with the anger I felt a surge of triumph. Did those two no hopers imagine that my phone was the only place the photos had ended up? The first thing I'd done when I got back to Sailor's that morning was to download them into my laptop, email them to myself and copy the files onto a memory stick, belt, braces and a safety pin for good measure.

Derek was by the reception desk as I went to leave the building. "Anything missing, then, loser?"

"You know it."

"I wouldn't know it, not me." He laughed. "It's just you look sort of down. I'll call you if anything turns up before we close. You know, lost property?"

Ha ha. I walked out, leaving him to enjoy his smirk. When I got back Sailor had gone to bed but Mary was still up. She let me use their printer and before I went to bed myself I'd made two grainy A4 sets of the photos. They looked even more tawdry printed out. I blagged two envelopes from Mary, put a set of the photos into each with a short note, 'Staffroom, 5pm, make sure no one else is there', and wrote Anthea's name on one and Derek's on the other. I was on my usual afternoon-plus-evening shift the next day. Something to look forward to in the middle of the shift.

When I arrived the following day I put the envelopes into Derek and Antheas' pigeon holes. As I started my afternoon work Anthea was neutral and Derek all pally. "You don't look too good, little Jolyon. Why don't you," here he paused and pretended to crease up, "phone a friend?"

"You should be on TV, Derek darling. You're so funny. Only, have you heard the saying, 'he who laughs last...'?"

"Oh, I'm laughing, sonny, I'm laughing. How many days more have you got? It's five, isn't it? Me and Anth were just talking about it."

"Nice piece of counting, all the way up to five. That must have been Anthea?" I was ready to run but with an obvious effort he controlled himself.

If Derek had looked angry then, it was nothing compared to the way he looked an hour later, talking to Anthea, the envelope in his hand. This was going to be almost as good as beating 'Tripper' Clarke at squash.

The two of them were standing waiting when I entered the staffroom at five. They didn't respond to my relaxed, "Sit down, sit down." I sat down myself, put my feet on the table and looked at them.

"Whose idea was it to nick my phone?"

No answer.

"How come you don't deny it?"

Still no answer.

"It's one more thing I can't prove, so you don't need to worry."

"We don't need to worry anyway," Derek said. "We've worked out how you got those photos. From the CCTV, wasn't it?"

"Oh Derek darling, I'm impressed."

"And the only time you could have done it is after closing."

I was a little worried that I wasn't in a position to run, but I couldn't resist the temptation. "Miss Marple couldn't have done any better."

"Miss who?"

"Never mind. Go on. So I was in the building when I wasn't authorised? Which will get me another disciplinary?" I looked at the notably silent Anthea. "I'm surprised at you, Anthea. You must have worked it out. The point is, Derek dearest, for sure I'll be fired if any of this CCTV business comes out. All that'll happen is I'll get another poxy little job somewhere else. Inconvenient, that's all. You, you and Anthea that is, it's your careers. And those pictures mean you'll be fired, absolutely no doubt about that. Without a reference. Think about it. And absolutely no doubt, too, I won't hesitate to use the photos."

Anthea sat down and I went on, "It's not in your interests. And destroying the CCTV tape wouldn't work, even if you could find it. I don't need it any more. The date and time are printed on the photos. It's obvious where they were taken. Get used to it. I've won."

"Okay," Anthea said. "You've made your point. Only, we'll want all the copies of the pictures."

"Anthea, don't you see? Why should I give you back the pics? They're electronic anyway. How would you know they still weren't in some folder somewhere? The pics mean that once you've got me through the disciplinary, you'll have to treat me like a human being. All up to the time *I* decide to leave this place. You should be able to manage that. It may be a problem for Derek, obviously.

"Now, one more thing. I need a phone."

They exchanged a glance. "Go and get it," Anthea said.

Derek went round the corner. I heard him open his locker. A moment later he came back and tossed the phone to me, or more accurately, at me. I caught it, very deliberately took the back off and extracted the SIM. Then I tossed it gently back to him.

"You didn't listen, Derek darling. I didn't say I wanted my phone. I said I wanted a phone. What I want, by the end of next week, is an iPhone 4S, SIM free, max memory, I think that's sixty four gig."

"That's ridiculous," Derek said. "They're six hundred quid."

"Welcome to the big bad world, Derek darling. You started this."

Chapter Nineteen

Sussex Argus, December 3rd

Squash - Local Boy Returns

Ex-Redbrook pupil Jolyon Jacks returned to Brighton at the weekend for the South of England U-19 squash championships. It was a winning return. Still only sixteen, Jacks left Redbrook in the summer after his GCSEs to train full time at the English Institute for Sport in Manchester. Jacks must be doing something right in Manchester, and he made short shrift of a quality field at the Brighton Squash Club.

In the semi-final Jacks slaughtered the top seed, local boy Dan Moore 11-4, 11-4, 11-0. The final was a complete mismatch, a rerun of Man U against Brighton in the cup. Jacks ran out the winner 11-5, 11-3, 11-3 in only 25 minutes, and this was against the fancied Brummie, third seed Billy Stamp. Jacks said afterwards he was sure the fitness he'd gained from his cross country running in the Downs around Redbrook was now helping his squash.

I'd almost pulled out of the South of England on Sailor's advice because the field was a weak one. For various reasons several of the top under nineteens had withdrawn. But it was an opportunity to say hello to Grandpa, and he had sounded anxious the couple of times I'd phoned him through the autumn.

So I took an expensive taxi ride over to see him after my semi-final win. We had a cup of tea, made with actual leaves and not a bag, and he asked me how I was getting on. His eyes sparkled when I talked about the wins I'd had, and the satisfaction of making the final in Brighton, with every prospect of taking the title.

"That's what I wanted to hear, Jolyon, you do the business, and keep going. Remember, this is early days. You're doing well, as Sailor expected. We'll know better after you've had the odd setback, and recovered. There'll be setbacks, there always are. It'll be injuries, loss of form, who knows. Call me if you're ever struggling. You know I'll listen."

We chatted about other stuff for half an hour, and I headed back to Brighton in a cheerful mood.

The Times, January 22nd

Jolyon Jacks won the British Open Under Seventeen championships in Sheffield at the weekend, to prevent a clean sweep by the strongest team of Egyptian juniors ever to enter the tournament. According to the seedings, the result was a surprise. Jacks, who only took the game up seriously in the summer of last year, was seeded in the bottom half of the draw, as low as number six. However, anyone who has been following his progress through the autumn, and the way he has been destroying opponents in under nineteen tournaments, would have expected something special from the sixteen year old.

The final was certainly special. Jacks broke the spirit of the elegant Hatem el Gabaly in the first game, which lasted a punishing fifteen minutes. The next two games occupied a total of all of nine minutes. The score of 11-7, 11-2, 11-3 tells something of the ferocity of Jacks' play. Jacks never allowed el Gabaly the time to weave the wristy spells that had taken him so effortlessly through to the final. It was to the Egyptian's credit that he fought so hard in the opening game. It wasn't enough. Jacks played more like a young man than a teenager still learning the game.

We shall be hearing a lot more of Jolyon Jacks.

The Times reported the triumph. Fortunately it didn't cover the disaster. If some journalist had picked up the other half of the story, it might have appeared in the front of the tabloids. The incident involved the Bentley family. Dick Bentley, I suppose because Sheffield was his base, was one of the principal organisers of the Open Juniors. A big job, and, I gathered, his first time doing it. I'd overheard him in his strong Yorkshire accent talking to Tim Graham about the size of the task. This was on the first morning of the tournament as people milled around in the old-fashioned Abbeydale Club.

"Bloody hell, Tim. You didn't warn me it was going to be like this."

"Welcome to the hard part of squash, mate. It's worse than running round the court, as you can see."

"I'm worn out and it's only day one. I had more than two hundred emails this morning, can you imagine it, two hundred and six emails. The press is constantly on my back. There are too many coaches here and they all want special treatment. There are parents from countries I haven't even heard of. And at least half of them are making complaints about the marking. Already. I've had to pacify a couple of the referees too, for Pete's sake. Then of all things, did you hear about this one, there's the dietary requirements of the Muslim players. Someone didn't pass the message on when the bar manager at the Hallamshire went sick. We had to send out to a Halal supermarket."

If Dick had known on top of everything else what I was going to be like as a guest, he wouldn't have invited me to stay at his place during the tournament, but normally I wouldn't have been much of a distraction.

The Bentley house was a large one, half way up one of Sheffield's big hills, ten or fifteen minutes by car from the three tournament clubs. Dick's wife had apparently died several years earlier, and his two sons were away at their universities, so it was just Paula and him rattling round in the family home. During the tournament Dick left dead early each morning and returned late so I fitted in with Paula's to-ing and fro-ing to the courts. She had a beaten up little diesel Renault that she drove far faster than I ever would. A lift is a lift though, and a lift with a fanciable girl who smiled at me, that was more, especially in my Samantha-less world. What's more, her poor dad had been looking increasingly sorry for himself and even ill as he zoomed between the three Sheffield clubs sorting out the tournament problems, someone to be avoided.

After a couple of morning matches my quarter final was scheduled more comfortably for two o'clock, on the fifth day of the tournament, this time at the Abbeydale. It was against Ross Fitch, a tall boy from New Zealand who had quite a reputation in the junior squash world. Paula had lost the previous day, but she happily took me in to the club in the late morning. She stayed in the gallery to see me beat Ross pretty comfortably three nil. It was about five o'clock by the time I'd stretched, showered, had a drink with Ross's parents, really decent folk, and met up with Sailor in the bar for a debrief.

"Why did you let up in the third, son? It shoulda been eleven love." Ross's single point in the third game had come when I'd caught Paula's eye as she sat on the crude scaffolding that acted as a gallery behind the ancient glass back court.

"I lost concentration for a moment," I said truthfully.

"Well you're no' here to be 'losing concentration'," Sailor tried to mimic my voice. "You're here to win the squash tournament. Scare the wits out of the international folk in the junior game. Let the folks in the professional game know you've arrived. It's all part of the top two inches. If people are scared to play you they'll fold at the start of the match when you do your whirlwind thing." He tapped his forehead. "Beat them up here and you'll beat them easy on the court."

Sailor had started talking up my 'whirlwind game' some time before Christmas. He said he'd put the word out about it to signal to my opponents what they could expect, and to make the point, as he explained it, that I was different. I'd never thought psychology came into what I was doing, but I'd already started to see the benefits as perfectly capable opponents started to hit the tin long before they'd become seriously tired. Any game won quickly in a tournament is good news. The accumulation of effort, usually five rounds over just three days in the juniors, could leave you tired and vulnerable during the later stages, if you got that far.

Paula came up while we were talking about my semi-final opponent, a Malaysian player called Chong How Joon.

"Mind if I join you? I was thinking of heading home if you wanted a lift."

"Give us two minutes," Sailor said. Nothing gets in the way of squash talk.

When Sailor had finished dissecting Chong How Joon's game, the main message being that the Malaysian was crude, physically dynamic and tended to hang back, so shots to the front of the court should tire him more than an opponent with more orthodox positioning, Sailor signalled to Paula that we'd finished.

"What are you doing about an evening meal, son?" Sailor asked me.

"I'm cooking something for him," Paula said.

Sailor's comment came with a half smile and a half frown.

"Well don't give him anything that'll slow him down tomorrow."

Paula laughed, "Of course not." Then she looked at me. "Jolyon will be energised for sure."

As we drove out of the car park I said, "You don't have to cook for me. I wasn't expecting anything like that."

"Well, now I've been knocked out I'm going to make sure someone in the household does well. Daddy won't be home till late and it wouldn't be fair to expect him to cook with all the tournament stuff going on. He was looking awful today, wasn't he? He does miss my mum. Misses her still. I miss her tons, but they were so close. I think she'd have packed him off to bed the way he's looking."

"You going to do enough food for him too?"

"I guess so, just in case he wants something when he gets in."

After stopping at a local supermarket we staggered into the house with several bags of provisions in addition to my squash bag.

"It won't take long," Paula said, standing rather close to me in the large kitchen-cum-parlour. "It's a bit early to eat. Any idea how we might pass the time for an hour?"

"Well, I've got to decant my kit and put new grips on a couple of racquets."

Paula rested her hands on my shoulders and locked eyes with me. "That should take less than five minutes. Can you think of something that will fill up the other fifty five?"

The penny well and truly dropped. "Well, I can think of something that might last, ooh, all of five minutes."

"Five minutes, that won't do. If it's going to be like that it's not going to happen." Her hands moved behind my neck and she mumbled into my lips as she pulled us together, "A first snog's going to take longer than five minutes, all by itself."

And it did. We collapsed onto an ancient sofa that occupied the opposite end of the room to the AGA and lost ourselves in a spectacularly intimate snog. It was at least five minutes before Paula's hands were inside my tee shirt, and mine inside hers. She took a deliberate age with the zip of my jeans. Then another tantalising five minutes before her hands were into my pants. And mine into hers, I wasn't going to be outdone in undoing. Not many more of our minutes and we were mixed up naked all over the sofa.

"My you're fit, Jolyon. You have the stamina for this as well as squash?"

I lay back with my arms above my head. "Gotta do my stretches."

"How would you like me to stretch, then? Methinks this must be a good exercise if semi-finalist Jolyon Jacks does it." She sat up beside me and stretched her arms over her head in a parody of my parody, cosmic breasts. This took me past the limit of playing games and I wrestled her onto her back. The look on her face as I pushed into her was a further turn on and I knew I was only going to last a few seconds.

"Stop," she said.

I couldn't.

"No, I mean it, stop."

I did manage to stop, but it wasn't going to be long term. "What's going on? Don't be such a fucking tease."

With her hands on my shoulders she pushed me away. "Don't be silly. I want to enjoy this too. We'll do it at my speed, that's all. The way I like it. Or not at all. What's it going to be?"

She looked really serious. "Come on, Jolyon, get off me. Get off."

"That's what I thought I was doing."

She giggled as I pulled out of her. "It's all right, Mr Willy," she made a ticking off gesture to my dick. "You can go back in in just a moment." She got off the sofa, still staring at my dick and stood for a moment rubbing her breasts. Then she slowly made her way to the end of the sofa and bent over the arm, hands on the cushion with her back arched like a stretching cat.

"Come on, Jolyon. We have one rule now. I do the moving. You stand still."

Weird, I thought as I positioned myself behind her, I can't believe this. I wasn't going to argue, though. I was starting to see the point.

"That's it," she said, "slowly, slowly."

Once I was in her again it was pleasurable torment. She told me to stand still and for ages just wiggling her bum, ever so slowly.

"Do you like that, Jolyon?" At last she started to rock herself gently backwards and forwards over her outstretched arms, looking round now and then. *Teen squash player's head explodes.* I was forced to content myself with holding her hips. This went on for further ages, help! She'd talked about this taking an hour, but in the end I couldn't control myself and started to push.

"Oh no," Paula said, "I'm not ready yet. Any more of that, boyo, we stop."

You can't fight nature though. As she resumed her rocking I felt my balls tightening. "Oh Jesus, I'm losing it."

I was indeed about to lose it, shit I was, but not in the way I thought. Without warning the door into the hall gave a loud creak. My heart lurched.

Nooo!

We both looked across as the door swung open. And we both froze. A dishevelled figure in an ancient tracksuit appeared in the doorway.

Paula managed a strangled squeak, "Dad!"

Dick Bentley blinked at us as if he couldn't believe what he was seeing. Almost certainly true. His face transformed in a few silent, agonising seconds from influenza grey to an intense, sickly purple.

"Get out, you cunt, get out. Out! And don't come back. And you, Paula. Upstairs. Now!"

Your girlfriend's father, I thought, the world's best cure for premature ejaculation. I suppressed a complaint that he should have arrived a bit sooner to help me hold out and for an instant considered the one saving grace in a totally unsavable situation: the appearance of my host had caused my erection to disappear like a burst balloon. Dick deflates dick. Prick pricked. So-called cunt exits cunt. Paula held a tee shirt over herself as she ran out of the room, leaving me with what would in other circumstances have been a further pleasing image of her naked bum. I rushed around the sofa in a panic, gathering items of clothing, pulling on my pants, tripping over myself. Then it was three at a time up the stairs to my bedroom where I crammed kit, racquets and the few spare clothes I had into my overnight bag.

Dick was waiting downstairs by the front door, quivering, face still purple. He wasn't there to wish me a polite good night.

"Get the fuck out of here, boy, and don't come back."

Plain spoken as usual, with the message reinforced by the way the door slammed behind me.

I trotted out of the drive into the road, anxious to get away. Then I took stock. Any other evening the frost that was already forming on the grass would have looked pretty. Now it was one extra negative in a truly negative situation.

Where was I to go? The only places I knew in Sheffield were the squash clubs. It had to be one of them. Even that wasn't simple. I'd not paid enough attention during trips in Paula's car. I wasn't confident of the route to any of them. And, I then realised, the situation was even worse. I'd left my warmest garment, my hoodie, on a hook to the side of the Bentleys' front door. I shivered as I felt the cold air on the back of my neck. A further problem, my mobile was in the pocket of the hoodie.

The first part of the route from the Bentleys' house was obvious, so I set off, feeling thoroughly sorry for myself. What would I do when I arrived at one of the clubs? Would they even be open when I got there? What was the time now? My mobile would tell me that, ha ha. It couldn't be too late in the evening, surely. When had we started snogging, half six? If Paula hadn't been so keen on the drawn out Cosmo sex-and-simultaneous-orgasm crap we'd have been dressed and half way through supper when her dad had appeared. The arrival of Mr Bentley must have been around seven thirty. Something like eight o'clock now, I thought. And what about Dick? Why was he there? He must have come back early to sleep off his flu. How unlucky could you get?

I took further stock as I walked. My squash bag was on my back but my arm was starting to ache from carrying my overnight bag. My hands were freezing. An awful thought was the possibility of a night outside. Too grim to contemplate? Yes, hopefully I could at least get into one of the clubs.

Not so encouraging now was the prospect of the semi-final against the dynamic Chong How Joon, with my preparation disrupted. Make that preparation utterly ballsed up. Then there was the prospect of explaining to Sailor what had happened. That was worse than all the other prospects put together.

I dithered at a road junction that was only half familiar. If I remembered correctly, the Abbeydale was nearer the Bentleys' place than the Hallamshire, and it was downhill from there to the Hallamshire. So I took the uphill road. The Abbeydale would do. There weren't many streetlights, with dark banks of trees on either side, not houses. Pretty discouraging.

Ten minutes later I stopped to give my shoulders a break. At least I was warm now, apart from my ears and my hands. Hungry too, I realised. Paula's still-born spaghetti Bolognese was an enticing thought. If only. Well I could get something at the Abbeydale bar, as long as the club was still open.

Oh no!

Oh no comma FUCK! Something else dawned on me. I wouldn't be able to get *anything* at the Abbeydale bar. There was another item nestling safely in the pocket of my hoodie. Also enjoying the warmth and comfort of the

Bentleys' hall was my wallet. Not much in my wallet these days, but not much was a whole lot more than nix. And nix was what I had with me. A thorough exploration of the pockets of my jeans produced not even an odd coin.

I came to another road junction. Had I seen this one before? I wasn't sure, so I crossed over and went straight on. I was starting to feel weary. Although the score against Ross had been decisive, the points didn't reflect the big effort I'd had to make in the first game, something like twenty minutes of it. A decent meal and an early night were what I needed, what a dream.

It must have been a mile before I reached the next junction, twenty minutes, and by that time I knew I was lost. I thought of flagging down one of the occasional cars that went past. Or maybe it would be easier to call in at a house to find out where I was. First find the house.

A car horn nearby startled me, and a small red Renault pulled up. The window wound down. For an awful moment I thought it must be Dick, kitchen knife in hand on a castration mission.

"Come on, jump in!"

Not Dick at all, it was Paula. Thank goodness! Apparently she'd been driving round for half an hour looking for me. Her father had gone back to bed after giving her a mighty earful and once she was sure he was asleep she'd slipped out to see if she could find me. Even better, my hoodie was on the back seat.

"Phew, thanks, you've saved my life. I was heading for the Abbeydale but I seem to have got lost."

Paula put the car into gear and pulled away. "Abbeydale was a good idea. You can't come back to our place obviously. Even though Dad's dead to the world now. You're not so far away from the club in fact. You're on a parallel road. Not the one you should have taken."

She ran her hand through her long hair. "It's too bad about Dad. That was so embarrassing, awful, I just can't say. I can't imagine what's going to happen in the morning."

"God, what'll he do to me? I suppose he slipped home to try to shake off his flu."

"Yes, his car was in the garage. I never thought to look. It's not as if he minds me having boyfriends, but I guess he doesn't dwell on what I do with them." She giggled. "And in the parlour. And over the arm of the sofa."

"If you'd let me go at my speed we'd have been well finished. Showered and dressed."

"You'd have been finished too. With me, that is, for sure. Sex isn't something you do in sixty seconds."

"The way we left it, next time it'll take about two seconds."

Paula rested her hand on my leg. "We'll have to try again, but not at my place. Not an option, is it."

"No way. I'm not looking forward to bumping into your dad, here or anywhere."

She pulled in to the entrance of the Abbeydale club, its lights blazing. There was the familiar sound of squash balls blatting onto squash court walls as I got out of the car. The club was very much open.

Paula got out too, and handed me my hoodie as I struggled with my bags. "What are you going to do about somewhere to stay?"

"I don't know. I'm too scared to call Sailor. I thought maybe I could doss down somewhere in the club. Anyway, you'd better get back home before your father wakes up. I don't want to be responsible for his death due to a seizure or something."

"I wish I could help, Jolyon. I can't really ask any of my friends."

"You have helped. I could have been wandering around Sheffield all night. I'll get something to eat, that's the first priority. Then I'll see what can be done about sleeping.

"Now push off, and thanks, it was nearly a great evening."

She gave me a quick kiss and got back into the car. I felt lost as she drove off.

Oh well, food first, I was starving. It turned out I had enough money for two club sandwiches, a jumbo Mars Bar and as much tap water as I could drink. I'd leave what to do about breakfast until the morning. Fifteen pence wouldn't buy much. While I ate I tried to look as though being there at that moment had always been a major part of my life plan, the most natural thing in the world. Luckily the place was still busy. No one was paying attention. I felt a tinge of envy every time someone walked purposefully out of the building with their bags and their car keys. It wasn't good not having anywhere to go. Not at all.

I took stock round the club. The last tournament matches had long finished and it was just late evening bookings for members. Was there a corner where I could lie down without being noticed? Nothing much on my first circuit. The changing rooms were barren. I'd wondered whether there might have been some towels I could use as blankets. None.

This wasn't looking good. I explored the rest of the club, along ancient improvised corridors past anonymous administrative offices. Nowhere you could easily hide from staff and, equally bad, nowhere remotely comfortable for a half decent sleep.

I sat myself down again in the darkened bar area. A large plasma screen was showing a professional tour game from the PSA circuit. It was a recent tournament in Doha, lots of prize money, lots of ranking points. I recognised an up and coming American, Julio Mattaz, being demolished by Jan Berry. The squash was even more depressing than my current situation. The Hatchet indeed; Jan Berry was well named. How could anyone live with that frightening energy? Mattaz looked just as far away from my squash, even under the immense pressure. His casual skills delayed the inevitable three nil thrashing. How could I ever hope to beat players of the quality of Mattaz, let alone Jan Berry?

"Trying to see how it's done?" A voice beside me with a strong New Zealand accent. I looked round to see Ross Fitch's dad, Colin.

"Oh, hello Mr Fitch. I'm surprised to see you still here."

"Same about you. We've come back to collect the half of Ross's kit he didn't take with him. Are you on the same mission?"

I wondered what I could tell Colin Fitch. It was such a relief to see a sympathetic face, and before I could stop myself I blurted out, "No, it's a long story, but I don't have anywhere to stay tonight."

"That's radical. What happened?"

It was too dark for Mr Fitch to see me blush. "I, er, I upset my host, I have to say."

"Who is that? Oh, I know, Dick Bentley." Then a long, slow, "Oh yes."

He smiled. "I think I can see, mate. You were staying with Dick Bentley, weren't you? And that was his daughter here, nice player. She was taking quite an interest in you during the match with Ross.

"And you didn't want to call Sailor McCann, I suppose?"

Unseen, I blushed some more, and didn't reply.

"Well, I guess not, let's not go into that. I've probably got the wrong end of the stick anyway. Point is, you can't stay here tonight. That wouldn't be right. We're in a B&B only a few minutes away. There's a second bed in Ross's room. Why don't you sleep there?"

I felt a surge of relief. "Oh thanks, Mr Fitch, that's almost too good to be true. I was feeling pretty down."

"If you're staying with us you'll have to call me Colin," was his response. Ross soon joined us, with a large bag of kit, and in a couple of minutes we were in the Fitch's hire car on the way back to their B&B.

The goodnight formalities didn't take long. Moments later in Ross's room the spare bed looked absolutely wonderful.

"What happened?" The second Fitch to ask me that, as we were undressing.

"Dick Bentley, you know, the tournament director, well I was staying with him. I went home with Paula, she's his daughter, she's been driving me everywhere. And I'm like making out with her in the kitchen. Sort of kitchen living room, it is. On this large sofa, or not exactly on it. He wasn't going to be back for hours. Then he appeared out of nowhere, in the middle of us doing it, he'd been there all the time, upstairs. He's got flu and he must've gone home for a sleep. You can imagine the rest."

"She wasn't that girl watching our match, was she? Yeah I remember. You were doing all right there."

"That was what I thought until, well, that was embarrassing with a capital E, a big time no-no. Can you imagine it? Anyway, he threw me out. Inside thirty seconds."

I paused. "I can't believe your dad now. He's saved my life."

"We've always got someone or other staying back home in Matamata. This is just normal. It's been a long four weeks, this. I'm looking forward to going home now I'm out of the tournament."

"Yeah, well, I'm sorry about that. You know what I mean."

Ross laughed. "No problem. It wasn't as if I played badly. It hacks me off if I play badly and lose. I hadn't heard about you. I was fancying my chances against Chong How though. I've beaten him twice. You won't have any trouble."

"I may not now, thanks to you lot. That's if I don't get chewed up and spat out by Sailor tomorrow morning. He's sure to have heard about it from Dick Bentley."

"Sailor looks like a hard nut."

"The hardest."

I was not looking forward to my next encounter with Sailor.

Chapter Twenty

In the morning Sailor's body language said it all the instant he saw me. What I recalled used to be referred to in gymnastics as body tension. I was desperately trying to look unconcerned as I walked into the Hallamshire. My semi was scheduled there that evening, and we'd agreed the previous day to have a gentle hit on a practice court at midday.

He jerked his thumb. "You, sonny, outside." Several people looked round, more embarrassment for me. Sailor marched away from the club till we were standing by a statue of Queen Victoria on the edge of the park next to the club. He was bristling like Rascal, my mother's thankfully deceased Yorkshire terrier.

"Right, sonny, you explain yourself to me, no bullshit." His face would have been right in mine but for his lack of height. Looking down at him slightly, regardless of the consequences, I lost my rag.

"Hold on, Sailor, just hold on a minute. It's you now. You're just like everyone else. Jolyon Jacks, everyone's blank canvas. See here, Jolyon Canvas, exactly what you want him to be. Jolyon Cardboard Cut Out. Colour him in yourself, people. Just look at him, Jolyon Jacks, the perfect teenager."

I didn't care what Sailor would say now, how he'd react. I was letting a whole lot of frustrations spew out and gave him no chance to interrupt.

"Why do you think I was so happy to leave home? No secret there, you know that, my mother. Then there was my school, my prick of a housemaster. Mr Pomp-Pomp-Pompous Middleton. Maybe I haven't told you about Mr Middleton. A scheming bastard, pardon my language. Why is it that everyone expects me to be something *they* want and something I don't happen to be? It's true my mother's the worst. All I ever am to her, I realised when I was quite small, is an extension of *her* personality. An object to increase *her* status. 'Look at my wonderful toy, it's called a Jolyon.' God knows how screwed up her own life must have been. To actually *need* that.

"Then I'm faced with a situation at the Bentleys. It's normal this, Sailor, it's what teenagers do, and yes I was wearing a condom. It was a normal situation with a normal boy and a normal girl. There was no way we could have known that her father was home, no way. Not during the tournament. You've seen the hours he's putting in. Neither of us wanted that to happen. Neither of us would have taken any *sort* of a chance on that. And now you're looking at me as though I've committed some crime against humanity. I know it was an appalling muck up last night, but just, just," I petered out, "just don't look at me like that."

For a moment, Sailor said nothing. The terrier capable of the Doberman bite. Plus rabid. Brace yourself, Jolyon.

When it came it was entirely different from what I was expecting.

"Okay, son, you've made your point. You messed up last night, you know that. We both know it. I'm afraid there are some important boats burned there.

We'll come to that but it's history now. I hear what you say. We put it behind us."

He stepped even closer. "But now you're going to listen. I won't say this again. This sort of thing, there won't be any next time. First, you're at an important tournament. Whatever the story, you've let yourself down. You've let me down. If you want to be world champ by twenty one, by any time, you've no margin, absolutely no margin. During a tournament there's no room, any room, for messing around."

He looked around. No one was paying any attention, thank goodness. "This is your launch tournament for God's sake, and you're prepared to take a chance on the semi-final? You win this tournament the way you're playing, it's the first piece of the jigsaw, the five year jigsaw, and it's a big piece. This is where your reputation starts, sonny.

"Second, whether you like it or not, I'm loco parentis. That's what I do for all my players. I'm responsible. And what you did is not acceptable. Do you hear me? Not acceptable. However you dress it up, it was abusing someone's hospitality. I know I'm old-fashioned, but some things don't change. You make the bed. You clean the toilet. And you don't take advantage." *You don't shag the host's daughter over the sofa.*

All that I could cope with, and Sailor was right. Then he laid the bombshell on me. "Third and last. Any chance of a lottery grant for you, son, next five years probably, that's gone, torpedoed, blown out of the water. I know Dick Bentley. He's a good man, but he doesn't forgive and he doesn't forget."

No, not possible, oh no! "But that's not fair. What about the others on the committee? If I win here they'll vote for me won't they?"

"Where are you based? North of England. Who's the man in the North? Dick Bentley. I can mebbe start to influence things when you're playing senior tournaments, but up to then, the man is Dick Bentley, and he calls the shots. You've pissed the man off. End of story. It's unfortunate."

"Unfortunate. What am I going to do about money?"

" You'll be getting to know the Fallowfield Pool even better, won't you. It's no' tiring and it fits with training."

Of all the things I'd been really looking forward to with my lottery grant, not having to go to the Fallowfield Pool was number one. I was about to start a rant but Sailor just said, "Cut it," and I did. It would have been a waste of energy.

"Come on, son, we'll get changed for our practice."

Chong How Joon had eyes that appeared totally black behind his science fiction mask. He had come to squash, Sailor had told me, from a promising junior career in badminton. I hadn't taken on board the implications for his squash, and to be fair, Sailor hadn't said much either. He'd just talked about Chong How's positioning. In the gallery, as I struggled against the Malaysian's first game onslaught, Sailor kept mouthing the word 'think' at me. It took many minutes before I realised that anything I was hitting high was being smashed away to a back corner or short to a front nick, and I was 7-2 down before I realised that Chong was very ordinary if the ball was below shoulder height. After that, by diligently keeping my shots low, I was able to impose my own game. Chong had less heart than Ross the previous day, and this time, without Paula distracting me in the gallery, I ran through him and finished with an 11-3 win in the third game.

Sailor surprised me in our debrief. I was expecting to be complimented with the way I'd finished the match off.

"What were you playing at?" he said. "You don't serve French fries to the class fatty. You don't play to your opponent's strength. He was murdering you with those overheads."

This really pissed me off. "Why didn't you warn me about it?"

"You've got to grow up, sonny. You have to think on court. Think. I knew you'd beat him, but I wanted to see how quickly you caught on. You have to use the top two inches, remember. Think as well as play."

He was right. It was something that Zoë had already talked to me about several times. She said how important it was to her. It was just that actually doing it, practice rather that theory, doing it on court in the middle of a match, was a different matter.

"Okay Sailor, point taken."

I had phone calls from two journalists after beating Hatem el Gabaly in the final. They wanted to know about the so called whirlwind training I was doing, plus more normal stuff, my background, how long I'd been playing squash, where I'd met Sailor and so on. It was strange having people taking an interest in me. I wondered if my mother ever saw the resulting articles. I'd had no contact with her in weeks, and little with my Dad, who was away at sea. I did get a call from Grandpa, full of encouragement.

Returning to Fallowfield Pools after the British Junior Open was hard; dreary shift after dreary shift. I'd been given a written warning in my disciplinary hearing, and had been desperately looking forward to handing in my notice.

"When are you leaving then?" Anthea asked. "It was your big competition last week wasn't it? The one that was going to 'free you from your shackles'? That was what you said to Derek."

"Well soon," I muttered.

"How the mighty are fallen, my my."

Had she heard anything about the events in Sheffield? I couldn't see how.

In other respects back in Manchester things returned to normal. A month later, sure enough, I heard via a formal letter signed almost illegibly by 'R Bentley' that I'd been turned down for a lottery grant, 'Dear Mr Jacks, we regret to advise you...' Regret my Aunt Sally. It was more like, '*Dear Mr Jacks you horrible shagger, I'm positively thrilled to be the one to inform you that not only have you not got a poxy little lottery grant, as long as I have anything to do with it you'll have more chance of winning the lottery itself than getting a penny of the money it provides to Squash England.'*

After Sheffield I started to take a greater interest in what was going on in the squash world. What I'd seen that evening on the plasma screen at the Abbeydale had fired me up. I'd become an avid watcher of any squash I could find on television. I was soon able to recognise the top players, one or two of them after they'd visited the EIS. The world number one was an Egyptian, Magdi Gamal, and the number two the Australian Trevor Cooper. Third of course was Jan Berry, whose manic face in close ups was almost frightening. The one who really interested me though was Julio Mattaz, the American Berry had been beating in the match I'd seen at the Abbeydale. Mattaz was ranked no higher than fifteenth, but there was something about his style of play that set him apart from players above him. Unusually too, he never argued with the marker, just shrugging and throwing himself a gentle catch with his racquet if he got a bad decision.

I mentioned Julio to Zoë one afternoon when we were out for one of the occasional runs we did together, during a pause to admire the view of the Hope Valley from halfway up Kinder Scout, the highest peak in the Pennines.

"Oh yes, Razz. He's a bit tasty, isn't he. He'll be top five next year, I'm sure of it. Watch the way he moves, no effort, and it seems to me he's intelligent, too, which counts. And he trains at altitude, Salt Lake City, that's bound to make a difference. He's the one you're going to have to beat in the end. He's going to go past the others. I'd put money on that if I bet."

"What do you mean, Razz?" I said. "Where does that come from?"

She smiled. "Julio Mattaz. Razzmatazz. You should see the way he dresses. He was destined to be called Razz. You focus on Razz Mattaz, Jolyon. You'll see him live pretty soon, maybe the English Open. Watch him."

"What about Joe Jackson, or Jan Berry?"

"Joe won't be up there in two or three years. He's got a bad knee, he'll have to stop. As for Jan Berry, ugh, the world's most boring man." Zoë grimaced. "I had a meal with him once."

"Not your boyfriend, then?"

"Jan Berry? No, no way." Her shoulders dropped a fraction, and she gazed out over the hills. "Boyfriends. You know what, Jolyon." She wasn't looking at me. "I don't know if I'm right for boys."

Without thinking I said, "You'd be right for me."

"No, I'm being serious." So was I. "For one thing," she said bitterly, "where's the darned time? You know the life by now, maybe it *is* the squash, what I put into it. I wish, I wish, oh I wish. I wish I knew. And, you know the score, the absolute basics, you have to fancy someone. Want someone, really want them. That's not happening. That doesn't happen.

"I wish," she paused, "so many wishes it's silly. I've tried but it just doesn't work. Nothing works, darn it, being close to someone. It doesn't work," 'work' almost shouted. "It's not that I don't, well, there's always possibles. You know what I mean." I certainly did. "I'm not sure why I'm telling you this, just you're okay, Jolyon, my little brother, we're alike." She was silent for a moment, and I noticed the wind, which was drying my sweat cold inside my tracksuit. "There was this girl, way back, I was in the sixth form. Looking back, something could have happened. I don't know. It's such a mess."

Then she looked at me fiercely, shaking off the moment. "Don't you say anything, right? To anyone. Not anyone. Not a word. Understand? If you do I'll kill you. I mean that. I'll kill you."

I just said, "Hey, Zoë," and cupped her shoulder with my hand. I so wanted to give her a hug.

She turned away and became the usual Zoë. "Jan Berry. The first time you play Jan you'll have an insane match, and if it's in say the next eighteen months you'll probably lose. He's horrendous, there's no one like him. You won't believe the bruises you get."

"Bruises?"

"Oh yes, it'll be physical. If it's two years away, what, you'll be nineteen then, you'll probably win. You'll do his thing better than he does, and you'll work him out anyway. He doesn't think. I don't think he's capable of thinking, he just grinds away on automatic. Automatic frenetic. You'll see things in his game, I'm sure. You'll work him out."

"You'll know you've been in a match, though."

We set off again. I let her set the pace on the narrow track, always happy to watch her move in front of me, glide really. I didn't know what to think about what she'd said. Not that it made any difference, if I was realistic. It was so much more than wanting to shag her, which I did, violently and gently at the same time, if that made sense. I wanted to make things right for her. But the door was again tight shut as she pushed on with the run. It had only been open a crack, and only for a moment. I didn't think I'd be seeing past that particular door again.

If only.

February came and went, March and April. I was loving the training. I was soon doing more in a day than Dave and I had been capable of in our three whole sessions a week when we'd started. I was always conscious of Zoë's way, everything at match point intensity. My first trip abroad was to the European Junior Championships in Brussels. I was just into the under nineteens, after a quiet birthday on March the tenth. 'Time enough wi' the children', Sailor had said. To his irritation I lost a game in the quarter finals to an incredibly clever Danish player, Bjarne Funck Rasmussen. For a start I couldn't work out his name. Then more importantly I couldn't work out where he was hitting the ball. His body language would say one thing and the ball would go somewhere else, making me look a right prat.

"You just have to force yourself not to commit," was Sailor's unsympathetic comment as I moaned about this afterwards.

"But if I don't anticipate I'll never reach the ball in time."

"Move quicker, son, move quicker. An' rough him up. Once you do that he'll hit the tin like everyone else. Clever doesn't work if you're hitting the tin."

I suppose that had been true. Bjarne had tinned a lot in the later stages of our game. Unusually the semi was less trouble than the quarter and the final easier still. I had the pleasure of taking home a smallish winner's cheque as European Junior Champion, some non-Fallowfield earnings, quite a landmark. I'd have to make ten times as much to be able to give up the lifeguarding though. Maybe I could pawn the engraved silver Frisbee that came with the cheque and skip a session or two at Fallowfield.

Chapter Twenty One

"Where did you get the phone?" It was Dave. I hadn't seen him for months. We were in the changing room at the EIS where he had come along to a weekend training session.

"Sort of a present from the staff at the pool."

"No way."

"Well, not exactly. I'll tell you afterwards."

I was going to stay Saturday night with the Kemballs, have a mix with Dave and avoid Channel Four with Mary McCann as my weekend entertainment.

I gave Dave the details of my disciplinary, what had led up to it. With Anthea's convincing support, she really did try, and I think she was feeling guilty, I had got off with the formal warning, to remain on my record for, ha ha, two years. I told him about the CCTV and the hold it had given me over Derek and Anthea.

"You sly dog," he said. "What a nerve."

"Well, in Zoë's language I was match point down. It would have been a pain to have to get another job even though it's a pain working there. Then it's not exactly thrill a minute at Sailor's, but I'm usually too fucked to worry. My entire recreation these days, apart from an occasional mix, is playing with this."

"What apps have you got?"

"Not much. I can't afford them. But see, I've got Facebook permanently on. I get everything straight away. And look at this video. The display's fantastic. Look at Zoë."

I showed him sixty seconds of Zoë doing routines on court with Riley, who was clowning around when Zoë wasn't looking. "She's all right, isn't she."

"Stop dreaming. It's time we got you a girlfriend."

"It's true, fat chance Zoë. Anyway, girlfriends cost. I wouldn't mind catching up with Paula though."

Dave laughed. "Paula Bentley? I thought you'd had enough trouble with her."

"It wasn't her. It was her dad."

"I tell you what," Dave said. "Me and a couple of others. We're putting on a party over in Sheffield. Three weeks time. Spring Detonation, we're calling it. You can have a set."

"What's that, last weekend in May? I think that's okay. Sailor's entered me in my first Challenger, but that's the weekend after."

"Let's do it then. Can you get over to us on the Saturday?"

"Mid-afternoon. I'll be training till one."

"That's fine. I'm heading off at about six. Did I tell you I've got a van?"

"A van, blimey. You can really pull with a van."

"It's not that sort of wheels. My mum and dad didn't want me in anything fast when I passed my test. I said all right, how about a van, not such a silly idea. One thing a van is, it's not fast, or not this one. It hardly gets up hills. But it fits a whole lot of gear, especially the speakers. You'd never get them in a car. It's S reg, really old. The insurance isn't bad. Amy doesn't mind."

"Amy? Is there something you haven't told me?"

"Kind of girlfriend. She's doing Art A level. We're in the same class. You'll see her tonight."

"She must be okay if she doesn't mind slumming it in a Transit van. Or maybe she's desperate."

"Ha ha. Are you going to walk to Sheffield?"

"Okay," I said, reflecting on the time I already spent at bus stops. "Any sort of wheels is good. What time will the party start?"

"We'll do the setting up at nine or ten. People won't arrive before half eleven, midnight."

"And packing up?"

"Six or seven, depends, could be later."

"I dunno if I can. Training is late on a Sunday. Not till one. But I'll have to get some sleep or I'll be wasted. Sailor's letting me do some weights now. It's hard. Then we finish with court work, and you know about that. You can't hold back."

"I can see it," he said. "It's okay. You can do your set early. I'll fix with one of my Sheffield mates for somewhere for you to crash. By the time we've loaded the van it'll be eight at least Sunday morning and I can drop you off at Sailor's, I guess before ten. You can grab another couple of hours if you want before training."

Sailor would be curious but it wasn't as if I'd be doing anything wrong. From time to time I spent the night at the Kemballs'. As long as I went okay at training on the Sunday there'd be no problem. I didn't want to give Sailor any reason to question my commitment. I knew Grandpa called him from time to time, as well as me. Sailor was far too straight to cover up.

I found myself thinking a lot about Paula in the days leading up to Dave's Spring Detonation. I was sorely missing female contact. There wasn't an app for that on the iPhone. Steve Jobs might have dreamed up a 'Happiness App' for socially challenged nerds and monkish squash players. I don't suppose Apple would now.

I helped Dave load up the van for the drive over to Sheffield. Firstly there were two huge pairs of speakers. "Not enough, these," Dave said, "I'm renting four Funktion Ones over there." Then there were several large amps, a sturdy table, some laser light gear and, carefully cushioned on some old blankets, his precious decks.

"How much did this lot all cost?" I asked as we ground our way up the Snake Road into the Pennines.

"I haven't worked it out. I was lucky with the speakers. I got them for five hundred quid. This guy going back to Australia. I knew he'd left it too late so I made a stupid offer. To give you an idea, today it's costing me two hundred and fifty just to rent the gear I'm picking up over there. Pair of bass bins and a pair of mid tops."

"Two fifty, that's a lot. That's ten weeks living expenses for me, give or take. How do you get that kind of dosh?"

"I do pretty well renting out my own kit for functions. Big pubs, a couple of football clubs. I should break even tonight. 'Pound for the sound.' We're expecting five hundred, maybe even more."

I was amazed. "Five hundred people? Where is it?"

"It's a disused warehouse. It's well scoped. There's no houses around. I'm not putting out the location till ten this evening. Police aren't likely to turn up."

It was a grimy part of Sheffield we drove through to reach Dave's warehouse. Eventually we crawled along a pitted road between two long, dirty red brick buildings. On a wall of one of these you could make out the name 'Washbrook Steel' painted in letters that must once have been white. At the far end of the road we had to stop at a chain link fence. Dave hopped out and opened some gates. Once through these we crunched across a huge empty forecourt in front of another long building similar to the ones we'd passed.

"Here we are," Dave said. "It used to be a factory. When that closed it was used to store materials for the railways. Something like thirty years ago. It's empty now."

He pulled up by a door in the side of the building. The door opened with a metallic screech. Enough light was finding its way through the partly grimy, partly smashed windows to reveal a vast empty interior. The building was all of fifty metres long. A single stack of pallets near a pair of large double doors at the end we'd entered was all that suggested the building had ever been used.

"We're going to set up at this end," Dave said. "It's pretty wet down there." His voice returned in a distinct echo. Light was reflecting from a pond-sized puddle at the far end of the building.

"Let's unload the van. Then I've got to pick up the generator."

It took us fifteen minutes to carefully unload the gear and hump it in, with any sharp sound we made inside the building bouncing back to us.

"Great acoustics," I said.

"Beggars can't be choosers. It's a rock solid venue. We won't be interrupted. You stay here while I get the gennie. Robbo will be along soon with the other four speakers. Make a platform for the DJs here with some of those pallets. Two rows of three, three pallets high, that should do it. Then put the table for the decks on there and a couple more pallets for steps.

"I shouldn't be more than fifteen minutes."

When Dave had gone I had some fun hearing how the life of a hand clap was extended as it travelled several times up and down the building. This place was going to pulsate. Robbo arrived as I was completing the platform and I helped him with his speakers. We finished setting up, using lengths of mighty copper cabling to connect the amps to the speakers. Then Dave came back with lighting for the rig and some green lasers for atmosphere. They wouldn't show much in clear air, *but there would be smoke.* By this time Amy had arrived, a short round girl in wispy clothes who had a scowl for everyone, including Dave, and Dave's two co-organisers, Mike and Don Don, 'twice the value of the normal Don'. Don Don had brought some burgers, which mercifully Sailor wasn't around to pass judgement on. I was starving.

As the light outside faded Dave got everyone together to make sure of the organisation. "Party line?" he asked Don Don.

"Just like we said. It's ready to go live."

The previous weekend, in the usual way, Dave had put out general information on Facebook that a party would be taking place. No details because the one thing the perfect party didn't need was the police. Word of mouth would circulate the number of a pay-as-you-go SIM bought just for this event. Anyone ringing the number would go straight through to the answer message, which, close to when the party was due to start, would be activated to give directions to the venue.

"Do you think there'll be much dealing?" Dave asked.

"The usual small time," Don Don said. "And Billy Smith."

"E?"

"E all round, several of them with E. There'll be dope. Dope's dead cheap in Sheffield these days, dunno why."

"Someone's got a growing set up locally," Mike said. "Rumour is it's Chinese kids. He frowned. I'm hoping one of those K arseholes won't be here. You any good at martial arts, Joll? We'd like to see them away if they turn up. There's nothing like K to kill a party."

"No way," I said. "I'm a pacifist."

"So am I, except when it comes to K dealers." K was ketamine, wobble juice, horse, bad news big time. With ketamine you end up in a K hole. You don't know where you are. On a fun scale you're at absolute zero. You can tell if someone's on horse, eyes wide, jaw slack, totally out of it. I'd seen friends in Sussex addicted to K. You need more and more to keep the effect. Someone told me it cruelled not just your nose but your bladder. With a drug like E on the other hand the feeling was wonderful, a party would surf the atmosphere. Even cocaine, bad shit in anybody's language, added its sparkle.

So none of us wanted anyone dealing K at the party.

Everything else checked out. It was dark when people started to arrive. Word had certainly got round. The area in front of the warehouse was soon looking like a commuter car park, except that the cars were a minimum of twenty years old. Mike stood at the warehouse entrance with a bucket and most people tossed coins into it as they passed. Unlike the cars, nobody I could see was more than twenty, pretty normal.

Don Don played the first set. Amy was on the mike and got the crowd going with some great vocals. Peculiar to have an MC over techno, but it worked, she really came alive. As for Don Don, he was good. He looked cool, headphones on, bouncing to the beat, fine tuning the faders, from time to time selecting another disc from a box on the crate beside him, expertly dropping the next tune with no break to the rhythm. I felt the usual excitement as a party got under way. Nothing scratches the music itch like several thousand watts of amplification, a big crowd and a classy DJ.

Don Don was playing techno. The beat was physical, leaving room for nothing else in your consciousness. Thud-thud-thud-thud-thud: my chest vibrated; my guts vibrated; I could feel my scrotum vibrating. Before long a hardcore, mainly male, group was dancing in front of the left hand stack of speakers, the stomp, an amorphous organism controlled by the DJ's beat, arms pumping overhead in unison, ay-ay-ay-ay-ay! The lasers provided a surprising amount of light, eerie green. They were controlled by the beat, pulsing on and off, reinforcing the rhythm. Even now the beams were stronger in the places where they cut through the rapidly thickening smoke, the familiar mix of tobacco and weed. One of the lasers was trained on the facets of a glass ball suspended from a stand and the resulting reflections lit up the dancers with green spangles.

The people not dancing stood around watching, grasping glass bottles of beer and plastic bottles of water, feeling the music. Dave joined the DJ who had replaced Don Don and picked up a mike. His educated voice morphed into something that wouldn't be out of place, "Everybody up now, c'mon, 'ave it you animals!"

The deck crew were lit from low in front of the stage. Their shadows, three times human size, bounced on the wall behind.

"Everybody dancing. Yeah that's better. The next DJ will be Steady Freddie. Come and get lively!"

As the party really got going there was less watching, more dancing. The smell of sweat became another element in the throbbing atmosphere. Two characters were head to head like rutting stags, completely out of it, on whatever. Two others were leaning back to back. Must be a different substance, I thought, with an opposite effect on brain chemistry. I was due on fourth to play my set and made my way round to the platform. The vinyl Dave and I had chosen was in an old plastic LP box he had picked up in a junk shop. I sifted through the discs to remind myself what was there. Without a spliff I was surprisingly nervous. There was so much dope in the atmosphere though, the lasers now searing through it, I hardly needed to smoke my own. A few deep breaths should do it.

Then I was mixing, fulfilment behind the decks, drum'n'bass. This was a million miles better than doing it in your bedroom. The cans on my ears were just right, the decks and the mixer the best you could get. The sound was *that* clean, the tunes were coming to life. The stomp was huge now, several hundred individuals, pulsing with the music. I could sense the appreciation as I made a precise drop, the beats in perfect sync, the high hat patterns matched just right. "Ave it', I thought as the synced arms, the cilia of the beast, doubled in number. I'd invented the image of the party beast when GCSE biology revision, or more accurately my mother, had prevented me from going to a rave close to home. Before long I was on fire. I didn't need dope now. I was controlling the organism, making it do what I wanted. Even the crew around me were dancing.

Eventually I got the nod from Dave. "That was DJ Jaxx, wicked set, big-up!"

In the momentary silence as the next DJ moved into place and put the cans on, someone from out front shouted, "Replay that DJ!"

I felt great. The new DJ started playing some gabba, not everyone's favourite, but I loved its frenetic rhythm, two hundred beats a minute. "I'm going to 'ave it," I shouted into Dave's ear.

"Yeah, Paula's down there somewhere."

Nice thought. I didn't see her though as I started dancing. Even apart from the absence of Paula, this activity should please Sailor. Thoroughly aerobic. 'Don't f'get to rehydrate, son', he'd say. For many minutes I was lost in the savage pulse of the gabba, feeling it as much as hearing it. Tinnitus wouldn't be a problem with a quality sound system like this. Homogenised insides might be. Then there was a hand on my shoulder, Don Don. He motioned me outside.

The relative quiet in the dark Sheffield night was overpowering. "The K dealer's here," Don Don said. "He's got an old Renault, a green one. I want to take care of the tyres. Will you help me find it?"

Finding one particular old Renault in the more than a hundred cars outside the building would take some doing. It was dark and a fair proportion of the crocks seemed to be old Renaults. I nodded. Don Don gave me the car's number and we started off in separate directions, hunting the dealer's wheels. Ten minutes of peering at number plates and I came to my fourth or fifth old Renault, pretty obviously red even in the minimal light, wrong colour. Someone was in the driver's seat, oops.

Then I realised it was Paula.

I knocked on the window. Paula's hand flew to her mouth. As much as I could see, she looked terrible. It took her several seconds to recognise me but she showed no sign of getting out of the car. I tried the door. Locked.

"Paula," I shouted. "Come on, what's the matter?"

"Go away," she mouthed. "Go away."

"No way," I shouted. "What's the matter?"

She turned and slowly wound the window down.

"What's going on?" I said. "You don't look too good."

She started crying, hands over her face, great big sobs.

"Hey, Paula, tell me about it. It can't be that bad."

"I can't. Just leave me alone. Go away."

What could I do? I squatted so I wasn't looking down at her. "This is just stupid. I won't leave you till you tell me what's wrong."

Then it all came out between the sobs. "I'm in trouble with a dealer. He's pressuring me."

"What, you owe him money?" She nodded. "How much?"

More sobs. "Two fifty."

Two hundred and fifty, uunghhh! out of my league. Two pounds fifty would stretch me.

"Can't you put him off?"

"I have. Over a month now. He's threatening to tell my dad."

"What about your friends?"

"I already owe them. Much too much."

"What is it? What have you been on?"

"It started with occasional coke, that's when it got bad. Before that it was just a little dope. Then one night, it was only a few months ago, this guy introduced me to horse. I didn't know he was a dealer. I'd seen people using it.

"It was cheap at first, it is cheap, but soon I was needing more. The habit crept up on me. I didn't realise till it was too late."

"Is your dealer, is he one of the dealers here?"

She nodded. "Mick Petman. He lives in a squat, not far from here. He's cruel." She wiped at the skin under her eyes. "And sick. He enjoys me wanting it. I've given him sex, anything. I just don't know what to do."

That was all she could get out. Her hands went to her face again.

What a mess. I felt some sympathy for Paula, seeing her like that. But for Heaven's sake, she was prostituting herself with an arsehole of a drug dealer. For that I felt disgust.

"Fuck's sake," I said. "You're letting yourself down, totally. Giving it away for a few snorts of horse? Where's your self respect? You need to take a good look at yourself, Paula. I wanted to see you tonight, looking forward to it. The main reason I came. That was before."

She let out a great wail and wound her window up.

What could I do? The dreaded red mist developed and I stood up. This was different from what I'd been used to back home. There dealing had mostly been a service. I'd been mates with my suppliers, mixed with them, and it had only been weed. The bad people had been further up the line, out of sight and mind. Here one of them was in mind, in my face, or would be soon if I could arrange it. The night had turned sour and I felt a strong urge to do something.

Nothing I could do for Paula though at that moment. I left her crying and went to find Don Don. It took several minutes and I almost stumbled over him. He was kneeling beside a small car, operating on its front tyre with a screwdriver.

"Fucking tyres. They shouldn't make them so strong."

"Special side walls for drug dealers I expect."

There was a loud hiss and Don Don said, "Ah, nice!"

He stood up. "That was the last one. He won't be going far tonight."

"Do you know him?" I asked.

"Do I know him? We all know Mick the Prick. Never welcome, always there."

"Do you know Paula?"

"Yeah vaguely. Paula Bentley. Skinny, nice body though. She's often at our parties."

"Well Mick the Prick is giving her some grief. She owes him and she hasn't got it."

"She's in doodoo then. Mick doesn't let go. How much?"

"Two fifty."

"Could be worse. I'd have thought a girl like Paula could raise two fifty."

"He's bled her. She's up to here and she's used all her friends."

"Well I can't help," Don Don said.

"You already have with this little operation on the tyres. Making me feel better. I'm going back inside."

I wanted to find Dave. The red of my personal mist was intensifying over this Mick the Prick. Michael the fucking Prichael. I really wanted to do something. Back inside Dave was playing a set, and I soaked up his drum'n'bass, standing with the stragglers rather than dancing. When he'd finished I dragged him outside.

"What is it?" he asked. "You ready to crash?"

"No, not yet. I bumped into Paula. She's got herself into some deep shit with the K dealer."

"Mick the Prick?"

"Yeah, apparently. She owes him and he's putting the squeeze on, two fifty."

"Not good. He's not one to mess with."

"There's nothing I can do," I said. "I'd pay him off if I could. And then do something to him for afters."

Dave shook his head. "I said, you wouldn't want to mess with Mick. He's seriously bad."

"Well I'm seriously pissed off. You wouldn't have... you know, you couldn't lay your hands on..."

"Come on, Jolyon. That's a whole lot of cash."

"I'm playing in a Challenger in a couple of weeks. Sailor thinks I'm going to do okay. First prize is five hundred."

"Yeah, but who's entered. Riley for one, I bet, and you won't beat Riley. Then there's those guys from the South. Two of them got through qualifying for the British Open. You'll be lucky to get past the first round."

"Hey come on, Dave. This is an emergency. You should have seen Paula. She's in her car. She's a wreck, crying her eyes out."

"Whose fault is that? Paula's a big girl." An image of Paula in her dad's kitchen flashed through my mind. Not big. Just the right size in the right places.

"Not when she's been manipulated by a Mick the Prick. Come *on* Dave, I'd pay you back. You know that. For absolute sure, absolute certain."

We argued away for another ten minutes. In the end it was like steamrollering someone on a squash court. I wouldn't let myself lose. I knew Dave had a fair bit of cash on him, to pay for the speakers and other gear he and his mates hadn't been able to bring along themselves. They'd done okay with the pound for the sound, enough to cover the evening's out of pocket expenses. So Dave's reserve wouldn't be needed.

Reluctantly he handed over the money, all of two hundred and fifty quid.

"Thanks, mate. I owe you."

"You owe me two hundred and fifty. And exceedingly soon." Dave stomped back into the party, not happy but he'd live, and I went to find Paula.

Problem was, Mick the Prick had found her first.

I saw them both from a little way off. Mick was leaning against Paula's car with Paula kneeling in front of him. It was too dark for the detail, but obvious what was going on. Mick's hand was in Paula's hair, holding her to his crotch. I crept closer, the other side of a car next to Paula's, till I could hear him grunting over the noise from the party. Then he straightened up and said, "Aarrgggh!" in an incredibly deep voice, the deepest I'd ever heard, before pushing Paula away.

"That's bought you an hour, Paula darling." It came as a deep rumble, from somewhere in Mick's belly.

Paula was on her hands and knees, spitting and wiping her mouth on her sleeve. "But you said you'd give me a week if I..."

"I said it might buy a little time, darling. Now I'm telling you, it's an hour."

"I've asked all my friends here."

"Not my problem, Paula darling, no, no, NO!"

His voice rumbled quietly along as he played with her. "Whose problem is it? Mmmm, not Big Mick's. Big Mick's a little short, see, just temporary. And we know we don't like to keep big Mick waiting. That's not part of the game. We said we'd have the money tonight, didn't we? Eh Paula? Then we disappeared. Soon as Big Mick arrived. Antisocial, wasn't it? To do that to one of our friends."

His voice hardened. "I know you want more. You can have more, course you can. Think of it, a lovely long line, all white, two big snorts. It's good gear, too. You know me, nothing but the best. First though, my two fifty.

"Now I've an idea. Why don't you go inside? Have another word with your rich friends, tell 'em it's urgent. They know me and my little ways. Someone will help you out. You wouldn't want me having to raise the subject with your dad, would you? He'd be so surprised, your dad, his darling Paula is a K head. All that guilt about neglecting you. Do you think he'd start to wonder what's been happening to the housekeeping money? Do you think he'd pay more attention to his building society accounts?

"I'll see you inside, darling. With the money. Then you can have another line if you want. Tell you what. I'll knock a hundred off if you come round to my place tomorrow and take it up the bum, can't say fairer.

"See you inside then."

With that he zigzagged away between the cars towards the party.

Paula was still on her hands and knees when I approached, taking deep breaths and repeatedly spitting. Couldn't blame her. When she saw me she slowly got to her feet. "He's a..." but she couldn't finish the sentence and started to cry again.

There wasn't much I could do. A hug from another male wouldn't help. After a couple of minutes she opened her car door and found a bottle of water. She took several swigs and spat them venomously away.

"I'll do something to that prick. I'll find a way."

"You won't do anything unless you stop your habit. K is so no good."

"I want to stop." She clenched her fists. "Want to, want to, want to."

"Will you get help if I find the money, like find it tonight?" I didn't think she'd seek help for a moment, but I was determined not to give the dosh away without some sort of commitment. Her problem was an eye opener for me. I was appalled at the side of drugs I knew about but hadn't seen close up. This sort of thing must be going on all over Brighton, but not among the people I knew.

Paula gave me a sly look. "Oh God yes. I hate all this. I want to stop so much."

"Will you tell your dad?"

"My dad? No way, I couldn't. He'd die if he knew about this."

"Maybe if you told your dad it would help to cement it. Make you really follow it through."

"You know him," she said. "The idea of his little girl fucking is a no no." It wasn't exactly the missionary position, I thought. "Doing horse... explaining that to him... I just couldn't."

"Everyone wants to stop," I said. "You *have* to. It sounds like you've just about run out of friends. Me too, giving head for it, Paula, take a look at yourself, I can't believe it. You absolutely have to stop. What a prick. I'll be putting myself out big time with my own mates if I'm going to get the money." I didn't want to tell her I already had it. "I won't do it if you're going to be in the same place next week.

"Now, this is what I want to do."

The relief on her face was pathetic when I explained what I had in mind.

"Come on," I said. "Let's go and find him."

"He'll be in there somewhere, on the fringes. He's always there."

The noise in the building assaulted my ears again. Someone was playing speedkore, and I must admit I sometimes thought it was like a full military fire fight, savagely percussive. Paula and I skirted the heaving mass of dancers. Then she said, "There. There he is."

"Okay, give me five minutes and then bring him down the other end of the building."

Mick the Prick was watching the dancing, smoking a cigarette, his back to the factory wall. Definitely a big bloke, but not in a muscly Derek sort of way.

With Mick it was simply his frame. I studied him as well as I could in the semi-darkness. He was older, maybe twenty five, nothing special about his face, a couple of seedy eyes in the usual places, a flattened nose and an ordinary mouth that I'd like to fill with something big-time distasteful. As we'd agreed, Paula went up to him and I melted away, heading for the far end of the building. I was glad to be wearing black jeans and a dark tee shirt, which wouldn't be seen so easily down there.

A couple of minutes later I saw Paula and the Prick separate themselves from the noise and head my way. Paula appeared to be pleading with him. They stopped on the edge of the puddle, not far from where I was crouching. What happened next was horrible. Without warning Mick gave Paula a mighty slap across the face, knocking her to the ground. She remained there kneeling, both hands over the side of her face.

My mist went crimson.

"All right, darling," Mick said. "I'm not waiting any more. Where's your guardian angel?"

Time to move. I mooched as casually as I could into Mick's line of vision.

"Here I am, prick."

A 'fuck me', rumbled clearly out of Mick's chest over the throbbing music. "Is this your baby brother? With his pocket money?"

My heart sank. I was hopelessly out of my depth.

"Come on then, boy." A further rumble, with emphasis on the 'boy'. "Hand over the money. Then you can watch if you want. Daddy's decided to give little Paula a seeing to right here. On account of then she can have a line. Free gratis, all on Mick. Can't say fairer."

I think it was the authority he was assuming, that what he said went, no questions. And the contempt. Inside I lost my rag, not at all what I'd planned. On the outside I made a show of hesitating, locating the notes in my pocket. Mick seemed to relax when I held the wad out in front of me. Then I took two quick steps and kicked him as hard as I possibly could in the crotch, a fifty five metre conversion from the touchline at Twickenham, with added feeling. It was incredibly satisfying to sense the contents of Mick's underpants being squashed flat against the instep of my shabby left Converse. Just as satisfying, Mick went down with a rumbling 'huurrrggh'. No one really deserves that, but he was genuine filth.

I stayed well clear of the wheezing figure and said, "Paula, out of here. Leave. Go. I'll call." She scrambled to her feet with one hand still holding her face and left at a joke of run.

Then I addressed Mick with a script I thought afterwards must have sounded like a low budget police drama. "You made a mistake there in pissing me off, Mick my friend. All I was going to do was to pay you the money and give you a message. Leave Paula alone."

Looking up at me, and without taking his hands away from his crotch he said, "No sonny, the mistake was yours."

He started hauling himself painfully off the wet floor. "I'm going to have you."

"First you'll have to take your hands out of your crotch," I sensed an advantage, "and catch me. Here's the money, prick. Come and get it."

He let out a growl and started for me, still half doubled up. Needless to say, I moved away fast, towards one of the exits. I wanted to be able to taunt him, and he wouldn't be able to hear much where we were.

But shit he was fast. He almost had me before I'd gone ten metres. The near miss, me with my back arched for a moment to avoid his groping hand, served to keep my adrenaline levels at max, but even better, to convince Mick that he'd be able to catch me. I doubt if anyone enjoying the party noticed me as I ran along the right hand side of the warehouse in the semi-darkness. I reached the door to the car park in time to get out well in front of the lumbering prick. As soon as he emerged I shouted, "How's yer balls, Mick baby?" and sprinted down the outside of the building towards the end where we'd been moments before.

I had time when I arrived there to turn and shout encouragement. "Come on, Mick love." I set off round a couple of cars parked nearby, again as fast as I could go, and ran back towards the music end of the building. Mick was still following but my lead had increased.

"Aw Mick," I shouted, "you've slowed down. I'm disappointed."

As further encouragement I let him get close in his pathetic attempt at a run, dodged him easily and sprinted all the way back along the building, mentally thanking Sailor for the training. This was a doss.

Not a doss for Mick the Prick though. It was ages before he pulled up short of me and bent to rest his hands on his knees. He was close enough for me to hear his, "All right cunt, your card is marked." His chest was heaving.

"Oh Mick, my precious, you're not giving up already? The word's going to be all round Sheffield. Big Mick was made to look a total prick by a seventeen year old boy. I only just started shaving last year. Think of it, on Facebook, 'Mick meets his match'. That's called alliteration, arsehole."

I picked up a handful of the compressed clinker we were standing on and approached Mick cautiously. "Come on, Mick. Wouldn't you like to get your hands on me?" Then I threw the grit at his face. Mick swore and again took me by surprise with his speed of movement. Luckily I was able to knock a groping arm out of the way as I started running.

Seconds later we were back at the top end of the building, with the incensed Mick still trying to catch me. "Tell you what, Mick," I said when he stopped. "Been studying you. I know your sort. You're a secret pillow biter, aren't you? Girls are for show. It's boys you're really into. Here's an offer. Keks down and bum up over the car there. I'll give you one then hand over the dosh. No more running around. I'll rub your balls, too." I tried to mimic his deep voice. "Can't say fairer."

Off we went again. Mick was so easy to provoke. Then again we stopped. A different suggestion, this time that he had several forms of simultaneous venereal disease, inspired him to a further fruitless lunge and half minute of pursuit. I varied the route, taking a whole circuit of the car park. Eventually Mick's excuse for running became comic and like a dog that's had enough of chasing a ball, he refused to go any further. He stood, outside the old factory, bent forward, hands on knees, helpless.

For all I knew Mick was having a heart attack. I was on a roll, but still with unfinished business. Here he was at a total anaerobic standstill and in no shape to fight. What next? Marquis of Queensbury? Not flipping likely, not with a character like Mick. Marquis maybe, but de Sade not Queensbury. It was time to give him one for Paula. With the mental image of this revolting individual forcing Paula to suck his smegma-smeared cock I nipped forward and delivered another kick, as hard as I humanly, or more accurately inhumanely, could.

This time my foot connected with the bridge of the Prick's nose.

The front of the human face isn't as soft as the human crotch. The kick really hurt, me that is, on the top of my foot. The crunch I felt told me it must have hurt Mick too. His head snapped back and he collapsed forwards onto his face. Not dead, thank goodness. His carcass remained collapsed, but it was still heaving.

What to do next? I had an idea, but I'd need help. I went inside, found Dave and shouted into his ear. Dave laughed.

"Okay," he shouted back. "Let's do it."

He went up to a couple of people hanging round the stand and passed on my message. More laughs. Mick was a popular fellow in Sheffield.

"I need that rope then," I shouted to Dave, "and probably some help."

Dave, Mike and Don Don headed with me out of the factory and over to Dave's van. Dave unlocked the back doors and pulled out a sizeable length of twine.

"This should do," he said. "Where is he?"

I led them over to where Mick was still lying, no longer the Prick, now Mick the Motionless Hulk. His breathing had settled down. Don Don and I each grabbed a leg and we dragged him over to his disabled car.

"That was a waste of time with the tyres, Don Don," I said. "He's going to get a lift now, with the pigs."

Don Don laughed. "Win a few, lose a few."

We'd reached Mick's car. I found his keys in a pocket of his ruined leather jacket and opened the driver's door. It needed all four of us to manhandle him, now grunting and snorting through the bloody mess of his face, into the driver's seat. I then made an over-thorough job of tying his wrists to his steering column and his feet to the pedals. I didn't want him missing the appointment we'd arrange for him.

"Right," said Dave. "He's not going anywhere. Let's get back."

"Anyone seen Paula?" I asked.

Negatives all round. She must have taken me at my word and pushed off before the Prick's multiple failures to catch me in the parking area. "Just as well," I said. Rightly or wrongly, I didn't want further complications from Paula that night.

"I'll call the pigs when we're leaving," Dave said, "before I ditch the SIM. No hurry with Mick, I'll tell them. He'll wait."

How satisfying. It made sense to use the party number to let the police know about the prick. The SIM would no longer be of use and would as always be thrown away, with the message about the party location deleted, eliminating any small chance the number would have led to any of us. As for Mick, the police would love it. We knew he had a good stash of several different drugs with him, some E, some draw, some coke and of course the horse. The coke I'd come across in a pocket when I was hunting for his keys. He'd have expected to clear a good few hundreds of pounds at the party, over and above Paula's two hundred and fifty. Almost certainly a grand, I reckoned. Even if he hadn't been busted before, he'd receive a custodial sentence for the cocaine. Neither Paula, nor indeed I, would have to worry about a visit from Mick for a couple of years.

Dave said that he would be driving home mid morning so I prepared to crash out on some blankets in the back of his van. I should be in just about adequate shape for thirteen hundred o'clock, or whatever it was, with Petty Officer McCann. I handed back the money Dave had lent me and said good night.

Chapter Twenty Two

The next event I was looking forward to was my first PSA Challenger tournament, the SweetSuccess Open, at a new club in Lancaster. The SweetSuccess was sponsored by a confectionary company run by a squash enthusiast. The prize for winning was five hundred pounds. The money was important. It meant ranking points. For a lot of the players, especially the ambitious ones on the up, the ranking points *were* the point. You weren't going to survive on the prize money.

I was almost sorry I'd asked Sailor again about ranking points. Mary had left for work. Sailor was reading the Independent. I was still eating breakfast.

His first response was, "Read the Tour Guide, son. Read the Tour Guide."

"It all looks so complicated."

"Well, ye paid yer money."

Sore point. I'd only just managed to pay Sailor back for my Professional Squash Association, 'PSA', Junior Membership fee of a hundred and fifty pounds. Now I'd had to fork out, or rather borrow, another three hundred for Continental Membership. Otherwise I wouldn't have been eligible to enter the SweetSuccess. Country Membership, one category down at only two hundred pounds, in truth would have been enough, but Sailor had advised me to go for Continental so that I could enter tournaments across Europe. "Next year yer'll be a World Member, but there's no need now."

Among the benefits of PSA membership, apart from the ability to enter tournaments, was the Tour Guide. It was the Bible of the tour. The Tour Guide explained... well I didn't know what it explained because I'd only dipped into it. I'd found a complicated table about ranking points and immediately bailed out. You got, I remembered it exactly, ten point six two five points for fifth to eighth place in a 'National Closed Challenger Tournament', whatever that was. Time now to bail back in. Ranking points were about to become the obsession of my life.

"Ranking points for a tournament depend on the prize money. And size of the entry. Each stage, last sixteen, quarters, semis and so on, you get more points. It's calculated as a proportion of the sponsorship, the whole pot, hotels, food, limos."

"Limos? You mean I'll have a limo to take me to Lancaster?"

"Dream on, son. Big tournaments, Hong Kong, Canberra, Delhi."

"What if the prizes are in different money?" I was thinking of the Challenger I was hoping to enter in Holland. If I could afford the travel, I thought, a big concern. "That Maastricht tournament I'm supposed to be in. The prizes are in Euros. You get more of them so you get more points than a UK tournament?"

"It's all calculated in dollars. Evens things out worldwide. In most places it's dollars you get paid in, specially the big Middle East tournaments. Plenty of prize money there. Dubai, Qatar, Sharm el Sheik. Ye'll have to be there soon. At least in the qualifying."

"Do you get points in the qualifying?"

"Aye, ye do, not many. You also get tired. So yer going to need good results as soon as possible. Automatic first round entry. That's essential. And that depends on your ranking." He fixed me with his piercing eyes. "No time to waste. Lancaster's important. Let's take some time before we head for Eastlands. We'll look where you need to reach, every three months going forward. Ye need to understand how tight the timing is."

"What do I get for Lancaster?"

"It's an open Challenger, fifty two point five points for a win. Twenty one for a losing semi." He opened his laptop, put on his reading glasses and after a few moments said, "Come here. Let's see. If you won in Lancaster you'd be ranked world three hundred and twelfth, alongside a feller called Samson Khama of Botswana."

"You mean I could get a world ranking, just from Lancaster?"

"Aye, above Mr Khama, see the list. It's on the PSA website. You can send your mother a text wi' the good news. If you make the quarters, you'll be," he clicked his mouse a few times, "around four hundred and twenty fourth. Above," he looked again, "Ian Cooper of Australia."

I peered at the columns: rankings, names, countries the players came from, points. "What's this?" It was a random single digit number in each row, a two or a three or a seven or a four.

"Number of tournaments played in the calendar year. Yer points total's divided by ten. So it's no good getting a good result in a single tournament. It's still divided by ten. After that you can discard yer worst results. Then, I forget the detail, if you play a lot more tournaments the divisor goes up. Max sixteen for twenty five tournaments, but no way could you play twenty five in a year. Ye'd be shredded."

"How many points do I need to be, say, top hundred?"

"Here we are, Manuel Montego, ranked one hundred. I know Manuel. He's a Mexican, never gives up, his knees are shot to pieces though. Manuel averages forty nine points. So if you win ten Challengers in a year ye'll be inside the top hundred. You'd be ninety two right now wi' fifty two point five average."

Sailor's accent had become thick as he talked, his eyes fierce. He went out to his study and came back with his briefcase.

"I've planned it out for you. It's tighter than I thought. Ye'll need two years among the big boys, I mean the top ten, top fifteen mebbe. No way you could break through to number one faster than that. So you've got to be up there by yer nineteenth birthday. Less than two years. That means, see here, ye'll need to be averaging three hundred and fifty points by then, give or take. For fifteenth in the world."

"Three fifty points?" It was scarcely believable. Here I was planning to scrap for a couple of tens of points at a highly competitive Challenger tournament, maximum fifty in the improbable event that I won it. Then in less than eighteen months I'd have to be disappointed with fewer than three or four hundred for every tournament I entered.

"What sort of tournaments will I have to be in?"

"For winning a Two Star it's three fifty points. Three star, five two five; four star, seven hundred. Semi in a World Series, five two five. You've got to be up there.

"And so, start with a bang. Ye can win the SweetSuccess, send out that message. You can't mess around in Challengers for long, but you'll struggle to get into the bigger comps without some outstanding results.

"Have a look at this. We'll have to modify it as we go along, but it's your tournaments for the next eighteen months." Sailor took an A4 pad from his briefcase. I moved round the table and looked over his shoulder. In his heavy handwriting there was a list of something like twenty five tournaments, with their classifications, first a range of Challengers and later some Internationals with higher prize money. Towards the bottom of the list, more than a year on, the so called Internationals were of the '50' and '70' varieties, with prize money of fifty thousand dollars upwards. They felt as far away as their locations, across the Middle East and the Americas. The early tournaments were mainly in the UK, with one or two in Holland and Germany. At the beginning of the following year there was the British Juniors, where I'd be in the under nineteen, and mid-year the World Juniors.

"I've worked this out on the basis ye don't lose much. You can't afford to."

I looked at the second page of the list, the final months before my twenty first birthday. If I could get close to the top, that would be where I'd have to make the last push. There was the PSA World Open, the world championship in Grandpa's terms, in December in India. Winning that would be job done. Or, maybe less unlikely, I'd accumulate enough points to be top of the rankings. The Tournament of Champions in January in New York would be the last realistic chance of winning big points. As I stood behind Sailor in his little dining room, it seemed absurd.

Sailor turned back to the PSA ranking list on his laptop. "Right, son, it's time to re-commit. You've got to do it. Think of your granddad." *Think of my mother, more like.* "See here, Magdi Gamal, little genius, world number one, one thousand five hundred and ten points. He's beatable, I'm telling you, Magdi's beatable."

"What, *averaging* one thousand five hundred?"

"Aye. It's tough. There's only three categories of tournament where first prize points is over fifteen hundred." He reeled off some numbers from memory. "World Open, two six two five; World Series Platinum, two one eight seven point five; World Series Gold, one seven five oh. Magdi had a good run at the end of last year, and a couple of the others were injured, Trevor Cooper, Jan Berry. Trevor's second, eleven sixty six. Another Egyptian's third, Hosni el Baradei, solid. He hasn't won a tournament for two years but he always make the quarters; usually the semis."

"What do you get for a semi in a top tournament?"

"World Open, over a thousand. Some World Series, as little as five hundred. Quarters, you're talking about three to six hundred. Like I said, it depends on the prize money." Sailor looked at me. "I know what it feels like, son. It seems a long way off. Do you know what it was like with Zoë? She was a skinny little bairn, nothing on her when she first came here. But she fought, from day one. You've seen her at training. Once she'd come here, she didn't have any doubt. She knew. I didn't have to tell her. She made *me* believe, not the other way round. She made it happen. I'm a wee bit wiser now, an' it's me telling you." He separated each word: "You are going to do it."

It gave me a surge of adrenaline. He wasn't making this up. This was Sailor McCann and this was what he really did believe. I was going to be number one.

"Now, bottom line. Win a couple of satellites, soon. The SweetSuccess would be a good start. We need you in the qualifying in the star tournaments. By the end of this year. Then next year, you'll be eighteen, qualifying's no' enough. Automatic first round entry so yer not tired. Flights paid, hotels paid. Those limos. Chance to play the big boys. Chance to *compete*. You'll have a year then to make it to the World Series, top eight. January. That's as far as I can get you.

"Listen to me." He turned round from his seat and his eyes bored into me. "That's where I will guarantee to get you, Jolyon Jacks. After that it's down to you. Everest, last five hundred metres. The death zone, they call it. I'll take you as far as the death zone. After that yer on yer own. But you'll do it."

I knew about the World Series. It was a separate scoring system through the year that culminated in a tournament in London, two sets of round robins, for the season's top eight players. The top two from each of the round robins went into semis. There was big prestige and big prize money for the winner.

Fortunately the short term pressure was off me financially. The two hundred and fifty Mick the Prick pounds were back with Dave where they belonged. I didn't have to replace them by two hundred and fifty semi-final pounds from the SweetSuccess. The prize money there rose from twenty five pounds for a first round loss to the five hundred if you won. Paula hadn't answered my texts, so there was less chance I'd have to part with any winnings to help her. I'd resigned myself to the fact that further contact with her would involve paying out rather than making out.

I didn't know my first round opponent in the SweetSuccess, a twenty one year old named Ben Tors from Hampshire. "Blitz him," was the instruction from Sailor before I left, and that was what I duly did, a guaranteed fifty pounds for the win. After the same result in the second round I was sure of a hundred pounds, more than two full days pay from Fallowfield. Next it was to be none other than Riley O'Callaghan, ranked in the world's top ten. Not the in squash world's top ten. This was a Jolyon Jacks ranking, the World Total Dick Scale, for arseholes and other scum. At squash Riley was eighty six in the world, with an average of fifty seven point six points. His best result had been in Canada, thirteen hundred dollars and a hundred and fifteen points as runner up in a One Star tournament. I'd done okay against Riley in practice sessions. We'd never played a full game, but I knew I wouldn't be outclassed.

But oh dear. It turned out I *was* outclassed, comprehensively, though not exactly at squash. This was Riley, remember. Riley's mother must have seen something in him the day he was born. *'What are we going to call the ugly little we'un? Oh yes, Riley.'*

The priest who baptised him would have been in on it. *'I name this little bastard Riley, may God forgive my soul.'* What did the label say on the Riley tin? Riley, Born To Rile. He was probably fortunate to have made it out of Belfast. In the week following our match his risk of a kneecapping was back up to highly probable. This time by me.

It started with routine Riley as I walked into the changing rooms at Lancaster. He'd been getting increasingly offensive at training, especially when I practised with Zoë, and now he simply carried on.

"Ah the Golden Boy, Golden Jolly. Come for a lesson today, jolly Jolyon?"

As far as names were concerned, I was coming to the view that my mother and father could have done better for me. John would have been okay. Or Eric or something. Nothing quite as poncy as Jolyon.

"A little tedious, Riley. I suppose this is going to continue through our game?"

"Indeed it is, my boy."

Indeed it did. I learned afterwards that tournaments at the satellite level had to have at least one international class referee. Whoever he or she was, they weren't looking after my match. Early on in the first game, Riley played a good drop shot. I'd get to it, but as the ball was so close to the wall, all I'd be able to do was to push back a return drop with the end of my racquet. The problem was, Riley hesitated ever so slightly before clearing the ball as the rules obliged him to do. The result was minor contact between my hip and his which unbalanced me enough to make me hold back from playing my return.

"Let please," I asked automatically.

"No let. Three two." I gave the referee a look. He was a non-descript man, part bald, in his forties, standing halfway up a gallery of seven big steps behind the glass backed court. There were ten or twelve spectators dotted around, Sailor included, and nobody looked surprised. It wasn't a big incident and I put it out of my mind. A marginal bad call. They happened all the time.

As Riley prepared to serve he smiled at me and said quietly, "Good marker."

My way of dealing with irritation was to ignore it. I was playing really well, feeling good, keeping Riley behind me, making him run. Several points later I tried to play a ball with Riley close. My racquet clipped some part of him on my backswing and even as the ball was going down at the front wall I raised my hand and pointed to the end of my racquet.

"Let please. Contact."

This is normally a routine let. Maybe Riley had been a little close for me to have played the shot. If he'd been closer I'd have stopped and asked for a let. Almost certainly in those circumstances I'd have been awarded the point. The rules say you have to be given room to play your shot, even if it means the non-striker must disadvantage himself by leaving the court open. Perhaps I should have asked for a let on this occasion; it was a fifty-fifty call.

Strangely the ref asked, "Was there contact, Riley?"

Riley stood there with one hand indicating apparent bemusement. "No. No contact."

"No let. Hand out. Five Six."

Another big smile from Riley as he retrieved the ball. "Justice," he said quietly. "This guy's reading it just fine."

I was furious. Careful now. Ignore it. Focus on the squash, Sailor's formula, take the ball early, hit it hard, keep the opponent behind, attack, attack, attack. Riley's game was different from mine, subtler, probably better to watch, full of little drop shots and clever angles at the front. It was a risky form of the game because if the shots weren't perfect the court was opened up for the opponent. On the other hand, it took a lot out of the opponent with all the scrambling, and Riley had excellent control. A couple of rallies later I played a perfect return at full stretch to one of Riley's drops. Six months earlier I'd never have reached it but I was getting quicker all the time. Riley made no proper effort to reach my return but bumped into my back.

"Let please."

Quite correctly the marker said, "No let, seven all."

"I was all over it," Riley said. "I'd have reached that easily."

"You were short, Riley. No let."

"Not a good one," Riley said, loud enough for the marker and the scattering of watchers to hear.

Something similar happened the next point. Again, no let. This time Riley opened the door of the court. "He's not clearing the ball. What do you expect me to do?"

"No let. Nine seven."

"Hey ref, that's harsh." He closed the door and took his time preparing for my next serve. I knew what Riley was doing. He wasn't trying to get the decision reversed. That never happened. He was putting pressure on the ref to influence decisions later on. Good refs could deal with that. Bad refs, which to be fair was most refs, it was the most difficult job in the world, always shaded one or two later decisions in favour of the complaining party.

I duly won the first game. In the interval, Riley spent some time in his what-a-jokey-fellow-I-am mode telling the referee how quick he was and how I was preventing him from reaching the ball. Sailor came down to talk to me. "Just keep yer concentration."

As we went back on court Riley said a few words to me, too quietly for anyone else to hear. "See what I'm doing. I'll have this fellow. Then I'll have you. Match to Riley, probably three one."

Riley started a campaign of minor delays in clearing the ball in the second game, especially after his short shots. Spectators who weren't players wouldn't have noticed. Nor apparently would low grade referees. Riley was too subtle. The slight hesitations made the ball harder to reach, and harder then to do something effective with. The first couple of times I squirmed past him. The next time, at three all in the second game, I stopped.

"Let please."

"No let. Hand out, four three."

I said as reasonably as I could, "But I wasn't able to get through."

"You have to make an effort to reach the ball. No let."

Riley came in loud enough for the gallery to hear. "Come on, golden boy. Play fair. You'd never have reached it."

I suppressed another surge of anger, said nothing and prepared to receive serve. The next rally was a long one, long and satisfying, with Riley desperately scrambling as I volleyed the ball deep into the corners. Eventually he played a loose defensive shot well away from the side wall. It was an obvious opening for me to win the point with a short volley and Riley was half way past in anticipation when once again I hit the ball deep, not short. Make him run some more, Sailor's mantra. Riley's effort to change direction involved charging into me, racquet theatrically outstretched in the direction of the ball.

"Let please."

"Yes let."

A hundred times out of a hundred with a decent referee it would have been no let.

"Hey," I said. "There's no way he could have reached that."

"You were in the way. Plenty of contact. He couldn't get through. Let ball."

"See the way it's going?" Riley said quietly. "You might as well give up now."

I gritted my teeth and played on. Several more hard points, yesss, that's better! It was looking as though Riley wouldn't be able to keep up. Sailor's formula.

Then Riley contrived another block. "Let please," I said.

"No let. Hand out, Four seven."

This was too much. "Come on!" I shouted. "What do I have to fucking do?"

"Conduct warning, Jolyon. The score is four seven. Riley to serve."

"Now come on, Jolyon," Riley mimicked, loud enough for the gallery to hear. "You're not playing with boys any more." He made a calming motion with his free hand. "Settle down."

That's exactly what I did. The next point finished with Riley just failing to reach a short angled shot and scraping it back, so clearly on the second bounce I didn't consider going for it. To my amazement the referee called, "Five seven."

"That pick up. I thought it was down."

The referee hesitated for a moment. "I couldn't be sure. Play a let, four seven."

Standing in the service box Riley grinned his infuriating grin and said quietly, "You were right. Double bounce."

That was as much as I could take. I drilled the next return of serve into the tin. The following point I bumped Riley as I went for a short ball.

It must have been too obvious. "Stop," the referee called. We both turned. "Conduct stroke, Jolyon."

"What do you mean?"

"That was deliberate. I'm awarding the point against you. Please play squash. The score is seven all. Riley from the right box."

The referee has the power to give different so called conduct sanctions, a warning, a point, a game or even the whole match. He'd just awarded a point against me on a conduct stroke. How could this be effing happening? I'd heard of conduct warnings for 'racquet abuse', someone smashing his racquet against the wall or floor, but never a conduct point. Riley went through a show of stretching the side I'd knocked. Then he bounced the ball a few times, grinned his grin, quietly said, "I never realised you were a cheat," and served. After a few shots another subtle block resulted in minor contact and prevented me from hitting an obvious winner, though I managed an average shot. Riley didn't go for it but stopped.

"Let please," he demanded. "More contact."

"Yes let. Jolyon, there's no need for that."

I'd had enough and opened the court door. "Can't you see," I said as patiently as I could, only a couple of steps down from the referee. "It's him getting in the way. He's just not clearing."

"I'll worry about him. Your movement's up to you and I want to see you making more effort to reach the ball. Now play on."

Riley acted as an obsequious doorman and murmured, "You just can't hack it, can you? Riley wins, definitely, three one."

"Seven all," the referee called. Riley did a pantomime stretch, bounced the ball a few times and served. Four close points later it was nine all, with Riley seriously out of breath. I knew I had him for that game, and he must have known it.

But Riley dug deep, on the rule-bending front. "Racquet," he called to the referee, holding up an apparently intact Dunlop. Without waiting for a response he left the court and spent an age pulling spare racquets out of his bag, removing the covers and testing the strings. He finally returned, comfortably back in aerobic territory. I controlled my temper. The next point was epic, with both of us up and back and side to side. Riley finally won it with a fluke, leaving me game point down. Riley though was wasted, first bent over and then down on his haunches. I was out of breath, certainly, but nothing I couldn't manage. Next point, simple formula, keep him moving. He might win it with another fluke off the frame or a nick, but the odds were against.

I couldn't believe what happened next. Again Riley said, "Racquet," left the court and started fiddling with his spares. By all rights the referee should have told him to get on with the game. Squash rules say play must be continuous. The referee could award a conduct stroke or even a conduct game against him if he didn't comply.

After a short interval, while I stood ostentatiously waiting to receive serve, I gave up on patience, went to the open door and said to the referee, "He's got to play. He's taking advantage."

The guy looked harassed. "Riley," he said, "that's enough time. On court please."

Riley raised a hand and carried on with his deliberations over his racquets. Finally he methodically zipped the unfavoured ones into their individual covers and meandered back onto the court, without shutting the door. He reached the service box, took a deep breath, grinned at me and said quietly, "Ah, that's better."

The next instruction from the referee was, "Please close the door."

Riley said, "Go on, you do it." A spectator closed the door but I was too far gone for it to help.

"The score is ten nine, Riley to serve, game ball."

All my control, so carefully tutored during my months in Manchester, disappeared in a few rabid seconds. I flayed the ball round the court. The harder I hit it the easier it bounced. With a few simple strokes Riley worked me out of position and played the easy winner to take the game.

"Game to Riley, eleven nine. The score is one game all."

"All going to plan," Riley whispered as we left the court.

I sat fuming. Sailor had a word with Riley and joined me. "Ye know how to win this. Keep yer temper, keep yer temper."

I made a big effort to control myself at the start of the third game. Successfully too until Riley managed something you see footballers do every Saturday on Match of the Day, but which I'd never heard of on a squash court. He contrived a dive as he brushed past me on the way for a short shot and ended up in a mixture of dropped racquet, hairy Irish legs and absurdly false indignation.

"Ref," he said immediately from his sitting position. "That was out of order. Way out of order."

"Jolyon," the referee said. "I've already warned you for physical contact. I'm awarding a conduct game, eleven six to Riley. Riley leads two game to one."

In four strides I was out of the court, hands on hips, looking up at the referee. "That's ridiculous. He did that deliberately. That wasn't my fault at all."

"It was clear to me that you tripped him. I'll have to come down hard on you if you carry on with this."

"You already fucking have, mate. You're missing his double bounces. You're calling the lets all wrong. If I were you I'd be booking in to the optician, prompt on Monday morning."

Not the best way to prepare for the fourth game, but the fourth game never started. For long moments the guy said nothing. His face went red. Eventually he came out with, "I'm sorry, you've gone too far," then raised his voice. "Conduct match to Riley O'Callaghan, three games to one, seven eleven, eleven nine, eleven six and no score.

I was astonished. How could I have let that happen? How could the referee not have realised what was going on? I wanted to grab him and shake him till he changed his mind. Luckily it was Sailor who did the grabbing, "Come on, son," and ushered me towards the changing room.

"What about my kit?"

"I'll get your kit. You shower." Minutes later, after the quickest possible shower but no towel, I was face to face with Riley in the changing room.

"What did I tell you?" he said. "Riley wins it three games to one. A triumph of strategy. Over youthful impetuosity. It's like a song by Manu Chao. What a great forecast I made, don't you think, jolly Jolyon? Riley wins it three one."

I noticed Sailor coming into the changing room with my bag and I merely said, "Piss off." Sailor extracted the towel from my bag, handed it to me and addressed Riley.

"You. Monday morning. My house. 10am."

Riley started to say something, but he wasn't encouraged by the look on Sailor's face. Finally, after a staring match he just said, "Okay."

Sailor turned to me. "You. Don't forget your stretches. You'll take a meal wi' me later. Here, twenty hundred."

We were staying at a bed and breakfast near the club. I didn't want to watch the squash and mooched back there. At the B&B I threw my kit into my room and not caring who was about shouted, "Fuck," once at the top of my voice, and listened to some mixes on my iPhone. I timed my return to the club for eight o'clock on the dot.

Sailor surprised me during our meal. I was expecting to be flame grilled like my burger. "Ye don't need me to say anything, son," he said. "That's out the way now, mebbe a good thing that it happened today. We don't see that sort of behaviour again. There's plenty more Rileys out there. They won't beat you at squash. You just show them, your two inches are tougher than theirs. Only reason they do it, mess you around, they know you've got their number.

"But remember, yer representing me when ye play squash."

"So's Riley."

"I'll take care of Riley. You take care of not having to find another place to live. And last thing, go and find Sid French tomorrow and apologise."

I don't know what went on between Sailor and Riley, Monday morning, 10am. Sailor never said, and nor did Riley, who conspicuously ignored me after that in training, and at tournaments, and anywhere we saw each other. I was to find out, though, that he hadn't lost his capacity to annoy.

Chapter Twenty Three

My embarrassing efforts at Lancaster had left me with twelve point seven five points as a losing quarter finalist and a less than vertiginous world ranking of four hundred and sixty six, just below a Venezuelan, Hugo Crespo. At least I was on my way, just four hundred and sixty five rivals to pass. *Watch your back, Hugo my man, I'm gunning for you.* On the credit side, there were already thirty eight hopefuls, or perhaps not so hopefuls, below me.

At my next tournament things significantly improved, on two counts. It was a PSA Challenger 10 event in Cologne. The squash count first: I played out of my skin, reaching the final. I only lost there because I was tired after a marathon semi. I gained one hundred and fifteen points, all at once, think of it. My total was now one hundred and twenty seven point seven five, and I had leapt to a world ranking of four hundred and twenty seven. Hugo Crespo was crisped.

The other count was something else, up there with Count Basie and the Count of Monte Cristo. The former I was familiar with because my father was a jazz fan, the latter because my English teacher Mrs Crabtree had forced me to read Alexandre Dumas after catching me with a copy of Nuts in one of her grammar classes. The tournament was at the ACR Sportscenter, a large friendly club on the outskirts of Cologne. The ACR was a large centre, consisting mainly of random add-ons that can never have been part of any master plan. There were areas for table tennis and badminton, and squash courts on no less than three levels. The tournament squash was confined to the ground level, with two pairs of glass backed courts at right angles to an irregularly shaped area that included the bar, a small viewing area and some canteen-style seating for food and socialising. It was in this area that I first noticed an Indian guy with the whitest teeth I'd ever seen, hanging around with the two Indian players in the tournament. My semi was against one of the Indians, Pradhan Prasana, a hairy bundle of energy, the other end of the fairness spectrum from Riley O'C. You didn't need to cheat when you could move as fast as Pradhan, I supposed. Fortunately, his stroke play was predictable, so he often failed to win the points he had earned. It made for a long game, nearly two hours, and neither of us would be fresh for any final.

It was after the semi that I was approached by the dude with the teeth. I was anxious to do some serious stretching, and force down a protein drink, mindful of Sailor's instructions. "No problem," he said. "Let's have some food when you've stretched and showered."

So we met at the back for the excellent buffet the club was providing. "Well played," he said. "You always know you've been in a game with Pradhan. I'm Suresh Haladkar."

Suresh turned out to be the sales director for a Mumbai sports company that was breaking into both the European and North American markets. Squash was growing rapidly in India. It already had one World Series tournament and there were rumours that the World Open would be played there soon. Suresh's company, AllSports India, had already captured a big slice of the Indian market for racquets, shoes and clothing, he told me. Now they wanted to take on the Donnays and Adidases in their major territories. They were moving into soccer and golf, but they wanted to cover the sports that had given them a start in India, tennis and squash. With squash they were looking to sponsor three up-and-coming PSA players. I was less highly ranked than the players pencilled into their business plan, but Suresh liked the way I played and reckoned I was going to make rapid progress. Would I be interested?

I held myself down in my seat, and tried to play hard to get. "What sort of a deal do you have in mind?"

"It goes like this. We provide you with kit, racquets, shoes and so on. That's taken for granted. We'll also support you in your PSA tournament activities, travel, out of pocket expenses. Depending on your arrangements in Manchester, we'll also give you access to our support team, physiotherapy, massage, the full health package."

My astonishment must have shown, and Suresh put up a hand. "This doesn't come for nothing. In return we'll expect you to make at least three trips per year to India, either for tournaments or separately to do promotions and activities to support the company, get involved in clinics with kids, show yourself at events we're promoting."

Suresh saw my frown. "It's all right. We wouldn't want to disrupt your squash programme. Our interests are your interests. You're with Sailor McCann in Manchester, that's right?"

I nodded.

"We'll work the dates out with Sailor. I know you've a tight schedule, all the training and the practice and the tournaments. But imagine not having to work to pay your way. Imagine being able to relax after training, or put in extra sessions."

"How do you know all that?"

"We've done our homework, Jolyon. This whirlwind style of yours. That appeals to my fellow directors. AllSports India, we're a whirlwind company. We don't hang around. This is only our seventh year. You're a perfect fit for us. The word is, you're going to get to the top. This is, what, your second PSA tournament? And you're in the final? Pradhan's no pushover, either. Pradhan fights for every point. I'll be interested to see how you get on against Rainer Rasch."

"So you've been following me?" It was flattering but a bit scary, the thought that this company, in India of all places, had me on their radar.

"We keep in touch with the scene. We didn't get where we are by sitting back and expecting the world to come to us. We have to know what's going on in our markets. Anyway, what do you think about the offer?"

I swallowed. It was such a big deal. "It's too good to be true," I said. "It will take away a lot of my worries. It's just, it's just sudden, I suppose."

Suresh smiled. "I understand. I tell you what. I'm going to be in Manchester next week. Let's meet. I'll bring along some written details. Nothing formal. We'll do a formal contract when you break into the top thirty. The only commitment I'll want from you at this stage is not to sign with anyone else without talking to me first.

"So." He checked the time on his mobile. "You need to get back to your hotel."

"I guess so. It won't take long. The trams are brilliant."

"No tram. I'll give you a lift. And I want to give you some racquets to try. Two different weights, a light one, one ten grams, and the Hi-Per, one two five. We do two professional strings, Hi-Per Touch and Hi-Per Power. Four racquets. Try them out for a few days. Let me know which you prefer. And let us know your preferences for the grip."

It was great to be driven back to the hotel. In spite of all the conditioning Sailor had put me through, I was weary. The next day it showed, and I lost to the elongated Rainer Rasch in less than half an hour.

Sailor always had us debrief to the others after a tournament. What was the opposition like? How had we played? What had we learned? What would we do better next time? We were sitting in a group in the canteen area at the EIS, ready to do some court work. Most of Sailor's squad was there, Paul White, Ahmed, James Lovegrove, Riley, Carmen and of course, Zoë.

"So you lost to Rainer three oh," Sailor said, and looked at me. "Journeyman German, disappointing."

"Oh come on, Sailor, I was on court two hours against Pradhan Prasana in the semi. I was tired."

Sailor seemed to know everyone on the circuit. "Aye, he's a tenacious feller. Still, there was a hundred and seventy five points there for the taking, an' you came away with a hundred and fifteen. What's the lesson?"

"I dunno, train harder, I suppose."

"The lesson is, a tournament's a full week. Ye have to win smart in the early rounds, ruthless, conserve energy. Plan to arrive in good time. Travel hassles? No good. Not enough sleep? No good. Three two wins? Three one is better, three oh is best. Double yer stretching. Take the massages. Eat properly. It's not just what happens on court. You have to manage yourself."

I nodded. "I do have one bit of good news. I've got some sponsorship. AllSports India."

To my surprise, Sailor frowned. Zoë asked, "How did that come about?"

I told the story about Suresh, and showed everyone the racquets he had given me.

"AllSports India," Zoë said. "I know them. They're due to launch in the UK soon. A sharp organisation. I heard they put a lot of pressure on Beth La Salle after she'd signed for them. It was turning up early for tournaments and doing clinics. She said it was okay, but they're very pushy."

"Can't have your programme disrupted. Ye don't have the time," Sailor said.

"Suresh said he understands that. He's here in Manchester later this week. Wants to arrange a couple of trips to India for me. Thing is, they're going to pay all my travel, and give me all my kit. Just think. I'll be shot of Fallowfield Pools"

"What have you done to deserve that?" Paul asked enviously. He was five years older than me and struggling at mid thirties in the rankings, a victim so often of the qualifying round trap. He'd had some fine wins but was usually too tired to follow them up.

"They're investing in gold," Riley said. "Golden Jolyon."

I smiled. "Something like that. Style. Have they approached you yet, Riley?"

"Can it fellers." Sailor turned to me. "You say this man is coming here? Let's meet him and lay down some ground rules. I'm no' having you commit to anything that'll hold your squash back."

I was doing some routines with Zoë later. In a pause she said, "Watch those people, Jolyon. It'll probably be great, and I like that racquet, the light one. Thing is, they're very sharp, very pushy. I've seen them at tournaments. India, Malaysia, Hong Kong. If something's too good to be true, it usually is."

I was relieved at the end of the week when Suresh finally turned up. He took Sailor and me out for a meal in the middle of Manchester. Quality meals with Suresh were going to become a regular feature of my life.

"We won't fix anything with Jolyon without talking to you, Sailor. As I said to him, his interests are our interests. Our board has decided to invest in three young players, a special extra promotion for three years. One Indian, of course, one Egyptian, you can't ignore the Egyptians, and one simply whom we like. We'd started to hear about Jolyon. Then he really impressed me in Cologne, *carpe diem*."

"Carpe what!" Sailor said.

"We like to act fast. I see a big future for Jolyon. He's young but he has huge potential. Why wait? Seize the moment. Now the object is for him to progress as fast as possible."

Sailor spoke to me at the weekend. The meal had gone well, and he and Suresh had had a long phone conversation the following morning. "I'm reluctant to admit it, but we've a good arrangement. Suresh Haladkar understands squash. Your work for them is no' set in stone. It'll depend on how you're going. When you're away, it'll no' be a vacuum, I won't allow it. I've seen them, money first, no attention to the squash. But it'll be fixed that you train with local players, proper players."

"I'm just pleased I can say goodbye to lifeguarding."

Sailor gave me the look I had learned meant that something unpalatable was coming. "Listen to me, son. Hang on to your job at Fallowfield. Six, mebbe nine months. Wait till ye know this is going to work out. You'll no' get back in, or not easily. Sure you can cut down the hours, do that."

"It's so grim. I could cope with that. But honestly, I'm knackered. I know I sound like a wuss. I'm pushing hard, Sailor. I'm not holding anything back in training. Sometimes it's all I can do to get out the door to go to Fallowfield. I talked about it with Suresh. He understands."

"Aye," he said softly. "I've been impressed. With the odd exception, ye've exceeded my expectations. I think you're going to do it, son, I really do. I worry, that's all. When something comes too easily. In the end it's your choice. Don't come to me if it turns round and bites you."

Chapter Twenty Four

Far from biting me, the sponsorship from AllSports India, and even more the support from Suresh, quickly developed into a major boost. Fallowfield was out, done, gone, finito, thank goodness. Without the financial imperative I just couldn't bring myself to carry on there. After two more weeks I told the management I was leaving. Anthea wasn't there on my last day. Derek was. He refused to shake my hand as I said my goodbyes and lumbered away, his huge neck muscles knotted, reeking of stale, testosterone-tainted sweat.

When I was out the door, finally on my way with my P45, I raised a finger to the forecourt CCTV camera and happily caught the bus home.

Squash Online, November 30th

...and in the world of Challenger tournaments, everyone is taking notice of the teenage prodigy Jolyon Jacks, from Manchester, England. After a poor start to his senior career, he was disqualified in September for abusing the referee in his first tournament, Jacks, not yet eighteen, successively reached two finals in Challenger 10s. Then astonishingly, he won the $12,000 Challenger 10 in Maastricht last weekend. His defeated opponents included two consistent performers from inside the top hundred, Dutchman Pieter Spaargaren, ranked ninety one, and in the final world number sixty Robin Norris, from Preston. Jacks' run of form has rocketed him to a ranking of sixty five on the world list.

How far is Jacks going to go? Watch this space.

Sailor had been with me in Maastricht, and had helped me through a grim patch against Pieter Spaargaren, when I lost the third game. 'Come on, son. He gave everything there. One more push. Don't let up. First three points, break his heart.' It had almost burst my heart, and my lungs, but Sailor had been right and Spaargaren faded when he found he'd have to exceed his effort in the third game to make any progress in the fourth. The final had been easier. Robin Norris had tired himself out overcoming the top seed in a long semi. My turn to benefit from the draw. The only down side was that I had to say some words of thanks at the presentation. Robin was a good guy and listed the things to say: 'Compliment the club and the quality of the organisation. Thank the staff. Thank your coach. Above all thank the sponsors. They put up the prize money.' I managed to mumble through the necessary words, and I made sure the AllSports logo on my kit was prominent in the photographs.

Sailor must have let a few people back home know about my win. While we were waiting at the tiny airport at Maastricht for the flight back to Stansted I had a text from Zoë. Gulp. It read simply, 'thats the way you do it x Z.' Next morning I had a call from Grandpa. 'It's a big step, Jolyon. Your first tournament win. I'm proud of you.' A couple of weeks later I heard from my father, who was just back from somewhere in the seven seas. 'Well done, I'm thrilled for you. Keep at it.' Of course I had a text from Suresh. 'Congratulations from all of us at AllSports. It will be the first of many victories.'

From my mother? Nothing.

December was a quiet month. The World Championships were being played in Saudi Arabia, beyond me at this stage. I'd have to be there within two years, preferably next year. What a thought: me competing in the world championships! In three years, just months before my twenty first birthday I'd have to be winning the thing. Financially I was doing okay. What a relief that was. I no longer had regular money coming in from Fallowfield, of course, but AllSports were giving me enough to live on. I received a monthly payment into an account they'd asked me to set up with an Indian bank, and all I'd had to do so far in return was to wear their kit and hit balls with their racquets. I was due to spend two weeks in Delhi and Mumbai in the spring. Part of this would be to play in a big Challenger tournament, and part to do some promotional stuff at two new clubs. These were being opened in Mumbai following the success of squash at the Commonwealth Games. In between there'd be training with two of the Indian players supported by AllSports. I couldn't wait.

There was one big down to life, no girlfriends. I was too tired, too poor and I didn't have the time. No girls was a massive ache. It had been so easy back in Sussex. If I'd split up with Samantha down there I'd have got going with someone else, no sweat. But up in Manchester, where to meet anyone anyway? Even if I found the energy, scraped the dosh together and made the time. Added to which, with Zoë around, I didn't want to meet anyone else. Oh Zoë! There'd always been something about Zoë for me. Rid-flaming-iculous, but there it was. Apart from the usual things, I imagined us just being together, having a laugh, planning how to play an opponent, watching TV. Getting up together in the morning. If only.

I brewed the idea for ages. I knew Zoë liked me. Did I have the nerve, though? At last I had some money in the bank, tournament winnings. I'd ask her out for a meal, that wouldn't be too blatant. Why then was I so nervous? One afternoon she and I had a brilliant session of court routines together. I wouldn't get a better opportunity.

"Are you going to be around this weekend?" I said as casually as I could while we regained our breath.

"Yes, why?"

"Well, I wanted to pay you back for that meal, the Indian, you remember, when I was first up here. I'm not totally skint right now. That's after Maastricht. Probably won't last, so how about another curry? Taj Mahal?"

The smile she gave me turned my insides into a smoothie, a non-veggie one, trashed tripe. "All right. How about Friday evening?"

I managed to get to TK Maxx on Thursday and spent some money on clothes: a pair of All Stars, my current ones had a hole, some jeans, my current ones had several holes, and a thick fleece, I'd been feeling the cold, Manchester's damp cold. More importantly, I didn't want to look totally tatty going out with Zoë. As an afterthought I got some new boxers.

On Friday we did a light session in the morning because it was performance testing in the afternoon. Sailor's entire squad was there. As usual, he organised us into two groups for the tests. Zoë, Carmen, Riley and I went off to do the jumps and the VO$_2$ max. Ahmed, James, Paul, Louise and a young Australian who had joined us, Doug Kafalias, went to do the bleep test. It was my fifth set of performance tests since coming to Manchester. I was looking forward to seeing how much I'd improved. My autumn training and competition had gone really well. I was feeling a lot stronger, even than six months previously, a kind of bursting-out-of-my-skin feeling. Energy to burn, speed to burn, power to burn. I had them all.

I was surprised that Sailor had put Riley and me together. Riley hadn't been too offensive since Lancaster, but he was always niggling. I didn't mind though, as I expected to do better than him in the tests. That's how it turned out. I was a full three centimetres above him in the standing jump, forty seven, a new PB. It was impossible to tell straight away with the drop jump; we'd have to wait for the print out for that. After the VO$_2$ max Riley started whinging about not feeling well.

Then there was the bleep test.

Some things in life, just occasionally, worked out perfectly. Zoë and Carmen were cooling off, hands still on knees, when Riley and I started. The audience was completed by Sailor. The name of the game for me was to appear nonchalant. This was easy for the opening levels. What's more, I knew, and Riley knew too, that I was going to trounce him. I sensed that he was torn between nonchalance, not wishing to appear less than comfortable, and early physical distress, to provide an excuse for when he stopped before me. He did start off with nonchalance. It was like arm wrestling, with the competitors making no impression on each other and only their distended forehead veins telling the true story. Still like arm wrestling, when the end can be sudden, at level twelve Riley started to grunt at the turn-arounds. I was bouncing. In level fourteen Riley fell behind a couple of times. He made it to halfway through level fifteen and suddenly stopped.

Ooh that had been fun! Now to rub it in. I was having to concentrate, fighting back the fatigue and making sure the enemy, the merciless beep, didn't gain on me. Through sixteen. Into seventeen. I had been frustrated previously in not beating the seventeen I had managed in that first session eighteen months ago. Once I'd been tired from Fallowfield, once I'd had a niggling injury to my ankle, and once I'd just lost concentration and stopped before I needed to.

This time, the pleasure of carrying on well past Riley's score kept me focussed. I was okay at the end of seventeen. "Come on, Jolyon," from Carmen. Eighteen was horrible but I made it. At the transition to nineteen, Zoë's voice cut through my pain. "Right, now it's match point!"

I was determined to do nineteen. I promised myself a night with Zoë if I made it, *will you undress me, Jolyon, or would you prefer to watch me do it?* Agony, my whole body rebelling, lactic torture, two more reps, turn, just one more. Yesss!

I collapsed with my lungs heaving, face screwed up, desperately sucking in air. The pain rapidly disappeared as my hyper-efficient biochemistry dealt with the lactic enemy, that ally of the bleep. As I hauled myself to my feet Sailor said, "Good going, son. That's a record in my squad."

Zoë said, "That's right. That's the way you do it. Twenty next time?"

I felt great in the shower, endorphin heaven. I'd dumped on Riley. He'd slunk away. I'd done a fantastic score in the bleep test, maybe twenty next time was a possibility. And I was taking Zoë Quantock, world squash champion and the most beautiful woman on the planet, out for a meal. I surfed the euphoria as I got dressed in my new clothes.

Sailor had summoned everyone to the canteen area afterwards for rehydration, re-carbohydration and re-something with protein, so we pulled a couple of tables together and sat down. Sailor extracted some result sheets from his briefcase, put on his reading glasses and peered over them at us.

"Pretty impressive overall. Particularly well done to Carmen and Jolyon. Your best scores all round. I know these tests aren't the same as winning matches. I said that before you said it, Riley. But they tell me what you're putting into your training. You have to invest to succeed. Big session tomorrow for those of ye who don't have a tournament next weekend. Have a good meal tonight. Early bed."

Riley said, "Zoë mentioned your curry, Jolly One, great idea, my social life has been lacking. I've asked around and everyone's up for it except Sailor. You sure you don't want to come, Sailor?"

My heart sank. Nooo! What was going on? Somehow my date had been hijacked by a suddenly cheerful Riley. Not that Zoë would have considered it a date, my private fantasy. She must have mentioned the plan, no big deal, to one of the group, and it had found its way to Riley. It was impossible now for me to say hey, this is a personal arrangement; I'm having Zoë all to myself. Piss off you lot. Find yourselves somewhere else. To make matters worse, Zoë didn't seem bothered. I felt as deflated as I had been inflated only moments earlier. Pox, in spades.

And sadly, things were going to get worse. Sailor said that he wouldn't sully his guts with spice-defiled food, or something like that. The rest of us worked out the transport. Zoë's car was having a service; she had apparently been given a lift to the EIS by the manager of the garage that sponsored her. Riley had come in his car. He claimed Zoë and Carmen. Doug would take James and me; Ahmed had other plans and Paul was on his pushbike. As we were leaving the EIS Riley said quietly to me, "Clever trick, that, Jolly One, trying to slip away with the princess. That's my territory, understand? Leave Zoë to the grown ups, someone who can handle her. She needs a proper seeing to and I've nominated myself."

At the Taj we sat at a long narrow table. Somehow I was at the other end from Zoë, and on the same side, with Doug in between. I couldn't even see her, pox again. Opposite Zoë was Carmen, and beside Carmen an increasingly jovial Riley. Smug, smugger, smuggest.

"Okay," Riley said to the waiter when the menus had arrived. "Bring us some poppadoms."

Then he addressed the women, rubbing his hands. "Indian food is Riley territory. If I may, ladies, I have some recommendations. Mix and match is the word. Nothing too spicy. A korma, coconut there, a bhuna, we'll go for a sag aloo, chicken tikka masala, pilau rice for six and six nans. What about you fellows? Let's start with some onion bhajees."

And so on and so on. The meal turned out to be a disaster, a royal command performance by Riley O'Callaghan. Riley King of Dicks. Still worse was to come, the sting in the disaster's scorpion tail. We'd all put in to pay the bill and at last, I was thinking, the Riley road show is coming to an end. As we were finding our coats the question came up about getting home. Riley came over to Doug and me and said, "Could you give Carmen a lift. I've, er, been invited for breakfast."

What did that mean? Stupid! It dawned on me. No, no, nooo! Riley and Zoë? It wasn't possible. I'd thought he'd been joking earlier. Irish excrement. I couldn't believe that he would be going home with Zoë. She wasn't even interested in men. So I thought. Neither was she shy about the arrangement, as everyone said their goodbyes, and she gave me what I would previously have classified as a warm smile. Normally I'd have smiled back but I must have looked as though my balls were at that very moment being chewed by a rabid conger eel. So the rest of us joined Doug and he did a circuit of south east Manchester dropping everyone off.

I tried to be quiet as I let myself into Sailor's house, but back in my bedroom I flung my kit against the wall. I'd get a bollocking in the morning. Sod that. I had a savage mix that blasted deep into the night.

Zoë wasn't overly familiar with Riley at training the next morning, and Riley wasn't overly cocky. Perhaps his cockiness had all spurted out of his cock the previous night, I thought morosely. Perhaps it had just been buddy sex. That's all right, then? Far from all right, it was a dense sensation in my guts, a leaden angst. Riley and Zoë? I couldn't help picturing them in bed, this way and that way, legs entwined, licking and sucking, straining and sweating. Cumming and cumming and cumming and fucking cumming.

Over the following weeks I put everything into my training, pushed myself to anaerobic extremes, up before breakfast for a run, doubling the repeats Sailor had prescribed for me in the gym, attacked the routines on court. One afternoon I absolutely crucified Zoë in a simple drive boast exercise.

"Is there anything wrong, Jolyon?" she asked as we came off court.

"No," I replied casually. "Just trying to push myself. It's only what you said."

She shrugged. "Okay."

The extra effort paid off in the British Junior Open in January. As usual it was played in Sheffield. This time I was staying in a bed and breakfast near the Abbeydale club. No favours from Dick Bentley, I could cope with that. Harder to cope with, there were no favours from Paula B either. I'd been hoping to see her. Someone said she'd given up squash, which didn't surprise me.

Ranking points were not on offer for the Junior Open but it was an immensely worthwhile trophy. Past winners were a roll-call of players who had made it right to the top. I got to the final without conceding a game, and had to play the previous year's winner, the elegant Hussein el Kashef, who during the previous year had come through qualifying at several major PSA tournaments. Sailor was laconic. "Ye'll have to earn this one. Usual formula will do it, but expect some resistance. Get in front of him."

I was optimistic. El Kashef had won his semi against Neeraj Solkar, a talented Indian player nobody had seen before at European junior tournaments. Neeraj played a high risk game, going for outrageously attacking shots. El Kashef had eventually reached enough of these to set up his win, but he had been pulled all over the court for a while. It surely would have taken something out of him.

Suresh had been there right through the tournament. He had seen all my games and was full of support. It gave me a boost to have someone else on my side as well as Sailor. Against el Kashef Suresh was desperate for me to do well. "I think you'll win, Jolyon. You must beat him in three games. Come on!"

Thankfully, three games were what it took. The pressure against juniors was nothing like as intense as in PSA tournaments, I'd found. There were some incredibly quick juniors, but you tended to have a fraction of a second longer to play your shots. Theirs were never quite so tight. So I was able to impose my game on el Kashef, and long before the end a look of desperation had appeared on his face behind his trendy eye mask. I'd have to ask Suresh about the mask. The AllSports one I'd been given was no more than functional.

Chapter Twenty Five

My angst-inspired training, with the lump in my stomach not abating one bit, continued to serve me well through my eighteenth birthday and the first half of the next season. During a trip to India in February, where I was treated like a prince by AllSports, I actually stopped thinking every moment about Zoë. Suresh drove me round Delhi and his brother Mital navigated me through the incredible traffic and the heat and the pollution of Mumbai, where AllSports was based. The staff I came into contact with were fanatical about squash, with never-ending questions about the tournaments and the cities where they were held and the players who played in them. I spent some brilliant times with kids, showing them the basics of squash. No one realised how little I knew myself. The final responsibility of the trip turned out to be good fun in its own right. Suresh arranged for me to play several televised exhibitions with Neeraj Solkar, the guy I had seen at the Junior Open. Through his teens Neeraj had been held back by his wealthy family because of sore knees, which explained why we hadn't seen him in Europe. I wondered what my mother would have done if sore knees had interrupted my progress at tennis. I once saw a teenager crying with pain as his father shouted at him to get on with it. Anyway, Neeraj's knees had sorted themselves out and he was trying to make up for lost time. Even with crippled knees, I thought, he'd win points anywhere. He blasted extraordinary nicks, far harder than I could hit the ball, but also played delicate angles that reminded me of Dave. His percentages inevitably weren't good, and I won all the games, but not before we'd done lots of running and been given enormous applause.

After India I had a successful month, four tournaments in Canada. I won in Calgary, lost finals in Edmonton and Vancouver, and reached the semis at my first three star tournament, in Toronto. It all added up to six hundred and thirty seven point five points, raising my ranking to forty eighth. I was inside the world's top fifty!

Zoë wanted to hear all the details when I got back to Manchester. I told myself to get over my ridiculous attitude. We were sitting in the canteen at the EIS, with Carmen and Ahmed.

"It's a big country, Canada," Zoë said. "You must have covered thousands of miles. I was worn out on my first trip there."

"It wasn't too bad. I had a lot of help from AllSports. Even apart from the flight tickets. They had reps in each of the cities and they met me at the airports, drove me around and so on."

"You don't know how lucky you are." She grimaced. "The travel, it takes it out of you. It held me back at first. Cheapest possible tickets. Dogleg flights via stupid stop offs. I had to scrape for the first two years, every last penny. I used to sleep in airports, the bigger ones anyway, where I felt safe. Anything to let me make a trip, an extra tournament."

It hadn't occurred to me what a difference AllSports was making. It was certainly true I was playing in tournaments I'd never have reached with my own financing. I'd not considered that arriving in comfortable time, and being able to relax and practise without hassles, contributed to my good results.

"Well I'm signed up with them for eighteen months more. And then further if it all goes well. Suresh said they were pleased with how it went in India. He says they want me to get as high as possible as soon as possible. He and Sailor have agreed a good schedule for me for the rest of the year. It's all good."

"Is sure good, Jolyon," Carmen said. "Can I come with you to Gran Canaria?"

I'd been looking forward to playing in an International 25 in Las Palmas, and Carmen had got very excited. Apparently she had family there.

"Sure thing, Carmen. You can be my minder. And my practice partner. And my masseuse."

"What's this mass... masseuse?"

"Massage, you know, tired arms, tired legs."

Poor Carmen blushed.

"It's all right," I said. "Zoë can come too and act as chaperone."

Zoë arched an eyebrow. "I see. Jolyon's harem. How will that go down with Sailor?"

Everyone agreed that that would not go down with Sailor. Zoë changed the subject. She wanted to ask me about my opponents in Canada, what had I learned, what would I do differently against each one next time. We chatted for ten minutes. Ahmed had some interesting thoughts on the two Egyptian players I'd met. It certainly made me organise myself. From then on I decided to emulate Zoë and record snippets about players in a loose leaf folder.

One pleasant chore on my return from Canada was to call Grandpa. I'd kept him updated while I was away, but I wanted to tell him about being inside the top fifty.

"You've made remarkable progress, Jolyon," he said, in a voice as strong as I'd heard for ages. "It's the next year that's going to be tough. You'll have to prepare yourself for the odd setback."

"You know what. I've been feeling so good for these past few weeks, I'd like to come and see you play. Can you tell me if there's a suitable tournament. I mean in England, all this jet setting you're doing. I'm hoping your father can come. If he's ashore. I know he wants to see the new Jolyon."

"Not my mother, though." It wasn't a question. It was a statement.

"Well, I don't need to tell you the answer to that."

I promised to let him know when I was sure to have a decent game, a definite date. I didn't want to line him up for a final somewhere and then go out in the quarters or the semis. As I put the phone down I thought, there's me now, look at me, worrying not about first round draws but high quality quarters and semis. I'd progressed so quickly, in spite of several self-inflicted muck ups. In Sailor's plan I was not due to break into the top fifty till the end of the year. Maybe I'd been lucky. Maybe it was the AllSports deal. The intensity of the training must have had something to do with it, especially since I'd been so pissed off with Zoë.

Just for the fun of it, I called my mother. "Hello Mum, it's me."

A grunt from the phone.

"I wanted to tell you how I'm doing."

"If you must. I don't have long."

"Well, I've made it into the world's top fifty. Think of it. I played four tournaments in Canada last month and did really well. I won one of them. In Calgary. It's the second open tournament I've won."

"I lost count of how many tennis tournaments you won."

"Oh come on, Mum. That was just juniors. I'm ranked forty eighth in the world, how about that, forty eight in the professional squash rankings."

"Bully for you. There's no money in it, is there?"

"That's not true. I've won nearly twelve thousand dollars this year, and that's after paying the PSA levy. I've got really good sponsorship, all my travel paid."

"You'd get twice that as a first round loser at Wimbledon. You're not going to convince me that there's any significance to this, Jolyon. I'm still expecting you to come to your senses sometime. I don't know when but it's bound to happen sooner or later. Sooner would be better."

"Thanks, Mum; all the encouragement."

"Don't get sarcastic with me. I've made it perfectly clear what I think about your... your folly. You'll regret it soon enough, believe you me. You'll come to your senses. Just don't come running when it all falls apart. You'll have to get yourself an education eventually. And you'll have to do it all by your foolish self."

"Well I'm on the squash track at the moment, and doing all right. But I think I'm boring you with the *foolish* details."

"Too right, Jolyon. Now I have to go. Good bye."

Bang. Ooh I enjoyed that one. I could picture the phone wincing at its abrupt return to the charger. I hadn't listened to a new rant for ages, now the 'your folly' rant. I made up my mind to call her again when I got into the top twenty. Then when I made the top ten. My money was on repeat performances, 'you'll come to your senses... just don't come running...' Knowing my mother it would be verbatim.

My Carmenless Gran Canaria trip didn't go as well as I'd hoped. I beat one of the three-to-four seeds to reach the semis, but was taken apart by the top seed, a good Spanish player called Leandro Ramós. The entry Leandro earned in my smart new folder was, 'Left handed/unbelievable forehand/next time hit it more the other side!' I'd not played many left handers. On the flight back I determined to take it up with Sailor, and Zoë.

Zoë was late for training on my first day back, unheard of. Someone saw her arrive in a BMW X5, they said, which then sped away. Maybe sponsor business. Anyway, she had some positive thoughts about the Leandro problem when a group of us were sitting down at the canteen for lunch a couple of days later. "They can be strong at the front left, lefties. You shouldn't worry about their power otherwise, especially you since you're left handed. I'd maybe give them less at the front forehand. It's always an idea to give less pace on that side too. Upset their timing. But you don't do less pace, do you? The other thing is, lefties are sometimes less strong on their backhands, you can explore that."

Carmen had other ideas. "Is just, all Spanish players are too good, no?"

"Only you, Carmen," Riley said.

Carmen pouted. She hadn't been thrilled either by Riley's familiarity with Zoë.

The World Junior Championships were a big fixture for me in the middle of the year. I'd wanted to enter the previous year. They'd been held in Dubai and I'd not been able to afford the trip. This time they were in Cairo, and AllSports were very keen for me to enter. Suresh explained in one of his regular phone calls that it would be great publicity for AllSports to have a World Junior Champion. They were introducing a new range of kit that they wanted me to wear, and new racquets. The racquets, the Stinger range, he explained, were physically the same as the ones I'd been using. The difference was in the artwork. They were covered in lurid black and yellow stripes, resembling hornets. "You get it? The Stinger?"

I got it. I couldn't care less how the racquets looked. As long as I had several that behaved in the same way I was happy. If you broke a string during a game, the replacement racquet had to feel identical, same weight, same balance, same string tension. Happiness was being provided with them free.

The World Juniors was a big tournament. Like the British Junior Open there were no ranking points at stake. There would though be strong opposition, and Sailor wanted me to blitz it. "It's the *manner* ye do it. The word gets round. It's another chance to put the fear of God into the journeymen ye'll meet in the smaller international tournaments. We want them beat before they go on court."

So off to Cairo it was, sadly not with Sailor but with plenty of support from Squash England, who had sent out a manager, Brendon Robinson, the equivalent in the South West of Dick Bentley, and a physio, Graham Hayes, who I'd seen at several junior tournaments. Luckily, I hadn't needed Graham's services so far in my career, if you could call it a career, beyond the advice he gave on warm ups before, and stretching after, matches. He was a man who you listened to, and Sailor had good words for him.

The England party, the two adults plus six of us in the boys' draw and two in the girls, was staying in a hotel in the middle of Cairo. It was hot and noisy, with traffic that was almost as crazy as Mumbai's. The facilities were excellent though, in two air conditioned centres with high quality courts. Suresh was around everywhere, brilliant smile, open neck shirt, immaculate suit, talking now to players, now to officials and now to managers. He checked that I'd tapered my training properly back home. Had the travel been all right? The hotel comfortable? Was there anything I needed? Did I know about my first round opponent?

The answer to the last one was yes. I was seeded one and playing Ross Fitch in the first round, my opponent from my first Junior Open back in Sheffield. Ross greeted me with a smile. "Time for payback for the room, mate. Ross to win three love. Shock exit for first seed."

"Nah, you only let me have the second bed, the small one. Otherwise..." I shrugged and smiled.

As I hoped, it was me who won three love. It was a hard game. Ross wouldn't give up, scampering every which way with his long legs, mainly behind me as I applied the pressure. Sailor's pressure, I thought. Anyway, the game didn't take much out of me. Nor did the thirty twos, nor the sixteens, nor the quarters. Sailor had insisted I call him before each game. Who was I playing? A New Zealander, an Egyptian, an Aussie. What was the plan? That was easy. 'Blitz him.' Make sure you eat at the right time. Yes, Sailor (I was). It may be hot out there but don't forget to warm down properly. Yes, Sailor (I was). Are ye behaving yerself? Yes, Sailor (I wasn't).

My behaviour problem centred on the junior English number two girl, Nikki Maltin. I'd noticed Nikki at several tournaments back in the UK. Any bloke less than a hundred years old with at least one functioning eye would have noticed Nikki. She was blonde and blue eyed and lovely, not in the subtle way that Zoë was lovely; Zoë's looks took a moment to make their impact, and were all the stronger for that. Nikki was in your face gorgeous, an absolute fox.

"Would you like a hit with me?" she asked, after Brendon had assembled the English group in our hotel the day before the tournament. We were planning the transport and the practice times.

"Sure," I answered casually. "As long as practice means practising hard, not rehearsing rubbish." What a dick.

Nikki met my gaze. "They said you were like that. Rubbish it won't be."

Rubbish it wasn't. At first I made a fool of myself because I was watching Nikki more than the ball. You would, given the choice, a small bit of hollow spherical rubber, black with two yellow spots, and a perfectly sized eighteen year old girl, white with two... Well, Nikki *was* distracting. She wasn't as lean as Zoë, which may not have helped her squash, but her less-than-lean bits were sensational. She hit the ball very hard for a girl and had been well drilled, so her shots tended to be tight. We got a good feel for the courts during our hit, and as a group we did a brief session of ghosting afterwards, perfect preparation for the next day. Back at the hotel, where we had a chance to relax together, I asked Nikki why she wasn't the number one English junior.

"That's simple. I'm not as mobile as Rita. I've lost to her three times this season. She gets so much back."

"Well I'm glad I practised with you rather than her," I said lamely. "You hit the ball so well."

She looked very directly at me. "Oh, there's lots of things I'm better at than Rita."

"On court or off court?"

"I've never tried on court. Have you?"

My brain exploded. This was going in a wholly unexpected direction. In my tediously focussed little world I sometimes mixed my priorities up. Manchester was great for the second priority, squash: winning matches, becoming world champion, that sort of thing. But Manchester had been a desert for social relations. All of a sudden I seemed to be in sight of a surprise oasis.

"No, and not behind the Pyramids either," I said, "which if I'm catching your drift might be our only opportunity." We were going on a sightseeing trip to the Pyramids later in the week. Opportunities for social relations in the hotel would be negligible because we were all in shared rooms. Nikki and Rita had been put together as the only two girls. I was with Art Ballingall, a rangy junior from Devon, whom I didn't know too well.

"It's okay," Nikki said. "Art and Rita and me, we go way back. Art and Rita want to spend some time together. I said to them, sigh, big sacrifice, I'd see what I could do. Then eeny, meeny, miny, mo, and you're mo, it turned out to be you." She smiled. "No, only joking. And I saw you looking at me on court. Don't tell me you wouldn't."

"Well Ms Maltin, seeing as it's helping out your friends."

That was how I found myself alone with Nikki in her room, after some chicanery with Brendon to make sure he didn't realise what we were up to. Nikki and Rita had gone up first, and when I slipped into the girlie bedroom, it was no surprise that Nikki was by herself. What did come as a surprise was that she was wearing one of her short squash dresses.

"Now you can take a proper look," she said primly.

I duly did as she spun round a few times, arms above her head. Then she went over to the television in a slinky walk and bent over in an exaggerated way to pick up the remote. What a jolt. She wasn't wearing any knickers. No bra either, I soon discovered, although it was a while before she removed the dress. "Not until you've got your own kit off." As I dropped my tee shirt on the floor she came right up close, circled her arms round my neck and pressed herself against me. "And then maybe, if you're lucky. Or I might just leave it on." Big blue eyes just inches from mine. "Do you think you're going to be lucky tonight, Jolyon?"

Boxers were said to avoid sex for at least a month before bouts. I hoped that twelve hours would be enough for squash players. The morning end of the Brendon avoidance plan was for Rita and me to return to our rooms at seven prompt, and we passed each other as I left the girls' room, with Rita giving me a complicitous grin. My game was at one o'clock, and Nikki had till four for hers. She hadn't displayed any of her claimed lack of mobility, or flexibility, the night before, and she had booted me out into the other single bed so we got a proper sleep, right up to the alarm at ten to seven. No time for further sex, although I was tempted as I watched Nikki walk naked round the end of my bed to pick up her discarded dress.

Finagling the sleeping arrangements became routine for the four of us through the week of the tournament. The night before my final was slightly complicated by Suresh, who invited me out for a meal. Nikki and I were too randy to be fazed, and when Suresh picked me up I already had a spare key to the girls' room in my pocket. Nikki's parting words to me were, "For fuck's sake skip the dessert."

Suresh took me to a swanky French restaurant in the middle of Cairo. "Don't worry, Jolyon, I won't keep you late. I know you'll be wanting your rest before the final." Strange words in view of what he had to say at the end of the meal. My opponent was another of his protégés, my friend from my Indian trip, Neeraj Solkar. To the huge disappointment of the local crowds, Neeraj had unexpectedly beaten good Egyptian opponents in both the quarters and semis. I was looking forward to playing him, and completely confident of a win.

"Neeraj has been really catching up over the last six months," Suresh said. "At last he's been able to train properly."

"We should have a good game, but I reckon I'll be too strong."

Suresh looked at me intently. "I'm not so sure. He's a talented player, and when you ally that with some real fitness, he's been training like a fanatic, no one would be surprised if you lost."

He dismissed the thought with a wave of his hand. "That's by the by. What I want to talk to you about this evening is your relationship with AllSports. My fellow directors have been very pleased with you. They love your enthusiasm. They love your style. It's a perfect match for our marketing boys. The trip in February was a huge success. We recorded a fifteen percent boost in sales in the month after the exhibitions. The television audience had doubled for the last TV show. We had a lot of enquiries from distributors. It's all positive.

"So what we want to propose, we're taking a chance here, we want you to sign with us for the next three years, to commit yourself, to become the face of squash for AllSports."

"What does that mean?"

"Oh, don't worry. The number one priority will still be your squash, progressing your career. We want you to make number one just as much as you do. Any success for you will be success for us. The kids are going mad over here for squash, and I'm not even thinking yet about the USA. We want you brash. We're developing the kit to reflect that. We want you hip hop. We want you Bollywood. This is the time for our big push. Nike, Head, Dunlop, we're going to take market share from all of them, plunder it. Our equipment is good, up there with anyone's, that's not the question. It's going to be our image. We're targetting the youth demographic. You're in the middle of that. You are brash. We're brash. You are flash. We're flash. You sting. We sting."

He hissed the word 'sting' at me. "I can see that, Suresh, but I don't see what it means for me. Me personally."

"For you, Jolyon, not too much in the sense of changing what you're doing. You're life is too bound with training and tournaments and winning and ranking points, and let's not forget, rest at the right times. We've factored in the trips to India. We won't add to them. We can take advantage of more PSA opportunities in India. Within the next two years there'll be two World Series tournaments in India, two minimum. You're going to be in the country anyway. Perfect opportunities for AllSports with no extra wear and tear on you. It all fits."

"It sounds fantastic." It did sound fantastic. Enough money to pay my way day to day, and the all important travel support.

Suresh's eyes gleamed and his teeth flashed. "Wait till you hear what we're proposing for you. We want you to be out there in front of our customers, our market, all the time, even when you're not in tournaments. Your wardrobe will be important, whirlwind on court, whirlwind in the fashions. So we'll triple your regular financial support. You have to look good. We want the boys to want to look like you." Here he laughed. "We want the girls to want you! And a little intrusive, but we think you'll like it, we want to be with you as you travel to tournaments, 'Jolyon en route to the Hong Kong Open, Jolyon arrives in Singapore, Jolyon heads for the Tournament of Champions, Big Apple here we come'. So we're going to have you travelling business. I told you it would be brash. We must work on your Facebook profile, and I want you to start a blog."

I tried to hide my gulp. I'd walked through business cabins on a couple of my transatlantic flights and it was a world apart.

"But listen to me, Jolyon." Suresh dropped his voice. "The bedrock, the very bedrock, is your squash. If you don't feel comfortable, if Sailor doesn't like it, then we don't do it, simple as that. You have to get to number one. We know you don't get to number one by showboating. A full length bed in an A380 across the North Pole is no use if you lose to a hungry opponent in the semis at the other end."

I thought for a moment about my mother, and then of Grandpa. "Don't worry on that score, Suresh. I want to do well. I *have* to do well."

"Good. I've already told my board that. We know we're investing well."

"How many other players are you supporting?"

"In a major way, it's just three. You won't have heard yet but we're on the verge of signing Razza Mattaz. Keep this under your hat. Razza as you know will be the next number one, liquid class. Too good an opportunity for us to miss. He's the one you're going to have to displace, Jolyon. Grace and guile, what a combination. Another wonderful personality, too. Just what we need in the USA. The potential in that country is enormous. They have some radical thinkers in squash. They're developing the game. We want a piece of that. Must have. AllSports is a natural in the US. There Razza will be the catalyst for us. Then there's Neeraj. You know Neeraj is with us. Neeraj is gold dust for us. An Indian and good enough to be top ten material, maybe even better. Neeraj is well connected. That matters in the Indian market. His father is a senior judge, wealthy. Like you Neeraj is good looking. That matters anywhere, London, Lucknow, LA, photogenic, charismatic. If he reaches his potential he will be the Tendulkar of Indian squash. Or maybe the Virat Kohli, the swashbuckler. There won't be a day when Neeraj won't be in the news."

It seemed like a fantasy, as I listened to all of this. This was a passport to the fast lane, to my achieving what I wanted, maybe the difference between success and failure in my dream, my world championship dream. I had already seen what a difference the support from AllSports was making. Winning or losing vital matches often hinged on the odd point. One percent more speed might be all it took at ten nine game ball when you were at your physical limits, and one percent more speed could easily come from perfect preparation.

"So you see, Jolyon," Suresh said as he paid the bill. "Yourself, Razza and Neeraj, what a trio. And just a word about Neeraj." He dropped his voice again and leant towards me. "In terms of worldwide exposure, right now Neeraj is behind Mattaz and yourself. This knee problem held him back. He needs a high profile performance to fix his place on the map, to confirm he is at the top table. It would make a huge difference if he were to win the World Juniors. Do you understand what I'm saying?"

I frowned. "I can see it would be big publicity if he beat me tomorrow. That's not going to happen. I could imagine losing to him down the line. When he's fitter. Right now for all his shots he's going to get tired. You know that."

Suresh's smile had gone. "You don't understand me. There aren't any ranking points at stake. This doesn't make any difference to you. Not in the grand scheme of things. This won't hold you back. My board will take a very favourable view of a Neeraj win. It fits with our Q-three Q-four promotions, that's your autumn into winter, In addition to that," here he leaned right forward, with his eyes only inches from mine, "there are some powerful influences in India that are expecting a Neeraj victory.

"I'm depending on you, Jolyon. You understand? It makes sense. You need our support. I know you won't let me down."

Uunghhh! I did understand, of course. If it's too good to be true it probably isn't true. Who had said that? I was being asked to throw a match, in exchange for an unbelievable support package, a pot of gold. The AllSports deal would last well beyond my twenty first birthday. It would make a significant difference in my achieving my goal.

"All right, Suresh," I mumbled, "let me think about it."

"Good man," he replied. "You had to see sense."

We were silent in the taxi back to the hotel, where I thanked Suresh for the meal, why ever did I do that, and headed for the lobby. I didn't go directly to Nikki in the girls' bedroom, which had been our arrangement. I wanted time to think, so I slumped in a chair in the lobby. I tried to call Sailor, but got his voicemail. I knew what he'd say anyway. I wanted to speak to Zoë. She'd understand the pressures. She knew from her own experience what a difference the AllSports deal would be making. Now it would be even better, business class, what an idea. To me the AllSports difference might be fundamental, success or failure in Grandpa's challenge. I pictured my mother's gloat if I didn't make it. 'What did I say? I've been telling my friends all along. Of course you'd never do it. Hair brained, I knew that from the start. The bridge group, they've been surprisingly sympathetic...' Could I take the chance of facing *that*? No way.

Unfortunately Zoë's phone went straight through to voicemail too. Oh well, it had to be Nikki. I'd enjoyed the time with her over the previous few evenings, not just the sex. Nikki was grounded, realistic about what she could achieve at squash, keen to do well but keen to have fun, to enjoy the experience, and I really had to talk to someone. In a few moments she was letting me into the room, in a short, pink cotton nightie.

"You're later than I expected. Good meal?"

"Sorry, the meal was fine. It's just, well, some issues."

Her frown was almost comic. "What do you mean, some issues? We haven't been found out, have we?"

"No, it's okay, nothing like that. I'm sure you'd have heard from Brendon. No, it's to do with AllSports."

I kicked off my All Stars and lay down on the bed with my hands behind my head. "They want to involve me much more." I told Nikki about Suresh's proposal.

"That's sensational," she said, sitting down on the bed and leaning over me. "You'll be made with all of that. Can I come in your hand luggage?"

"That wasn't the end of it." To an incredulous Nikki I finished the story of the meal.

"You mean they want you to throw the final?"

"Yup. Apparently it's important for AllSports that Neeraj's image gets a boost. I'd love to talk to Tafiq."

"The one he beat in the semi?"

"Yes. I wonder if AllSports got at him. It didn't look like it. Neeraj played well. It does make you wonder, though. I got the impression from Suresh that there's betting. It goes on in cricket big time. Betting is illegal in India, but that's where most of it goes on, serious money. I had the feeling this evening that Suresh is under pressure."

"So what are you going to do?"

"I don't know."

"Are you sure the AllSports thing depends on you losing?"

"Suresh didn't say that in so many words, but he made it pretty clear. They know Neeraj can't win if I play properly."

Nikki bent down and kissed me on the lips. "Sleep on it."

"So you want me to go to sleep?"

"No, you need a cuddle."

"Just a cuddle?"

"Up to you," she said as she pulled her nightie over her head in a single, sensuous movement.

Squash On The Web

Jacks Triumphs In Cairo

In Cairo this evening Englishman Jolyon Jacks trounced Neeraj Solkar from Mumbai to add the World Under Nineteen Junior Championship to his rapidly expanding portfolio of titles. This was not so much a victory as a demolition. The score of 11-4, 11-0, 11-2 reflects the one sided nature of the contest, which lasted only twenty five minutes. Solkar had done well to make the final. In the quarters he beat the second seed, home town favourite Omar Abdel Sulieman, in five punishing games, and he had a long semi final against Tafiq el-Barak, in which he eventually triumphed 9-11, 11-8, 12-10, 13-11. Nevertheless, a lot of smart money had been on Solkar, who has improved rapidly following his return to full time training nine months ago.

In the event, Jacks dominated from the opening point, ruthlessly confining Solkar to the back corners. The Indian had no chance to unleash the array of attacking shots that had accounted for his powerful Egyptian opponents. "Neeraj has been unplayable when he gets in front," Jacks said afterwards. "I saw both his games, against Omar and then Tafiq. I knew I had to keep him deep. I think he was probably tired, too. I had the easier semi final."

As far as I was concerned Neeraj wouldn't have got more than a handful of points even if he'd been properly rested in a king sized bed with satin sheets. I'd realised, lying awake during the night after Nikki had booted me out, that if I went along with the AllSports plan I'd be in their power for as long as I was in squash, my entire career. There'd never be a way out. Business class seat and first class hotel in Sydney? Yes. Never mind the surprise loss in the quarters. The British Open in Manchester and the big dollar bonus? Yes, but again an upset loss. I couldn't do it. I wanted to give Suresh, and more to the point the figures behind him, a message. The corruption side was awful, but even more, it was the knowledge that I would be controlled. I didn't want some faceless Indian businessman or bookmaker or anyone pulling my strings. I'd made too many sacrifices getting away from my mother. And I didn't want to lose squash matches without being properly beaten. Winning was hard enough. I wasn't going to sacrifice even an occasional victory. The timetable for my world championship dream was too tight, anyway.

It was obvious there was no chance that Suresh's fabulous promises would be realised if I beat Neeraj. Worse, I guessed that my established AllSports sponsorship would come to an end. Nevertheless, I was determined to play all out. Before I came off court I noticed Suresh hurrying away from his front row seat. Out of character. Suresh was always around after a match to congratulate, with his flashing smile, or commiserate with an arm round your shoulder.

Later that evening Art and I found out why Suresh had left the court so quickly. We were due to leave early the next morning for the airport, and had decided to forego the bedroom exchange for the last night. I'd never have admitted it to anyone but between them, seven rounds of squash, each match lasting up to forty five minutes, and six nights of Nikki had worn me out. Sleep had become the number one priority. Art was of the same mind. He and I headed straight for the lift when we reached the hotel, and he was first down the corridor to our room. I lagged, slowed by my squash bag and my big glass trophy. When Art opened the door to our room he uttered an awed 'f-u-c-k-i-n-g heck'.

Chapter Twenty Six

Fucking heck it was. The first thing you noticed was the smell. Paint. Then Art turned on the main light. His side of the room was normal, a mess, but it was Art's mess. My side of the room was a mess too, but in a different league. My side had been trashed. I'd left five of my eight swanky new-style AllSports racquets in the room. They were on the floor, no longer in their lurid black and yellow covers, each one snapped neatly across the shaft. My spare kit, my spare pair of AllStars, my clothes, my toiletries, the soft bag I used as a suitcase, all of them had been piled beside the racquets and smothered with red paint. The paint had been over-budgeted, five litres. The remainder lay in a pool on the duvet on my bed, with the empty tin dumped on my pillow.

It was a powerful message.

It took half the night to sort things out. First we contacted Brendon, then security, then the hotel manager. Then it was the police and finally after all the questioning, the move into our new room for all that was left of the night. I had said, truthfully, that I didn't know who had done it. I had had a disagreement with my sponsor, nothing else. Brendon had looked sceptical and so had the policeman who interviewed me. He was going to track Suresh down for an interview, he said. Fat lot of good that would do. Suresh was too smart.

The scariest thing only emerged afterwards. At my next tournament I heard that Suresh had disappeared. In the squash world at least he was never heard of again. I spoke to someone from AllSports India, who said he had resigned suddenly. It left me hugely relieved that I hadn't gone along with the plan to lose to Neeraj. Nothing emerged from the investigation. The Cairo police apparently came to a dead end. A couple of weeks after we returned to England I was contacted by the Egyptian embassy. They told me on the phone that the case had been closed. They were sorry I had been inconvenienced. A Dutchman took over as AllSports' European representative. He pointedly ignored me whenever our paths crossed.

So I was left with my iPhone, which fortunately had been with me in the club, about half my minimalist collection of clothes, three black and yellow striped racquets, a couple of pairs of squash shorts and the real choker, zero sponsorship. Financially, I was on my own again, this time with a credit card bill to pay off.

"Will ye listen to me next time?" Sailor wiped his hand wearily over his face as I talked him through what had happened in Cairo. We were sitting down together over a cup of tea at home after Mary had gone to bed. "It was always too flash. Ridiculous, this AllSports India."

"That's easy to say now. It worked out pretty well for me for a year, a bit more, didn't it? And it's got me inside the top fifty."

"Ay but this is where you have to be pushing on. An' that means winning. An' that means being there in the first place, where the tournaments are. How are you going to get there?"

"Well once I'm winning, I know it's never much, there is the prize money."

"Ye can't win prize money in Nottingham and Freiburg and Rotterdam sitting on yer backside in Manchester. You have to be there. How much have you got left?"

This was embarrassing. "Nothing, actually. I'm skint. I was expecting my monthly transfer from AllSports tomorrow. It might still come through."

"No, don't hold yer breath for that, son. These people don't do charity, and they're sharp. They won't overlook something like that. Not after ye beat their boy. I'm hearing rumours. There's been a lot of betting interest in India on squash. They've moved into it after all that publicity in the cricket. It's said that PSA results have been manipulated. No' hard to do. It's all down to money, and some of the players are desperate," he grimaced, "like you."

"Hey, that's not fair. You've seen what I did in Cairo. I'm not into losing squash matches on demand. It was a big offer, too."

"That's all right, son. I'd never have taken you on if I saw that in you. Good win over Solkar, by the way. I've seen the lad play. What was it? Six points? People will hear, people will listen. Thirty three six against Neeraj Solkar. An' that's not just the shady folk in Delhi and Bangalore and Mumbai. That's squash folk. It's a good message.

"Now listen. Mary's become very fond of you since you've been here, can't see why. We were talking about Cairo after your news came through about AllSports. I don't go along with this but Mary wants to tide you over, so you can get to tournaments, pay us for that matter. She agrees soon ye'll be making enough from winning tournaments.

"What do you think of that?"

"What can I say? Mary's an angel. And it's true I can't win prize money if I'm not in the tournaments. Chicken and egg. I won't need long, though. I'm feeling good."

"You tell Mary that, son. If I had my way you'd be back to Fallowfield Pools."

I spoke to Mary at breakfast the next morning. Sailor had left early for a meeting in Manchester. "It's strange," Mary said. "I've never really engaged with Sailor's world before. Not personally. We're chalk and cheese him and me, different interests, very different lives. It's just, we've always clicked. So his players have mostly been only names to me. I've always wanted him to do well. His passion, squash. I just let him get on with it; I've not been interested. I didn't see much of Zoë Quantock when she was coming up through the ranks, the rankings. Until you came along she was Sailor's pinnacle. She made Sailor; she gave him confidence. You'll be better in a way, if you make it to the top. You'll show that Zoë wasn't a fluke. It's been lovely having you here. I've seen how hard you're trying. Then this setback. AllSports, it must be a huge disappointment. It sounds like a good thing you're out of it, but it leaves you in a mess, doesn't it?

"So for three months I'm going give you what you need to get to tournaments. You'll pay me back, plus the interest." I scratched my head. "Don't worry. I'll work it out, Bank of England minimum lending rate. That's a bargain by the way. If you do half as well as Sailor says, paying me back won't be a problem.

"It will be so exciting if you make it," she said. "It'll put Sailor on top of the world. You too," she smiled warmly, "of course."

There wasn't much time to thank her before she headed off for work. Mary's money would be a lifeline, but it racked up the pressure another notch. Someone else not to disappoint. I vowed to take the campaign in the coming European tournaments extremely seriously, the preparation, the concentration, the recuperation. It was to be the full effort, all the ingredients, nothing left to chance.

Chapter Twenty Seven

I had Mary's generosity in mind on the way to Rotterdam for the Blooming Autumn Championships, if I'd got the gist of their flowery Dutch name. It was a PSA International 25 tournament, plenty of blooming euros, anyway, worth doing well in. After winning a hard quarter final I was stretching out in the changing rooms at the excellent venue, the Victoria Squash Club. I was unaware how well I was about to be served by my, or should that be Sailor's, zero tolerance to recreational substances. I looked up to see a heavyset dude walking directly towards me. He greeted me by name and said that he was from the Dutch national anti-doping agency: I'd been randomly selected to provide a urine sample.

Wow, me being dope tested!

The dude showed some identification, Pieter Wittens it said on his Netherlands Antidoping Agency badge. I remember wondering where the errant 'i' had crept in. Anyway, I was clean. Bring it on, Pieter.

It was a novelty to witness the well organised, highly detailed sample process. My passport provided the necessary photographic identification. I declined the opportunity to have a representative with me throughout, but accepted the offer of a free cola. I had as always been careful to take in plenty of glucose electrolyte drink during my match, so I wasn't dehydrated, but I might as well get something out of this. The manager at the club, Caes Edelman, had been appointed as the 'Urine Collection Witness'. Lucky Caes. Caes was looking apologetic.

We followed the procedure laid down by Mr Wittens. The three of us had the washroom to ourselves while I peed into the sample container. It was Caes' job to look on. Mr Wittens was busying himself with the paperwork. I'd had to remove my tracksuit top before providing the sample so that nothing was covering my lower arms. Mr Wittens explained that it had not been unknown for athletes to use a reservoir of innocent urine taped under the arm and connected to a tube that served as a secret parallel willy. He didn't say parallel willy, he just said penis. With his accent it came out explosively as 'benis'.

When that was done we sat down at a table in the large lobby. I was surprised to be given the choice of so called sample collection kits. They all looked the same. When I'd made my choice, Mr Wittens opened the sealed package and took out two bottles the size of small jam jars. These were the 'A' and 'B' containers you sometimes hear about in big name drug cases. In Mr Wittens' correct but Dutch-sounding English the 'B' container sounded like the 'P' container. How apt. He filled each container with some of my sample. Still according to the procedure, I was the person who had to seal the bottles. Mr Wittens then completed the Doping Control Form, pages and pages of it. Was I taking any prescription drugs? No. Did I want any concerns about the procedure recorded? No. Was the sample code number correct? Yes. And so on and so on. Eventually the form was complete, the three of us signed it, Mr

Wittens gave me a copy, we all shook hands and off he went. There had apparently been a couple of earlier victims. I was the last.

Mr Wittens' parting words were, "Put that copy somewhere safe."

'Whatever,' I thought.

The dope test was a sort of highlight for me in Rotterdam. I was disappointed to lose in the semis. Two weeks later though I had another chance in an International 25 semi. This time the tournament was on home territory, Nottingham, and it was something big for me, not because I expected to win, which this time I did, but because Grandpa was going to be there: my father was bringing him. I'd been longing for a chance to show Grandpa what I could do. The time with Sailor had changed me so much. I was sure Grandpa would be impressed. After the collapse of my AllSports India deal he'd said in one of our regular telephone chats, "You didn't expect this to be plain sailing, did you? It's just one more thing to overcome." I wanted to show him that I was really capable of overcoming.

My opponent for the semi was another English player, Mark Goodrich, the world number forty. I'd be disappointed if I lost a game to Mark. It should be plain sailing in Grandpa's terms. However, I was about to encounter the least plain of all the sailings, Storm Force Twelve.

Mark and I were due on at five o'clock. My dad and Grandpa had arrived at lunchtime, while I was showering after my practice hit on the show court. We'd lingered over lunch in the large upstairs bar area overlooking the Park Estate. Grandpa was in fine form. "You've no idea how much I've been looking forward to this. I've never seen proper squash before."

My father laughed. "Huh, you saw me play once. That Jesters match."

"No, I mean proper proper."

Sailor perked up. "Jesters *is* proper. I belong to the Jesters Club. Right attitude."

"Well, I'll save 'proper' for when I'm in the top twenty," I said.

"If," said my father, "not when. It's what they drum into us in the Navy. Always anticipate the unexpected."

"I know," I said. "But I'm more confident than I was a year ago. I've been getting good results. I'm number thirty two. In the world, think of it, Grandpa. I'm feeling so strong. And I can see where I can improve. Honestly. I've had a run of tournaments in the last two months so I haven't been able to do any proper training for a while. I know I can improve the fitness side, and the speed."

Sailor and my father had been chatting in lowered voices, excluding the other two of us. "That you can, son," he said. "Right now it's time for your pre-match. I'll look after these gentlemen."

Ninety minutes later I'd completed my warm up and visualised my way through successfully countering Mark's strengths and exploiting his weaknesses. I sought out Grandpa and my father in the gallery behind the show court. Sailor was with them.

"All set, Jolyon?" Grandpa asked.

"I think so." I was feeling more nervous than usual, with two people there I so wanted to impress.

"Good. Sailor's expecting you to win. We've taken a chance and booked into a hotel. We're going to stay for the final."

"Excuse me," Sailor said. He pulled his phone out of his pocket, looked at the screen, got up and moved away to the gallery above the adjacent courts. Something about his body language intruded as I carried on chatting. I looked across just as he snapped his phone shut and set off towards us. His face was like thunder.

"Come here, son, now!"

He hurried away and down the stairs. I followed at a run. He didn't stop till he'd gone through the lobby and out of the club.

"What is it?"

"You eejit." His eyes blazed at me. "You complete fucking dead-in-the-head eejit. Ye've tested positive for cannabis. Rotterdam."

What? Rotterdam? No way!

"That's it for me. You're done. Yer history, son. I'm finished wi' you. I cannot effing believe it. How could you be so stupid? I've staked my reputation on you. I've put myself on the line. I've supported you. I've apologised for you. I've had you living in my home. I've all but changed yer nappies. I've made you something. Now this. It's almost three years I've invested in you. Gone. Wasted."

Sailor's eyes were beyond flint. "Well? What ha' ye got to say fer yersel'?" His voice was getting louder and his accent stronger.

"I dunno, Sailor. I just don't know. It's not true, that's all."

"Don't make me puke, son, that's what they all say." Spittle was gathering at the corners of his mouth. He was on a roll and all I could do was stand there.

"Marion Jones?" 'Maahrion Joorns.' Louder still. "The smiling Miss Jones? Innocent? Floyd Landis? Innocent? Ben Johnson?

"'It wasn't me!' They all said that. 'Someone spiked my food!' 'It was in a supplement!' Flo-Jo fuckin' Joyner?" He looked around. "I'm sorry but I've heard all the stories. They're all bullshit. Yer finished, son. It's a two year ban, minimum. Does nae matter how long. Two months. Two years. I don't care. I'm having no more to do wi' you.

"Yer tainted. Tainted."

"Hold on, Sailor. What about my B sample? I can have that tested. We don't know if that'll be positive."

"Do me a favour." He wiped his sleeve across his mouth. "Just get out o' my life."

As he turned to go back inside my father came out of the club entrance. "What is it? Has something happened?"

Sailor didn't stop. As he passed my father, he jerked his thumb at me and said, "Ask him."

"What is it, Jolyon?"

"It's, well, it's…" I couldn't bring myself to say it.

"Come on. It can't be that bad."

"It is. I've tested positive for cannabis. I've no idea how."

"Oh God. You fool."

"But it's not true."

"Your mother was right. She said this would never last, committing yourself to squash. Your going up the rankings. Her exact words, I remember them when she first told me, 'He doesn't have it in him'. I said, for heaven's sake, cut him a bit of slack. He's done okay.

"She was right. I'm sorry to have to admit it, I was wrong. You've made a fool of yourself, now, and of all of us. A complete arse. I suppose this means you can't play any more?"

I welled up. I was so disappointed. And so angry.

"This won't help. Pull yourself together. You'll still be able to play today but you'll have to get a grip of yourself. There'll be some sort of a hearing, I'm not familiar with the process. That'll be in due course. But right now I don't care. I'm going to take your grandfather home. We're not going to watch you after this."

He turned and went back inside. I wandered down the wooden steps from the entrance balcony, past a couple of rows of cars in the narrow car park at the front and sat against the wall.

What could have gone wrong? Could my sample have got mixed up with someone else's? It didn't seem likely. Maybe my B sample would be clear? Fat chance. I thought back. Cannabis. I could do with a joint right now. But I'd been saying no ever since that conversation with Dave, on the bus, what, three, four years ago. I'd had opportunity, small time dealers, plenty of offers, spliffs and the like. It just hadn't been worth it, wasn't worth it, too much at stake. Had someone found a way to spike my sample? No, I couldn't see it, and anyway, why? I was a minnow in squash terms. So where and how could the drug have got into my system?

Then it dawned on me with an awful certainty. It was obvious. It just hadn't occurred to me until that moment, never crossed my mind. The free party in Manchester, and, I smiled to myself for a moment in spite of everything, its aftermath.

Before Rotterdam the series of European tournaments facing me was intense. I was determined to have at least a little relaxation, my world was so narrow. There was the EIS, the track running, the weights sessions, drills, stretches, practice games. 'Take care to warm down.' Yes, Sailor. 'Mind you rehydrate properly.' Yes, Sailor. 'Mind you eat properly.' Three bags full, Sailor. Beyond that? Just my little bedroom, falling into bed exhausted every night, too tired even for a wank, then up with the alarm for the Faslane-punctual breakfast. The succession of tournaments was providing some diversion. Some. Ah look! A different changing room. See here! A different squash court.

Occasionally I had to break out.

The break out didn't have to be extreme. I'd resigned myself to staying off the weed and I'd lost the stomach for a bellyful of lager. But when an opportunity came up, a change of scene, a gig, an occasional party. You had to go for it.

And this one was a beauty, a comfortable two days before I departed for the tournament in Rotterdam. Dave had arranged for me to play a set at an event in an old school building destined for demolition not too far from the centre of Manchester. Dave had got into university there after an appeal and it hadn't taken him long to extend his music connections all round the city. I checked, the small hours of the night wouldn't be involved. My set was early, before the arrival of several heavyweight DJs, notably a dwarf from New York called The Small Blitz!z!z! I'd bought a whole lot of vinyl online just before AllSports pulled the plug, and I was well up for a mix through a proper sound system. The headphones in my bedroom were sterile.

To make matters better, this particular sticky cake turned out to have icing on it. Paula Bentley was there.

I spotted Paula from behind the turntables. She was dancing at the edge of the heaving mass of ravers in front of me. In the semi darkness and the smoke, fifty percent tobacco, fifty percent weed and fifty percent goodness knows what else it was that thick, I'd normally have done well to pick her out. But you couldn't miss Paula that night. She was in a vivid yellow tee shirt and a narrow strip of equally yellow skirt. Her friends in contrast you could hardly see. Paula was looking great, great spelt s-e-x-y.

I caught up with her after my set, as soon as I'd safely packed my vinyl away. She put her hand on my shoulder and shouted into my ear, "I wanted to say, fantastic set."

"What?"

"Fantastic set."

"Did you say you wanted fantastic sex?"

In the semi darkness, music pounding, smoke swirling, she put her head back and laughed. Then she made the sort of eye contact I'd have fantasised about back in my bedroom if I'd had the energy, and I could clearly read her mime. "No, I said I wanted to take you to bed."

"Unfinished business?"

Her lips were all over my ear. "Yes, and I hate to leave things unfinished."

"I'm not driving to Sheffield for the pleasure of getting interrupted again in your dad's kitchen."

"Oh yes, the kitchen? I like my dad's kitchen."

"I've been allergic to kitchens since. They bring me out in a rash."

"It's much nearer than that." She tugged at my arm. "Come on."

"Wait," I shouted. "I've got to get my vinyl."

I didn't waste long on goodbyes to Dave and the other organisers. "You going to get your beauty sleep?" Dave asked.

"Sort of," I shouted. "See you soon."

Paula quickly parted from her friends and seconds later we were outside. It was cool but not cold. She had slipped a long thin sober grey woollen garment, with buttons down the front, over her minimalist rave clothing. I had brought an AllSports-funded leather bomber jacket. We didn't stand out in the busy centre of the city. Manchester was alive with clubbers.

"I'm borrowing my friend's apartment," Paula said, grabbing my hand. "It's only ten minutes." If I'd had my way we'd have made it in five. A female hand in mine, the prospect that none of the rest of its owner would be off limits. I hoped no one was staring at my ooh-what-a-give-away crotch.

"My friend works for a bank here but she's on holiday. Her parents set her up in this place."

"Lucky her. What are you up to?"

"I'm back with my dad. I can't thank you enough for the Mick the Prick thing. What a prick. I'm still asking myself, how could I have fallen in with that? I guess he was the complete opposite of my dad. I was like seriously in a mess. It kind of jolted me, that night. I went home and told dad what had happened. I'd been so beastly. He's not so down on you now."

How much not so down, I wondered. "So are you going to uni?"

"No, I can't see the future in it, three years of handing over borrowed money to a place that doesn't give a toss. Then paying off the debt for the rest of your life. If you can get a job, that is. It doesn't add up. I'm starting a management training scheme with Marks and Sparks in Sheffield. And get paid to do it."

"What about squash?"

"I'm playing again. I'm out of the rankings now. Not sure about that. I may just stick to the club.

"How about an update on you?"

No time for that. We'd passed the typical town centre shops and arrived in front of a large brick building at least five stories high. "Here we are," Paula said. She fumbled in her tiny yellow bag, found some keys and let us in through a door with an intercom buzzer system, perhaps thirty buttons in all. Inside there was a spotless vinyl-floored lobby with a door marked 'Janitor' and two lifts. We snogged on the way up to the fifth floor, or rather I attempted to snog and Paula giggled, "Mind out, the CCTV."

"Oh yes, I know about CCTVs."

As she let us in to the flat I said, "No CC anything in here I hope."

"Not unless you'd like me to set something up. We could do it on my mobile?"

"Phew, next the Internet?"

We'd entered a smart carpeted hall with an open door through to the main living area. Two other doors led to a bathroom and a room that if I had been asked to assign rankings would have come in comfortably at one. The bedroom.

Paula closed the curtains and switched on a reading light over the double bed. "Now Jolyon sweetie, same conditions as before." She came over close to me and looked intensely up into my eyes. "This is for me as you know. That's the deal. I know that you're *quicker* than me, oh my all that *hard*," 'hard' said with great exaggeration, "*hard* conditioning Sailor makes you do. So we'll have to go at my speed, slow, slow."

True to her word she was ever so slowly unbuttoning her cardigan. "You can sit on the bed and watch me undress. Just so you're ready to put on one of these." She fiddled in her bag and tossed me a condom. "We'll have to make sure you're *hard* enough to get it on." Job done, I thought, about fifteen minutes ago outside the club. Knowing Paula as I did I stifled any argument, sat dutifully on the bed and prepared to watch. She eventually let the cardigan fall in a heap on the carpet and stood in front of me. "You choose," she said. "My shirt or my skirt?"

"Hmm, if I said skirt, would I get to choose again? I take it you're wearing some knickers?" I knew she was wearing knickers, yellow ones, from when she had bent down to slip her shoes on at the club. Her skirt was that short.

"Yes, just for the moment, you're in charge."

"You're not wearing a bra, are you?" Even the most needy of Specsavers customers would have worked that out.

"No."

"What, you didn't have a yellow one?"

"As a matter of fact, no."

"So if I said shirt you'd be naked apart from that shockingly skimpy skirt and a pair of yellow knickers?"

"How do you know they're yellow?"

"Just a guess. I know you have excellent colour sense."

"I don't believe you."

"What, your colour sense?"

"No, you've sneaked a preview of my knickers."

I smiled. "Aha, a preview implies a proper view to follow. I'd better make a decision pronto or I won't be able to get the condom on."

"Well?"

"Take your tee shirt off."

She crossed her arms, took hold of the hem of the tee shirt and pulled it over her head. Theatrically, she let it fall on top of the cardigan. Wow! She was a little rounder than I remembered, perhaps the absence of recent squash.

"Two down, two to go," I said.

"What about my wedges?"

"I forgot about those."

"With what I have in mind, they're staying on."

"What is it you have in mind?"

"You'll find out when we're both undressed."

"Okay, skirt off then."

Reaching behind for the zip of her skirt brought Paula's breasts into greater prominence in the oblique light from the reading lamp. In this case 'reading' didn't accurately capture what the lamp was doing for us: it wouldn't be illuminating any text that evening. Paula shimmied her hips, the skirt fell to her ankles and out she stepped. Her knickers were of the no VPL variety, lacy at the front. They weren't skimpy, I assumed since they were an essential back up to her skirt.

They were indeed a vivid yellow.

"I've never seen yellow knickers before," I said.

"Liar. If you don't admit you've seen *my* yellow knickers already I won't take them off."

"All right, it was only a glimpse, I promise. At the club. And let's face it, if you go out with a skirt that short, you have to expect that your knickers will be clocked."

"Well before they come off, you're going to have to do some catching up. Stand up."

She was staring at my crotch. "Ooh look, it obeys me too. I have the power."

"At your service, Miss. Me and my knob, that is."

"Good." She undid the button of my jeans, then slowly unzipped them. Her touch was electric. Finally she pulled them down.

"Your pants aren't doing a very good job." This was a fair observation. The waist of my pants was designed for 'S', but it was being stretched to 'XL'.

"I'd better take them off before they pop." This she duly did.

"Ah yes," she said. "I remember this." She looked up at me. "Oh my, has it grown? Jolyon's hard on, what fun. Where's that condom?"

She retrieved the little packet, extracted its slippery contents and worked it over my dick while I watched her breasts gently wobbling. "Good." She looked up. "You seem to be ready?"

"Just about, Miss. Now it's time for your knickers to come off. I'll do it."

I knelt down in front of her, hooked my fingers into the waistband and pulled off the third last item of her yellow attire, counting the wedges. The wedges elevated her by about three inches, bringing my face into close proximity to the curve of her half-in-shadow mound. She smelt sexy.

"Is it okay if I steal a kiss?" I asked.

"All right, if you must. It's not part of the plan, so just a quick one."

"In the nick?"

She giggled.

I reached round to her bum, pulled her towards me and planted a soft kiss just where her long legs met. After a brief moment, more giggling, "Hey, put your tongue away. I didn't give you permission. It tickles. We've got to get back on plan."

I looked up at her. "And what *exactly* is 'plan'?"

"I told you. We're going to carry on where we left off."

She turned away, round to the end of the bed, bent forward, legs straight and wide apart, with her bottom exaggeratedly in the air and her hands on the wooden foot board.

"Surely you can remember this?"

"Yes," I said as I moved behind her, "graphically."

"And the other thing is. You have to remember this too. *I* do the moving." Strong emphasis on the 'I'.

"Oh Paula, that's not fair."

She turned to look at me. "What's fairness got to do with it? That's the deal, anyway. Take it or leave it."

I was more likely to leave it than a banker leave his bonus, and being an adaptable fellow, I coped. No one burst in, I succeeded in preventing my balls from bursting, in spite of the hyper stimulating sight of Paula's rounded bum and my dick sliding in and out of her. On subsequent engagements in the bed, rather than over the end of it, I was allowed to do some of the moving. We were at it for ages. When we'd eventually shagged ourselves to a halt I had to deal with the only debit note of the night. I couldn't share Paula's fat spliff.

We were both propped up against the headboard, with Paula sucking deeply on the joint. As we watched the smoke slowly drifting upwards she said, "You were pretty good, Jolyon, for a young bloke."

"You usually do it with geriatrics then? That's a perversion."

"No, one older guy, just one. He was pretty good, too." She smiled. "Experience does count." She turned to me and rested her head on my chest. "But your body's much nicer, much sexier." She sat up and pushed the sheet back. "You've a beautiful body."

"Why thank you, Miss."

"No, I mean it. Squash players have the best bums. Not those wimpy little flat things you see on male models."

"That works for girls too."

"And nice hard legs," she went on. "And nice arms." She traced the veins on my arms. "These too. Look how your veins stand out."

"Talking about bums," I said, "well, talking about your bum, it's not just my veins you make stand out. You're making me hard again."

"Relax, I'm too sleepy to do it again." She blew smoke in my face. "Take a puff."

"No, I can't. I really, really can't."

So, I'd said no to proffered spliffs at the party. Then no again in the bedroom. But it had been smoky as hell at the gig, and no less so after Paula and I had made love. Combined, that had to be it. I must have taken in enough passively to register in the test. Not that it mattered. No one would believe me. Talk about hero to zero. What was I going to do?

First I had a match to play. I wasn't banned yet. I got up and made my way back up the steps to the club. Grandpa and my father were coming through the entrance in the opposite direction, bleak faced. Grandpa stopped and said in a voice that wasn't overburdened with sympathy, "What a fool, Jolyon, and I've misjudged you. I'm so disappointed."

Not Grandpa, oh dear. I could take it from Sailor, just. I could take it from my father. I could take it from my mother, no problem there. But Grandpa. His harsh words made me realise how much I depended on the support from him and the enthusiasm he always added.

"But don't lose touch," he said, looking back as my father helped him down the steps. "I'll be wanting to know what you're doing. This is something else you're going to have to deal with."

Why should I bother, I thought during the knock up against Mark Goodrich. The whole project was coming to an end. My *life* as I knew it was coming to an end. What was I going to do? I didn't have a clue. There wasn't anything else as far as I was concerned. My head had been filled with squash, to the exclusion of everything, apart from Zoë, and the occasional Nikki and Paula. They didn't count. I duly lost to Mark for a handful of points; my heart wasn't in it. I couldn't be bothered to do any stretches afterwards and showered quickly. Sailor had apparently departed so it had to be the train back to Manchester, what fun, and too late to get one that evening. I walked back to my B and B, picking up a McDonald's en route, who cares, and crashed out, feeling exhausted. Next morning it was three hours and fifty five minutes via Sheffield to Manchester, then twenty five minutes by bus out to Sailor's.

I wished I hadn't bothered. Sailor was there, back for lunch. He emerged from the kitchen as soon as I was inside the front door.

"So you lost?"

"What do you think?"

"I think you should have tried."

"What's the point?"

"You enter a tournament, you give it yer all. You compete."

"I didn't feel like competing."

"Well no. And I don't feel like supporting you. Here," he handed me a letter. "Came this morning. Registered. It'll be your notification from the agency. There'll be a hearing. If you want, I'll represent you, I'll do that for you, not that it'll do any good. But I'm no' having you under my roof any more. You're out of here, son, as of now. Today."

"What do you mean?"

"I mean, son, that you are moving out. This afternoon. I will not have a drug taker living in my house. Understand?"

"Where will I go?"

"That's for you to decide. Home, mebbe."

Something in the way he said it triggered an explosion, everything I was feeling. "For fuck's sake, Sailor. You've condemned me without even listening to me. You may be throwing me out but you're going to fucking listen for two minutes."

"Don't start effing wi' me..."

I felt this colossal indignation. I'd been judged without the slightest chance of providing an explanation, of making a comment. "I will effing eff as much as I like. Just this once. There's another side to this story. I know you won't believe it but I'm going to give it to you anyway." I took a deep breath. "Now listen. I-did-not-smoke-any-dope-before-Rotterdam. Hear me? Did not. I've not smoked anything, not even a cigarette, not since I've been here in Manchester. All that time. I was at a gig the weekend before Rotterdam. I told you. A lot of dope was smoked. And socially afterwards. I think it's possible it got into my system that way."

"Got into my system that way?" He sneered like a bad actor. Another time it might have been comic. "I said at the club. Everyone has an excuse, some story to tell. Everyone pleads innocent. It won't work with me. The system's good. The cheats get caught, some of them anyway. Only shame is, some of them come back. Two years. It's no' enough."

"It's not cheating, what I'm supposed to have done. Even if I did do some dope. It'd be more likely to slow me down, cannabis. Not increase performance."

"Yer wasting yer time on me, son. Get yerself packed. You can leave anything you can't carry. Pick it up later. I want you out of here before Mary gets back."

Oh dear, Mary. I hadn't thought about Mary. She had supported me to the extent of giving me money. How on earth was I going to pay her back?

"I'd like to say goodbye to Mary."

Sailor hesitated. He appeared to be thinking. Then he turned away. "Save it," he said over his shoulder. "She won't want to see you. She'll be as disgusted as I am."

I trudged upstairs to my bedroom. Disgust. That wasn't fair. I didn't deserve that. Disgust. It wasn't as if I'd done anything bad, anything to be ashamed of. In two days I'd gone from number thirty two in the squash world, with brilliant prospects, some sort of chance at least of meeting Grandpa's challenge, to this. Contempt, disgust, nowhere. And nowhere to go. What had Sailor said? Go back home? And face my mother? Not in a zillion years, no way. I could picture her smug satisfaction, hear her words. 'What did I tell you?' 'Never had it in you.' 'It was always going to end in tears.' I wouldn't be able to control myself. *Teen drug fiend in matricide tragedy.*

But what were the alternatives? Maybe I could doss at Zoë's for a couple of nights while I worked something out. She might not be unsympathetic, hmm, but I wasn't so sure. What about the Kemballs? They were my best bet. Russell didn't seem too judgemental, and I couldn't imagine Marion not being helpful.

So I called Dave, hoping he wasn't in a lecture. "What happened?" he said when I started to explain. "Je-sus, that's bad."

There was a pause. Then he went on. "I doubt if it will be a problem with Mum and Dad while you sort yourself out. But what are you going to do?"

"I have no idea. Life after squash. I've been thinking about it every minute since yesterday afternoon and I've come up blank. It wouldn't be so bad if I could go home. That's one thing I couldn't face. Not my mother."

"Well look," Dave said. "I've got to go. I'll text you the numbers. Talk to you soon. Let me know what's happening."

"Thanks."

I managed to get hold of Marion later that afternoon. She listened without saying much as I told her what had happened. "Yes of course you can come over. Dave's not here, he's at the university but you know that. Do you want a lift?"

"No, that's okay, I'll get the bus. There's one in forty minutes." I'd have loved to have accepted a lift but I was being offered huge hospitality as it was. The relief at having somewhere to go, even if only for a few nights, was enormous.

On the bus I opened the letter. It was indeed the official notification from UKAD, the UK Anti-Doping body:

Dear Mr Jacks

<u>Re Urine Test, October 29th, Victoria Squash Club, Rotterdam</u>

I am obliged to inform you that the A Sample taken from the urine sample you provided at the Victoria Squash Club, Rotterdam during the Golden Tulip International 25 Squash Racquets Tournament, October 26th-31st, has tested positive for cannabinoid metabolites. Cannabis is included on the current World Anti-Doping Agency list, Version 33.01 dated September 30th, of Prohibited Substances the presence of which in an athlete is proscribed under Article 2.1 (Presence of a *Prohibited Substance*) of the World Anti Doping Code as adopted by UKAD, the UK Anti-Doping body.

Please note: While this positive test for a Prohibited Substance is under investigation, you are ineligible to compete in any competition regulated by any sports body that is registered with UKAD or the World Anti-Doping Agency.

In order to establish your eligibility to continue competing in sports competitions under the auspices of affiliated sports bodies, you have two options:

1) Your B sample has been retained by the Dutch Anti-Doping Agency at Capelle aan den IJssel, Rotterdam. You may request to have your B Sample tested. A positive result will oblige you to attend a hearing organised by UKAD as described in 2), below.

A negative result from your B Sample test will terminate this investigation in your favour.

2) If you elect to forego analysis of your B Sample, an early hearing has been provisionally scheduled for 10.00 a.m. on November 25th at the offices of the

English Institute for Sport, Sportcity Manchester, Gate 13, Rowsley Street, Manchester, M11 3FF.

Please reply as soon as possible by recorded delivery to indicate the option you have chosen.

Yours sincerely

Abraham Charlton
Test and Performance Section
UKAD

The letter felt awfully official, although it didn't tell me anything new. It left me feeling completely in the power of the authorities. The actual date for the hearing was a surprise though, only two weeks away. Close but on the whole a positive angle. I would soon know where I stood, whether the last four years had been a total waste of time, whether I was going to have to find an alternative life, whether I'd have to crawl back home to my mother.

Oh dear, dossing down in a passage near Manchester Piccadilly Station would be preferable to that.

Chapter Twenty Eight

That evening, sitting at the Kemball's kitchen table, I went through the whole sorry story with Marion and Russell.

"The thing about cannabis metabolites," Marion said, "is they're persistent. They have a long half life, that's the technical way of putting it. So it is plausible that if you inhaled some at that gig…"

"And afterwards," Russell interrupted with a smile.

"…it is possible that the cannabis persisted in your system till the time you provided the sample."

"What are we going to do then?" Russell asked.

"We?" I said. He and Marion exchanged a glance.

"Yes, we. We can't let this go on. It's just unfair. Just unjust, you might say." He turned to Marion. "Can you get chapter and verse on cannabis, especially how long it persists and the levels that can be detected by tests? We need to be able to prove that whatever quantity was picked up in Jolyon's sample, it could have come from passive inhalation.

"You say you don't know about the tribunal process?"

"Not much," I said. "Only the date. And it's going to be held at the EIS."

"See what you can find out. I'm going to look into it too." He was all enthusiasm. "Do you remember that French tennis player, what was his name, Grass… Gass… Gasquet, that's it, Richard Gasquet, top ten, I think. He got off, didn't he, and that was cocaine. He said he'd got it from a girl he met in a bar in Miami. From a kiss. Quite a kiss, I guess. There must be other cases. I really think you should fight this. The other angle is the girl, who's she?"

"Paula Bentley."

"Oh, Paula. Is that Sheffield Paula?" He smiled again. "Well, good for you. We can get a statement from Paula. Maybe get her to attend the tribunal. It depends on the process. Could you get anyone from the gig? One of your fellow DJs. It would be great to have a statement from one of them. About you not smoking while you were there."

I could hardly believe this. After all the hostility, from Grandpa and my father and Sailor, the assumption I was guilty, all the condemnation, here were Marion and Russell on my side, working out how they could help. They believed me.

"You don't know what this means," I said. "You're the first two people who haven't branded me as guilty right from the start."

"Well we've got Dave," Marion said. "It probably makes us more understanding."

"All Dave makes us is poorer," said Russell. "We won't worry about that though. I want to explore this tribunal process, top to bottom."

"And I'll do the cannabis stuff," Marion added. "Let's compare notes tomorrow evening."

Daily Telegraph, November 12th

Teenage squash star Jolyon Jacks has sensationally tested positive for cannabis. Jacks underwent a random test last month at a PSA tournament in Rotterdam. Jacks' coach in Manchester, Sailor McCann, last night confirmed the leaked result. Jacks' abrasive manner has not endeared him to the squash authorities, but in the last twelve months he has shot up the world rankings and was tipped by many to be a future world champion. Jacks has been suspended from competition pending a tribunal. He faces a two year ban.

Oh dear, the Daily Telegraph. I'd picked it up online. It meant my mother's friends would know. I could hear her savouring my discomfiture, the 'Jolyon never had it in him' theme. Trouble was, maybe she was right.

Not if the Kemballs had anything to do with it. They must both have spent ages in their research. That evening Marion launched into the relevance of my quoted cannabis levels. "The information available is varied. Your urine level, twenty two nanograms per ml, was low, which is helpful. I've found a report that says the presence of cannabis metabolites in urine is not," she looked at some notes, "'unequivocal proof of active cannabis smoking'."

"That's great," said Russell.

Marion went on. "Cannabis is taken up in fatty tissue and released slowly from there. It can hang around in the system for up to thirty days. That's in persistent users. For a single exposure we're talking up to six days." She looked at me. "How long was it for you?"

"I was tested on the Thursday. That makes it five days, or four really. I was with Paula well into Sunday."

"Four sounds better. The other thing is, with cannabis metabolism people vary a lot. That's in your favour too. You might be a slow metaboliser. I think there's a plausible explanation in there.

"So," she said, putting away her folder. "It would have been possible for THC to remain in your system all the way from the Saturday night at the gig, let's say Sunday morning, to the following Thursday in Rotterdam. Your reported levels there were certainly low. On that timetable the experts will conclude that you hadn't had the marijuana equivalent of a skinful. Alternatively, you might have had a skinful say two weeks before Rotterdam. So nothing's proved. Except that the gig and what you did afterwards could have, potentially, accounted for your failed test. You're not off the hook but there's real doubt about being guilty."

She turned to Russell. "What have you got?"

"I have a process that at least I understand properly now. I've reviewed a lot of cases. Two things usually happen." He raised his eyebrows. "The first is the accused pleads innocent." Then he frowned. "The second is he or she gets convicted. It's not sympathetic, the world of dope testing. The system is desperate to nail you. What we're up against specifically is UKAD. This is a subsection of WADA, and as I'm sure you know, WADA rules are tough. You can get done for using a steroid cream, just a cream for goodness sake, rubbed into your skin. That's if you don't have a therapeutic use exemption, or TUE they call it. The one that catches out a lot of athletes is asthma medication. Ventolin? *Yes. TUE?* Okay then. *No?* Quick as a flash, you're banned. Recreational drugs, let's say cannabis for example, are considered no less bad than performance enhancing drugs. Which is to say, lower than the belly of a worm.

"There is some good news. Firstly, it's specifically stated, the hearing panel has to be fair and impartial. That gives me scope if the hearing goes against you, an appeal with reasonable chances of success. I can dig up some stuff on the panellists' backgrounds; there's usually something there. Next, you're given the right to respond to the supposed rule violation by presenting evidence. That can include calling witnesses, or if the panel allows it, introducing phone or written testimony. Thirdly, this is the real good one, you have the right to be represented at the hearing by your appointed counsel. That'll be me. For a huge fee." He must have seen the look on my face. "It's okay, I'm only joking. My fee will be a pint of Theakstons, on a no win no fee basis.

"Now, you're going to be found guilty under WADA rules, that's the way they're written, that's inevitable. There's no point in us contesting. There were cannabis metabolites in your urine. You, the athlete, are responsible for what's in your body. Doesn't matter how it got there. For a first violation it means two years ineligibility, as they call it, from competition. But, section ten point four of the rules allows what they refer to as elimination or reduction of the period of ineligibility under specific circumstances. This is where there's a great big opening. We're going to have to demonstrate that you were exposed to a lot of cannabis smoke over a protracted period on Saturday October the twenty fourth."

"And Sunday October the twenty fifth," Marion added.

"Does it mean I can bring witnesses to the hearing," I asked.

"That would be the best way. Like I said, Paula would be good, both for being at the gig and explaining the afterwards. And if you could get someone else to say you were at the gig and that you didn't smoke, and that it was smoky, that would be perfect."

"Let me give Paula a call."

I managed to get hold of Paula straight away while Russell and Marion made a pot of tea. She was reluctant, but when I explained what was at stake she said she'd help. She'd be willing to appear in person at the hearing. One in the bag, I thought, good. As for the local DJs, I had Facebook addresses for two of them, and I messaged them.

We sat down again over the tea. "It would be best if I could speak with Paula pretty soon," Russell said. "Where is she based?"

"She's in Sheffield. Working nine to five I think."

"We could go over one evening," he suggested.

"Really? That would be great, if you wouldn't mind. It's so kind of you, of both of you."

Russell laughed. "It's a worthwhile project." He put on a pompous voice. "I always want to see justice done."

"And it could so easily be Dave," Marion added quietly. "On top of that, I don't think you've had a fair deal from your parents. You could do with a bit of support."

Russell and I fixed to go over to Sheffield the following Saturday to see Paula. Russell said we should take her to lunch. Her presence at the hearing was assuming greater importance because neither of my DJ contacts wanted anything to do with authority. They didn't want to attend the hearing in person and they wouldn't sign their name to any statement. If someone was going to come good it had to be Paula anyway, as she could talk about my further passive cannabis intake after the party, as well as what had gone on there. I was starting to feel that I had a chance at the hearing, with the Kemballs on my side. They were a good combination, Marion with her knowledge of medical tests and Russell a lawyer. And I had what was surely a decent story to tell.

Problem was, I hadn't considered who the story was going to be told to. I had a call from Sailor the following day, with the message that another recorded delivery letter had arrived for me. Russell offered to take me over that evening so I could collect the letter and pick up the rest of my stuff. Sailor was terse when he opened the door.

"Here's the letter. My offer still stands for the hearing. Your kit's in the hallway."

"Thanks, Sailor. In fact Russell has said he'll represent me, and it would be a big chunk out of your day. Is Mary there?"

"Mary will no' be seeing you."

"What? Isn't she here?"

"I said, Mary'll no' be seeing you."

Oh dear. One of my objectives in calling at the McCanns was to try to square things with Mary.

"I owe her some money. I want to tell her that I will pay it back, maybe not too soon, but I will."

"I don't think she's wanting your money, son. Neither of us, for that matter."

"Hey, that's not fair." My voice was loud and fortunately Russell intervened.

"Come on, Jolyon. That'll do for now. Let's get your stuff."

My stuff was my decks and my vinyl, the rest of my squash kit plus a few clothes, so it didn't take long to load it into Russell's car. I called goodbye to Sailor as we were leaving. He had disappeared into the kitchen.

As we were driving away I opened the letter:

Dear Mr Jacks

<u>Re: UKAD Hearing, November 25th, 10.00am, EIS, Sportcity, Manchester M11 3FF</u>

Thank you for your letter dated November 14th, with regard to your positive urine test for a Prohibited Substance from a sample taken on October 29th in Rotterdam. I note your decision not to have your B Sample analysed, and confirm therefore your forthcoming attendance at a UKAD hearing at 10.00am on November 25th.

I am writing to remind you that you may chose to be represented at the hearing by a lawyer. If you chose to be represented, please send me details of your legal representative.

The UKAD panel will consist of three members, one of whom will be myself. The other panellists will be:
Mr Frank Walsh, LLB, as UKAD's legal representative,
Mr Dick Bentley, representing Squash England.

Yours sincerely

Abraham Charlton
Test and Performance Section
UKAD

My heart sank. Dick Bentley. Why did it have to be Dick Bentley? If ever there were a hanging judge, for me it would be Judge Bentley. *Should we be lenient with this fornicator? Certainly not! It is our duty to throw the book at him, preferably at his deviant crotch. Will the squash world be better off without him for two years, or even four? You betcha!* Even overlooking Dick's attitude to someone he'd caught shagging his daughter doggy style over a sofa in his kitchen, what effect would his presence have on Paula?

The Paula question was promptly answered when Russell and I sat down with her in an Italian restaurant in the middle of Sheffield.

"My dad's going to be there? You've got to be joking. I'm sorry. I'm not going to do it. No way!"

The best part of an hour's persuasion and a bottle of wine extracted a promise from Paula to give us a statement. She had seen me at the party, yes. It had been full of smoke, yes. Not all of the smoke, she believed, could have been attributed to the combustion of tobacco. Some of it, she thought, might have come from cannabis.

"Our story, it's pretty thin now," Russell said as we drove glumly back towards Manchester. "Not having witnesses will make the passive inhalation story," he shrugged, "…it'll just sound like a legal argument. Clutching at a straw," here he laughed, "…a spliff-sized straw. I guess it's all we've got now, that and your marginal levels that Marion talks about."

The days leading up to the hearing were dreadful, in the literal sense, especially with Russell's confidence so obviously gone. We had talked about objecting to Dick's presence on the panel, in view of his and my acquaintance, but decided it would be counterproductive. I went out for several runs, but I was listless without the level of physical activity I was used to. I helped as much as I could round the Kemballs' house. The evening before the hearing I had to scrub emulsion paint from my hands.

Approaching the EIS felt strange after a gap of several weeks. I had spent so much of my time there over the previous two and a half years. I noticed details that had previously lost their impact. The Mercedes dealership that had provided me with fantasies of owning a lairy AMG. The enormous sculpture from the Commonwealth Games of a sprinter starting, not from blocks, but from a huge globe. And there was the looming futuristic presence of the Man City stadium and its Etihad advertising. How long would it be before I was flying off anywhere again?

We were early. The letter-writing Mr Charlton appeared in response to a call from Russell, who was looking unusually formal in a grey suit, and led us up the stairs to a meeting room on the first floor. The walls were decorated with photos of athletes. A shaft of morning sunlight did nothing to cheer me, mourning sunlight, I thought.

"Please wait here," Mr Charlton said as he left us. "The panel will convene in about ten minutes."

Dread. I was at the mercy of a system that didn't care what happened.

"Cheer up," Russell said as I mooched around the room. "I've seen good results in worse cases than this."

"I don't feel like I've got a chance."

"You're entitled to a fair and impartial hearing, as the words say, and I'll see you get it. Don't forget, you are actually innocent in natural law. We just have to show it. In the end it will come down to whether they believe you or not. Tell your story, like it happened. I'll do everything else."

At five to ten the three panellists joined us. Dick Bentley blanked me as he sat down with the others at the large table, the three of them side by side, opposite the two of us. An attacking posse, I thought, *they've got the numbers and we ain't got the guns.* There was no standard size for panellists. Mr Charlton was small, apart from his Adam's apple. I was no good at ages: he was nearer thirty than fifty. He meticulously parked four large lever arch files and a laptop in front of him and introduced his colleagues. First Mr Frank Walsh. Large, Adam's apple lost in the folds of his chins. Mr Walsh wasn't anything like my image of a lawyer. He was cheerful looking, happily stressing the seams of his pinstripe suit. He was also a file man, two thick manila ones in his case. Then there was Dick Bentley, skinny, just about managing a nod as he was introduced. In the file department Dick, with just a notebook and a pencil, was outgunned. Did that mean that his mind was made up? He was the one I was going to have to convince. Finally Russell introduced the two of us, with Mr Charlton making some notes. He asked whether Russell had any objection to the hearing being recorded.

"No problem," Russell said, "provided that we can have a notarised transcript within three days."

"We don't usually have a formal transcript done," Mr Charlton said.

"Well I'm not happy you'll have access to a resource we don't have in the event of an appeal."

"I tell you what," Mr Walsh said in a deep, burbling voice. "If it comes to that we'll have a transcript done. The recording's just to simplify the clerical side. Mr Charlton and his minutes. We find it helpful to be able to review what was said."

Russell nodded. "In which case that's fine by me." Afterwards he told me he had known the likely outcome, and simply wanted to be able to make a concession.

Mr Charlton opened his laptop, inserted a USB stick and made a few moves on the trackpad while we watched. "Right, the recording has started." He pronounced the date and time and some details of the hearing. Then he read from a script, summarising the allegation against me, citing various paragraphs from the World Squash Federation Anti-Doping Rules, summarising the possible penalties, listing the people involved in the collection and analysis of my sample, getting me to confirm that I had waived the right to having my B Sample analysed, and finally inviting me or my representative to respond.

In contrast to Mr Charlton, Russell sounded almost conversational. "Jolyon has asked me to speak on his behalf, and I'll get him to explain the circumstances that led to the positive test. I'll try to be brief.

"Now, firstly, we accept the findings of the urine analysis. That's why Jolyon hasn't asked for a B sample analysis. He has thought back over his movements in the days leading up to the test. He knows when he was exposed to cannabis smoke and we'll show that the inhalation was inadvertent. The point I'd like to emphasise here is the marginal level of THC detected. The urine level is compatible with passive exposure.

"This is the sequence of events. On Saturday October the twenty fourth Jolyon went to a free party in a building in central Manchester. I'll leave him to describe the party in a few moments, but first I'd like to ask if you'll accept a witnessed statement concerning Jolyon's presence there."

"Could I see it?" Mr Walsh asked.

Russell opened his briefcase, took out an envelope and extracted a single sheet of A4 paper with Paula's handwritten statement on it. Russell had suggested the message would have more credibility if she didn't type it up. He passed it over to the lawyer, who gave it a cursory glance said, "That's in order," and handed it back.

Russell put on a pair of reading glasses. "I'll pass this over when I've read it out. 'To whom it may concern'," he started, "'I was at a free party held in the hall of what used to be St Botolph's School in Manchester on the evening of October twenty fourth. Jolyon Jacks was at the party, at least between ten o'clock and one o'clock in the morning. There were at least two hundred people at the party. Many of them were smoking cannabis. The windows of the hall were kept closed to stop the noise getting out, so there was little ventilation. The atmosphere was very smoky.'"

Russell didn't specifically mention Paula as the person who had given the statement. He replaced the A4 sheet in the envelope and went on, "As you've seen, the statement is duly signed and witnessed. I'd like to submit it formally to the hearing." He handed the envelope to Mr Charlton, who took the statement out, made a note, and passed it to Dick Bentley. Dick's face didn't register any surprise as he too glanced through it. Maybe Paula had told him.

"So," Russell went on. "We've established Jolyon's presence at a party where a lot of cannabis was being smoked."

"Is that all you have?" Mr Walsh asked.

Russell appeared surprised. "Well, yes. How much do we need? It's pretty unambiguous. The statement, and Jolyon's evidence to come." Mr Walsh made a note in his file. "Carry on, please."

"At about one in the morning," Russell continued, "Jolyon left the party and spent the rest of the night with a friend in her flat, also in central Manchester. Regrettably this friend did not want to provide a statement. We wanted a statement from her as the period after the party is relevant. Specifically, during this period, Jolyon's friend smoked several cannabis joints. Since she and Jolyon were in bed together, once again he was exposed to high levels of cannabis smoke."

Mr Walsh interrupted again. "I would have thought you could have provided at least a supporting statement here, since as you say this has a significant bearing on the account. Without corroboration this evidence is worthless."

Russell ignored this and carried on. "Now, turning to the urine sample. Tetrahydrocannabinol, THC, is the cannabis metabolite that is picked up by gas chromatography mass spectrometry, GC/MS, the usual analytical method for this type of drug. I've obtained this paper from the American Society of Clinical Chemists, published in the journal, Clinical Chemistry." Russell took another A4 envelope from his briefcase and passed it over to Mr Charlton. "To summarise, three hundred and sixty six subjects exposed to cannabis use underwent blood and urine tests up to fourteen days after exposure. I'm particularly interested in the results from seven of the subjects whose exposure had been limited to passive inhalation. THC at low nanogram levels was detected in these subjects' urine up to seven days after exposure."

Russell took of his glasses. He was one of those people who made you want to listen. He paused and looked in turn at each of the three panellists.

"This isn't complicated." He gave a slight grin that removed any hint of talking down to his audience, drawing them onto his side. "We've shown that Jolyon was exposed to high levels of cannabis smoke for a combined period of as much as six hours."

"Three hours is what you've shown," Mr Walsh said.

Russell shrugged. "A substantial period on the Saturday and Sunday before the Rotterdam tournament. He will have been continuously inhaling cannabis smoke for the majority of this time, with a break between when he left the party and, if you accept his word, his time in the flat. We know he provided the urine sample at the most five days plus two or three hours after the end of his exposure. We know THC is slowly eliminated from the body and we know from the Clinical Chemistry paper that this level of exposure can result in detectable levels in urine, not just for the five days that are relevant in this case but for as long as seven days.

"So it is entirely plausible to account for Jolyon's positive test as coming from passive exposure, especially given the low level of THC that was detected." Russell paused. "Of course there is another plausible explanation for the positive test. Jolyon may have actively used cannabis. Again being led by the Clinical Chemistry report, this exposure could have been up to fourteen days before the sample was taken. This is the crux of the matter, and you'll have to be the judge. Any questions?"

"We'll do questions when you've finished," Mr Walsh said.

"All right. I'd like you to listen to Jolyon's own account. To help you make up your minds."

The panellists turned their attention to me. My mouth was parched, my saliva having been apparently diverted to my armpits and the channel down the middle of my back. No antiperspirant could hold back the three mini deluges.

Russell, Marion and I had debated how exactly I should approach this. The line we agreed was, why on earth would I put at risk the sole, single, burning focus of my life?

"I only started playing squash when I was fifteen," I said. "Almost by accident. I knew I was good early on, but it was just for fun. I entered a few junior tournaments, which was where I met Mr Kemball's son, Dave. I came to Manchester in the summer holidays to play squash with Dave and do some mixing." Mr Charlton looked blank. "Music, I mean."

I felt better once I'd got started. "We went along, Dave and I, to train with Sailor, Sailor McCann, here at the EIS. He gave us some performance tests and I did really well. Sailor told me then that if I wanted to I could be world champion. I couldn't believe it. I'd never imagined I could be any way that good at anything, maybe county standard at running, squash nothing really, not properly good. I always thought it was mixing I was best at.

"The problem was, I had to give up school to train full time. Otherwise I'd never make it. My Mum and Dad, well mainly my Mum, didn't want this. They, mostly she actually, my Dad's away most of the time, she said she wouldn't support me, no money, no nothing. But I made up my mind, and Sailor, well, Mr McCann, said I could stay with him and he's very strict, and he's very strict especially about things like drugs. Since coming here I've trained really hard, just about every single day since I came, and I'm on track, sorry I haven't told you this, my Granddad wants me to be world champion by the time I'm twenty one," Mr Bentley gave a little laugh, "and I'm on track for that, or at least I was until this thing happened."

"Where are you ranked, now," Russell asked.

"Three weeks ago I was world number thirty two. And I was going up pretty fast." Neither Dick Bentley nor Mr Charlton showed any response, but Mr Walsh said, "That's good."

It put me off my stride and I stopped, but Russell was great and prompted me again. "Now talk a bit about the music."

"Yes, the music. You see I was always really into mixing, ever since I was eleven or twelve. I had a good reputation as a DJ down in Sussex, round Brighton. I'd be at a gig or a party most weekends. I loved it, more than tennis, I used to play tennis, more even than cross country. I loved cross country. Most of all I loved the parties, they're what you read about as illegal raves, but no one means any harm. It's just most people my age can't afford tickets to proper music gigs, in proper venues, even if you wanted to go. These parties get put on in places the police aren't going to object. That's what we try anyway. Trouble is the police do object, and you can understand it in a way, there's lots of drug taking there, I want to say that. It's pretty harmless mostly. I do know the other side, people get into trouble." Dick Bentley wiped the side of his face and stared at the table. "Anyway, I have to admit, I did do cannabis, I used to, always when I was mixing. Everybody did, really."

Now all three of the panellists were looking at me intently. Russell had emphasised while we were preparing, don't hold back. Just tell them. So I went on. "When I came to Manchester, some time in the first couple of weeks I was here, Dave Kemball told me about the WADA list. And that cannabis was on it. I was surprised. I knew about steroids, everyone does, and EPO. No one down in Sussex had explained drug testing to me, maybe because I hadn't been involved in the county set-up. And I'd thought that cannabis would only make you worse, anyway, worse at squash.

"But I made up my mind, that time I was talking to Dave. I really, really want to do well, I really want to become world champ, and even though I've been to some parties up here, and I've had lots of offers, I've never smoked anything since I've been here. Not a single spliff. Why take the chance?

"And now I feel terrible. Everyone seems to think I've been taking drugs and I've blown it. But I haven't. I wouldn't do anything that got in the way of squash. It would be so silly. Especially now, after I've got this far. It was just the smoke that night, honestly, that's what it was."

There was silence in the room for a few seconds. Then Mr Walsh asked, "How often do you go to these parties?"

"It's only occasionally. They tend to last through to the morning, and that doesn't work with training. Or competition. I've been to maybe six or seven, in the two and a half years I've been here. Otherwise I just mix through headphones, or sometimes with friends."

"And you say that there's always cannabis at these parties?"

"Yes, people will always be smoking weed, and tobacco, and doing other stuff, and there'll usually be dealers, low level," I glanced at Dick Bentley, "and occasionally one of the more serious dealers, with hard stuff."

"What's stopped you at these parties?" Mr Walsh asked.

"It just hasn't been something I'd do. I love the mixing, and the chance to play through a big sound system. It's completely different from mixing through headphones. I dunno, it's the energy at a party, all those people out there dancing, it grabs you. But I haven't wanted to do weed any more. The squash is more important. Weed might affect my training, and I couldn't take the chance of that."

"Were there any dealers at the party in Manchester?"

"None that I was aware of, but I wasn't interested. Probably in the crowd. I didn't know many people there. I was offered a spliff by one of the DJs. I just said no. It wasn't a big deal. You'd always offer, up on the platform."

"I see. So you were offered cannabis and said no?"

"That's it. That's what I've always done, since coming to Manchester."

"Thank you," Mr Walsh said. He addressed his fellow panellists. "Do you gentlemen have any questions?"

"Why should we believe you?" Dick Bentley asked, looking at his finger nails rather than me.

I didn't know what to say. "I... I... I just want to be world champion. I wouldn't take the chance. It's not worth it." I felt myself going red. "I just wouldn't. I can't explain any more. I just wouldn't."

I looked at Mr Walsh. He was staring intently at me. "All right. You can understand Mr Bentley's point. Every dope-in-sport case I've been involved in, I didn't do Dwayne Chambers, in the end he was different, in every one bar none the athlete has had a story. This time it's supplements, this time it's tainted meat. We've had the jealous-rival-spiking-my-drink story more than once. You name it, we've heard it." His eyes were protruding now. "And I didn't believe any of them. Not one. We've had the passive inhalation story before, too."

Russell intervened, in a mild way, with something hard underneath. "We take the point, Mr Walsh. Dope is a problem, it's a shocker. But I hope you and your colleagues will simply look at the particulars of Jolyon's case. We're not disputing the test result. Not disputing the violation. I'm prepared to bet that Jolyon won't be going to these parties any more, and in the circumstances, first violation, strong mitigating factors, we're asking, under Para Four of the UK Anti Doping Code, for a reprimand and a waiver, no period of ineligibility from competition. We strongly assert that there was absolutely no intent on Jolyon's part to enhance his athletic performance with the THC in his system."

"Thank you, Mr Kemball, I know the code. Do either of you have anything else to add?"

I shook my head and Russell said, "No, that's all. Thank you for the opportunity to present the case."

Mr Charlton said, "Under the procedure, the panel members will now have a discussion in private. This won't be recorded. Please wait in the adjacent room in case we need to clarify anything."

Mr Charlton led us out and showed us the room. We hung around for a moment then went downstairs and bought teas in the canteen. Then is was back to the room and settling in for the wait.

"That was no good," I said. "Mr Walsh had it in for me. Mr Charlton doesn't seem anything and I won't get any help from Dick Bentley."

"It's too soon to fret," Russell said. "Mr Walsh is paid to challenge what's said. It may have sounded personal, but it wasn't. I still think the key is Dick Bentley. He's hard to read."

"We know the result already if it's down to him."

Russell grimaced. "We'll see." We were both quiet for a few minutes. I couldn't help thinking about the embarrassment of having to tell people what had happened. Russell eventually broke the silence. "It's an awful time, this waiting. You agonise over everything you said, and what they said. I admit, your story is thin. Even if we'd had a gallery full of witnesses, it was going to come down to whether they believed you. And you did just fine, don't worry about that."

After half an hour of broken conversation Russell sent me down for more tea. This whole process was agony. The morning of a lethal injection in an American prison. No, that's silly. But it felt not far short. At least you wouldn't have to explain things to anyone after the injection, I thought.

I just couldn't see what I'd do when I was banned. What was I going to say to people. They'd freeze me out. There'd be my mother's self-satisfied scorn. Grandpa's disappointment. Then there was Zoë. What would Zoë say? What would I say to her? It would be goodbye to Zoë. My glums were interrupted by the need to find a toilet. I lost concentration there and had to wipe up the miss with copious runs of poor quality EIS bog paper. Back to the condemned cell, more painful silence. Eventually, after almost an hour, I was startled by a movement of the door handle. It opened and Mr Charlton peered in.

"Would you gentlemen like to come back." *You may if you wish, Mr Jacks, prefer to jump out of a window and impale yourself on iron railings.*

The meeting table was tidy. Mr Walsh's documents were all back in their files. Mr Charlton had put away his laptop. There was a single sheet of paper at his place, with handwritten notes that were too small for me to read. Mr Walsh watched us as we rounded the table and sat down. Dick Bentley just stared at the table. He wouldn't meet my eye.

Mr Charlton cleared his throat. "Thank you for waiting." He picked up the sheet. "Mr Jacks, we have discussed your statement and all aspects of your case in detail. First, I'm obliged to formally ask you to confirm that you've had full opportunity to respond to the asserted anti-doping rule violation and call and question any and all witnesses." Oh dear, not a prelude to good news.

Russell grimly nodded. "Yes," he said.

Mr Charlton's Adam's apple aped the Grand Old Duke of York's ten thousand men, up to the top and down again. "I'm now obliged to inform you that the hearing has established your unambiguous guilt in the issue of ingesting a specified substance, in this case tetrahydrocannabinol. As you know, UKAD has an attitude of zero tolerance to such transgressions. For a first violation the period of ineligibility is two years."

Oh God, it really struck home. Two years. It might as well be two centuries.

"For a transgression with a specified substance," another return excursion by the grand old Adam's apple, "but a claim from the guilty athlete that the substance was not intended to enhance their sporting performance or mask the use of a performance-enhancing substance, we are obliged to consider reduction or elimination of the period of ineligibility. In your case, Mr Jacks, we accept," he looked up, "*marginally* accept, the modest corroborating evidence you have presented about your cannabis ingestion, in the context of the minimal level of THC detected in your urine, and we have taken into consideration the nature of cannabis as a recreational and not a performance-enhancing drug. We have decided to exercise our option, since we believe *on balance* that you bear no fault or negligence, to eliminate the period of ineligibility.

"Congratulations, Mr Jacks, you're a fortunate young man. You may continue to compete."

It took a moment to sink in. I'd given up the last hope that I'd get off. Paula's refusal to attend the hearing, the involvement of her father, not my greatest fan, the track record of harsh judgements in doping cases, the sheer formality of the process, they all had pointed in one direction.

Russell patted me on the back. "Well done, Jolyon. You're okay. It's back to squash." He turned to the panel. "Thank you, gentlemen. I'm passionately anti-drug, but I think you got it right here."

Mr Walsh said, "You should thank Mr Bentley."

Dick Bentley was still staring at the table but he sneaked a quick glance at me. "I know a bit about you, son. I know your attitude."

Chapter Twenty Nine

"I heard from Dick Bentley." I was sitting with Sailor in his kitchen, having a cup of tea. "He said some good things about you."

"When I found out he was on the panel, I thought it was the end."

"Dick wouldn't elaborate. Something earlier in the year." He raised an inquisitive eyebrow.

Not the time to talk about Mick the Prick, I thought.

"Well I owe ye an apology son. Too quick to jump to conclusions." He rubbed his chin, looking uncertain. "But Christ, pardon me, son, but Christ, don't put me through that again."

"*You* through that? Me too. Me too, Sailor."

The cannabis incident acted as a sort of spur. It took a couple of weeks for me to get over the missed training, but the rest had done me good and I had prodigious energy. At Christmas I played Riley O'Callaghan in a training game. With Sailor marking, and several of the squad including Zoë watching, Riley had to be on best behaviour. After five incredibly hard minutes he 'exceeded his aerobic capacity', as Sailor would have put it, and became what the rest of us called 'totally fucked'. In all I lost just seven points. The trick was to keep your opponent running, so he couldn't recover. I kept Riley running for the pure satisfaction. I repeatedly avoided pulling the trigger when I'd worked him out of position. More fun to exploit the step change in my speed and strength and make Riley look like an idiot.

"A triumph of youthful impetuosity, eh Riley?" I said as we left the court, he with his head down, having declined my handshake. Undiluted pleasure.

"That's the way you do it," Zoë said, walking past a few minutes later as I was doing my stretches.

"That was out of order, son," Sailor said more accurately as he sat down beside me in the changing room. "It does show you where you are. Time to forget the Rileys now. Focus on next year. That was top ten play, think about it, top ten. And if you're no' in the top ten by this time next year, you'll have let yourself down."

World Squash News, July 17th

Teenage Sensation Jacks Beats No 2 Seed

In one of the most brutal sixty minutes of squash those privileged to be watching have ever witnessed, nineteen year old Jolyon Jacks eliminated second seed Jan Berry from the first round of the $130,000 PSA World Series tournament in the New World Shopping Mall, Nanjing Road, Shanghai. The shock score of 13-11, 16-14, 11-7 gives some clue to the closeness of the contest, but no indication of the pace at which the game was played. Berry is noted for his remorseless attacking game, and it has been accepted that no one in the modern game takes the ball earlier. Not any more. That crown has gone to Jacks.

In a sensational contest, the teenager with his whirlwind style beat Berry at his own game, cutting everything off at the service line and volleying to a deadly length on both sides of the court. The dynamic South African fought to the end, but it was clear in the last few points that he had nothing left to offer. PSA Chief Executive Pierre Dentressangle said, "We have seen the future. Jacks has raised the bar tonight. For sure he has a lot to learn, but his sheer physicality will take him right to the top."

The measure of Jacks' achievement is that he had already come through two qualifying rounds. Admittedly they were both swift 3-0 victories. The teenager was thrilled with his win. "I knew it would be hard against Jan. I've seen him play and we have similar styles. My coach Sailor McCann said, nothing to lose, just go for it. I had to dig deep at the end of the second."

A bitterly disappointed Berry had no excuses to offer. "I came into the tournament in good shape. He executed better than me this evening. Good luck to him. He should have a great future on the tour if he can continue with that intensity. For me, it's back to the gym."

"Bl**dy h*ll, J*n B*rry! :-)" It was a text from Dave that came in while I was showering after my game with Jan. I was elated with the win and had wanted to tell people back home. 'People' meant, automatically, Dave, who would tell Russell and Marion, and diffidently, Zoë. Would Zoë be interested? Probably not. She had been mainly stand offish since my dope test scare, which I thought was unfair. I shouldn't have told her about the second phase of my passive ingestion. I knew where Zoë was while I was in Shanghai, defending her title in a tournament in Philadelphia, so I probably wouldn't hear from her anyway for a while. Right now she'd be asleep.

The Shanghai was my first ever World Series event, and Sailor had generously decided to come all the way over to China to support me. "I want you to stay on the rails, son. And stop you from getting big-headed."

"What do you mean, big-headed?"

"I've a good feeling about this one," he said before the tournament started. "You're going to surprise yourself."

It was more than surprise. Less than a year before I'd been scrabbling around in Challenger tournaments, delighted to pick up anything more than a hundred points for reaching the semis. Here I was with the scalp of the world number two, the renowned Berry the Hatchet, with a minimum of three hundred and twelve point five points for getting into the last sixteen, and the prospect of playing an unseeded opponent in the next round because of the PSA's recent decision to halve the number of seeds in their tournaments. They'd done this to mix the entries up and prevent the top players from becoming complacent in avoiding hungry, unseeded challengers. I was due to play another qualifier, an unknown Chinese called something like Fu Wi.

Being in Shanghai itself was a thrill, the twenty four hour action, the noise, the sheer energy of the streets. Per the PSA rulebook, I was having my accommodation paid from the night before the first round, and free meals.

This Shanghai result, even if I lost to Phew-wee, combined with the success I'd had in the first half of the year, should see me into the world's top sixteen, with automatic first round entry into any PSA tournament. Event organisers would take care of my travel and hotel bills. By scrimping and scratching, by the start of summer I'd finished paying Mary back for her subsidies. The money side was looking all right.

After Shanghai, so should the squash have been. Phew-wee had reached the end of his road by the time I played him, following three consecutive five setters. For him, oriental pictograms aplenty in the local media. For me, five hundred and thirty one point two five points, in fat Arabic numerals, even if I got no further. But I was on a roll. In the quarters I beat a good Frenchman, Serge Colson, guaranteeing eight hundred and seventy five points.

Those eight hundred odd points were the ones I finished with. I lost the semi in straight games. Mansoor Ali Khan, a seriously quick guy from Pakistan, short, intense and with a seriously cool moustache, was too strong. According to Sailor, Mansoor was a throwback to the days when Pakistanis ruled the squash world. He had no trouble in ruling me in Shanghai. It had been a long six days and I simply ran out of gas. Nevertheless, the semi final points boosted my total to precisely three thousand five hundred and two, giving me an average of three hundred and fifty point two points, making me the world number sixteen. Nineteen months to go. On the surface, these were rosy statistics. You would think I left Shanghai in a positive frame of mind.

Not so.

"Ay, those are my thoughts, too."

I was chatting with Sailor over breakfast the day after we'd arrived back from Shanghai. I'd been saying how impressed I'd been with Razza Mattaz. Razza had won the tournament in Shanghai, having beaten the world number one, Magdi Gamal in the other semi, and then my conqueror Mansoor Ali Khan in the final. It wasn't the fact of the two wins, Razz after all had reached number five in the rankings. It was the ease with which he'd won.

"We're going to have to look at Mattaz specifically," Sailor went on. "I've seen people as quick." He looked at me. "You're as quick, son. I've seen the shots, not often, mind. That's quality. What set him apart in Shanghai, and I'd no' seen him enough before to recognise it, it was the man's intelligence, the way he put it together. Did you notice how much he hit it to Magdi's forehand?"

Sailor went on for a few minutes, maximum intensity, about the technical side of Mattaz's game. I was only half listening. I was looking forward, previewing the next eighteen months. I wasn't bothered at the idea of having to beat Mansoor Ali Khan when I next had to play him. Next time I'd be too strong. Jan Berry? It would be more of the same; both of us knew I had the measure of Jan. Trevor Cooper, even Magdi Gamal, I could see myself doing well against them, certainly with another year's strength and experience. But suddenly none of this mattered. I knew, as clearly as I knew my own name, that I'd never be able to beat Julio Mattaz on even terms. I reflected that in spite of my troubles, since I had committed to squash I had always believed, had always *known*, that I would make it to number one. I had always *known* that one day I would be standing in front of my mother saying, 'It may not be much, Mother dear, just a sweaty little game with a mere fifteen million players worldwide, but I am the best of all of those fifteen million, I am the number one, top of the tree'. It was arrogant but it made sense to me. After three years with Sailor I'd met or exceeded every one of his targets. Zoë had told me I was doing better than she was at a comparative stage. I was still improving in the physical tests. I had learned about reading an opponent. I was able to raise my game at the crucial moments of big matches. Everything was good. Everything apart from Razz Mattaz.

"It's your left handed factor," Sailor was saying, "that's where we'll have him. Him a lefty, you a lefty. There's no any other left handers in the top fifteen. We can prepare for that, better than him. Lefty backhands can be suspect. Yours is strong. We'll be working on it."

Bullshit, I'm afraid, Sailor. You know it, I know it. Bullshit. Dream on. Usain Bolt? I'm going to beat Usain over a hundred metres? Insane. I've the same chance of breaking down Razza Mattaz's sublime backhand. Razza is something else. Razza has moved the game on. Razza is a freak's freak.

I didn't say this to Sailor over the following months. It just hung over me like depression. Even so I stuck to the programme, clung on to it, really. Through the second half of the year I continued to improve my ranking, fourteenth after reaching the semis in Doha in August, thirteenth after Sharm el Sheik, and then a breakthrough in Chennai.

Chennai Vision, September 3rd

Newcomer Jolyon Jacks, the seventh seed, overcame Frenchman Armand Darnaud yesterday evening in the final of the $200,000 Madrassar Jewels PSA Squash Tournament. The score was 11-7, 10-12, 11-9, 11-6, a hard fought match lasting sixty five minutes. Jacks was eventually too strong for the giant Frenchman. Jacks, a whirlwind of speed and energy, is the current World Under Nineteen champion. He was sponsored for a period by the Mumbai-based AllSports India racquet company, and made many visits to the northern cities to train with the cream of Indian squash. His victory in Chennai marks a triumphant return to India for Jacks, with a performance that shows the value of the hard work he has put in, back home in Manchester with the renowned Sailor McCann, and in Delhi and Mumbai.

This was my first trophy, and more to the point, my biggest prize to date, twenty five thousand dollars in cash, unheard of. Admittedly it was reduced by the five percent levy I had to pay the PSA. Fancy having to hand over twelve hundred and fifty dollars, I thought, eight hundred quid! It was painful. It reminded me that I ought to take up Zoë's offer of an introduction to her accountant. Another fancy-that, me having to get an accountant. I'd been dreaming of winning significant prize money ever since I'd started with Sailor. What I hadn't considered was the hassle. It was a nice hassle, though, and I wanted to show Grandpa, and more importantly my mother, that I could be independent of them and independent of family legacies.

I spent a bit of time with Armand in Chennai before the final. His ambitions were hard to work out. I was to learn about those later from his father. Part of the problem was the language barrier. I couldn't say much in French to Armand, not with my fifty word French vocabulary, and neither could we get far in his English. Armand was never part of banter in the changing room, obsessively organising his spare racquets and his kit and the sticking plasters he was always applying to blisters on his feet. In Chennai, like me, he had done better than his seeding, noisily supported by his father throughout the tournament. He had unexpectedly beaten an off-colour Razz in the quarter final, so that my anticipated first encounter with the American was deferred. Eventually in the final I had silenced 'Doctor Marcel', as everybody called his dad, by running the legs off his son during the crucial, desperately hard third game.

I'd been feeling strong all the way through my half of the draw. I'd not been affected by the squits that had been jetting out of several of the players, and I revelled in the noisy atmosphere that I was coming to expect from tournaments in India. Now I had an average of four hundred and six points, and was tenth in the world. I texted Zoë, 'Wld #10. 9 2 go :-)!'. She texted back, 'And counting x'. I hadn't told Zoë of my fears, that the best I could manage would not be nine places higher, but eight. Just not enough. None of us could rely on Razza getting diarrhoea at every tournament. My pinnacle then, world number two? So what, some might say. So second best.

Back from Chennai I had a long chat with Grandpa. "Thing is, I'm a bit less confident now," I concluded.

"This Razza," Grandpa asked. "What sort of a fellow is he, I mean underneath?"

"That's part of the problem. He's a one off, a really decent guy. You should see the clothes he wears, crazy, long hair, red bandana, shirts in weird fabrics, shorts, sandals. He was halfway through a PhD in astrophysics when he decided to give it a go at squash. Not like me though. He'd played the game since he was a boy, in the army, all over America. He makes it look ridiculously easy. He seems to be as fit as me, and I'm fitter than anyone else."

"Sometimes the people it comes easily to fall apart when things go wrong. And don't forget, you're still improving. Sounds to me as though Razza has reached his peak."

"Huh," I said, "probably like Roger Federer. His peak lasted years. Flat as Table Mountain."

"Don't be a chump, Jolyon. Nadal could have come along sooner than he did, Djokovic. I've never heard you negative like this. It's one of the things I admire in you, you've always been such a positive person. This thing is still in your grasp. More than a year still to go. It's up to you to work out how to deal with Razza Mattaz. It was never going to be easy, never going to fall into your lap. Remember, you've given up your education for this. Are you going to wimp out at the first difficulty?"

First difficulty! It seemed to me as if I'd had plenty of difficulties. It was just that in the chapter of difficulties, this was a big one, north face of the Eiger in December rather than Mount Kilimanjaro in the tourist season. But Grandpa was right, no point in feeling sorry for myself. This wasn't something I wanted to talk to Sailor about, but armed with some of my Chennai dollars, which physically had disappeared into the hands of a teller in the mercifully air conditioned branch of the State Bank of India, I'd take Zoë out for a meal and see what advice she had. And once bitten, I'd make sure that the meal was exclusive. Riley wouldn't get to know about this one.

Zoë gave me a fantastic smile when I suggested the meal. We'd just finished a hard training session at the EIS. If I could bottle that smile it would be worth two points a game, even against Razz. I said that after Chennai I might find Manchester Indian food disappointing, so we arranged to meet in the city centre at an Italian restaurant Zoë knew. Good choice, it was a classy place with linen napkins, well separated tables and no music. Zoë looked spectacular in a short, red dress.

In response to my compliment she said, "If only I didn't play squash I'd fit better into clothes like this. My legs and bum."

"Rubbish. I've never fancied scrawny girls, on catwalks or anywhere else, and for goodness sake..." Enough said, I left it hanging, feeling pleased with the balance. Don't lay it on too thick. Jolyon Jacks, the personal relationships genius.

Genius? Zoë's next words left me utterly, totally shocked. Not just shocked. Want-to-die-now devastated.

"Don't say that. I've been wanting to tell you. You remember on that run, I mentioned that girl, the one at school, way back? Well that was then and I'd always sort of regretted not doing anything about it, not finding out. Well I've been seeing this lady and it's something marvellous, absolutely marvellous."

She smiled at me, lost in her mind's eye.

"Oh really? How..."

"She's the regional manager for the car dealership, my sponsors. She's never had any doubts. About her orientation. She says."

"Is she..."

Zoë's eyes were all lit up, happy. "She's thirty two, she's really going places in BMW, one classy piece of work, breaking through the glass ceilings in a tough business. But outside of work she's so kind. She doesn't impose herself or anything. She knows what a struggle it can be if you're a woman. There's parallels between what we do, the loneliness. With her I don't have to put on a show. I can just be me."

"I'm so..."

"I can even imagine a life after squash now. Not yet of course, no way, but some time in the future. It's a real change in my life, a turn around. Rachel has turned it round."

Rachel. I thought seriously bad thoughts about Rachel. Pox, pox, pox! Pox on Regional Manager Rachel. BMW? Maybe she'd be posted to Germany. If I remembered rightly, BMW were based in Munich. Southern Germany, too, a long way away. But it didn't matter. If Zoë really fancied women, what could I do?

Our food arrived and I made the almighty effort to pull myself together.

"That couldn't be better, Zoë."

It was up there with the great lies, the dog ate my homework; your bum looks fine in that dress; of course I'll love you in the morning. Why did this have to happen to me? I'd been longing for Zoë ever since I'd set eyes on her. Even before; when I'd seen her on television, I guess I was fourteen, at the Sports Personality awards, she'd perfectly fitted a set of receptors in my brain. It didn't matter then, she was just an image. Now it did matter. I'd always known that my fantasies about Zoë fell into the same level of probability, improbability, as winning the lottery. This was like not even having a ticket. Sure the lottery was an infinitesimal chance, but what a distance between that and no chance at all.

Now, Jesus, I had to force down some food. I just wanted to curl up in a corner.

I managed to launch into something normal. "Have you seen Razz Mattaz play recently?"

"Not for a few months. Why?"

"He's got so good. I just can't see myself beating him. I've played most of the others in the top twenty. Even if I haven't done them, I reckon I could. But Razz, I haven't actually played him yet, but the thing is, I can't see anyone beating him, unless he's sick." I shrugged. "Or doesn't turn up."

Zoë nodded. "I know what you mean. He's got class."

"Oh yes?" An attempt at a joke, well done.

"I don't mean like that. Although he is a bit of all right."

"Like Riley?"

"Riley? What are you talking about?"

"Before this, I'd thought you and Riley?"

"Riley, no way, do me a favour. He did doss on my sofa for a week. After he'd been thrown out of his apartment. Oh, I see," she said, "you thought..." She laughed. "I've got better taste than that, give me credit. Razza, maybe yes, in another incarnation."

"He's married," I said.

Zoë laughed. "You know I'm not worrying about that in this incarnation."

"The problem is," I said, "in my current incarnation, I haven't talked about this, I sort of promised my Grandpa that I'd make it to number one, I know it sounds big-headed, by the time I'm twenty one."

Again Zoë laughed. "When's that?"

"March the tenth, the year after next."

"I'd forgotten you were as young as that. My baby little brother."

"Thanks. Anyway, that's what I am. I've got, what, eighteen months."

"A lot can happen in eighteen months."

"Yes, Razz will ascend into the squash stratosphere. As far as I can see, he'll be winning most tournaments he enters. So he'll be getting anything between slumming it at thirteen hundred for a Silver to two six thou for the World Open. Golds, they're seventeen hundred and fifty aren't they? Platinums, two thousand one hundred. He'll be averaging close to two thousand points a tournament soon. Know what I've got? An average of four hundred and piddling footling six."

"It's hard to sustain, though," she said, with an achingly pretty frown. "There's always injuries. And what happened in Chennai?"

"Chennai, Razz got the squits. I can't rely on him getting the squits."

Zoë was eating her penne with unconcealed enjoyment. She would never be a scrawn in a magazine ad. "Well, let's think through what you've got to do. First of all, what about winning the World Open? Would that satisfy your grandfather?"

"Yes, that would do it, world champion. That's November, in Delhi. All I'll have to do, in all likelihood, is to beat Razz. Plus any combination of Magdi G, Trevor Cooper, Armand Darnaud, you name them."

"Armand Darnaud? He's always looked too lazy to me."

"Not any more. From what his father told me he's been training really well. He was no pushover in Chennai. And how about this? His father's had a glass court built specially for him. At his business, in Aix-en-Provence. Think of that, a private glass court. He has his own trainer, Lou somebody, and his father invites quality players there for practice. No expense spared for Armand."

"Well stop fretting about Armand," Zoë said, "let's think what you can do. You'll shed all your results to date by this time next year, so you don't need to worry about your four hundred and six. Which after all isn't bad; it's got you to number ten. Let's say you're going to need an average of at least fifteen hundred points to get to number one. If you don't win the World Open that is. Let's think about the calendar."

"You're sounding like Sailor," I said.

"Sailor talks sense, believe me. How many tournaments do you think you'll play?"

"Apparently there's usually some late changes, but for next year it looks like there are going to be ten Platinum events, the prize money's been going up with India adding three big ones, at least ten Gold and eight silver. Under PSA rules I can drop one Gold if I want to, and two Silver. That means I could be playing as many as twenty five tournaments, if I'm not injured, plus the World Series finals."

"That would be crazy. I'm going to do eighteen this year," Zoë said. "Under WISPA rules the women can drop their nine worst results out of twenty five for the divisor, and just count their best sixteen."

"It's the same in the PSA," I said. "And the problem is, even if I'm regularly runner up it isn't good enough." I'd done the calculations with Sailor. "In a Platinum event you get fourteen hundred and thirty seven point five points for runner up, eleven fifty in Golds and eight sixty two in Silvers."

Zoë gazed up and thought, for a moment looking incredibly young, mid teens rather than twenties. "So, for an average of fifteen hundred points over sixteen tournaments your target is twenty four thousand, aggregate that is. You're going to have to win a lot, just doing the arithmetic."

"That's what I've worked out." I was going to add something about needing Razza not to win too, but I became hugely conscious of Zoë's brown eyes. "Stop it, I'm losing my thread."

"Stop what?"

"Oh, nothing." What a waste of breath.

We carried on eating and chatting, about the other members of Sailor's squad and music and earliest memories. Finally we got onto training.

"When I'm really tired," Zoë said, "I think about losing, and how much pleasure someone's going to get out of beating me. You feel hunted when you're number one. I hate losing, hate it. The thought of losing really pushes me. Even so, I train smarter now. I used to do ridiculous amounts, right through the season. I still do when we've a break from tournaments, but when I'm competing, that's different."

"I know about your training," I said, having earlier that day continued with Zoë in a sequence of shuttle runs after everyone else had finished.

"Problem is," Zoë went on, as I ceased to take in her words, just bitterly enjoying her eyes, "maintaining fitness when there's a run of tournaments. What I do then is short, really hard sessions. Avoiding tiredness is the key then."

"That's all very well if you're winning."

Her eyes went fierce. "What's this 'if you're winning'? This is *you*, Jolyon, and this is your chance. You won't have more than one chance like this in the whole of your life. Why are you so negative tonight? Remember what Sailor says, the top two inches. If there's doubt in the top two inches you're never going to make it. Razza's human. At some point you'll make him realise, all that skill, all that finesse, they're not enough. He'll have to beat your will. Your will's mixed up with your commitment. You have to commit."

It gave me a boost, Zoë's passion. She thanked me sweetly for the meal and dropped me off at Sailor's, with me longing for another aspect of her passion.

If only.

Chapter Thirty

I had a pleasant surprise at the end of October while I was preparing for a sharp trio of tournaments in the Middle East, the Kuwait Open, Qatar Classic and then the biggie, the World Open in Saudi. The surprise came in the form of a phone call from Marcel Darnaud.

"Hey Jolyon. I'm glad that I was able to reach you. I never got to see you in Chennai after your win. Armand was so disappointed. You deserved it. I told him he had to be fitter. Why don't you come down here and visit us for a week, do some sessions, play some practice games? It will be great for Armand to see how you do it, and I promise you, it will be great for you too. We have a fine team here, Lou Kiefer, he does the conditioning, he's one you won't love. Pascal Neige is our dietician, Mary-Emmanuelle Colombey, physiotherapy. I swear she halves the time of any injury. One of my medical colleagues takes care of health issues, Gaston Miahle. You'll be well looked after, we'll have some fun. And one more thing, it's twenty two degrees here right now. I hear your having some bad weather in Manchester."

It did seem an idea, the south of France, and he was right about the weather, two degrees rather than twenty two, the dank cold that often affected Manchester. Problem was, what would Sailor say? Well sod Sailor.

"Wow, that sounds like a fantastic idea," I said. "Maybe the guy who works on Armand's wrist can do something for me while I'm with you."

Marcel laughed. "I'm sure we can work on your wrist. Give me your email address and I'll send you the travel arrangements."

That was how I found myself the following Friday in a huge country house just outside Aix-en-Provence, sharing a delicious meal prepared by the Darnaud's cook with Marcel, Armand and Madame Darnaud, whose English was of Armand rather than Marcel quality and whose looks were the quality of Marcel's English, phew. Clothes too; I knew about clothes from my mother. Of course Madame D bore no resemblance to that Sussex elephant. She was, I guessed, early thirties, too young to be Armand's mum. How often, I wondered, did Marcel change his wife?

"Have a glass of wine, Jolyon," Marcel said. I'd noticed Armand already had a small glass.

"No thanks. I had some issues a year ago, not with alcohol. Anyway, I made up my mind to stick to water."

"Oh yes, the cannabis."

"How did you know about that?"

"It was in the squash press. It was said you were lucky to escape a ban. I'd have known about it anyway. We make it our business to know about Armand's opponents." He rattled off something in French and Armand nodded, looking embarrassed. His wife wasn't paying attention.

"You see," Marcel continued, "Armand and, I must admit, myself, we take the squash seriously. We are after all following some great French players,

Lincou, Gaultier, the very best. Armand announced, well I announced actually, to L'Equipe, in January, I announced Armand's ambition, no his *intention*, to reach number one, to become the world's best player. I make no secret we will learn about you this week, Jolyon. Nor will we hold back, you will benefit also. You will learn about Armand. You will see the routines he accomplishes. He is a remarkable young man.

"You see, Armand has been playing squash since he had seven years, since he was seven years old. He has talked of becoming world champion. Even as a boy he dedicated himself. His mother, my second wife, she objected to how much he played. I would take him to the club every day, before I built the courts at the factory. She did not want his success. We fought," he shrugged, "sadly, divorce. But happily now, you see a formidable young man."

The formidable young man was staring at his plate.

"I can tell you," Marcel went on. "It is in my log book, Armand has missed, not trained, not played, on a total of thirty seven days since he began to play squash."

"Are you serious? Not since he was seven, surely?"

"Yes, it is true. You know the theory, ten thousand hours to produce a champion? Well Armand has spent more than sixteen thousand hours with a squash racquet in his hand. Sixteen thousand three hundred to be precise. That is the origin of his skill. Armand's technique is totally the best."

"You mean you've logged all the time he's been on court? Since he was seven?" I did the mental arithmetic. Sixteen thousand hours: it was two solid years.

"Of course. And his training, that is logged also. Kiefer has made it more scientific now of course, the last three years. He is the expert," he shrugged, "I am the amateur. But once I begin a project, my business, my passion for flying, this rare individual, my son," an open gesture with his hands, "I am dedicated to it. As you see, I am dedicated to Armand.

"And so you are too, my friend, dedicated. I know a little of your story. From your coach. That's a man I admire, Sailor McCann. He told me you only started squash when you were fifteen. Remarkable. Armand since the age of seven, you fifteen. Tell me more. How did you start? How did it happen?"

I paused as the cook, who I learned the next day doubled as Pascal Neige the dietician, came in to take away our plates and bring dessert, something delicious based on peaches. No cream, I noticed.

"Well, I started when a girl at school challenged me to a game."

Marcel translated. His wife looked at me and made a cheery remark. "She says," Marcel explained, "that there's always a girl involved."

"If only," I said. "There doesn't seem to be time for girls. Or else I'm too tired these days."

More from Madame D in her soft voice, all the while smiling at me. Marcel followed up: "Crudely translated," he said, "she says 'more fool then the English girls'. She is sure that French girls would find a way of making you forget your tiredness. I think you are a hit, is that what you say, with my wife."

I smiled back and managed a, "Merci, Madame," to which she inclined her head.

I carried on with the story of my arrival in Manchester, trying to work out how long I'd spent in total on court. It would probably be measured in minutes rather than hours.

"We do performance tests too," Marcel interjected when I described the day Dave and I did our first set of tests with Sailor. "We do them monthly, a little more sophisticated than yours, if I may say, and we include blood tests. Monsieur Kiefer is the expert. The aim is to balance the training against the athlete's physical condition, against tiredness certainly. There is a limit to what the body can tolerate. We know that exceeding that limit makes performance fall away; the athlete is open to infections; often he becomes unwell. Armand keeps himself, well let's say Monsieur Kiefer keeps Armand, just below the critical threshold."

Not long afterwards Madame Darnaud excused herself, kissed Marcel on both cheeks and left the room. Marcel said, "I have some work to do but you must be tired, Jolyon. Perhaps sleep now for you? Armand is never late. We will have breakfast at seven. I will leave for my office at seven thirty and Armand will drive you both to the plant in time for your start at nine thirty. You can take it easy before that, maybe a swim in our pool.

"For now, good night." He made a small bow. "Till tomorrow."

I'd already been shown my bedroom, up a wide wooden staircase that continued, I could see, for at least two more floors, it was that sort of house. I said goodnight to Armand, who shook my hand, and made my way up. My room was sumptuous, a suite. Notable were the vast bathroom and the four poster bed. I undressed and crashed between the posts. Marcel was right, I was tired. Unfortunately the mattress was too soft. If you'd been in there with someone else you'd have had to cling to the side. Unless it was Madame Darnaud, in which case you'd have happily let go, hoping to be joined by her in the valley.

I lay there for ages trying to get to sleep. What a strange set up, Marcel and Madame and Armand. Madame D was of an age to be Marcel's older sister. I wondered if they got on. They hadn't said much to each other at dinner, but no one could with Marcel around. Another thing to consider, the plan for Armand to be number one. He had nodded vigorously when Marcel mentioned his announcement to L'Equipe. Maybe I'd have to take Armand more seriously. He had always seemed destined to be just there or thereabouts, with his enormous frame and incredible wrist. He was capable of beating anyone, maybe even Razza, on his day, but to date he had never been consistent enough to make it right to the top. Now I'd seen from close up the way his father thought, and his father was central to team Darnaud.

Sailor had been positive about the trip but warned me about its purpose. He said that Armand, or more accurately Marcel, would use the visit as an opportunity to establish a psychological advantage over me. He mentioned home cooking, 'garlic-infused snails', the home squash court, the expected home town result in any competitive game. "Whatever you do, don't lose to Armand."

It would be interesting to experience Armand's training over the next few days. I was confident I could cope with any of Monsieur Kiefer's routines. Not so confident about playing Armand.

I was surprised to be wakened at half past six by Madame Darnaud. Disappointingly after my four poster musings, she was wearing a cover-everything dressing gown, not the négligée I'd have picked out for her. Fortunately I too was covered, by the duvet. I was in the buff.

"Here is a cup of tea," she said with her comically strong French accent. "For you English, no?" She smiled and glided out of the room.

The tea turned out to be fine, and so was the breakfast. There was melon, fresh grapefruit juice, croissants and delicious baguettes, with all manner of stuff to go with them. Marcel was there for a short time. He was in his usual linen suit and open-necked shirt, also linen. He didn't eat much and quickly headed off after a meticulous wipe of the lips on his napkin. More linen. Armand and I were able to take our time, with his appetite more than making up for his father's. I managed a joke about carbohydrate loading before he too disappeared.

Armand found me outside at about nine o'clock. I'd been chilling beside the magnificent kidney-shaped swimming pool.

"It is necessary not to be late."

"Okay. Same with Sailor. I'll get my kit."

It was a ten minute drive in Armand's convertible Peugeot. We were nodded into the site at a security gate. Armand drove through the main complex to a large building the far side. This appeared to have not one but two courts attached.

"Yes, the other one, it is a doubles court." Blimey, a bespoke doubles court.

Inside I was even more impressed. There was a gallery behind the courts, which both had glass back walls. To one side there was a changing room, luxurious I was to discover, and to the other a twenty five metre gymnasium. At the far end of the gymnasium there was a variety of multi-gym systems, free weights and exercise machines, plus a small office. A stooped figure in the office conspicuously didn't look up when we came in.

"Him, that is Monsieur Kiefer. He is my trainer. We must get changed."

I noticed Armand strapping a heart rate monitor round his chest while we were changing.

"Yes, for Monsieur Kiefer, for every session. I am all recorded. You too. I am the most recorded moine in 'istory."

"Moine?"

"I don't know. Priest?"

"Oh," I said, "you mean monk. That I can identify with."

I was starting to appreciate what was being invested in Armand.

We made our way out of the changing room and across to the office. With a glance at his watch Monsieur Kiefer came out and greeted me unsmilingly with a 'bon jour', and then pointing to himself, a 'malheureusement, not Eenglish'.

Indeed no Englishman would ever smell so strongly of garlic. Nor dress any more in a shell suit.

"First we are weighed," Armand said. Monsieur Kiefer led us over to an electronic scale. I followed him in removing my shoes and tracksuit and stood on the scale. Armand weighed in at a massive ninety two point seven six kilograms, exceeding my puny seventy two point three seven. I wanted to ask if they couldn't do it a bit more accurately, but I judged the joke wouldn't find its mark. The diligent Monsieur Kiefer noted our weights on an iPad, which I saw already had an entry in my name. Scary. Next he indicated that I should put on a heart rate monitor. My turn to indicate, a polite 'non'. I didn't want to give team Darnaud an insight into that. Sailor was big into the physiology, and insight was a word he used. Monsieur Kiefer shrugged.

Now it was the business of the day. We did a half hour warm up of movement and stretches on the singles court, and a half hour of hitting. Monsieur K prescribed the heights at which the down-the-wall shots should strike the front wall. Interesting in that you had to be continually adjusting the pace to keep a good length. Armand was very focussed, and I was amazed at how hard he could hit the ball. Next we did twenty minutes of high intensity ghosting, exhausting work, followed by ten minutes rest. All the while we were encouraged to drink a foul tasting electrolyte concoction, little and often. The final session before lunch was a best of five game match, with each game played to just five points. The object was to hit as many winners as possible. Armand won all five of these games, blazing the ball into the nicks.

Before we had a shower we were weighed, apparently so that we could be given the right amount to drink, and met Marcel in the airy works canteen for lunch, queuing up with the other workers for our food. The options looked pretty good but to my surprise, Pascal Neige appeared from the kitchen with a tray each for Armand and myself, loaded with two bottles, one of Badoit and one of the electrolyte drink, plus some risotto, delicious as it turned out, some fruit salad and separately, two bananas.

"So, how was the morning?" Marcel asked when we had sat down among the staff.

"Different but hard," I said. "He's a serious guy, Mister Kiefer."

"Ah, Monsieur Kiefer, yes, he is a conditioning genius, an artist. I took him from Castres, you know, the rugby club. He transformed that team."

"What, just for Armand?"

"You must understand by now, Jolyon. This is a serious project. I told you, if I make a project, I make it properly. Nothing is left to chance. For Armand," he looked at his son proudly, "the best. I searched all over France for a trainer with the right approach. The scientific approach." He grimaced. "Castres had been meat. You know rugby players? Neanderthals. See here, they say, I can do the enormous bench press. Watch me, I need the biggest pair of shorts. My thighs? They are nucleaire explosions. Now at Castres they are athletes, all athletes, not just the backs, the forwards, the front five. They move at speed. They leap. They rip the ball better than ever. Monsieur Kiefer was always my man. He was a good squash player, too, one of my best investments for sure."

Marcel paused for a moment to put some food in his mouth, and continued while still chewing.

"Kiefer says, with Armand, it will take another twelve months. He has been with us for twelve months already. He specialises, it is the application of plyometrics."

"Plyometrics?"

"You don't know? Plyometrics, as Kiefer tells me, plyometrics makes the maximum, in the speed-based power. It was his university thesis, Université Louis Pasteur, always the best. Kiefer is a world expert in exercise physiology. Speed-power, how quickly you reach the ball, this is the difference. There is a maximum amount of force a muscle can produce when it contracts." Marcel was animated now. Armand? He was looking the other way. "If the muscle is stretched while it is loaded just before the contraction, it will produce greater force. It is the storage of elastic energy. Kiefer concentrates on this with Armand. You will learn about this.

"Kiefer says it will take two years for Armand to reach his peak. This is why I have been announcing to L'Equipe, it will be the end of next year. Armand will win the world championship. Armand will become number one. I don't say this to insult you, Jolyon. Julio Mattaz, it is Julio and you. We see you as our greatest rivals."

These ambitions were awfully similar to my own.

"Yes, Razza," I said. "It's hard to see either of us beating Razz Mattaz."

Marcel looked at Armand, and then at me, intensely. "There you are wrong, my friend. Mattaz has his weakness. We have studied him. We know it. Kiefer has catalogued his movement, his patterns, his shot selection. If it all comes too easily, you have nothing to fall back on when things go, what do you say, go awree? That is his weakness."

"It's 'awry', and I'm not so sure. You've been studying me too?"

"Of course, we make no secret, as I've said. As if your Sailor, tell me Sailor McCann doesn't study your opponents, Armand naturally, also Magdi, Mansoor. We study you here, for sure, but tell me *you* don't study Armand. Tell me you don't learn from Monsieur Kiefer. And listen, Jolyon, I'm saying to you now, I am open. What I want Armand to learn from you, it is not your shots," a very French gesture with his open hand, "Armand has shots. Not your pace, Kiefer gives him pace. He has to see your *will*, to understand it, to learn from it. To adopt your will, your red *rosbif.*"

Jeez, the will again. Wills seemed to be on the agenda, even if Marcel's metaphor had strayed into underdone Sunday lunch territory.

"Manchester United," Marcel carried on, shovelling down the crêpes he had taken for dessert. "How often do Man U score in the last minute? It is their will. If Armand can duplicate your will, he has the world. I tell you this frankly. It is the end of the jigsaw puzzle, for me the last piece. I tell you too, you must add our science to your programme, you must adopt the plyometrics. That is what we will give you. We show you our science freely, we do not hide it, you shall learn, you are an intelligent boy. From you, Armand learns, he must. Maybe it is the one thing I cannot teach, he learns the goal in the eighty ninth minute. That is why we invited you here. You will see. The week is designed around the will."

He finished his crêpes. "I like you, Jolyon, I want you both to be successful." He acknowledged a colleague passing our table and leant forward towards me. "Now, tell me this, why do you refuse the heart rate monitor?"

"I don't know. It feels private."

"We will do some performance tests, on Thursday and Friday. There the heart rate is essential."

"I don't mind it in proper tests," I said. "That won't feel like spying."

Marcel looked hurt. "You disappoint me. Your heart rate in the entire programme, it gives an important insight, not for us to spy but for Kiefer to help you."

"Just the same," I said, "I think I'll pass on that."

Marcel's eyes flared for a moment, then he took a breath as though making an effort to control himself. "Have it your way, my friend. It is your loss.

"Now, let me explain the programme for the rest of the week. This afternoon you will go back to the house for ninety minutes, take some rest, the pool, the computer. Return here, a review of your physical status with Marie-Emmanuelle, we will take a blood sample, and then the serious business of the day, two hours of circuits, directed by Monsieur Kiefer. We finish with stretches, a cold bath and a massage. That will be Marie-Emmanuelle. As well as physiotherapy, she has trained in Japan for her massage. Then home and dinner and bed."

He addressed his son. "What do you think of the circuit training, Armand?"

Armand shrugged. "It is 'ard."

"It is carefully, how do you say, *tuned*, for the individual. Monsieur Kiefer has already planned your circuits, Jolyon, different from Armand's. He will refine them tomorrow when he sees how you have responded. This is where your heart rate would help. There is a big emphasis on monitoring, and also on symmetry, we must provide balance, to help movement. Squash is so one sided. I will be there at the start to give you the explanations."

"Well, thanks, Marcel." What could I say? "I'm looking forward to it."

"So, that is today. Tomorrow morning, a ten kilometre run, in the hills, some high intensity ghosting and then lunch. Before the circuit work in the afternoon, half an hour of racquet skills, we will practise hitting nicks. I think you will be surprised by Armand. Then always at the end of the day, a massage."

"I try to avoid those in Manchester," I said. "Henry Clark is too brutal."

Armand smiled and his father said, "I think you will find Marie-Emmanuelle agreeable."

The idea of someone with a name as luscious as Marie-Emmanuelle giving me a massage did have an appeal, at least in theory. She might turn out in real life to be a toughie, a Dee-Anne or a Charlie, but you could always hope.

"Wednesday," Marcel continued, "some practice hitting and ghosting, and then the performance tests. The main afternoon work will be a circuit. Thursday, more circuit work in the morning, ghosting, shuttle runs and another mini-match to finish. Friday a run paced by Kiefer on his mobilette and in the afternoon a full game, marked by Kiefer.

"Saturday…"

"Saturday," I interrupted, "the dream is over and I go back to grey old Manchester."

Marcel smiled.

Chapter Thirty One

It turned out that I would have a dream to take back with me to Manchester, Marie-Emmanuelle Colombey. We met Marie-Emmanuelle in a sort of medical suite attached to Marcel's main manufacturing building. We had already provided a blood sample to a serious looking guy in a white coat, introduced as Dr Miahle. Marie-Emmanuelle was also wearing white, a sleeveless tailored tunic that almost but not quite reached her knees. Above them it faithfully followed every exaggerated curve of her body. The tunic wasn't unsubtly tight, she was too, I struggled for the word, chic for that, but neither was it camouflage loose. It took all of my self control not to gawp. Marcel introduced us and said that Marie-Emmanuelle would spend five minutes checking Armand and would then 'interview' me. I sat around in the waiting room, speculating hopefully about Marie-Emmanuelle's interview technique. Would I be grilled? *Ooh please, ask me that again, Marie-Emmanuelle.* How strong the psychological pressure? *Dominate me, Marie-Emmanuelle, break me, mould me to your will.* Sleep deprivation? *I will not sleep in your presence.*

Marie-Emmanuelle turned out to be thorough and professional, with English that in most respects was adequate and where applied to anatomy, superior to mine. Anatomy dominated the interview. Mine in terms of my history, my pains and strains, my muscle tightness, where I was sore after hard matches. We went into detail about my flexibility routines. All the while my responses were carefully noted in a manila folder. As for me and *her* anatomy, no formal notes. My surreptitious but minute scrutiny of the downy dark hair on her arms, the lopsided dimples on her cheeks when she smiled, the ears half hidden by black hair, the quaintly uneven lower teeth, was all recorded in multi-megabyte detail in my memory. Occupying even more storage space (would my brain ever have room for anything else?) were Marie-Emmanuelle's bountiful bits, the ones the lads' magazines would have concentrated on. I would happily have continued adding to the folder, but Marie-Emmanuelle concluded the interview.

"So, I will be seeing you later, after the circuit training," here a smile, "and I will try to repair what Mr Kiefer has done."

"I hope the damage is extensive."

This elicited a cool look as I left the room.

I was apprehensive about the circuit work, afraid I'd be shown up by the weights Armand could lift or his one armed press up repetitions or something like that. I needn't have worried. Marcel explained that Monsieur Kiefer had devised a different programme for me from Armand's. Apart from being knackering, it was satisfying. There was an element of competition in the time we took for each element. Marcel stayed and watched for a while, shouting encouragement at me and surprisingly vitriolic abuse at Armand if I beat him, whereupon Armand would look sourly at his father but say nothing. Then we alternated, Monsieur Kiefer first demonstrating and then timing each routine. By the end of the two hours we were exhausted.

I knew well enough the importance of stretching after high intensity exercise, and we did twenty minutes. Then it was five hundred millilitres of protein slurp, and three two-minute dips in a tepid bath that felt far colder. We emerged in towelling dressing gowns. Armand made a call to Marie-Emmanuelle from a phone on the wall. Now, at last I thought, the massage.

When Marie-Emmanuelle arrived, same tunic I was pleased to see, she gestured to Armand to go first. "We will be twenty minutes," she said. I chilled during the twenty minutes, trying to read a copy of L'Equipe. No radical squash pronouncements in that edition. But it was hard to concentrate.

Then it was my turn. "Do you have any soreness?" Marie-Emmanuelle asked as I lay down on the table.

"No," I replied, "only all over. That was a hard session."

"Then I will attend to you all over," she said primly. *Ooh goody.*

Oh dear, more like. It was up there with the great disappointments in my life, for instance having the Sussex elephant for my mother. I'd thought Henry in Manchester was bad. Henry was *nothing*, a novice. This was seriously worse than Henry, quite intimate in terms of coverage, but so painful, real live pain.

"Deep massage," Marie-Emmanuelle explained in response to my protests. What did she have for fingers? Forged titanium rods? If it had been the interrogation I'd been dreaming about earlier I'd have confessed to everything inside sixty seconds. And then made stuff up for the next nineteen minutes.

"You are very tight," Marie-Emmanuelle said, "I have to tell these muscles to relax." *Let me tell them, Marie-Emmanuelle, I'd rather do it myself.*

When she eventually finished I croaked, "Thank you." It had felt far longer than twenty minutes. "You are very strong."

"Thank you," she echoed, with a flashing smile that propelled me far down the road to forgiveness. "You have nice muscles. I will see you tomorrow."

Armand also smiled when I emerged, as if he knew what I'd been through. "We get dressed and go 'ome," he said.

'Ome was where I wanted to be, and quickly, as far away from the massage room as possible and closer to food. On the credit side, I had to admit to a pleasant feeling of languor in my mangled muscles. Furthermore, I slept well that night in the valley of the four poster. At breakfast I felt really fresh, with no hint of tiredness. This was just as well, as Tuesday's programme was a hard one, starting with the 10K run on a hilly route above the town, paced by the dour Monsieur Kiefer on his Mobilette. The circuit in the afternoon was edgy with its competitive element. My weights and reps had been adjusted, and Armand and I invariably finished within seconds of each other. Towards the end I had to battle to maintain concentration. I was starting to dread the final act of the day's training, the massage.

Again it was Armand who went first. He emerged the prescribed twenty minutes later with another rueful smile, rubbing his shoulders. "She is, 'ow do you say, an assassin, a killer."

"Oh well," I replied, "my turn to die."

Marie-Emmanuelle was writing some notes as I went in. Without looking up she said, "I heard you say that."

"Oh no, Marie-Emmanuelle, you don't understand. That's English irony. Sometimes we use a word that's opposite to the meaning we intend. Having your hands on me will only be a pleasure."

A sideways glance from a brown eye. "So," she asked, "any soreness today?"

"Well strangely enough, I've reviewed my entire body. *Nothing* is sore today. Does that mean that my massage is gentle?"

"Of course not. Not sore today means my work yesterday was good. It's logic. We must repeat so you are not sore tomorrow."

"Can't you put some local anaesthetic in the oil? Aromatherapy or something?"

She put her hand on her hip and arched her eyebrows. "Do not say aromatherapy in 'ere." Her smile was like an astronomer's gamma ray burst. "I will have to punish you."

"I will shout."

"No one will hear. The room, it is, I do not know the word, *insonorisé*."

"I'm afraid you mean soundproofed."

"That is correct. Under data laws, in France, *nothing* leaves the treatment room."

"Not even to Monsieur Darnaud?"

"Of course not."

"So I can't expect any help?"

"Of course not."

It was probably worse than the day before, but with the banter it was better fun, and the twenty minutes were quickly over. Again through the evening, as the memory of the pain faded, the benefits of the treatment were apparent. Lucky Armand to have this every day.

The performance tests on Wednesday were not so different from what I was accustomed to in Manchester. There was though a greater emphasis on the performance of the heart. Armand and I were hooked up to an ECG machine while we were on the treadmill for the VO_2 max measurement. As in Manchester, scheduled last was the bleep test. Marcel had already visited us twice that morning, and he appeared again as we were about to start. Two strips of what looked like heavy groundsheet ran on the gym floor alongside the array of weights and multi-gyms. "It is for grip," Marcel said. There was no CD player. The beeps, Marcel informed me, would be played over the sound system. I didn't mind how they were played. I'd completed all twenty one levels of the bleep test the last three times I'd done it, eliciting a 'well done, son' from Sailor and a 'that's the way you do it' from Zoë. I'd refrained from asking Armand how he performed, confident that I'd beat him. Sailor told me that very few sportsmen can reach, let alone complete, the final stage.

We duly set off, and the early levels were jokey, as they usually are. It takes nine seconds to do each twenty metre length at level one. Not difficult. Usain

Bolt goes nearly five times that far in nine seconds. Around level seven or eight we went quiet, as you usually do. At level ten, not at all usual, I started to become aware that something was wrong, oh fuck, the ground sheet was shifting when I turned, making each interval harder than it should have been. I glanced at Armand. He didn't appear to be having any problem. By level fourteen, when you are going exactly twice as fast as level one, still normally a cruise for me, I was having to work hard. As I turned in the transition to fifteen I noticed Marcel whisper something into Monsieur Kiefer's ear. Armand was grunting but doing okay. Fifteen was a serious strain for me and by sixteen, with reduced purchase as I slowed and then accelerated at each turn, I could hardly keep up. I just managed level seventeen, utterly exhausted, and had to stop.

Armand carried on. Nooo! With a huge 'aarrghhh' at each turn he managed to complete level eighteen and collapsed.

Straight away Marcel was all over him as he heaved air back into his lungs. Effusive congratulations in excited French. As I sat and repaid my artificially severe oxygen debt with poxy Aix-en-Provence O_2 molecules, I saw Monsieur Kiefer removing the start and finish markers and rolling up both lengths of ground sheet. Getting rid of the evidence. I'd been set up. The bleep test had been rigged.

"So Jolyon," Marcel said, "maybe Armand has been learning the will from you this week. Level seventeen is impressive, well done, but I'm delighted that my son has made a personal best today."

"Good effort," I grunted, "he's very fit."

"These tests are nothing." *You creep.* "Don't be disappointed. What is important is performance during a match. We will see on Friday how you really compare."

"You are quiet today," Marie-Emmanuelle said during my massage.

It was true. I was totally, mortally pissed off about the bleep test. I should have quit as soon as I began to slip. It was just that it hadn't seemed serious at first; I thought I could cope. By the time I was struggling it would have been lame to pull out. What could be done? The only answer, I decided, as Marie-Emmanuelle's fingers probed down through my muscles to my very bones, was to thrash Armand on Friday, three games to love, minimum points. Marcel would see what will was. I would show will to both of them. And show that zombie accomplice in his shell suit. Not that it would have been Monsieur Kiefer's idea. The idea clearly came from Marcel. As for Armand, I doubted he had any notion of what was going on. I hadn't felt as strongly about anything since Riley had conned me out of our match in Lancaster. Poor Armand was going to have to be humiliated.

"Have I upset you?" Marie-Emmanuelle asked as she manipulated my feet. "You have said nothing."

"No, no, not at all."

When she had finished the massage Marie-Emmanuelle stopped at the head of the couch and surprised me by running her fingers down my cheek.

"Something has happened. You will be better tomorrow."

"I will certainly be better tomorrow. And then on Friday, I'm looking forward to Friday."

The circuit work on Thursday morning was seriously hard, at least for me. Armand appeared to have a lighter programme, though I couldn't be sure. Monsieur Kiefer had devised an intense programme for my legs. The reps were fewer but the loads much higher than I was accustomed to.

"Kiefer sees more potential for you," Marcel shouted to me when he popped in halfway through the session. "He tells me he thinks you can be significantly quicker. It will be a matter of strength, the major muscle groups in your legs, and the plyometrics. We will give you the programme to take home."

I grunted an acknowledgement, too knackered to say anything more. It felt weird afterwards in the light ghosting session we did before lunch. My legs had lost all their power. I knew this would be temporary, and that if I could sustain the bouncing movement at this workload for a month, doing it no more than three times a week, there might be benefits from my additional strength. Anything to make up the difference with Razza.

Armand and I were once again given a lunch prescribed by Pascal Neige. For the first time, I was issued with more drink than Armand. On the previous days he had been given at least half a litre more, which I put down to his size and the fact that he must have sweated more than me.

"A good morning, no?" Marcel said when he joined us.

"I'm going to need Marie-Emmanuelle this evening," I replied. "My legs are dead."

Marcel dismissed this. "What is it the Americans say, 'no gain without pain'? You will be okay."

We were just finishing the meal when Marcel took a call on his Blackberry. He listened and nodded and said a few 'ouis' before returning the phone carefully to its leather pouch.

"Okay," he said, "we have a change of plan. Tomorrow I have to visit my mother, in La Ciotat. An issue with her lawyer. I regret I will be away for the whole day. So we will play the match today, and transfer the afternoon's schedule to tomorrow."

Not a good idea at all, from the way I was feeling. "I'm a bit tired from the circuits," I said. "We can still play the match tomorrow."

"Oh no, my friend. For me this is the highlight, your match with Armand. This I must see. I must discover if Armand has learned to cope with your English whirlwind, your tornado as we say in French, your tempest. You must feel some obligation, Jolyon, of course you do. I would not miss this.

"It is important," he went on. "Take some rest, for sure. We will do the match at five o'clock. That is plenty of time to recover. Go back to the château, relax, chill out."

I knew even as I nodded agreement that I should have said no. Even in the week before a competition Sailor would never have given me a session like the one earlier. It was another set up, that was obvious. Marcel had manoeuvred me into another loss to Armand. This time not in an easy-to-dismiss performance test. What had Sailor said? 'Whatever you do, don't lose to Armand'.

"Until later, then," Marcel said as he got up from the bench.

Fuck.

Armand drove us both back to the château. I'd have preferred to find Marie-Emmanuelle and get her to massage my legs. Anything to get some life back into them. But there again, I reflected as I snoozed the afternoon away beside the Darnaud's pool, it would take a lot more than a massage to put me into shape for a match with Armand. What could I do? Drop the pace, play slow ball? There were some on the circuit who could change their game, throw in a stream of lobs and drops. Dave could do it, back in Manchester, so could Riley. It could be difficult for opponents to adjust to. Problem was, I'd never done it, didn't know how. I only had one pace, as fast as I could go. Only not today. Whirlwind today was going to be a limp force five.

We made it back to the centre at four. One thing was definite, I wouldn't go on court beaten and I went through my normal pre-match preparation. I visualised getting Armand behind me, dominating the rallies, crushing his spirit. I did a full warm up, ignoring the sensation that my quads had turned to blancmange. At ten to five Armand and I walked into the gallery area behind the main court. At least twenty spectators had distributed themselves on the four levels of tiered seating. Marcel introduced me to a young man with a shaven head whom I vaguely recognised.

"Here is Alphonse Manasset. You know each other?"

"Oh yes. I saw you in Hong Kong."

Alphonse was an up and coming French player who had occasionally made it out of qualifying into the first round of the bigger tournaments. I remembered him for the lurid shoes he wore. Then my heart sank. Sitting right at the end of the front row, unaccompanied, was Marie-Emmanuelle, luscious in a short skirt and tee shirt, looking more girlish than she did in her uniform. Not fair, I didn't want to lose in front of Marie-Emmanuelle. The ever present Monsieur Kiefer was there. Marcel explained that he was going to mark the match.

I paused for a moment before going on court for the knock up, pushing everything out of my mind apart from the game. Monsieur Kiefer threw us a ball, Armand and I shook hands and we were off.

I was taken aback by the sheer fierceness of Armand's hitting during the knock up. He was more intense than I'd ever seen him. The intensity carried through into the game. The control I knew about, and the brutal strength, but not the passion. That rarely if ever showed with Armand. I had to respond. Move up thirty centimetres, my squash brain knew it, push. Trouble was, my drained legs wouldn't do it. Something extra was needed and nothing extra was available. I resorted to an attritional game, fighting, scrapping, defending. Six all the score, seven all, then bang bang bang, a stream of unplayable winners from Armand. Fifteen minutes gone according to the big clock at the back of the gallery. First game to Armand 11-7. I had done my best but the result of the match was already written on the wall, or at least pencilled in.

I was going to lose.

I desperately considered the options as I towelled myself down. Normally I'd have concentrated harder, hit every shot tighter, pushed even further forward. Today pushing wasn't an option. I would simply have to make winning as difficult as possible for Armand. I would give him nothing. He would have to wring every point out of me. Maybe along the way he would start to have doubts, tighten up, make a few mistakes. Right now he was the opposite of tight, standing with Marcel and Alphonse, calmly taking in advice.

"Quinze secondes," Monsieur Kiefer called. Here we go.

For a while it worked. Two all after five desperate minutes became six all after fifteen. None of Armand's six had been errors from me. Seven all, eight all, a gut wrenching rally, come on! Then Armand did the ridiculous again. In quick succession, off tight shots that were all but clinging to the wall, he hit three clean dead nicks. Each time the ball fizzed off his strings across the court, and rolled without a hint of bounce. Unplayable. I felt my shoulders slump. Forty two minutes and I was two love down.

You'd never have thought twenty people could make such as much noise as we left the court, clapping and cheering. Marcel was beaming, Armand looking sheepishly pleased. I sat down with my towel over my head. What now? Well, take a drink, change your shirt, get on with it. More of the same was all I could offer. Or try to offer. The second game had taken so much out of me. Realistically, I had nothing left. I looked across at Armand and his team. Marcel was laughing.

"Alors, allez!" he said with gusto, pushing Armand in the direction of the court, and exchanged a high five with Alphonse.

At that something snapped in me. It wasn't Armand I was playing. Not at all. It became Marcel. For all his urbanity and his generosity, Marcel was a cheat. Not some euphemism: gamesmanship, professionalism, slanting the odds. This was naked c-h-e-a-t-i-n-g. I'd suffered several cheats in my short time in sports and I didn't like it. Cheating brought bile to my throat. Cheating was Ron Clarke in the Senior Steeplechase; that still rankled. Cheating was Siobhan in my first ever squash match, when I didn't know the rules. What a little tit she had been with her blatant obstruction. And worse than either of them, cheating was nobber Riley, the cynical one. Now here, cheating was Marcel Darnaud. He glanced at me then shared a self satisfied observation with Alphonse. He had won. He knew it.

I was incandescent. Would I *allow* it? No way.

The adrenaline took me all thirty of the centimetres forward that I needed. The first point of the third game, I was where I had to be, right on the T. I overwhelmed Armand through that long first point. He fought and fought, scrambling in the back corners. Finally he was late reaching the best struck shot I had played the whole game. What a satisfying way to win a rally. As I went to retrieve the ball from near the back wall, I found myself less than two metres from where Marcel was sitting. We locked eyes as I slowly wiped my hand on the glass. Eventually Marcel looked away. He was embarrassed.

I managed to sustain the effort through the whole of the third game. Armand raised his level too. It was the only game of the match of real quality. I kept thinking of the smirking Marcel, the high five with Alphonse. Sheer indignation kept me going. Armand meanwhile did everything that he did well, getting big applause for each point he won. It was never going to be enough. He led nine eight, two points from victory but there were no miraculous nicks at the finish. I took the game 11-9, another twenty knackering minutes. This time the crowd was silent as we came off court.

Now the attitude in Team Darnaud was different. A grim-faced Marcel was jabbing Armand in the chest. Alphonse had his back to both of them, scratching his head. Armand would be tired after that, I thought, and disappointed having got so close. He wouldn't realise I was spent. No amount of adrenaline could sustain me further at the level of the third game.

Sailor would often talk about a great player of the nineteen sixties and seventies called Jonah Barrington. 'Bar-rington' was how he pronounced the name, though apparently bars were the last place you would find the man. Barrington had wrenched the world crown from a stream of talented Egyptians and Pakistanis, and then defended it against some great Aussies in the second half of his career. On one occasion he took the British Open crown in a match lasting two hours, and had to be literally carried off the court. Barrington apparently was rock hard in the manner Sailor approved of. He later wrote a book, *Murder in the Squash Court*, maybe inspired by that two hour match.

What followed between Armand and me would have qualified for an extra Jonah Barrington chapter. The match became attritional on both our parts; neither of us would take any risks. My legs had gone and with them my speed, but so had the snap Armand had displayed in the first three games, the quality of his striking. There were numerous lets, to his credit accurately called by Monsieur Kiefer. Marcel was shouting instructions after almost every point. If he'd carried on like that in a proper tournament he'd have been ejected. There was nothing I could do about it, and anyway it wasn't helping Armand. I won the fourth game 11-8 after all of twenty more minutes, without making a single error. Coming off the court I was rewarded by a smile from Marie-Emmanuelle. From the spectators? Further silence. From Marcel, serious abuse for his son. Armand looked dejected.

Marcel's invective had an effect, though. Armand must have been tired, but anything he was suffering was magnified in me by the strain my legs had been through that morning. Armand tried to attack at the start of the fifth game. It must have taken some of his remaining strength and I managed to soak it up. We soon returned to boring make-no-mistake attrition. After every point, and every one of the frequent lets, I paused to visualise Marcel's face at the moment I won. A highlight for me was a lengthy argument between Marcel and Monsieur Kiefer about one of his decisions. To Marcel's fury Kiefer wouldn't back down. How sweet. I was beating Marcel through his agent Armand on the court. He wouldn't meet my eye when I wiped my hand and stared at him through the back wall between points.

Armand looked drained, pausing for longer and longer between points. I built up a good lead, seven four. Then Armand brought the audience to life with one of his runs of nicks. It took him to eight seven and I was three points from defeat. It was never going to be enough though and after exactly two hours and a mental nod to Mr Bar-rington I won my first match point to finish the most exhausting game of squash I'd ever been involved in.

Armand's handshake was heartfelt and he insisted I leave the court first to polite applause from the remaining spectators. Marcel wouldn't acknowledge me, and I went to thank Monsieur Kiefer for the marking. He wouldn't let go of my hand, repeating, "Good, good, good, formidable, very good."

As I separated myself from Monsieur Kiefer I was astonished to see Marcel frogmarching Armand away. Monsieur Kiefer also departed, leaving me on my own to collect three saturated shirts and the rest of my kit. Maybe some stretches before my shower, and was I looking forward to the shower.

I stopped to look at the court before I left. The floor was spattered with sweat, the glass back smeared where we had repeatedly wiped our hands. I wondered, why had I made such an effort? No ranking points at stake, no journalists to write about the game. It was, I think, an aversion to being controlled. Control was what my mother wanted. Marcel had tried to contrive control during the week with his manipulation of the training and the performance tests and this evening's match. Winning this evening more than made up for losing the bleep test.

"You did well."

I jumped with surprise to see Marie-Emmanuelle, now in her white tunic, at the entrance to the gallery.

"Hey, you gave me a fright."

"I'm sorry. I came to insist you make your warm down."

"I was going to do some stretches."

"Yes, and the ice bath."

"Oh, not this evening, Marie-Emmanuelle. I don't think I could face an ice bath."

"Today it is more important. Much damage to your muscles, that game."

It made sense. "I suppose so."

"And then I will give you a massage."

"No, that's kind. I simply couldn't cope with one of your massages this evening."

She laughed. "This will be different. This will be a healing massage. Come. Make your stretches. Have your shower. I will prepare the bath. And then the massage."

I was too tired to argue. As long as she moderated her attack.

Half an hour later I was stretched out on my front with a towel over my bum enjoying the most sublime sensations as Marie-Emmanuelle stroked the fatigue away from the muscles in my legs. She was using an entirely different technique from before. The high-tech table was lowered and she was kneeling while she worked. "I learn this in Turkey," she explained. 'Tourkay', but who cares. "It is a special oil. It is long strokes. It is therapy."

"Oh it certainly is therapy. It feels wonderful."

Next it was my back and shoulders and then I was ordered to turn over, my head comfortably on a pillow. I watched Marie-Emmanuelle through half closed eyes. She was lovely, maybe older than I had first thought, nearer thirty than twenty five, far too curvy to be a squash player. The massage was hard work, the continuous movement, the bending from the waist. I could see faint perspiration on her forehead and upper lip. Well, I was happy to lie back. I'd done enough perspiring myself that evening. Then I noticed something else. It came like an electric shock. Marie-Emmanuelle wasn't wearing a bra.

How had I missed that? Marie-Emmanuelle breasts were behaving as free agents inside her tunic. The women I usually saw, Zoë, Carmen and other squash players, had small breasts that didn't swing around much. Marie-Emmanuelle's did. It was lucky they weren't musicians because they were out of time, the swing of one slightly behind the swing of the other, depending on how she moved. Inevitably the notion of studying her breasts more intimately sprang to mind, and where springing was concerned my dick wasn't far behind.

Marie-Emmanuelle must have noticed. She asked directly, "What are you looking at?"

Oh well, in for a penny. "Your breasts."

She stopped the massage and knelt up, shoulders back, which brought the items under discussion into greater prominence. "That is not polite."

"That's true. You must suffer a lot of impoliteness."

"I don't understand."

"A lot of men must stare at your breasts. They are very attractive breasts."

"Thank you."

From the way my dick was behaving, it clearly shared my opinion.

"Please don't stop the massage," I said.

"So you can watch my breasts?"

"Well, partly, but the massage is wonderful after that game. I might be able to walk again if you keep going. Walk as far as the car park anyway. I don't know in whose car though. Armand has disappeared.

"But if I'm honest I would mainly like to watch your breasts. With your permission."

Marie-Emmanuelle shrugged and carried on with the massage. After a few more minutes of watching I became aware that the focus of her massage was progressing. It was closing in on the part of me that had not been stressed at all in the two hours of the match. Marie-Emmanuelle cast my tented towel aside. "Ah," she said. "You are not absolutely fatigued?"

"It appears not," I said.

"Then we must achieve a balance," she replied. She stood up, unbuttoned her tunic and let it fall to the floor. No bra, manifestly. Just a pair of plain white knickers. She walked over to the door and locked it, then returned, knelt down again and reached under the couch. This brought the twin subjects of our conversation disturbingly close to my face. With a whining sound the couch descended to what must have been its lowest setting. Marie-Emmanuelle moved astride me and sat back on my knees. In direct contrast to the couch my dick had assumed its highest setting.

"Have I your permission to continue?"

"It appears I have no option. I am at your mercy."

Continue she did, down my chest and stomach and then to the centre of my universe, if we consider my priorities at that moment. The cosmic rod was showing definitive signs of wanting an equalising two hour work out.

"You have a beautiful body, Jolyon," she said as she slid her hands up as far as my neck and down as far as my absolutely fatigued thighs, now trapped between her legs. This continued for several minutes until she stood up again, slipped off her knickers and without asking permission stepped over me and lowered herself onto me.

She bent forward, her nose almost touching mine, and looked into my eyes. "It is best like this. You do not have to move."

"Okay, if you insist."

Watching Marie-Emmanuelle do the moving was too much for me. I came straight away.

"I'm sorry," I said. "You're too sexy."

"It means nothing. I demand you make the massage on me."

"It would be ungrateful of me to refuse."

"Let me lie where you are."

We exchanged places.

"Now, it is necessary to apply some oil to my body." She giggled as I complied by squirting the oil into her deep navel, over her nipples and into her pubic hair.

"Is that the way?"

"Yes. Now, you have seen my massage. Make it the same way."

I think it was the sexiest experience of my life massaging Marie-Emmanuelle, from her neck all the way down to her feet and then all the way back, her skin glistening under my hands. She lay still, with closed eyes and parted lips. When I eventually concentrated my efforts halfway between her neck and her feet her breathing became progressively deeper until suddenly she half sat up with a series of grunts, her face contorted in a violent orgasm. When she had finished coming she lay back, breasts rising and falling with her breathing.

"Oh thank you," she whispered. "You are very good."

"Good teacher," I replied, and bent to kiss her lips. "I've never made love to anyone before without kissing them."

"Wait," she said, and stood up. She went over to a cupboard and took out some towels and pillows. These she spread on the floor and invited me to lie with her. This was much more normal and tender. I enjoyed the touching of our faces as much as the touching of everything else.

Afterwards while we were just lying there she said, "That was a hard game you had."

"It was the hardest. I really didn't want to lose. It was Marcel..."

"I know," she interrupted. "I heard him talking about it yesterday evening with Monsieur Kiefer. After you had gone. Kiefer was to fatigue you today and they change the plan. The match today, not tomorrow."

"Why didn't you warn me?"

"I was away all today, in Marseille." She looked at me with solemn eyes. "I didn't need to warn you. You won."

"Well I got a good massage out of it, anyway. Armand is lucky. To get a massage every day."

"He does not get this massage."

I smiled and kissed her. "Well I was dead lucky. Maybe he's not as lucky as that. It's hard to tell what Armand's thinking. My French isn't good enough to speak to him, not really, and his English is no better."

"I know him since three years," Marie-Emmanuelle said. "He hates his father." "'E 'Ates' is what she said, but I understood.

"Really? You can't mean that."

"It is true. Every time his father shout at him, he, how do you say, makes the grimaces?"

"Uh, I see, he pulls faces."

"Yes, when his father is not looking. But I notice. He is still a little boy. Some day this will stop. Maybe when Armand becomes mature."

"When he grows up, you mean. You're probably right. I wouldn't take it. My mother's like that. Except she doesn't have any good features. Marcel does. He can be a decent guy."

"He is a good man when he succeeds," she paused, "when he... gets his way?"

"That's it. Gets his way. I can see that. He's very generous. He's been very generous here. Apart from setting me up to lose."

"I worry," she said. "Since three months. Armand is heavier. I feel it in his muscles."

"What do you mean?"

"I think," she frowned, "I suspect, an anabolic agent." 'Anabolique' was how it came out but the meaning was clear in any accent.

"You can't be serious. He could get caught so easily."

"Marcel is too clever for that." 'Clevvair'. "Armand was eighty seven kilograms, always. Now since, I think, the summer, he is stronger for sure. He is what, ninety three, ninety four kilograms? I 'ave no proof. But it is not the cassoulet."

She looked me in the eyes, so seriously, and put her index finger on my lips. "You must not say. I 'ave no proof."

She presented an alluring sight as she sat up and stretched. "He is still not strong enough. That match this evening, that was to give Armand confidence."

"Didn't work, did it. I felt so pissed off being manipulated by Marcel. I don't mind being manipulated by you, though."

She smiled. "You are looking at my breasts again. No more manipulations. We must go."

Marie-Emmanuelle drove me back to the Darnauds' château. I got out, kissed her through the window and said my thanks. She smiled and drove away without looking back. Everything was quiet; some lights were on. The mighty entrance wasn't locked. I left my bag at the bottom of the staircase and went hunting for some food. I was starving.

Finding the kitchen was easy. It was next to the dining room, and huge. I retrieved the best part of two baguettes from a large waste bin and found some butter and pâté in one of the fridges, plus a carton of tropical fruit juice. With this lot inside me I felt better and heaved myself step by step as quietly as I could up the staircase to bed. Not quietly enough. Marcel emerged from a door on the landing.

"Where have you been?" His eyes were fierce.

"I had a massage with Marie-Emmanuelle. Then she brought me back. I've just had something to eat in the kitchen. I hope you don't mind."

"Why have you been so long?"

"I haven't been so long. I'm tired, you won't be surprised to know. That was a hard match. Then you and Armand disappeared."

"I had to speak to Armand."

"Well, I had to get back here and Marie-Emmanuelle offered." Better not go into more detail on the extent of Marie-Emmanuelle's offerings. This appeared to be a sensitive subject for Marcel.

"You should have called me."

"I didn't want to trouble you, and Marie-Emmanuelle was very friendly." I kept a straight face. Marcel looked at me suspiciously.

"Next time call me." *If the alternative is a massage from Marie-Emmanuelle Colombey, probably not, mate.*

What a day.

Chapter Thirty Two

My time in Aix-en-Provence had helped. I understood Marcel now, mighty rich and mighty generous with it, good company and watch out, alarm bells, sonny, utterly not to be trusted. He was far too passionate about his son winning. Armand himself, him I'd never understand even if I did a degree in French and a postgrad in psychoanalysis. How could anyone be so good at something and yet so passive? One thing, I'd never now lose to him when it mattered. Armand's will to win came from his father. Mine had its origins in my dominant parent too, my mother. Big difference: mine came from inside, founded on spite; Armand's from outside, founded on what, fear?

Marcel had phoned me during lunch on the Friday. 'It was your will, Jolyon, nothing else, Armand knows it. Armand learns. Thank you.' Hmm, the will wasn't something you could teach, I'd have thought. On the training front, the visit had been good for me. I had picked up tips from Monsieur Kiefer that I wanted to incorporate into my routines in Manchester. The principal gain came from the match against Armand, the knowledge that I could push myself further than I'd imagined. If it came down to murder in the squash court, it would always be me the perp.

After Aix-en-Provence it was the three year-end tournaments, Kuwait, Qatar and Saudi for the big one, the World Open. Good results in Kuwait and Qatar, including a win over Trevor Cooper, then ranked three, should have taken me into the World Open in a confident mood. Problem was, I was seeded to meet Razza in the quarter final. At least I'd find out if he was as good as I thought.

Was Razza good? Was the lake in Salt Lake City salty! Razza destroyed me. The score was 11-8, 11-6, 11-4. He pulled away in a depressingly arithmetic progression. I all but gave up in frustration.

I returned to a freezing cold December Manchester with the full-on glums. I'd been embarrassed on court against Razza, made to look a novice. He had ghosted about, never physically stressed, controlling the ball with supernatural skill. It wasn't as if I'd played badly. I had done everything I did well, moving better than ever, onto the ball so early, timing every shot with a subconscious ease that comes with peak condition. Fat lot of good. Razz had taken the ball as early as me, he had reached virtually everything, his length was immaculate, and as if all that wasn't enough, he was incredibly deceptive. Time and again I'd be wrong-footed as I set off in the direction his shot *had* to go, only for him to flex his wrist and send it in another direction at the last moment, or crack it deep with zero backswing. This took extra energy out of me, and for all the game was short, I was knackered when I shook hands and hurried off the court.

Coming up to New Year I shook myself out of the glums and made a resolution. Zoë was right about attitude. The way the calendar worked I had thirteen months. The big chance was next year's World Open in November. Even if Razz was way ahead in the rankings, he could always lose there. And if it was me who won, not an impossibility, that would be it, think of it, world champion! The far side of the World Open, the last big tournament before my birthday, was the Tournament of Champions at the end of the following January. The ToC in Grand Central Terminal New York, a glam tournament that all the players wanted to do well in. If for some reason the points were close at that stage, winning the ToC might be my final step onto the top rung. What a place to claim the number one spot.

The clichés came out as I looked forward to the next year. It ain't over till it's over. You've got to be in it to win it. Winning is not a result, it's an attitude. All hot happy clappy air but never mind, that would be my attitude.

On the credit side, at the start of the year my six hundred and thirty seven point five points as World Open quarter finalist had taken me to my highest ever ranking, number six, with an average of seven hundred and two points. Also, I had qualified for the season-ending World Series finals at Queen's Club in London. A great opportunity to kick the year off well. The season's top eight players competed for a huge prize by squash standards, thirty three thousand dollars, big prestige, too, and a fantastic venue, the all glass court erected on the main tennis court at Queen's. Not, that is, out in the open. The court was set up inside an enormous science fiction cube, a sort of mutated bouncy castle. That was how I found myself in the lobby of the nearby Hilton Hotel with a group invited out for a meal by Marcel Darnaud.

The meal became progressively more enjoyable. I'd wanted to be closer to Zoë, for the pleasure of looking at the loveliest eyes on the planet, and enjoying being on the same page as her in the rankings for the first time. Next best thing though: it was great talking to Sasha Cremorne, with her nose rings and her ear rings and her eyebrow rings. I told her about the music scene, down in Sussex and up where I lived now. I promised to take her to a party some time. I described the chaotic London markets, where to shop in Petticoat Lane and Camden Lock, yes Brick Lane, but avoid the restaurants. I told her I'd personally accompany her on a shopping expedition in Manchester if she'd make it up there. She surprised me by explaining that she and Trevor Cooper, my opponent at one o'clock prompt the following day, weren't really together now. He was a great guy, Trev, they'd had something going way back in Sydney, but it had petered out.

The meal didn't go on late: too many earnest squash players with matches to think about. Sasha and I fell behind the others on the short walk back to the hotel. Everyone had dispersed from the lobby by the time we arrived.

"How about a drink, Sasha?" I asked. It wasn't yet ten o'clock.

"Sure, I'd like that."

The bar had several Aussie lagers available and Sasha opted for a Swan, a west Australian beer apparently.

"What's that?" she demanded when my pint of orange squash arrived. "Jeez, you'll wash yourself away from the inside. Trev is always up for a beer."

"Nah, I find the only way to deal with substances is not to have any of them, at all. Anyway, Sailor would kill me."

Next morning, when I stumbled down to what I'd hoped would still be breakfast at half past eleven, having left Sasha fast asleep in the monster bed, Sailor did kill me, as near as. He was hanging around in the hotel lobby, the last person I wanted to see. I braced myself as he walked briskly up to me.

"What are you doing, son?" Each word emphatically separated from its neighbour, and he didn't care who heard. "I've been trying to phone you for three hours now. What is going on?"

My guilt must have been all too apparent.

"You horny, immature..." brace yourself, Jolyon, "...child." Phew, I got away with that one. "You friggin' idiot. This game today is key to your whole season."

Oh come on, Sailor, it's not that bad. "Trevor flippin' Cooper!" An effective variation on tmesis, though I doubted Sailor was thinking of it in those terms.

"Where do ye keep yer brains? In yer..." another hesitation, "...friggin' penis?"

He looked around and turned as if to walk away, and then turned back, waving a finger under my nose. "I'm done, done with you, son, Jesus wept."

I was saved by the arrival of Razza Mattaz, who appeared with Ruth from one of the lifts. "Hey Sailor," he said as he took in the scene, "the coach's burden is an onerous one." He signalled me away with his eyes, put an arm around Sailor's shoulder and ushered him off in the direction of the nearby café.

I hurried away. I was well knackered, well and truly. Sasha had been, how can I put it, demanding. We'd gone on for ages. At one stage just for the fun of it I'd asked her a pointless question.

"Sash, do you know what the word 'lascivious' means?"

"No."

No surprise there. Then when we were well and truly finished, and so was I in the other sense, with murky winter daylight just visible outside, since Sasha had insisted on having the curtains open, she switched on the TV. Porn for goodness sake. Half an hour into that I said, "We've done better than them."

"We haven't done it that way."

"For fuck's sake."

"Wouldn't you like it like that?"

"I've never tried."

I had to admit the idea did have its attractions. So it was one more time, like the lyric in one of my dad's songs, all the while watching the bored twosome on the TV. Eventually we flopped back and as I lay there with my chest heaving, *thank goodness for all those four hundred metre reps at the EIS, Sailor*, Sasha put her arms around me, kissed the end of my nose and said, "That was good." Then in her businesslike way she pulled the duvet over both of us and fell asleep, head on my chest, arms around me. I cleared her hair away from my face, reflected for a moment that Sailor would have insisted on proper fluid replacement, and fell asleep myself.

With hindsight I should have given more consideration to the advice Sailor would have given if I'd consulted him the previous evening. *I've the possibility of shagging my balls off with this crash hot Aussie girl, Sailor, all night. Or do you think I should simply go to bed?*

Well, son, I can see the dilemma. She certainly is a sexy piece of work, well stacked as we used tae say in the tenement, two o' the best. If ye can confine it to a quickie it might relax you, help you sleep.

No, it wouldn't have been that. At quarter past twelve, having eaten a bread roll pinched from a discarded room service tray in my corridor, I was getting changed in the splendid trad locker room in Queen's Club, as far on the other side of the room from Trevor Cooper as I could manage. Razza came over and sat down beside me.

"How are you feeling?"

"Awful."

"You look it. Some bridge building to be done there. Sailor is not pleased."

"I feel an idiot."

"Well, you can only start from where you are now. Maybe an apology. The best thing would be to beat Trevor."

The Times Online, January 9th

World Series Squash, Queen's

The first pool matches in the squash World Series finals were played today at the Queen's Club. World champion and world number one Julio Mattaz had a straightforward win, 11-9, 11-7 against Magdi Gamal. In the same group, Armand Darnaud surprised the seedings by beating Hosni el Baradei, ranked six places above him. This was the only one of the four matches to go to three games.

Darnaud was impressive in seeing off the lightning quick el Baradei 7-11, 11-8, 11-8. Afterwards El Baradei said, "Armand was impressive today. I didn't expect him to be so consistent. With Razz in the group it's going to be hard for me to qualify for the semis now."

In the other group Jan Berry dominated all the way against Mansoor Ali Khan, to win 11-8, 11-7. Earlier, in the opening match, Trevor Cooper reversed two recent defeats by Jolyon Jacks in a 11-6, 11-5 win in only twenty five minutes. A delighted Cooper said, "It was time someone put Jolyon in his place. He has come up so quickly." A tired looking Jacks said, "I just didn't have it today. Maybe next time."

Queen's was a disaster. I lost my other two pool matches, one of them watched by Grandpa, the worst possible start to my crucial year. You would think it marked a low point for me, packing my bags to leave the Hilton Hotel to return to Manchester. No. That came over a cup of tea with a belligerent Zoë after my first training session back.

"You bleeding idiot. That Sasha thing was a set up."

"What Sasha thing?"

"Oh stop it, you know what I mean. Everyone knows. You were set up. Trevor Cooper's been bragging about it. Along the lines of 'that stupid Pommie galah', you know what he's like. I can't believe you fell for it. She's kind of obvious, isn't she?"

Oh dear, how could I have been so gullible. Now it was twice as bad for being common knowledge. That's *not* the way you do it. I felt my face going red as Zoë regarded me coldly. I'd like to think it hadn't all been an Aussie plot for Sasha. I didn't think it would help with Zoë to say that even if Sasha was obvious, she was certainly committed.

Through the spring it appeared that my Zoë boats had been burned. She was consistently unfriendly on the rare occasions she wasn't away playing tournaments. Sailor, to his credit, treated me as normal, that is to say consistently sadistically, after having an almighty go at me the first evening I was back. Then after the embarrassment had faded and after I'd had Riley by the throat in the car park when his smirking had become intolerable, I adopted the Razza philosophy, 'you can only start from where you are now'.

My rebooted life was little changed. Training was even more intense, enhanced by some of the stuff I'd picked up with the Darnauds. There was regular travel to tournaments: my first 'Tournament of Champions', the ToC in New York; in February the British Nationals, which was my home competition, literally, at the EIS; there was another transatlantic trip to the North American Open in Richmond, Virginia; then the Canary Wharf Classic back in London. And all the while encouraging progress, I continued to improve: by July I was ranked number four in the world, squeeze that into your absurd little Prada handbag, mother.

And all the while the prospects were becoming bleaker. Inevitably, that was down to Razza Mattaz. Razz too was playing better, and his better bested my better, and everyone else's. Razza had acquired his own conditioning guru, his own Monsieur Kiefer, in Salt Lake City. This guy, one Cornelius Liszt, had imposed order on his training, according to Razz's wife Ruth. The free spirit Razz had become the serious, fully physically focussed athlete Julio. It wasn't so much that he beat you more easily now. His extra fitness seemed to protect him from injury. It enabled him to play a series of tournaments without the loss of form that eventually affected even the best players. Razza won in New York, beating me on the way, he won in Richmond and he won at Canary Wharf. As the second half of the year began, Razz had an average of one thousand nine hundred and fifty five points. Me for my fourth place in the rankings, eight hundred and three. I could catch Trevor Cooper, one place above me, I could catch Magdi Gamal, world number two, but as for catching Razz, the idea was beginning to become absurd. My chances of meeting Grandpa's challenge were narrowing: I couldn't do it in the rankings; I'd have to win the World Open. This year, good news, the Open was being held in New Delhi. I always did well in India.

I wasn't without hope for the World Open. Razza did get beaten occasionally. In the Australian Open, he sensationally went out in the first round to a qualifier. "I can't explain it," he said to the excited journalists afterwards. "There was nothing in my legs." Armand came through in Razz's half of the draw to play me in the final. It was satisfying to beat him, in one hour rather than two, under the nose of his father. Sadly my massage afterwards was not delivered by Marie-Emmanuelle Colombey.

So Razza could lose. So indeed could I to others in the top ten. So could Armand, but in his case ominously he was starting to lose his reputation for going walkabout during matches. I thought back to Marie-Emmanuelle's theory that he was on something. I remembered Marcel's implacable commitment to his son's reaching number one. Armand was responding, clean or drug-enhanced, and was on a collision course with me, not for the number one spot but for number two. Magdi Gamal was just Magdi, a lightweight with an always present grin, whom you had to beat over and over again, it seemed, to actually win. Magdi had come back from two nil down in more matches than anyone else in the history of the tour. Then there was Trevor Cooper, abrasive Trev, always a danger, though I'd enjoyed beating him comprehensively in our next match after the World Series finals. "Good night's sleep, Jols?" he'd asked before we'd gone on court. "How's Sasha, by the way?" I'd responded during his cursory handshake at the end of my three nil win. "Still hanging out with friends?"

The World Open became an increasing obsession through the autumn. As long as I didn't have an injury, in Delhi I was going to be at the highest physical level I'd ever reached. My training had gone well, I was 'in the stratosphere' as Sailor put it in the performance tests. My one blip had been in the Hong Kong Open. I was seeded to meet Armand in the semi and play Razz in the final. Foolish to take things for granted. I lost in the quarters to Serge Colson in a game in which my legs had no spring. Frustrating, and nothing I could do about it. It was Armand who underwent a demolition at the hands of Razza in the final.

Chapter Thirty Three

I loved it in New Delhi. Not the classic tourist stuff, Rajpath, India Gate, the colonial architecture. It was the stuff I'd picked up when I was with AllSports, the noise, the smells, the mad traffic; narrow streets bustling with people in every sort of colourful clothing. It added up to an energy I'd buzzed off ever since my first visit. Admittedly, in the Oberoi hotel we were insulated from the grimmer, grimier side, the legless beggars and the open sewers.

The seedings in Delhi had worked well for me: I was not going to meet Razz until the final. My semi opponent was due to be Trevor Cooper if the seedings worked out, and Magdi Gamal would play Razza in the other. Mentally I was even sharper than I was physically, which meant razor with a capital 'R'. 'Murder in the Squash Court'; I'd made up my mind, if anyone was going to beat me, even Razz, they'd have to murder me to do it.

The Daily Telegraph, November 27th

Tragedy in New Delhi

The world's number one squash player, Julio 'Razza' Mattaz is dead. Mattaz suffered an anaphylactic reaction in a Delhi restaurant yesterday evening and in spite of prompt medical attention passed away before he could be taken to hospital. Mattaz, the first seed in the squash World Open, was due to play today in the quarter finals. As a mark of respect, play has been suspended for the day and will resume tomorrow. The Pakistani world number eight, Mansoor Ali Khan now has a walkover into the first semi final, where he will play either Magdi Gamal or Jan Berry. In the other half of the draw, Australian Trevor Cooper meets Armand Darnaud and Egyptian Hosni el Baradei takes on the young Englishman, Jolyon Jacks.

"Razza has been the star of the tour for the last eighteen months," said Jacks' coach, Sailor McCann, summing up the feelings of everyone in Delhi. "He is the one the players all set themselves against. Razza in my opinion was the greatest player of the modern age. No one dominated in quite the way he did. Razza is irreplaceable."

It was the most horrible experience of my life. A bunch of us had gone out for a meal, the now traditional Darnaud tournament meal. Razz almost got lucky that Marcel was with us, and my opinion of Armand's dad went up several notches for the way he handled the situation. I was sitting opposite Marcel and Razza. Sailor was on the far side of Marcel. I had Magdi on one side of me and my old friend Neeraj Solkar on the other. Who knows what went wrong? It was an Indian restaurant. We had persuaded Marcel that to eat European would have been all wrong, and he had reluctantly agreed. If only we'd gone with his idea of a meal at La Table Orientale, a leading French restaurant, everything would have been okay. While we were ordering, Razza had specifically spoken to the head waiter about his nut allergy. He had not taken any of the huge plate of samosas we shared for a starter. He wasn't a confirmed veggie but he had ordered vegetarian. Afterwards Marcel said that it could have been the nan.

Whatever it was, Razza had sat up very straight and started stroking his throat soon after we were into our main course. "Hey fellers, I'm not feeling too good." Moments later he said, "I'm going to go outside."

Straight away Marcel was alarmed. "Are you all right?"

Razz stood up and bent forward with his hands on his knees, gasping. From that moment Marcel took charge. "Quick," he said to a waiter, "clear a space."

The restaurant went so quiet you could hear Razza's rasping breathing. The adjacent diners quickly got up and moved out of the way. Once their table had been shifted Marcel had Razza lie down. He undid the buttons on his collarless shirt.

"Razza, listen to me. Where is your EpiPen?"

Razza pointed to the beaten up leather satchel where he kept his money and his mobile. Marcel rummaged in it and came out with a box that contained two hypodermics. He took one and quickly broke off the plastic cover then made the injection through Razza's shorts into the side of his thigh. We all stood around, silently watching, not knowing what to do.

"Hospital, call the hospital," Marcel said urgently.

Neeraj made a call on his mobile and after a brief conversation said, "You must go by taxi. It will be quicker. Wait, I will flag one down."

He hurried out of the restaurant. Marcel kept checking the pulse at Razza's neck. "He is not responding. No blood pressure." Razza was pushing, desperately trying to exhale, his eyes staring, his face turning a ghastly colour in the dim restaurant light. Marcel injected the second EpiPen into Razza's other thigh. Then muttering 'antihistamine' he grabbed Razza's bag and emptied the contents onto the floor. It wasn't much, some coins, one of which we all watched roll away across the floor, a money folder, a mobile phone, a sachet of tissues. No more hypodermics. For the first time Marcel looked unsure of himself.

Neeraj returned. "There is a taxi outside."

Marcel waved him away and started heart massage. With Marcel pushing rhythmically on his chest Razza was otherwise still, his eyes staring, his face now swollen. Then every few seconds one of his feet would do an agitated burst of turning inwards and outwards. Most of the diners had left. A few joined our helpless circle, peering at Marcel's battle, Razza's battle really. Marcel persisted with the heart massage, but some minutes later, I've no idea how many, Razza half pulled his knee up, slid it back down and sort of flopped. His eyes remained open but they were lifeless. Marcel persisted a little longer but it was obvious to all of us, Razza had died.

Eventually Marcel felt a final time for a pulse, looked up at us from his kneeling position and announced the obvious. "Il est mort. It is useless. He is dead."

The tournament went on. It should have been my great opportunity, the world championship and no Razza. I had the beating of everyone else there. Trouble was, you had to want to play, and I didn't. Sailor went through the motions of talking me through my game against Ahmed. Hopeless. Sailor had taken it harder than any of us. He finished with a half-hearted, "Go on, son. Do yer best."

I didn't even do that. I might have had a faint spark of motivation in wanting to prevent Armand from winning, to defy Marcel. My heart wasn't even in that. Marcel had managed the Razza incident with such dignity and authority, both in desperately trying to save Razz, and afterwards in placating the police, dealing with the bureaucracy, arranging for the body to be collected, it went on and on. So my developing animosity had evaporated. I lost to Ahmed three love.

I needn't have worried about Armand. He lost equally tamely to Magdi Gamal. Trevor Cooper was the only player who didn't seem to be affected. He beat Magdi in the final to a half empty gallery.

Squash wouldn't be the same.

"What do you want to do?"

It was the day after Sailor and I had returned from thirty degree Delhi. I was on the phone to Grandpa, plumbing depressed depths in a wet December Manchester.

"I don't know, Grandpa. I just don't feel like playing."

"I can understand that. It's a shocking story, and actually to have been there. Why don't you come down to the South coast for a few days? Change of scene. I'd love to see you."

The idea of seeing Grandpa gave me a flash of optimism, a buoyant moment in a grey sea of couldn't-care-less. So with Sailor's blessing I headed down to Sussex, by expensive train rather than penny pinching coach.

The trip worked, even if not in the way I'd imagined. It was marvellous to see Grandpa, who was so much more robust on his latest drug regime than when I'd last seen him. His Zimmer frame was parked unneeded in the corner of the room, supporting some neatly folded laundry.

"Are you going to carry on?" he asked.

"I'm surprised you're asking that, Grandpa."

"What would you feel now if you got to the top?"

"I'd still feel I'd done something. It's a fit-for-playing, you go on whatever the circumstances. You've got to be there. You can only beat the person in front of you."

"It's devalued, though."

"What are you saying? Razz could have got injured. Or lost form. He's not the only player out there."

Grandpa smiled. "That's what I wanted to hear. You've got to look forward. If Mattaz is gone, so be it. You can't let anything distract you, even something like this.

"Now, are you going to see your mother while you're down here?"

"Yes, I'm staying for two nights."

"Good. She'll be glad to see you." Like a boxer welcoming a punch bag.

"The one thing I will not talk about," my mother greeted me as soon as I walked in the door, "is squash. It just goes to show what a miserable little game it is. If someone like you can win matches against top players..." 'Top players' said as if they were some sort of fatal food contamination.

"What are you going to do when you stop playing, anyway? Don't come back here asking for charity."

Hey, the charity rant. I hadn't heard the charity rant for ages. *So many young people these days...*

"So many young people these days, relying on their parents, as if the world owes them a living." *The Bank of Mother and Father...* "Money, the Bank of Mother and Father. I've been talking to your grandfather. His ridiculous commitment, that trust. It's not too late to change it. Even if it'd be just symbolic; the chances of you, what is it, becoming world champion? But I want him to give you a message, Jolyon. You have to earn things in this life. Not have them handed to you on a plate." *I haven't noticed you turning down your dad's dosh, dear.*

If ever I needed a stimulus, something to make me push for the number one ranking, this was it. My mother went on for the full two days, Rorke's Drift, we'd learned about it in History, wave upon wave of hostile Zulus. I'd been taken aback by her opening attack. After that I fended off the assegais by imagining the pleasure of getting my hands on the trust in March. Maybe I'd send her a bunch of flowers, with a note saying, 'such a *trivial* bouquet'. I'd like to send her an assegai, point first.

The plan was to avoid her as much as I could over the two days. Mostly successful, but I did have to undergo one humiliation. She had invited round my old housemaster, Mr Middleton, to meet some prospective Redbrook parents. They were a Mr and Mrs Wang, originally from Taiwan and lately apparently from the tennis club, where their little Master Wangster ponced around with the other juniors. The timing of the invitation must have been spite. My mother knew my feelings about Mr Middleton, pompous pillock that he was. Somehow I got trapped into having a cup of tea with the group.

The Wangs were formal and friendly when they arrived. Mr Middleton in contrast looked away during our briefest of handshakes. With a piece of cake in his hand he was quickly into his stride.

"Jolyon's the exception that proves the rule. Redbrook pupils," *ho ho I'm in stitches,* "are almost universally successful."

"You've got it there, I'm afraid," my mother said. "It's been so disappointing." She turned to the embarrassed couple. "But I've nothing but praise for Redbrook. And Tudor House especially. I can't recommend Tudor highly enough. Mr Middleton runs a tight ship."

The poor Wangs. Mrs W had the grace to ask me what I was doing now.

"He plays squash," my mother said. "Can you imagine it?"

I could have handled things better but I did keep my temper. "I play full time, on the professional tour."

"Jolyon was such a good tennis player." My mother couldn't let it go. "Like your little Lee. Now he imagines he's going to be world squash champion."

Mr Middleton laughed. "That's rich." He addressed the Wangs. "Not that we don't have squash courts at Redbrook. And Tudor are the current house champions. And at tennis too, I'm pleased to say. We're not just top on the academic side."

Mrs Wang still wanted to talk to me. "Are you really that good?"

"Well..." I got as far as saying before Mrs Large Hadron came in again. "Jolyon a world champion? It's about as likely as me parading round the bar at the tennis club in a Venus Williams outfit."

Everyone laughed, except me of course, and I did myself credit by saying some insincerely respectful goodbyes when mercifully I heard the horn of a friend's car. If he'd been on time I might have escaped my mother's bit of fun.

Overall the short stay was more good than bad, good for relaxation away from Manchester, good for catching up with friends, Samantha not included. As I was getting ready to leave I said to my mother, "Thanks for all the motivation, Mum."

"What do you mean?" The idea that she'd given me something clearly didn't appeal.

"I'd been wavering a bit. Your hostility, somehow it's given me the boost I needed. I'll let you know when I get to number one."

"Jolyon, I will not be spoken to like that." *Well not if I can help it either. I want to avoid having to speak to you at all.*

So there I was, after less than five years, in with a chance of becoming world number one squash player, before my twenty first birthday.

Sweet.

And with a chance of sticking a very big one indeed up my mother.

SWEET!

Chapter Thirty Four

All I had to do was win the ToC in New York. I worked out the permutations with Sailor before I left, but it wasn't difficult. Trevor Cooper was number one. He had an average of eleven hundred and thirty two and a bit points. Magdi Gamal was second with eleven hundred and one and a few fractions, I was third just a couple of points back and Armand fourth, with only three points fewer than me. It couldn't have been closer. A Platinum tournament win was worth two thousand one hundred and eighty seven point five points, seven hundred and fifty more than second place. We were so bunched that if any one of us won the tournament, we'd take over as, or in Trevor's case remain, world number one.

New York Times, January 23rd

Squash Returns to Grand Central Terminal

The J P Morgan Tournament of Champions brings squash back to Grand Central Terminal for a week of the highest quality squash racquets competition. Once again the all-glass court is being erected in the lofty Vanderbilt Hall, with a gallery for nearly five hundred squash fans. The matches will be seen by many further casual observers, the thousands of commuters walking past the front wall of the court as they head between the main concourse and 42nd Street.

The Tournament of Champions marks the traditional start of the year for the Professional Squash Association tour. It will be played under a cloud following the tragic death of the undisputed world number one Julio 'Razza' Mattaz from Salt Lake City, UT. Mattaz tragically died of anaphylactic shock due to a food allergy during the World Open squash championships in New Delhi, India in November.

In Mattaz's absence, the competition is wide open. At least four players have a realistic chance of winning. The first seed is the Australian, Trevor Cooper, from Sydney, New South Wales, who took over the number one ranking from Mattaz. Then successively there are Magdi Gamal, from Sharm el Sheik, Egypt, the twenty year old Jolyon Jacks, from Manchester, England and the giant Frenchman Armand Darnaud, from Aix-en-Provence.

The qualifying rounds take place on Monday and Tuesday. The competition moves to the show court on Wednesday. The event is already a sell out.

I'd been looking forward to the ToC, even beyond its overriding significance for me. New York itself, the amazing Grand Central venue, the hospitality, it ticked all the boxes. You could add the proximity of the luxurious black clad Grand Hyatt Hotel where the players stayed. Its dark marble lobby, supported on opulent gold columns, seemed the height of luxury and it was an easy stroll from the venue. None of the players wanted to miss the ToC. I would also have added the tournament's sheer razzmatazz, but not this time.

The ToC had been a highlight the previous year, my first visit to New York. There'd been the spectacular sightseeing. This included the flimsiest pair of knickers I'd ever had the pleasure of removing, from Connie, a hoot of a curvy red-headed hospitality waitress. Connie had tried to ply me with wine at the J P Morgan reception at the other end of Vanderbilt Hall. No to the alcohol, Miss. Is there any other hospitality on offer?

This time of course my eve of tournament nerves were way beyond the usual butterflies. It was a positive nervousness. For me this was it, the culmination of five intense years, and I believed I could make it. With Sailor's help I was approaching the best physical condition I'd ever be capable of reaching, and though I'd never be a Razz or an Armand in terms of artistry, the game I had was brutally efficient, I was confident of that. The draw had turned out okay. I was seeded to meet Trevor Cooper in the semis, and I'd disembowel myself if I lost to Trevor, though neutral observers would probably have put us fifty-fifty. If the other semi followed the seedings it would be between Armand, or should I say Marcel in the shape of Armand, and Magdi Gamal. Magdi I liked and I hoped he'd win. Any good feelings I had for Marcel after Delhi had not neutralised my revulsion over the way he controlled his son and over his role if Marie-Emmanuelle's suspicions were borne out. A Magdi win would mean Marcel's predictions were overturned even before the final. *Do you want me to phone it through to L'Equipe myself, Marcel?* As for playing Armand or Magdi, I'd happily go on court against either of them the way I was feeling. Again, neutral observers would probably call either match even. I'd hoped to be where Razza was coming into the ToC, the undisputed favourite. It hadn't worked out that way, but I was in with a big chance.

There was another five star angle to the ToC. The tournament traditionally included a women's invitation event, for just four competitors, two semis and a final. Zoë had inevitably received an invitation. It was always a thrill when I did well with Zoë watching, bittersweet these days, and this could be the all time top of the 'did wells'. If I could make it to world number one with Zoë there it would be the sweetest completion of the circle. I sometimes ran over the scene in my mind, at that Indian meal in Manchester, the time Zoë had inspired me to go all out for squash. Almost five years ago now. At first it wasn't one dream but two. More accurately, one dream, on top of world squash, and one fantasy, on top of Zoë.

The tournament started okay. The background announcements in the station, this arrival from here, that departure to there, were something you had to get used to. In addition there was the vague distraction of New Yorkers in their winter coats hurrying past just the other side of the front wall. It was the same for everyone and after two comfortable wins I was coping fine, quarter finals to come. I didn't at that stage pay much attention to the fact that Armand was coping even better. I did tot up the points: Armand had won his opening two rounds for the loss of fifteen fewer than me, a lot given our respective opposition, but so what.

The rest of the arrangements were good. Sailor was giving me space. I was enjoying Manhattan. I didn't always want to socialise with other players but when Magdi Gamal suggested a meal in the hotel after our respective matches on the Thursday evening I quickly agreed. As we passed through the enormous lobby Magdi called out in Arabic to another Egyptian player, Abdel el Tayeb, who earlier had lost to Trevor Cooper. Abdel hadn't eaten and said he'd join us.

"You know Jolyon?" Magdi said.

"Yes, not well. Our game in Hong Kong was too short."

That was the ice broken and as we ordered food we chatted about the tournament. Magdi was older than Abdel and myself and described his first ToC. "Back then it was sponsored by Bear Stearns. Before the banking crash. It was cool then too. It was my first time in New York, I couldn't believe the city. I went up the Empire State, and downtown to Ground Zero. Back then it was unusual to play a tournament away from a sports place. The ToC was radical. It's still special in Grand Central, I love it. Then J P Morgan, I think they took over Bear Stearns. We thought the ToC would finish but J P Morgan, they've carried on with it."

"How did you get on in your first ToC?" I asked.

He laughed. "I lost in qualifying. I never made it to the glass court. I said I'd be back. I wanted to play on the show court."

Abdel nodded. "It was Magdi talking about the ToC that made me go for squash. Do you remember? You were playing in an exhibition, at the Gezira Club. In Cairo. You'd just come back from the ToC and you talked and talked about it. I was a medical student then. I was only a year short of qualifying. After that I made the decision to interrupt medical school and play on the squash circuit. My father almost killed me."

"Talking of fathers," I said, "did you hear Marcel Darnaud and Armand yesterday? In the lobby here? It sounded as though Marcel was going to kill him. It was embarrassing. Armand started by just standing there, you know how he is, just taking it. Then he had a go back. I've not seen him do that before."

"What was Marcel saying?" Abdel asked. "Armand is playing so well, I can't see any problem."

"I don't know," I said. "It was in French. The general impression, Marcel wasn't happy, big time, something to do with a girl, I think. I visited them in Aix-en-Provence last year, a week's training and practice with Armand, everything laid on." Even the masseuse, I thought fondly. "Very generous, Marcel, but always hard on Armand, that's the way it seems to be. As for Armand, he's such a quiet guy. He never used to react when his father had a go at him; just stood there taking it. Maybe that's changing."

"Marcel's been helpful to me," Magdi said, "as well as all the meals, very good meals I have to say. Two seasons ago I was feeling bad. I kept losing, no reason, I just didn't have the strength. I lost to Armand, before he was top ten.

Marcel asked me some questions afterwards, while we had a drink, a lot of questions about my health. Eventually he said to check for malaria.

"He was right, It was malaria."

"Yes," I said, "on balance a good guy, but he makes me want to beat Armand twice as much."

Abdel leaned forward. "Good guy, bad temper. Did you hear this? I was laughing. It was at Delhi airport, you know, Indira Gandhi airport, after the World Open." His face clouded for a moment. "Well I wasn't laughing much, not after Razz. We were going through security. Dr Darnaud's attaché case was being searched. He had a jar of peanut butter. A Frenchman with peanut butter? It was taken away from him."

We all chuckled. It was so out of character, Marcel Darnaud of all people. Why on earth would he want to supplement his diet in Delhi with peanut butter?"

"It's a secret training supplement for Armand," Magdi said. "I must buy some tomorrow."

"You may not be able to find a Halal version," I said. Magdi was a committed Muslim, even to the extent of not playing during Ramadan. He'd told me he found that the daytime fasting, and even more, the inability to drink anything, left him unable to compete.

"Kosher if that's all right," I carried on. "You'll find kosher *anything* here in New York."

Abdel wouldn't let it go. "I can't understand. He is very French."

"And very organised," I agreed. "I've seen it. Nothing is left to chance for Armand. Armand is regulated. It's like he's an extension of Marcel. I wonder why the peanut butter."

"I like the supplement theory," Abdel said. "It's high energy, peanut butter."

Even as I was saying, "Yes, I guess that's it," I felt I'd been tasered. It was worse than the time I thought Riley was going home to bed with Zoë.

Fuck.

Fuck, fuck, fuck!

I didn't want to say anything to the others, but suddenly it was plain stark horribly obvious.

Awful. Terrible. Unbelievable. The nut contamination that had killed Razza Mattaz had come from Marcel Darnaud. Peanut butter. It made sense. Marcel had made a big show of trying to save Razza, even while he was making sure he was going to die.

No, surely not? I'd missed something. I had to be wrong?

He'd used the EpiPens. He'd done heart massage.

But why otherwise the peanut butter?

I had to check some facts. "Do you remember the meal in Delhi, when Razza died?" I asked Magdi. "You were there. Where was Razz sitting? It was next to Marcel, wasn't it? And Marcel did his best to save him; his EpiPen and

PASSENGER BAGGAGE must not contain:

Oxidising
Substances

Gases

Radioactive
Material

Corrosives

Explosives

Flammable
Substances

Toxic or Infectious
Substances

or other articles or
substances which
present a danger
during air transport

10/10

M920T

Supplied for British Airways by RR Donnelley - 013052

UPGR

BRITISH AIRWAYS

HILL/JEREMY MR
BA 2587 23JAN LONDON   LGW

SEAT	GATE CLOSES	GATE
04C	1915	20

CLUB EUROPE
SAPPHIRE/BA/SILV80448532

BOARDING PASS
CARTE D'ACCES A BORD/BORDKARTE
TARJETA DE EMBARQUE/CARTA D'IMBARCO

SUBJECT TO CONDITIONS OF CARRIAGE, COPIES
AVAILABLE ON REQUEST. SEE IMPORTANT
NOTICES ON THE BACK OF THIS DOCUMENT.

NAME OF PASSENGER
HILL/JEREMY MR
SAPP/BA/SILV80448532
FROM VENICE   VCE
TO LONDON   LGW

FLIGHT NO.	CLASS/DATE	TIME
BA 2587	C 23JAN	1940

GATE	GATE CLOSES	SEAT	SMOKE
20	1915	04C	🚭

PCS. CK. WT. UNCK SEQ NO
1   0   0   038

00 ETKT

everything. Do you remember the business just before, the glass of water he spilled?"

"I remember. Some of it went over my pants."

I could picture the scene. "Marcel stood up quickly. It was funny. He moved all the dishes, and the plates. He was helping to clear up as he called for a waiter. He was apologising." But I didn't want them to realise what I was thinking, and said, "A good guy, Marcel, trying to help."

"He spilt a glass of beer over me once," Abdel smiled at the memory. "It was at a meal also, in KL. I remember clearly. I remember because I lost in the quarter final, to Armand. I was third seed, he was seventh, eighth. It was disappointing that time, very disappointing. I had no energy."

"It can happen." Abdel looked at the ceiling. "Before I was more sensible and the coaches had taught me about nutrition, and I should have known from my physiology studies, I missed a meal before a match once. I ate two Mars Bars, half an hour before I went on court. I was playing a qualifier at that big tournament in Zürich last year. All that refined sugar, it made too much insulin in my system. It took away my energy. I was so slow."

Abdel's Mars Bars moved us on from Marcel Darnaud and peanut butter to Zürich and how everything cost so much in Swiss francs. That suited me. I needed time to think.

Chapter Thirty Five

I lay awake for ages, trying to convince myself it wasn't true. The whole idea was just too terrible. The peanut butter, could it have been an innocent supplement? Perhaps, although I'd never heard of anything like that. Strange for Marcel to be carrying it in his hand luggage. Then there was Abdel's remark, 'I had no energy', and the coincidence of the meal the evening before that game, one of Marcel's invitations. The loss of energy had happened to me too, in Hong Kong. I thought back, yes, Marcel had taken a party of us out that night, me included. I tried to remember. There'd been so many Marcel evenings. I was pretty sure I was sitting next to him on that occasion. What was not in doubt, my lifeless feeling next day on court. But the match wasn't against Armand; my opponent had been Serge Colson. Why arrange for me to lose to Serge? One reason might be that Armand had never lost to Serge. He duly beat him the next day, and he wouldn't have beaten me.

I had to talk to someone. Not Sailor, not until I was sure anyway. I'd not seen much of Zoë; maybe I could catch up with her. First I needed some sleep. I was playing an experienced Canadian, Jerome Bale, the next day. I should win but should wasn't enough. That I knew.

My heart gave a jump when Zoë walked in to the buffet the following morning while I was having breakfast with Sailor. She was just back from a series of exhibitions in Australia and was looking fabulous. What about the BMW exec? Zoë was coping easily away from her, I hoped. Not pining. I was scheduled for a practice hit on the show court at eleven thirty with Sailor but he suggested Zoë take his place. Yeeha, it was a deal.

"Is that an all over tan?" I asked as we went on court.

She laughed. "Wouldn't you like to see?"

"Well of course, here comes a monumental untruth, I'm more concerned about a good practice."

She laughed again and we got down to some concentrated but stress-free hitting. There were a few people scattered around the gallery, plus some possibly surprised Grand Central Terminal travellers peering at us through the front wall. I felt special just to be there in that amazing venue. And to be on court with Zoë, that was always special.

Then when I thought about the Marcel business, all my good feelings evaporated. It was awful.

"Have you got time for a bit of lunch?" I asked as we collected our kit.

"Good idea. Let's meet back here at one and we can go down into the food hall."

"What, here in Grand Central?"

"Yes, there's all sort of concessions. It's into the main hall and then down the stairs. See you at one?"

I wouldn't be late. We both went back to the Hyatt to shower and I returned to the court at five to one. Armand was knocking up with Lou Kiefer. Marcel was there of course, and I exchanged pleasantries with him, all the while wondering uncomfortably whether I was chatting with a murderer.

Zoë and I found our way down into the enormous food hall and ordered a couple of sandwiches and soft drinks from one of the delis.

"What's the matter, Jolyon?" Zoë asked when we'd sat down.

"What do you mean?"

"You're tense. Worried about playing Jerome? Or Trevor Cooper in the semi?"

"Jerome's a chicken I've not yet counted. He's too good for that. But what makes you think I'm tense?"

"You're like a harp string. I know you too well. You're twanging."

I hadn't thought it showed. "Well there is something. Not what you'd think though. It's not the squash, not exactly."

Without a pause I went through the conversation with Abdel and Magdi the previous evening. At one stage Zoë said 'slow down, slow down' but otherwise she listened intently and ate her sandwich.

"So," I finished off, "it's too grim to think about. And I don't know what to do."

"Let's see what you have," Zoë said. "First, the peanut butter. That is a strange one. Then Razz, who we know had a nut allergy, having a reaction at a meal."

"Reaction? The guy died. And it's a pretty big coincidence. Him sitting next to Marcel."

"But Marcel tried to save him," she said. "I'm trying to look at everything. Then we have the tiredness in games that might benefit Armand, directly or indirectly. People do have off days."

"It was pretty radical in my case," I said. "I felt dead."

"What could account for that?"

"Abdel talked about eating Mars Bars, too much refined sugar just before a match. Not what you'd think but it increases your insulin, he said. It made sense to him anyway."

"Marcel hasn't been handing out sweets to Armand's opponents," Zoë said. "Not that they'd eat them."

"It must be something else to slow you down."

"I'm not an expert. My dad might know, more likely my mum. She's the scientific one."

"Could you ask them?"

"I could try. They're away in South Africa. Sailor wouldn't know. Is there anyone else medical?"

"Doctor Darnaud, ha ha," I said. Then I had a thought, "I know, maybe Abdel himself, he's a down to earth dude. He wouldn't blurt it out everywhere."

"Abdel's not a doctor."

"No, but he was saying last night, he gave up a medical degree to play squash. From the way he talks, it's very medical sounding, he got quite far. He says his father nearly killed him when he stopped."

Zoë made her child-like grimace, with the corners of her mouth turned down, and I melted inside. "That sounds familiar." Then she nodded. "I don't know Abdel. Let's try him if you think so."

Abdel was on court after me that evening. We found him chilling in the lobby at the Hyatt, reading something on his iPad.

"What's that, Abdel?" I asked. "You watching one of my old matches online?"

A big smile. "It's the New England Journal of Medicine. My tutor told me to read it, to keep in touch. My father arranged the subscription. For when I retire as world champion, back to being a doctor."

"Here's a current world champion. Do you know Zoë? I train with her."

He stood up. "Only from seeing you on court yesterday. Nice win." He shook Zoë's hand formally.

"Something we wanted to ask you," I said. "Mind if we sit down?"

Abdel sat back down with a gesture to join him. "I'm curious, please."

"Let me do this," Zoë said. "It's delicate, Abdel. Please can we ask you not to say anything to anyone about this. You'll see why."

"No, that's okay. What is it?"

Zoë clearly explained the story, taking half the time I'd have done. "The question is," Zoë concluded, "is there something, some substance, that could slow you down a little, that you probably took the night before, but that in the end doesn't do any harm? Some drug. Jolyon says you talked about Mars Bars and insulin; so maybe insulin?"

"Insulin you have to inject," Abdel said, "you know, diabetes, and it doesn't last long enough. It's dangerous pushing insulin levels up, or even diabetic drugs, they'd be an idea."

"Is there anything else?"

"It's funny you should ask. The time in Kuala Lumpur, when I was so lethargic, I had some trouble with my breathing. It was like when I was a boy. I had asthma as a boy, never very bad but I had an inhaler. I grew out of the asthma, some children do. It was difficult on court at the KL Open, very hot, no energy and the trouble with my breathing too. I couldn't play, I knew from the first point. With childhood asthma it's never completely gone. Your airways are susceptible, perhaps when you get a cold or flu. I was worried that my asthma was coming back."

He paused and gazed into the distance. "You've made me think. There is a heart drug that can take away your strength, it's a whole family of drugs, very common. They're called beta blockers. They treat high blood pressure and angina, heart pain. They reduce the force of the heart muscle. Beta blockers, most heart drugs, have side effects. With beta blockers it is a tiredness, a lack of energy. There is something else, and I have to look this up. Beta blockers I think are not for people with asthma. I think. They can give you problems just like I felt in KL, breathing problems. If you are right and Dr Darnaud is trying to slow people down, if it was me I would chose a beta blocker.

"Give me a moment." Abdel picked up his iPad and within a minute had stroked some information out of the screen. "Here it is," he read out, "beta blockers, common side effects: cold hands and feet, tiredness, dizziness, sexual problems, wheezing, sleep disturbance. Wheezing means airways." He pulled the pages down on the screen. "Wait, listen to this, contraindications, beta blockers are contraindicated in patients with asthma or chronic obstructive pulmonary disease."

Abdel looked up. "It does fit. It's possible. What are you going to do?"

Zoë asked me, "What do you want to do, Jolyon?"

"We can't do anything without proper evidence," I said, "and I don't know where to start. I guess we need to keep Marcel away from Armand's opponents for a start."

"Who is he playing today?" Abdel asked.

"He's playing now," I said, "first session. It's against Mansoor. We're too late to do anything about that. Mansoor wouldn't have hung out with Marcel anyway. I don't think so. He spends all his time with his manager. No one sees much of them."

Abdel nodded.

"If Armand wins," Zoë said.

"Which he will," I added.

"If Armand wins," Zoë continued, "it'll be a semi against Magdi or Zhang Chao." Zhang Chao was from Hong Kong, the same age as me. I'd known him as a good junior and he'd come on in the last year. He'd almost certainly reached his limit this time in the ToC though.

"So Magdi's the one who has to be careful," I said. "Zhang Chao isn't going to win."

"Could Marcel get at Magdi?" Zoë asked.

"I don't know," I said. "How much of this, what did you call it, this beta blocker drug would be needed?"

Abdel thought for a moment. "Not much. It would be a tablet or maybe a capsule. One would be enough. It wouldn't be big. He could empty the contents of a capsule, or grind up a tablet. It wouldn't fill a tea spoon. Then it could go into a drink, or more likely food. You might notice the taste in a drink or it might not dissolve. Food would be better."

"Is Magdi likely to spend time with the Darnauds?" Zoë asked.

"I don't think so," I said. "He never has done, as far as I know. He's a strong Muslim, no booze. I know he prays a lot. It would be hard for Marcel to get at him."

"Marcel is going to have to rely on Armand beating him honestly, then," Zoë said. "What's your feeling?"

I was surprised by Abdel's answer, the detail of it. "Armand is looking very good. Have you noticed, he's strong, twenty centimetres further up the court. Moving so well. To me it looks very easy for Armand. If you play him," he looked at me, "you'll be under pressure. He has that short game, everyone knows, and he has been playing short early in the points, taking risks."

"That's precisely what Marcel tells him not to do," I said. "It was a constant theme when I was in Aix-en-Provence." I didn't mention Marie-Emmanuelle.

"He's been so accurate," Abdel went on. "Normally with Armand I would say that game would leave him exposed, giving his opponent openings. That's where I hope to beat him when I play him. But his short game, just now," he nodded, "very impressive."

"Armand to beat Magdi then," Zoë said. "So you're the one at risk, Jolyon? As long as you beat Trevor Cooper."

"It could be Trevor. It could be me. First I have to beat Jerome. That's as far as I'm looking."

"Far enough for now," she said. "One way or the other though, we need to look a bit further."

Was Zoë right, I wondered as I headed back to my room. What a mess. I glanced both ways down the corridor as I left the lift.

I was frightened.

Chapter Thirty Six

I did a Jan Berry job on Jerome Bale.

"Jolyon will go on to win the tournament if he plays like that," Jerome said in his post match interview. "That was one heck of a hiding he gave me. I was powerless. Well done. I'm off to lick my wounds."

I was starting to believe it again. It wasn't just a theory now. It wasn't the dream I'd lived with for five years, a quarter of my life. It wasn't Sailor's prediction. Suddenly it was there, a reality, so close. Jolyon Jacks, world number one, I could almost touch it. Looking back, all the way through my time in Manchester, all the ups and downs, the training, the travel, the self denial, well mostly self denial, it had always been the dream. Now it was just two days and two wins away, almost in my grasp. I so wanted it. I mustn't fail now. I couldn't cope now if I failed after coming so close. Trevor Cooper next. Trevor would be more worried than I was about tomorrow. No one wins a quarter at a major tournament as I had, for so few points, without being at the top of his game.

Then who in the final? It had to be Armand. The people who knew were all saying how well Armand was playing. Magdi was good too but you always felt that any one of Trevor or Armand or indeed I, certainly Razz if he'd still been alive, we all would have beaten Magdi at our best.

I was doing my stretches at the back of the gallery while Armand and Jan were knocking up, having decided to watch some of their game. Marcel Darnaud came over and congratulated me on my win. I felt surprisingly calm.

"You are playing well, Jolyon. It is the plyometrics, no? I spoke to Sailor. Your movement is exceptional. And I hope you will stay to watch Armand. That boy has taken a step forward, I have to say it. You inspired Armand with your performance in Aix-en-Provence. You inspired all of us. Tonight you will see your spirit in my son, your *rosbif* will. I love your will."

"Jan Berry? Tonight I fear for Jan."

Marcel called it correctly. I stayed for two games. One would have been enough. Armand was giving the great Jan Berry a lesson. The fearsome hatchet was at maximum intensity. Armand was impassive, physically untouched by the pace. He was consistently there in front of Jan, dragging the South African around the court with delicate drops and angles. Jan was exhausted after fifteen minutes, his spirit draining away. Armand meanwhile appeared not tired at all. Squash can look so easy. He was consistently reaching every ball with a giant stride, this way or that.

Bugger any beta blocker, I thought. Marcel had a better weapon than that. It was his son.

I was wary of intervention by Marcel over the following twenty four hours, but I couldn't be distracted from the more real threat of Trevor Cooper. A good hit with Zoë in the middle of the day left me feeling as well as any person could feel. I was bursting out of my skin with relaxed energy. Trevor and I bumped into each other a couple of times the next day, the second time mid afternoon in the Grand Hyatt.

"Hey Jols," he called from the upper level of the lobby. "Who did you shag last night?"

"Just a beauty sleep, Trevor."

Several people turned in our direction.

"What, can't you pull unless it's laid on for you?"

"Oh Trevor. Why don't you leave it alone? I've learned that lesson."

"My my, the humility."

"Take it easy. I'll see you at seven o'clock." That's when I'll score, I thought. I was at the top of the escalator from the entrance level when I saw Marcel Darnaud joining Trevor.

"Ah, Jolyon, you too, perfect." He made a sweeping gesture. "I want to invite you both, win or lose, to Smith and Wollensky's. Tonight. You know it, the famous steak restaurant? We have a table at nine thirty. Magdi cannot come, it is to be regretted, but there will be several others, Armand of course. It is only ten minutes, on third and forty ninth. We must celebrate a great tournament."

Trevor had no hesitation. "Jeez, Marcel, I'm up for that."

"I'm not so sure, thanks," I said. "Sailor is very insistent these days." I let it trail away.

"What a wimp," Trevor said. "Look, Jols, don't be scared. You afraid to be the other side of the table from a winner?"

I hesitated. Marcel said, "That is unfair. But you must reconsider, Jolyon. We won't be late tonight. It is necessary to eat. And Sailor has agreed to join us."

"So you'll have a chaperone, Jols." *Eff off, mate.*

I was torn. I wanted to speak to Zoë. The sensible thing would be to say no, I want a quiet evening, very kind of you, Marcel, *et cetera et cetera.* But I was driven by curiosity, and surely I could see to it that he had no opportunity to add anything to my food. Or Trevor's, if it came to that. Anyway, unless I had a disaster in my semi, it would be an opportunity for some fun at Trevor's expense.

It felt surreal, eight of us crammed round a circular table in Smith and Wollensky's. Marcel Darnaud's hospitality, and, I was pretty sure now, some inhospitality to come. Marcel had approached Sailor and me jovially while we were leaving the Vanderbilt Hall after the semis, my win against Trevor Cooper and Armand over Magdi.

"No excuses now, gentlemen. Monsieur Kiefer recommends a good protein intake and I assure you, that is what you will take from Smith and Wollensky's."

I still hadn't told Sailor about my suspicions. He was well up for the meal. Almost deferentially he said, "Ay, Marcel, after my boy has had his ice bath. We need to prepare for a hard final."

Marcel beamed. The final seemed to have been fated. Yet again, Armand and I had won our matches by three games to love. Yet again, Armand had lost fewer points. I hadn't seen his match, preferring to do a thorough warm up in the exercise room at the top of the Hyatt. Apparently for all Magdi's quicksilver movement, he had simply lacked the firepower to disrupt Armand's game. Scary. My match with Trevor had been closer but I never felt I wasn't going to win.

Smith and Wollensky's was packed. 'Steaks and Chops Since 1922', it said outside. Downstairs there was a noisy bar, with classy leather-covered bar stools, where Marcel insisted that everyone have a cocktail. Iced water for me, which came with a twist of lime. The decor was clubby, the walls decorated in pink and cream, hung with wood-framed pictures. There were several dining areas, which meant that it felt quite intimate in what was apparently a large restaurant.

I was feeling okay, not too tired after my match, looking forward to the food. I made sure I was safely separated from Marcel. Sailor was between him and me, to my left. The others in the group were Trevor, on my right, to his credit reasonably cheerful, Ruth Mattaz, who had accepted an invitation to present the trophies after the final, Gaston Guillot, a journalist from L'Equipe, Lou Kiefer, Armand and a spectacularly lovely girl with waist-long black hair who insisted on sitting beside Armand. Marcel introduced the girl as Stephanie Boumedienne. Stephanie told us she worked at the French consulate in Manhattan. Lucky consulate.

"Mesdames, Messieurs," Marcel said. "I am going to adopt a privilege as the host this evening and order for all of us. I know you will forgive me. Smith and Wollensky's is not," he looked up, "it is not subtle. It concentrates on what is does best. And what it does is the best, I assure you. I propose we all take the New York Cut Sirloin, on the bone, medium rare. This the Americans call the top sirloin. Here they understand meat. Here it is properly aged, perfect condition. Sirloin is from the French, I have to say, *sur la loin*, above the loin," he shrugged. "Of course there has to be a French connection. We will have baked potato, our boys must pay attention to the carbohydrates, no, from Idaho of course, broccoli and something else they do so well here, creamed spinach. I propose no appetisers. You will understand this precaution when your steak arrives.

"Armand, Jolyon, a glass of wine?"

We both shook our heads.

"A pity. Of course, we understand. The rest of us will enjoy a Californian Cabernet Sauvignon. Trevor? This may even be superior to your Barossa Valley."

"I'll have a beer thanks."

"Sailor, are you a wine drinker?"

"Me, I take an occasional glass of whiskey." He gave Marcel the full flint stare. "Tonight I'll stick to water. Mebbe something stronger tomorrow night to celebrate."

Marcel smiled. "Tomorrow we can celebrate together, the world's new number one squash player," he nodded to Ruth, "with due deference, Madame. It will be Armand," he paused and Armand looked away, "or Jolyon." I just smiled.

"Enjoy it while you can, fellas," Trevor said. "I'm getting it back. Most likely at Canary Wharf. Respect to Razza, Ruthy. We wouldn't be having this discussion if Razz was still going."

The Canary Wharf Classic was in March, now a Platinum tournament. It was held at another spectacular venue, the East Wintergarden in London. Razz would have been the defending champion.

Ruth replied, "Thanks, Trevor. I guess we all could do with having Razz here. I wanted to come because he regarded this championship as the best, the one he always wanted to win. Razz was so proud to be a US citizen. His grandfather's Mexican, Pedro. Pedro was always challenging Razz to make good in the USA. He did. And now he hasn't."

Armand was the only one not listening, doing his best to distract Stephanie. "It looks as though Armand's sorted," I said quietly to Trevor. "Can I take back what I said earlier. I need balance. Have you lined up any of your Aussie girlfriends for me?"

"I tried mate, believe me, I tried. As soon as they heard is was you..."

I couldn't help but laugh. Again quietly I said, "It's straightforward playing me, but you'd worked that out. Watch out for Marcel, though."

Trevor surprised me with his reply. "I wonder about that too. Not good vibes there. But Marcel or not, you're going to have your hands full tomorrow. The great lummox has finally got it together. I don't reckon he'd have beaten Razz. But look, Magdi got just eighteen points today, seven, seven and four. And Magdi's playing well. That is a cruel wipe out."

"I don't think Armand believes he can beat me," I said. "Not Marcel either." I told Trevor about the Aix-en-Provence match. "If you see what I mean, I'm more worried about beating Marcel."

Two waiters then arrived with a trolley, necessarily sturdy since it had to carry our food. The sirloins were massive, attached to pieces of bone that could have doubled as girders in a Manhattan bridge. The baked potatoes were sized to match, sliced crosswise, ready for butter or cream with chives. The second waiter put a bowl of steaming broccoli on the table followed by another one with the creamed spinach.

"Is that everything?" he asked.

Marcel laughed. "You understand now about the appetisers?"

Gaston uttered some oath in French. "Three countries I have visited, Australia, that was the rugby; Argentina, rugby also; and the United States, the first time for cycling, Lance Armstrong, now for the squash. These countries are the champions for beef, but here we have the winner. My wife insists on my diet. Regrettably," he smiled, "she is not here."

Sailor muttered to me, "Go easy, son. Ye could still be digesting this lot back home."

Stephanie asked me, "Do you eat steak now in England? The beef scare?"

"That was a long time ago. I think. It never affected me. No one pays any attention now." Marcel helped Stephanie to some broccoli and spinach, then he leaned across me and put some on Trevor's plate.

Stephanie smiled directly at me. "Marcel says you have the *rosbif* spirit. I think perhaps," 'per-aps', "he is right. You are very English Jolyon. Is that an English name, Jolyon?"

"Greek originally, I've been told. It comes from Jupiter. He was the king of the gods."

Another smile. "So you are a god?"

Armand was looking pissed off.

"I wouldn't go as far as that, though if you were a goddess..."

"For Christ's sake," Trevor said, and we laughed. Not Armand though.

Then fuck. Oh fuck.

I'd realised that Marcel had put some broccoli and some spinach on my plate. Pay effing attention, Jolyon! How could I get out of this? The food didn't look as though it contained any hidden extras, but seeing it there on the plate made me nervous. The steak? That should be okay. It had gone nowhere near Marcel. The mighty baked potato? Ditto, if I avoided the add ons. The broccoli looked okay, but that *had* come from Marcel. Then there was the spinach.

The spinach looked delicious.

No way was I going to eat the spinach.

Problem was, I was starving and I didn't want to make a scene. The steak and the potato at least should be safe, surely. Then I had an idea.

"Hey Armand. I've too much spinach here. You must have some of mine." As I half stood up with my plate there came a sharp 'no!' from Marcel.

"Why not?" I asked. "He's twice as big as me and he needs twice as much greens."

"Surely it is not polite," Marcel said smoothly, "and there is still some here." He pointed to the bowl. Then he locked eyes with me. Everyone else looked on, sensing the tension. As for me, I'd gone cold. If I'd needed proof, this was it. Marcel had sabotaged my food, almost certainly the spinach.

And Marcel knew I knew. And he knew that I knew he knew. Knews travelled fast, I thought. No knews would have been better knews.

I looked away. "Sorry, out of order," I held up my hand. "I'm sure if Armand finishes his steak he won't have any room for more spinach."

That was the end of the general tension, if not my own. Inside I was back where Zoë had seen me, twanging. As the meal carried on, Trevor asked me quietly, "What was all that about?"

"Not here. I'll tell you tomorrow."

As I was finally setting my knife and fork to one side, defeated by the massive potato as much as the steak, Sailor said, "What's wrong with the greens, son?"

My bloody vitamin balance. Would Sailor never let go?

"You into the Floyd then Sailor?"

He frowned. "What Floyd? What's that?"

Ruth perked up. "Pink Floyd." She did a passable attempt at a Scottish accent. "'If ye don't eat yer greens you can't have any pudding.' Another brick in the wall, that's right?"

"Bravo," said Gaston.

I agreed. "That's impressive. Avoiding my greens isn't an issue, anyway. I'm not up for pudding tonight. When did you become part of the Floyd fan club, Ruth?"

"It's not me really. It's Razz. Sorry, was Razz. Razz was Pink Floyd crazy. And I come at it from another angle. I'm an IP attorney."

"IP?"

"Intellectual property. I did some work for a file sharing outfit. I had to advise them: stay very clear of EMI. They were in dispute with Pink Floyd at the time. Big bucks and potentially big lawsuits if you made the wrong move."

"So you're a lawyer?"

"Yes, it's a specialised field, but an attorney as we call it, that's what I am."

I suddenly felt embarrassed for Ruth, on behalf of all of us. Her husband had been murdered to further someone's pathetic ambition, in something as trivial as a sport, two guys whacking a ball against a glass wall. I didn't know how things were going to turn out with Marcel, but I wanted to tell Ruth the story. She might even be able to help with nailing the man.

Eventually we had all had enough steak. I guess Stephanie had eaten ten percent of hers, Ruth fifteen, me and Gaston doing well, in the fifties. My spinach was conspicuously untouched. Armand was the champion, with just the bone remaining on his plate. I didn't take any comfort. I'd seen in Aix-en-Provence how much he ate.

Looking at the unfinished steaks while we were all declining desserts one of the waiters asked, "Anybody want a doggy bag?"

"Oh certainly," Stephanie said. "My dog will love the steak."

While the waiter was attending to this I said, "I'll have one too."

"Of course sir."

For an instant Marcel looked poleaxed. "Jolyon, Jolyon, I'm disappointed. You are more cultured than that. A doggy bag and no dog? What are you going to do with it?"

"This has been just fantastic, Marcel. Best steak I've ever had. I'll finish it later."

"Me too," said Trevor. I was grateful for that. It took some attention off me. Not Marcel's attention though. Without asking, the waiter transferred my spinach as well as the pink hunk of meat into separate sections of a plastic container and into my doggy bag. Marcel was uncomfortable; anyone who knew what was going on would have seen that. The waiter wanted to take the bags away but I put mine on the floor beside Trevor.

"I don't want to lose that," I told him while everyone was ordering coffees.

The conversation meandered comfortably on as we enjoyed our coffees, decaff for me. Ruth was so composed. She had some funny stories about Razz. Lou, poor fellow, didn't have much to say in English. Gaston explained that he had been specifically sent by his editor to record the ascent of another French player to the top of the squash rankings. Armand didn't contribute much. Everything Armand wanted to say was into Stephanie's ear and she was enjoying the monaural input.

Eventually Sailor said, "Okay, Marcel. It's time for a beauty sleep for Jolyon here. Wonderful evening."

"Of course," Marcel said. "It is a big day tomorrow." He summoned the waiter and took care of the bill while we waited for our coats.

As we left the restaurant I clung on carefully to my doggy bag. I'd felt safe in there. Now I was worried. I had to get through the next twenty hours to the final. Surely the spinach was Marcel's final effort? It was scary: sure I was not.

I was planning to walk back, it wasn't cold, and was amused as we milled around outside the restaurant to see Armand hailing a cab. A yellow monster pulled up immediately and he made to get into it with Stephanie.

"Non. Non, non, non!"

I couldn't believe it, Marcel shouting. Armand paused and received a further volley of French. Stephanie was half into the cab, trying to pull Armand in with her. Monsieur Kiefer got between Marcel and a now belligerent Armand like a boxing referee. Eventually Armand, looking as animated as I'd ever seen him, stood up, waved Stephanie away, said some strong words to Monsieur Kiefer, the meaning of which was pretty clear, and astonishingly shaped to deck his dad.

Now it was Trevor who intervened. "Come on, mate. It's probably for the best. I'll walk back with you."

"Ay," said Sailor. "This is no' helping anyone."

Together he and Trevor dragged Armand off down the street. Meanwhile Monsieur Kiefer hailed another cab in which he, Gaston and a livid Marcel departed.

I was left standing on the pavement with Ruth. "You up for a walk?" I asked, "or shall we get a cab too? Plenty of them."

Ruth was well protected with a dark coat and a Cossack hat. She looked up at the sky, swung a colourful wrap round her shoulders and said, "Let's walk."

Chapter Thirty Seven

"All sweetness and light in the Darnaud camp," Ruth said.

"The domineering dad and Armand's hormones finally surfacing."

"Stephanie's an attractive girl."

"Certainly is. It would have been better for me if they'd gone off together."

"Yes," she said. "Boys will be boys." Then, "Oh damn. Oh damn, damn, damn."

"I know." I wanted to put my arm round her. "I haven't had a chance to say something about Razza. I wish I'd known him better."

"I'm almost sorry I did," she said bitterly. "It wouldn't feel so bad. What a human being. What a waste, and how darned stupid. I was always reminding him about his EpiPen. In some ways he was like a boy. He needed someone there, to remind him about all the little things."

"But he did have his EpiPen. Two in fact. Marcel used both of them."

"What?" Ruth stopped. "It was explicit in the PM."

"Uh?"

"Post mortem. We had a post mortem done back home. There was no evidence that an EpiPen had been used. Let alone two. Who said?"

I was shocked. "It was me. It's been bothering me. A lot of questions. There's some stuff I need to tell you and you're not going to like it. Let's grab a coffee."

We went into a diner a little way on, joining a couple of lonely figures at either end of the row of benches. A cheery waitress with big hair approached. She turned around our coffee order and brought two glasses of iced water in about thirteen seconds straight.

There wasn't much colour in Ruth's face and the light in the diner didn't help. "Well, what is it?" she asked in a resigned voice.

I stirred some full fat sugar into my coffee, postponing the moment. "I was only able to work this out yesterday. Before that none of it had crossed my mind. Some of the stuff this evening confirmed what I've been thinking. Rock solid, I can't dress it up," I took a deep breath. "Marcel Darnaud murdered Razz. I'm sure of it."

Ruth's hand flew to her mouth but it couldn't stifle her shriek, "No. Oh no!"

The waitress came over. "Are you all right, Miss?"

Ruth started sobbing, face to the table, her whole body shaking. The sobs evolved into a continuous keening, horrible to hear.

"It's okay," I said to the waitress. "Some bad news."

She nodded uncertainly.

"Could you bring some tissues?"

The tissues arrived in seven seconds.

"I don't really know her," I said. "Could you... could you hold her for a moment?"

She nodded again, sat down beside Ruth and put both arms around her.

It was so awkward. The other two punters had left at the start of the commotion. I felt utterly inadequate and just sat there, watching Ruth in her distress, with the waitress stroking her back. It took long minutes before Ruth's composure returned.

"Thank you," she said eventually. "What's your name?"

"Patsy."

"Well, thank you, Patsy. I'll be okay now. May I keep the tissues?"

"Of course."

Patsy moved away.

"I'm so sorry," I said. "I didn't know how to tell you."

"There's no way to sugar that one. Give me the whole story. I want to know."

First I described the scene in the restaurant in Delhi, and Marcel's convincing act of trying to save Razz, including the use of the two EpiPens. Then I repeated Abdel's tale of the peanut butter, and our theory that Marcel had from time to time been using a drug to hold Armand's opponents back.

"It happened to me once. And I've a strong suspicion he tried it again tonight."

"Oh my god, are you all right?"

"I think so. I think it was in the spinach. But I didn't eat any of it. Did you see how agitated Marcel was when I pretended to offer some to Armand. And then when I asked for the doggy bag?"

"Yes, I didn't understand. Oh my God! Do you still have some of the spinach?"

I patted my bag. "All of it."

"We could get it analysed. I did my law school here in New York. I know some guys in one of the forensic labs." Her eyes were fierce. "First thing is though, you've got to beat Armand. Got to, got to. That creep has been making such a big thing of his son being number one. Now Gaston Ju... I can't remember, whoever, all the way from France to write the story. As if Armand would've come within a million miles if Razz... oh God, oh fuck." She broke down again and this time I moved to the other side of the table and stroked her as she sobbed.

Patsy came over, hesitantly. "More coffee?"

I signalled yes. She brought two fresh mugs and filled them. Ruth slowly composed herself again.

"I'm so sorry. We've got to get you back to the hotel. You won't beat Armand without a good night's sleep."

"It looked like Armand was a near miss for a good night but no sleep."

"Yes, that was sad. I've seen the way his father controls him. Razz used to laugh about it. He said that sort of motivation never works.

"Anyway, come on." She took a sip of the coffee, found a wallet in her handbag and took out a fifty. We went over to the till. "Thank you, Patsy," Ruth said. "You're a sweetie in the best way I can say it."

Patsy smiled. "You're so very welcome, Ma'am."

We were back at the hotel in a few minutes and arranged to meet for a late breakfast. I said I'd try to get Zoë and Abdel to join us.

In the lift Ruth said, "Watch out for yourself," and departed a couple of floors below my level.

I felt like someone in a spy thriller. Thrilling it was not. It was *scary*. Marcel wouldn't actually try anything, would he? I breathed a sigh of relief as I firmly closed my bedroom door, clutching the doggy bag. Darkness. Peace and sleep at last, it had been quite a day.

Darkness?

The thing about the Grand Hyatt, and any decent hotel, I'd learned over the last couple of years, was the way the cleaners and valets and minibar managers were constantly in and out of the rooms. A premium was placed on the early evening preparation, pillows plumped, beds turned down, sometimes an insincere good night note and a chocolate.

And the bedside lights? On. Why no lights?

I felt a stab of fear like nothing I'd ever experienced. Pure electric terror. I heard rather than saw the bathroom door opening.

Out!

Thank goodness I hadn't fixed the security lever. It was a heavy door, heave! I hit my shoulder on the frame going out and spun. Slam it shut, quick. But a foot in a leather shoe thrust through the opening. A violent kick to the attached shin brought a grunt and the withdrawal of the foot. Using all my strength against the pull in the opposite direction I hauled the door closed. Still clutching the doggy bag I ran down the opulent corridor. The emergency staircase. The lift would take too long.

Up or down? How high was the hotel? Twenty five floors? I was on the ninth, I'd go up. I sensed someone back down the corridor as I pushed through the door into the utilitarian stairwell.

What to do? It was hard to think.

First, run! I'd be quicker than Marcel or anyone he'd employed.

Could it be Kiefer? No, I reckoned he was a decent sort at heart. It had to be Marcel. There'd not been time for him to make other arrangements.

Should I seek help down in the lobby? The threat was too sinister.

Sailor? Sailor was back on the ninth. The ninth was unhealthy.

Zoë! Yes! What floor was Zoë on? The seventeenth. Zoë was in 1707.

In no time I was five floors higher, bounding past fourteen. I stopped to listen. Someone below was on the stairs, leather soled shoes.

The terror gripped me again. He was taking his time. What did he know? Why was he so certain?

I exited on the fifteenth and ran down the corridor to the other stair well; the room numbers started at that end. Then up the two remaining floors to seventeen and out into the corridor.

Here it was, 1707, quick!

It was close to one o'clock now. Would Zoë be asleep? Probably. I knocked, not hard, I didn't want to make too much noise, but continuously, urgently.

Come on, come on!

"Who is it?"

Ah!

"It's me, Jolyon. Let me in."

My voice must have signalled that whatever it was had brought me to Zoë's room at 1am, it was urgent. The security lever clicked and the door opened. Zoë stood there in a white knee length silk nightdress, sleepy and perplexed. I pushed past her and violently shut the door.

"God, thanks, you've saved my life. I'll explain."

I grabbed the room's single lounge chair and jammed it under the door handle.

This must have convinced Zoë I was either serious or mad. She went into the bathroom and emerged in a dressing gown. "What on earth is going on?"

The shock got me then. I sat on the bed, still panting from the stairs, sweating, and I started shaking violently. Just a couple of minutes ago I'd thought, I'd *known*, I was going to be killed.

Killed.

Ending up dead. The end.

Finito.

Then the flight, the frantic ascent of the aptly named emergency stairs. Footsteps following, pursuit, someone tracking me. Horrible, I'd never not shudder at the phrase 'man hunt'; that's what I'd been, hunted. Then the relief, the elation as Zoë opened her door.

My breathing slowed, and with it my shakes. "Give me a moment. It was the dinner. It all started in the restaurant."

"Smith and Wollensky's?"

"Yes, how did you know?"

"Marcel invited me, 'nuff said?"

"Yup, 'nuff said and the whole thing's moved on."

I told her about the meal and the spinach and the doggy bag. "Here it is. I hung on to it." Then about Ruth and what she'd said in the diner about Razza's post mortem. Then about the moment I realised how sinister darkness was when you returned to a posh hotel room. After you'd shut yourself in.

Then I started to cry.

I couldn't help myself. Not in front of Zoë, I thought, how embarrassing. More shakes, this time with added sobbing. Stop!

What happened next was as surprising as anything that evening. Zoë sat on the bed, pulled me to her and started to rock me and stroke my head. The relief was as intense as the terror. I stopped thinking and gave myself up to it. Safety. Another concept that had moved on for me. Zoë was so gentle, her hand, over and over, stroking my close cropped hair and the side of my face. She was smoothing away my sobs. Slowly they subsided. And as they did the relief turned into plain prosaic happiness, Zoë with her arms round me. I dreamed about this.

Eventually she said, "Come on. Get your stuff off, into bed. You need some rest."

A moment later I was in bed beside Zoë. I enjoyed the thought for about five seconds before I fell asleep.

The next thing I was aware of was Zoë's whisper and her hand on my face.

"Wake up, come on, wake up."

It took me a few seconds to realise where I was. I opened my eyes. There were Zoë's, close, regarding me seriously.

"You could get me into trouble with Sailor," I said.

"I don't know if we're going to give Sailor all the detail."

"What detail are we not going to give Sailor?"

"Jolyon, this is very peculiar."

I reached out. A naked shoulder, that would do.

"Do you mind?"

Her big brown eyes came even closer. "I'm not sure. I don't think so."

So I pulled her into my chest and started to stroke her hair, roles reversed. She wriggled into me and rested her hand on my face. Then she said, "Wait, I need a pee."

"So do I, before I have to do a handstand in there."

"What?"

"To point it at the bowl."

She laughed. Moments later, back in bed, we were off; her nightdress off; her pulling my pants off: getting off. "What are these?" she asked. "I never thought you were going to be shy."

"It wasn't on the agenda."

Her body was so hard, small boobs, rippling stomach, nothing soft about her bottom, strong legs. She made love like she played squash, with an overwhelming intensity. "Fuck me," I exclaimed in surprise as she quickly slid onto me, "match point down?"

The slightest of nods. Then she closed her eyes. Concentration, Zoë's major strength. It didn't last long for either of us. For me it was the culmination of an incredible twelve hours. The transcending memory of those twelve hours was Zoë's face as she came, straining, an agony of pleasure.

"Phew," I said, as we held each other when we'd finished. "I didn't expect that."

"Neither did I." She kissed me on the lips and slipped out of bed. "No time for post mortems. Sorry, bad phrase. We'd better get on or we'll miss breakfast."

Ruth was finishing a cup of coffee, reading the paper, when we entered the dining room. "Ah, there you are," she said as we approached. "I thought I'd missed you. I see you still have your doggy bag."

"Not for breakfast though. It's my evidence bag. I was hoping to hand it over to you."

"I called my contact at the lab this morning," she said. "I'm meeting him for lunch. I'll give it to him then."

She raised an eyebrow. "Are you two together then?"

"Just last night. I'll explain."

When we had collected some food I filled Ruth in about the night's events, or most of them anyway.

"Phewy, scary."

"You just don't know."

"Are you sure it was Marcel?"

"I think so. I'd probably recognise his right shoe. And pick out the bruise at a shin identity parade."

"Has he had breakfast?"

Ruth shrugged. "Not that I've seen. Gaston was here, Sailor. He came over and said hello. Said he was going to do some work in his room."

"If it was Marcel," Zoë said, "whoever it was, I wonder how long he was looking for you before he gave up. We've got to keep him away from you today."

"Yes, only I've been thinking. You know the attaché case he always has with him? I'd love to get a look inside it."

"How?"

"That's where I have absolutely no idea."

"He'll be at the court when Armand has his practice," Zoë said. "That might be an opportunity. What time are you on?"

"One o'clock. Till half past. Armand's on after that."

Ruth sounded positive. "Best chance we've got. I should be back by then. I'm meeting my friend early, round the corner. On forty second. Can you help too, Zoë?"

"I suppose so. It would help if I wasn't on court with Jolyon. I could just be there. Watch out for an opportunity."

"Sailor will do the hit. Or even Trevor. Have you seen Trevor?"

"Yes," Ruth said. "He was going off to Central Park for a run."

I explained what I'd heard from Trevor at Smith and Wollensky's. "He seems to have had the same idea about Marcel too, some suspicion at least. Said he'd tell me about it today. It would be good to have Trevor watching out. I don't want to tell Sailor yet. He'll go up and confront Marcel. Too soon."

"Is Abdel still here?" Zoë asked.

"I think so. He was supporting Magdi during his match."

"You should get Abdel to keep an eye out as well."

At that moment Trevor came in and strolled over to our table. He was wearing a heavy hoodie and thick tracky bottoms. "Mind if I join you?"

"Sit down," I said. "Strange evening, wasn't it?"

"Too right."

"And it got stranger, wait till you hear. How did you get on with Armand?"

"He was spitting fire. Sailor and I managed to frogmarch him back here. Ha ha, sorry about the joke. Frog. Halfway back he was all set to turn around. I told him his dad had got into a taxi. I guess he went to bed in the end. All by himself." He laughed. "You nearly got lucky there, mate, big time. That Stephanie. But you know that story, excuse me ladies. Armand would have been wrung out. We left him in the elevator. Going up."

I told him about the end of my evening.

"Jesus Christ," he said when I'd finished, "you're not kidding?"

"What we were hoping," Ruth said, "is you'd kind of ride shotgun with Jolyon today. We don't know what Marcel might do. We don't know for certain it was Marcel last night. But you haven't heard the rest of it, certain now, from what Jolyon's found out." She took a deep breath. "Razza's death wasn't an accident."

"No?"

"No. Marcel murdered him."

"Jesus Q Christ, excuse me. I thought Marcel'd almost saved him."

"It seems it was peanut butter," I said. "Abdel el Tayeb saw him with a jar of the stuff when he was leaving Delhi, in airport security of all places. Razza's nut allergy, a lot of people knew. Thing is, I think he's been fixing some of Armand's matches, too, slowing his opponents down, with a drug, not enough so they can't go on court but enough to stop them performing. I've no idea how many, or how, but it must be at the Dr Darnaud meals. There are enough of those. Abdel thinks he knows the drug it might be. It happened to me once; I just had no energy. And Abdel, he said."

Trevor became animated. "That's what I wanted to tell you. I'm convinced that happened to me. I was playing Armand in Toronto. What is it, the Canadian Classic? I was second seed, two years ago. We did go out the night before I played Armand, Marcel and all, the usual. Then it was the quarters next day, fuck, what quarters, good night Gertrude. I couldn't raise a sweat. There was something about the way Marcel looked at me as I went on court."

"A beta blocker," Ruth said. "Abdel thinks so. It makes sense. It's a common heart drug. My father's on a beta blocker. It's supposed to slow the heart down."

Trevor was wide eyed. "Just let me get at him."

I rested my hand on his arm. "Not yet. He must be putting it in our food. That was the spinach story last night. That's why I didn't eat my Pink Floyd greens. The spinach is in the doggy bag now, along with half a ton of New York fillet. Ruth is going to have it analysed.

"Today though, we want to see what's in Marcel's attaché case. We'd like you to help, Trev. Would you do my practice with me, one o'clock? That'll leave Zoë free with Ruth as soon as Armand goes on at one thirty. They're going to see if they can distract Marcel so one of us can have a look in the case."

"If it's not locked," Trevor said.

"We'll have to take a chance on that. I haven't seen him lock it."

Ruth added, "Or just take the case? Mystery theft?"

"That's a thought."

We didn't need to steal the case, or not for long; it was just borrowed. Zoë was all over Marcel in the gallery while Trevor and I were having a hit. She filled in the details afterwards: 'please tell me about Armand's training'; 'would you have any advice for me as a woman'; 'what's the best way of coping with my period?' *et cetera et cetera*. According to Ruth, Marcel was beginning to think he'd hit the jackpot. Sailor hadn't a clue what was going on.

It was Ruth who did the actual borrowing during Zoë's performance, and she did the inspecting of the case's contents, under the main stand. She was apparently able to return it in less than two minutes. Inside the case there were various papers, a copy of the New York Times, a pair of reading glasses, a packet of antacids and a small bottle.

The label on the bottle apparently said, 'Corgard 80mg'.

We arranged to meet in the Grand Hyatt lobby at four o'clock. I was comically careful through the afternoon. Marcel didn't try anything, either in Grand Central or at the hotel. He'd have had to get past a belligerent Trevor, who didn't leave my side. He'd come back to my room for his shower. Abdel, whom we'd managed to contact, had sat outside the room, among other things checking out what Corgard was on his iPad.

At four we were sitting at one of the low tables in the lobby, Zoë, Ruth, Trevor, Abdel and me. "I thought I recognised the name," Abdel said. "It's a drug called nadolol. Corgard is the brand name. It is a beta blocker, like I thought. It's a perfect drug for the job because it's long acting. An eighty milligram tablet would easily last for twenty four hours. The other thing is, it's known to affect the breathing in people like me who have a medical history of breathing problems."

"Marcel could be taking it himself," Ruth said. "Let me give my contact at the lab a call. I'll tell them to look out for it, what did you say, nad...?"

"Nadolol," Abdel confirmed.

Ruth took out her mobile and made the call. "Well, what are we going to do now?"

"We have to go to the police," I said, "but where? Here? New Delhi? In France?"

"The sooner the better," Ruth said. "It has to be here. Let me worry about that. I'm going to speak to someone I know at a downtown precinct, now, today." She addressed me. "Come on, it's time you started preparing for your match."

I laughed. "It's ridiculous. I've not been thinking about the match. I'd've been bricking it all day normally." I checked my iPhone. "I'm due to meet Sailor in fifteen minutes. You'd better go too, Zoë. You're on first."

We agreed to get together after the squash for something to eat. By then, Ruth said, the cops would have made a move on Marcel, if she could get them to believe the story. She solemnly told me to take care in the meantime. So, chaperoned by Trevor, I went up to my room for my kit. The red light was blinking on the room telephone: a message for collection at Reception.

It was the message that brought my nerves back up to the twanging level, the way I'd expect to be feeling before the most important squash match of my life. I'd had a lot of posts on my wall, and several texts, one from Grandpa saying, 'I'm proud of you, win or lose but the deal doesn't change. Go for it and good luck! With love, Grandpa'. Another was from Dave, Russell and Marion, much shorter, 'Go Jolyon!' The message at Reception was in an envelope from the British Consulate-General, New York, 845 Third Avenue. The message was typed on a sheet of swanky cream paper. "Good luck in the final. Somewhere in the deep I'll be thinking about you. All my love, Dad.'

That brought a lump to my throat.

Chapter Thirty Eight

Break out the booze and have a ball – if that's all there is.
Jerry Lieber and Mike Stoller

My nerves were making up for lost time. Zoë's match was over. She'd beaten the local girl Beth LaSalle, less convincingly than Sailor had expected. She hadn't had her normal focus and it had taken five games. There wasn't a single space left now in the boisterous gallery. An extra crowd had gathered on the travellers' side of the front wall. I'd done my warm up. Various people had come up to me with the usual 'good lucks'. A pink and sweaty Zoë had looked at me fiercely and said, "Believe it, Jolyon; you *know* you can win." I'd had some final encouragement from Sailor, "Go on, son. Do the business, yer physically ready for this," and from Trevor, "For Christ's sake, Jols. This one's for all of us, especially Razza."

Armand and I hadn't spoken. He was standing to one side of the court arguing with Marcel, a radical departure from the normal Darnaud pre-match routine. I'd not heard Armand answer back to a single one of Marcel's instructions before. Not at tournaments, not in Aix-en-Provence, not at Marcel meals. Had Stephanie brought this on? She was sitting in the front row, with Gaston beside her with his laptop. Armand turned away from his father to Monsieur Kiefer, who was talking with a series of emphatic hand gestures. Marcel was almost hopping at being ignored; I wasn't the only one who was tense. Earlier he had given me a nod and then tried, and failed, to stare me down. His shoes I didn't recognise but the size looked right.

At last the announcer went on to the court with his microphone.

"Good evening, folks and welcome to the Vanderbilt Hall in Grand Central Terminal. This is the final of the J P Morgan Tournament of Champions, magnificently organised once again by Event Engine. This is the final we all wanted, between arguably the two most exciting players on the PSA circuit. Currently ranked two in the world, a semi finalist from last year, can I introduce to you from Aix-en-Provence, France, winner of five PSA titles, Mr Armand Darnaud."

Thudding music started, disco lighting, big applause. Armand jogged onto the court, waving acknowledgment. He stood to the announcer's right.

"And contesting the final with Armand tonight, from Manchester, England, the physical sensation we all know as The Whirlwind, the twenty year old Jolyon Jacks."

More music, more applause. I walked forward slowly, taking in the atmosphere. This was it. Where had the five years gone? If only my stomach would stop churning. In the front row of spectators Marcel glared at me as I passed, Stephanie smiled, Gaston nodded. Monsieur Kiefer was looking at Armand. Sailor, Zoë and Trevor, my team, were to the side where I'd left my kit. I took my place to the announcer's left, turned to the audience and tried to look nonchalant, in body language terms a whopper. Armand had resumed his jogging on the spot. How was he looking so calm?

"May I remind you," the announcer continued, "that this match is also for the privilege of the world's number one ranking. Neither Armand nor Jolyon has been there before. These are big stakes tonight at the ToC.

"The marker is David Dolman, the referee Robert Vaughan and the two assistant referees Ian Fuente and Charles Hodgson. Let me hand you over to David Dolman."

From his seat a few rows back in the centre of the gallery David threw the white ball down to us. "Five minutes knock up."

Armand and I went into the familiar routine, banging the ball across to each other, hitting a few returns back down the wall, moving up to a few short balls to get the tension out of the legs. I was vaguely aware of the spectators sitting to the sides, hardly more than a metre beyond the court wall, and I noticed the guys crouched low with their cameras on either side of the front wall, behind the two rectangular areas left clear for photography.

"Half time."

We crossed over. Seeking inspiration I thought of my mother. This is for you dearest M. Not even she could dissipate my nerves, this must be bad. Then, "Time!"

We stopped, Armand shrugged, I nodded and he spun his racquet. Me to serve. We returned to the court after our final adjustments. David announced the match, finishing with the standard, "Best of five games, love all."

I went to the right service box and smashed a serve as hard as I could, straight at Armand.

BlackBallBlog, January 28th, by MatchPoint

ToC Final

I'm in the gallery at the ToC, high up in Vanderbilt Hall, Grand Central, looking down at the final. And now I've seen everything. Armand Darnaud, as tall as the Empire State with the seven league stride and the titanium wrist. He's playing Jolyon Jacks, the kinetic energy phenomenon from England who has been rewriting the laws of physiology. The first rally, the scene is set. It lasts for, read this carefully, seven minutes and thirty five seconds, I timed it, four hundred and ten strokes. Darnaud eventually takes the point. Most players would have died. These guys battle on...

I'd never played a point quite like that. If you had to calibrate it, it was mid twenties in the bleep test. This was a different Armand. He'd never struck me as confident before. Here his stroke play was full of confidence. It was as if he was out of the shadow of his father, just doing what he wanted to do, in the way *he* wanted to do it. He seemed the taller for it, stronger, with an aggressive, bullying attitude.

Not that Armand was going to bully me. I didn't mind losing that point. It was bound to have damaged him already. I was the only player on the planet who could sustain that pace.

BlackBallBlog...

It goes on, no less explosive. This is NOT going to be one of those tedious play-the-ball-down-the-backhand-wall-and-wait matches. The two players are vying for who can take the ball earlier. Normal traffic for Jacks, but what a difference it makes to Darnaud's game. I've not seen him play like this before. All that skill, and now the aggression to convert it into a score. Not that it's easy scoring points. No freebies today from Jacks. 1-1, 2-2, 3-3, the score inches forward. The gallery is alive, uproar after every point. And this is only the first game!...

I lost the first game, but I didn't mind. The doubt would only set in later. Armand took it thirteen eleven on a fifty-fifty penalty point decision. It should have been a let, but there you go; I knew the refs and they were a good team. In credit was that Armand would never be able to sustain this. Never. I was dripping when I came off. I rarely had to change my shirt after a first game. This time I did.

"It's okay son," Sailor said, as I took in some drink. "Keep working him, that game's damaged him. He's tired already."

"You've got to push," was Trevor's advice. "Take the front of the court away from him."

"If I get any further forward I'll be into the front wall."

"Then do it, mate, do it."

Zoë said, "Come on! Match point, match point, remember."

As I walked past Marcel onto court he was looking smug. *Enjoy it while you can.*

BlackBallBlog...

The second game is following the pattern of the first. How can two athletes sustain this energy? The consolation for Jacks and Darnaud is the applause at the end of each point. At least it gives them time for a breather...

I'd never known support like it. Noisy New Yorkers, all partiality, shouting for one or other of us. You could pick out individual voices: Marcel's constant 'Allez, allez'; Trevor's 'Go on, mate, push'; and sharp as an arrow into my consciousness, Zoë's 'Focus, focus'. Seven all, eight all, nine all; this time a big fifty-fifty decision went my way. Game point to me, yesss. I could visualise one game all. Above the noise I heard Marcel's excited, "Non, non, ce n'est pas possible!"

Someone called out, "Sit down."

I couldn't clinch the game though at ten nine. Armand won the rally with one of his exquisite feathered drops. Can he keep that up for the whole match? No, leave the thought, not a good one.

I might not win?

No, no, no. No way, of course not. But Armand took the game twelve ten. I was two nil down.

I followed him off court mentally patching over the cracks. I've been here, Aix-en-Provence, remember. I didn't lose then. I'm not going to lose now. Repeat it: I am not going to lose.

If Marcel had been smug after the first game, the expression on his face after the second was smug squared. It made me want to puke. *No way, my friend no way. Even if I have to die!*

"Steady, son," Sailor said as I towelled down. "Ramp up the pressure. The boy's gone. He's done as much as he can."

"More pace," said Trevor. "Pour it on. Make him know. You're in it to win."

I looked across at Armand. A different dynamic there. Marcel had remained seated, apparently not welcome. Armand was talking with Monsieur Kiefer. Stephanie was up with him, holding his arm, urging him on. *No luck, Stephanie, babe. Your boy knows how this one's going to turn out.*

I still believed that.

BlackBallBlog...

I can't imagine I'm writing this. The third game is surpassing the first and surpassing the second. If the first point in the first game was hard...

That first point in the third game. It gave me a sense of déjà vu. It was me against Dave that afternoon back at the EIS. Dave had fought and fought, but I had been implacable. I would not lose that point. Finally Dave realised it. A single point had broken him. Now Armand was me, fierce, frowning and Zoë's word, focussed, reaching everything with his huge stride. Didn't the guy get tired any more? What training had he been doing? Marie-Emmanuelle must have been right, he was on something. Armand was positively devouring my shots while maintaining his unbelievable control.

It is not going to be enough though. It is not going to be enough.

It's not going to be... enough?

BlackBallBlog...

Jacks puts his life into this point. Three times he's full length on the court to retrieve impossible balls. Now he makes the crowd laugh with an absurd diving backhand, back wall boast from a ball that's gone, out of reach, give it up fella, regroup, point over. Jacks fights and scrambles. But it's Darnaud who is applying the pressure, keeping his concentration. And this point. You won't believe this. I still don't believe it. Eight minutes and ten seconds, I have to check my stopwatch. Another four hundred and thirty two strokes. Watch it tomorrow on YouTube. A last dive from Jacks. Not quite there, 1-0 Darnaud...

Nooo! That point was important. Armand knew it. I knew it. Armand is off script. How can he be playing like this? Come on! I cannot lose this match. Not after everything I've been through.

BlackBallBlog...

2-0 Darnaud, he's controlling this now. Jacks is looking frustrated... What's that, a disturbance behind the front wall? Never mind, this squash is unbelievable.

Remember Aix-en-Provence. Make it difficult. He's going to run out of belief. He must. He must?

BlackBallBlog...

3-0 Darnaud, another superb point. You have to admire Jacks... Hello, it looks like cops back there. There's a posse of New York's finest the other side of the front wall.

Uunghhh! Marcel was standing applauding after that one; I watched him through the back wall as I wiped my hand. I cannot tolerate the idea of Marcel seeing the see sawed: me lose, Armand win. *His* Armand, *his* win.

BlackBallBlog...

Jacks is lucky there. The ball jams out from the front wall nick. 1-3 Jacks.
Now he's lucky again, Armand should have had a let. 2-3 Jacks. Maybe this isn't over.
Yes it is. It must be now. That was a cracker of a rally, another long one. Armand had the Brit on a string, but he wouldn't give up. Then the ball comes off Darnaud's frame for a fluke winner and the Brit's shoulders slump.
Who is *that?* Armand's dad again, on his feet, shouting. What a jerk...

That mishit winner hurt. It was bad enough dealing with Armand's properly hit shots. This was no longer Aix-en-Provence, with my fate in my hands as long as I had the will. Now my will wasn't enough. Armand had the game to overcome everything I willed and the luck was going his way too. My fate was in his hands.

Armand played another delicate drop. How could they be so consistently tight? I got a bang from his hip as I lunged past, in hope rather than certainty that I'd reach the ball.

Worth a try? Yes. "Let please?"

There was a pause, the three judgements made, "Yes let."

"No!" A loud shout from the gallery: Marcel.

"Quiet please," David Dolman said. "Two four. Jacks."

BlackBallBlog...

Then can you believe it. Darnaud hits three cross court nicks in succession, two silky ones on the back hand and a triumphant two hundred mile an hour smash on the forehand from a Jacks lift. 7-2 Darnaud. Surely it's all over... Even the cops are watching. I'm counting five of them.

I kept Armand waiting at seven two, checking my socks, adjusting my wristbands, replenishing my oxygen. Then I glared at him. You're still going to have to win this. I am not going to lose it for you.

Then it was more of the same game. I was still strong; problem was, I wasn't good enough. One of my defensive shots came out, just a little. Not too far?

Armand: "Let?"

It was a fifty-fifty call at best. The pause for arbitration.

"Yes, let."

Phew, I'd thought that one would go the other way.

BlackBallBlog...

Who is this jerk? It's Armand's dad again and he's shouting at the marker. Sit down!

I exhaled big litres of carbon dioxide, took in volumes of oxygen. Keep on, Marcel, it all helps. Then he subsided. Armand served.

BlackBallBlog...

Jacks is getting lucky. Where does this decision go?

Close up behind Armand, I took a chance and anticipated one of his backhand drops, yet another as tight as tight could be. Anyway, I couldn't get through.

"Let, please?"

Please give me a let, pretty please.

"Stroke to Jacks, three seven."

No way, not a stroke. They definitely got that wrong.

Marcel was up again. "You cheats. You are cheating. It is a conspiracy."

A slow handclap started, and some booing.

"Sit down, Mr Darnaud. For all of us. Let the players play. If you persist you'll be removed. Jacks to serve, three seven."

BlackBallBlog...

This guy is seriously out of order. Someone's going to have to throw him out, he's spoiling the match. And it's not over. Now I'm starting to wonder. Looking at

Jacks, he's bouncing. He's still so competitive. Might do something remarkable. I've never seen such determination...

A shout from Zoë, intensely personal, "Come on Jolyon. Do it for me!"

It gave me a surge of adrenaline, a jolt like the darkness in my bedroom the previous night. We were connected.

BlackBallBlog...

No one can believe Jacks and I've never heard this much noise in a squash gallery. This is physically impossible. Darnaud is superior. Everyone can see that. But now Jacks is winning the points. 3-7 becomes 4-7 and I'd swear that was a dead nick he picked up there. 5-7, Darnaud looks bemused. 6-7.

Nooo! Eight six.

BlackBallBlog...

Another great point. I take my hat off to Jacks. He is possessed but Darnaud still has the force. More accurately, Darnaud has the skill, another feathered drop. 9-6, it must be all over. Now 10-6, a back wall nick from the serve.

Oh God, the back wall nick, the ball rolling, that's not fair. Come on! I *will* not lose.

BlackBallBlog...

10-6 match point. That must be it. Not even Jacks can come back from this and let's face it he's two games down. Oh dear, another tight let decision...

Maybe I shouldn't have asked for that one. Two love and ten six match point down, you have to or you've lost. Worth a try. Armand had wrong footed me and I crashed into him as I turned.

The pause was longer than usual.

"Yes, let. Ten six, match point."

A big disturbance at the front of the gallery, Marcel again. He was standing up and shouting at the marker. A slow handclap took hold, with shouts of 'sit down' from all over the gallery. What a prat. You don't need to do this. Your son's two oh and ten six, he's won it, all but!

I took some deep breaths.

BlackBallBlog...

What's happening? They're shaking hands. Darnaud's coming off court. He's giving his father the stare as he walks past...

We'd been standing in the middle of the court, waiting for Marcel and the noise to subside. I felt Armand's big hand on my shoulder. I turned. He gave one of his shrugs and shook my hand.

"Zat's eet," he said. "Is enough, my fuzzeur again, 'e push too much." Another shrug. "Eet ees finished. Sank you."

What?

He opened the door and left the court.

The whole gallery went silent.

"Mr Darnaud, Mr Darnaud." This was David. "Armand?"

Armand didn't listen. He collected his kit, headed off down the side of the court with everyone's eyes on him. Through the semi-opaque wall I could just make him out turning left towards the street exit of Vanderbilt Hall. Stephanie shouted his name and ran after him.

David stood up, looked round and announced, "Hold on." He picked his way down to the front of the gallery and hurried off after Armand. The buzz restarted. I looked through the side wall at Zoë and Sailor. Zoë mouthed 'stay there' so I started hitting some shots to myself. After a couple of surreal minutes, David returned. The buzz subsided. Everyone watched him climb back to the marker's position and take the microphone.

"Ladies and gentlemen, I'm sorry. Mr Darnaud defaults. Jolyon Jacks wins, eleven thirteen, ten twelve, six ten," a pause, "Retirement."

The buzz intensified. I saw Marcel stand up and look around, opening and shutting his mouth like a fish. Then he grabbed his briefcase and scrambled off, head down, past the spectators along the side of the court. Moments later there was a mighty commotion beyond the front wall. I couldn't see clearly but Marcel was shouting again, surrounded by the NYPD. Ruth had obviously got through to them.

I felt embarrassed and went to leave the court. Some tentative applause started.

David said, "Wait." I stopped at the open door and looked around the big gallery. Now everyone's eyes were on me.

"Jolyon Jacks," David repeated, raising his voice. "Our new champion, J P Morgan ToC champion!"

I looked across at Sailor, sitting with his hands on his knees, shell shocked. Beside him Trevor was shaking his fist in celebration.

"And let's hear it again, Jolyon Jacks, ToC champion and NEW WORLD NUMBER ONE!"

Huge applause, it must have gone on for at least a minute solid.

I looked at Zoë as I took it all in. And oh, this was best. Zoë was clapping, hands raised, and smiling warmly at me with her eyes.

Chapter Thirty Nine

A couple of hours later we were in Michael Jordan's, another of New York's famous steak houses, at a table overlooking Grand Central's main hall. It was a superb place, Ruth's recommendation, high up on the station's north balcony. What a spot to celebrate. Across the vaulted hall you couldn't miss a mighty reminder of the squash, the four huge ToC banners that had dominated the main terminal entrance during the tournament. Through the archway to Vanderbilt Hall you could see the lights of the court, and hear the pneumatic drills that were already disassembling the structure.

There were seven of us, Ruth, Zoë, Sailor, Trevor, Abdel, Gaston Guillot and me. You'd have thought after such an extraordinary end to the match we'd have been deflated. Not this time. I was zinging, still pinching myself, world number one, the best in the flipping *world*. You could argue about the circumstances, but not about the fact. I'd made it and it had been such a pleasure sending messages to Grandpa and the Kendalls.

Ruth was upbeat too. She'd told me outside the restaurant that discovering Razza had been murdered had taken away the guilt she'd been feeling. It didn't ease the pain but the pain was more bearable. Horrible as it was, Razza's death hadn't after all been the accident she might have prevented. As for Gaston, he was as thrilled as I was: he had a major scoop, mainstream, not just sporting; Marcel was a prominent figure in France. It wasn't the story he'd expected but his byline would be on L'Équipe's front page. And I'd never seen Sailor so high, after a couple of glasses of the normally reviled red wine. He was sitting next to Zoë, who was directly opposite me, the only one of us, I thought with some concern, who was quiet.

"Well, Jolyon, son," Sailor said, "now I've two number ones. But work to do, I logged six errors, three in the second game and three in the third." He flung back his head and laughed. "Happy days, what am I quibbling over, eh Zoë?"

"It's the coaching that's responsible," I said. "I'm thinking of moving on."

"Where to? Aix-en-Provence? Marcel Darnaud?"

"I believe he's unavailable." I turned to Ruth, sitting next to me. "How did you fix it with the police?"

"Not so difficult. I called an old friend at Midtown North Precinct. It's only a few blocks, on West 54th. Maria had met Razz once. She said she'd need more than just my word, but it all fitted together. Trevor and I went over there during Zoë's match."

"Oh, I never realised you'd gone."

"It was only ten minutes in a cab."

"Hold on, hold on," Sailor said. "Would one of ye take me back to the beginning."

So we pieced together the Marcel Armand story to an increasingly incredulous Sailor, who hadn't fully understood the background to the arrest.

Gaston was furiously jotting stuff down in his notebook, eyes darting to whoever was taking up the tale. Marcel was not going to look good. After Ahmed had described the effects of nadolol Ruth said, "Yes, the result came through really quickly from the lab. Jolyon's spinach was loaded with it. He'd have OD'd if he'd eaten it all. That helped us down at the precinct. Enough for Maria to get an arrest warrant."

"Did you mention the shin?" I asked. "There's no way it won't be bruised if it was Marcel in my room."

"Yes," Trevor said. "And they want all of us down there tomorrow morning to make statements. We fixed it for ten o'clock. Ruth managed to block their first proposal, to interview us all tonight. Your friend, Maria, she's a squash player, that's right?"

"She won't be troubling Zoë, but yes, she's a regular player. She had tickets here for the second round. She's looking forward to meeting you, Jolyon."

"Another of your women?" Zoë said with a raised eyebrow.

Ruth laughed. "Give him a break. I guess he'll be a bit tired for that."

Zoë was looking at me intensely and I decided it wasn't the time to describe Marie-Emmanuelle's ministrations, and what the tired body could be coaxed into accomplishing. I did want to mention Marie-Emmanuelle's suspicions, though.

"There's something else," I said. "When I was staying in Aix-en-Provence I found out some interesting stuff about Marcel. Mainly the lengths he'd go to to improve Armand's chances. I suppose we know that now anyway," I was conscious of Ruth stiffening beside me, "but have any of you noticed? Armand's bulked up a bit. The physio there, I'm not sure Marcel's so popular among his staff and she was quite forthcoming, she said she suspected Armand was on something, maybe a steroid. She said he's put on some kilos just recently."

"No way," said Sailor. "He'd be picked up."

"Marcel's a doc," Trevor said. "And he's into all this drug stuff."

"It's all very scientific down there," I went on. "There's a dietician, Pascal something. Everything Armand eats is controlled. I wouldn't put it past Marcel. We've seen what he does. Excuse me, Ruth."

"Is it that Armand knows about this?" Gaston asked. "The drugs?"

"I really don't know," I said. "It's a good question."

Trevor nodded. "Does he know is one thing. *If* it's happening. My feeling is no. Armand's not a cheat. The other is, I'm still wondering why he pulled out when he did. For Christ's sake it was match point. Think what was at stake, and he had it won. Pardon me, Jols, but not even I could have come back from two nil six ten. Not against Armand playing like that."

"I've been watching him over the last few days," Zoë said. "Armand is okay with Lou Kiefer. He seems fine in general with squash people. But he absolutely loathes his father. It's physical. He's been doing a good job hiding it, but you can't altogether. He flinches," she made a small finger thumb gesture, "not much but it's been there, whenever his father gives him orders. As he does. He treats Armand like a ten year old. And have you noticed the way Armand looks at Stephanie?"

"I have," said Ruth.

"He's besotted," Zoë went on. "There's a lot happening in Armand's world." She looked round. "And someone said his father wouldn't let them go off together last night."

"Almost a fight," Trevor said.

"If you add it together, Stephanie, his father's pressure, and he must have been so embarrassed this evening," Zoë grimaced in the way I loved, "I'd have been cringing if my father had started giving off in a squash gallery like that."

"Also," Gaston added, "the pronouncement to my newspaper, my boy will win this, my boy will win that. Armand the puppet, no?"

This time Zoë nodded. "I think in the end he reached his limit, just reacted against it. It would have been instinct. He's probably regretting it even now."

Trevor laughed. "He's probably with Stephanie right now, not thinking about it one little bit."

Sailor was pink in the face from the unaccustomed wine. It was still the normal Sailor's speech though. "Aye," he said, "maybe it was the pushy parent in the end. Pushed too far. That was you, Jolyon, eh? Ye've your mother to thank for taking up squash."

"Well, I have her to thank for not being a tennis player." I explained the full frontal details of my relationship with my mother. From Sailor there was a quiet, "Aye, I've met the lady."

"And thanks for reminding me," I continued. "I can't tell you how sweet this is. She's an avid follower of tennis, my mother. Do you know what she said a little while ago, it was when I was down there before Christmas? She said she'd parade around our tennis club in a Venus Williams outfit, of all things those are horrendous, in the impossibly improbable event that I made it to something as trivial as world number one in squash. She said it in front of witnesses, even better. Someone from my school was there. Well, I took the precaution of having a friend at art college in Brighton photoshop my mother's Medusa head onto Venus Williams' body, Venus wearing one of those does-she-actually-have-any-knickers-on outfits. He's created two full-sized cardboard figures. I'll text him now. We've agreed he'll put one up in the tennis club bar, and we've worked out how to get the other one into my school."

"Steady on, son," Sailor said sternly. "You're over the top there."

I sat up straight. "Over the top? That's what she's been, way way over, for the last five years for goodness sake. I've got to do something. She's earned it. And it'll only be this once. I won't do anything like this again. But imagine how I feel, Sailor, how I've felt all this time, since I came to Manchester, it's not been easy. If she'd shown the slightest trace of respect, or given me any support at all, just something, I might have felt like holding back."

"Aye," was all he said.

"Bear with me while I send the lady a text."

I'd thought about this. The others watched silently. Our excellent waiter, I think he was all the way from Serbia, collected our plates. I tapped out the message. I had Mr Middleton's mobile number and added him as a second recipient:

copy 2 MISTER middleton, hi mum Im world number1 tonite, tell your friends and its the Venus Williams outfit I believe? Is it a size 16 or a size 18? ha ha x your devoted jols, not yet 21 ;-) please tell dad PS theres something abt a LEGACY I believe...

SWEET.

I hit the 'Send' button and looked up at Zoë. She was fixing me with her beautiful brown eyes. I hadn't had time to reflect on where I was with Zoë. Maybe back to square one. Back to the ninth floor for me; I'd console myself with the ToC trophy on the other side of the bed. Zoë had been so reserved since we'd gathered underneath the balcony at Michael Jordan's. I'd have to arrange more escapes from attempted homicides.

Gaston started telling the others about the copy he'd submitted to L'Équipe, and the follow up stories he was planning. Zoë wasn't listening. She was still staring at me expressionlessly.

It was then that I felt it, hidden under the tablecloth, Zoë's shoeless foot pushing its way between my legs. All the way up to my crotch. Her eyes held mine as her toes began a slow circular movement.

Maybe I wouldn't need the attempted homicide after all.

Zoë smiled.

Seventeenth floor tonight, I thought, yippee, and a sleepless night to come.